Emma Jean's BAD Behavior

Emma Jean's BAD Behavior

Charlotte Rains Dixon

Roslyn,
Here's to our shared passion for writing!
Charlotte

Vagabondage Press

This is a work of fiction. Names, characters, places, and incidents are either the product of the author's imagination or are used fictitiously, and any resemblance to actual persons, living or dead, business establishments, events, or locales is entirely coincidental. All rights reserved. This book, and parts thereof, may not be reproduced, scanned, or distributed in any printed or electronic form without express written permission. For information, e-mail info@vagabondagepress.com.

Emma Jean's Bad Behavior

© 2013 by Charlotte Rains Dixon

ISBN-13: 978-0615738178
ISBN-10: 0615738176

Vagabondage Press
PO Box 3563
Apollo Beach, Florida 33572
http://www.vagabondagepress.com

First edition printed in the United States of America and the United Kingdom, February 2013

10 9 8 7 6 5 4 3 2

Cover images by Karl Redshaw and Sosnitskiy Evgen. Front cover design by Maggie Ward. Back cover image by Sosnitskiy Evgen.

Sales of this book without the front cover may be unauthorized. If this book is coverless, it may have been reported to the publisher as unsold or destroyed, and neither the author nor the publisher may have received payment for it.

To the ones who have gone before:

Lewis J. Rains
Barbara Rains
Meredith Johnson

Acknowledgement

I am blessed to have abundant support in my professional, personal, and creative lives, so much so that I cringe at the thought of leaving someone out of these acknowledgements! Please forgive me if I've omitted your name—you know who you are.

I'm grateful to the entire staff of Vagabondage Press, who plucked Emma Jean from the random submission pile and fell in love with her. Thanks especially to my editor N. Apythia Morges, who answered my many questions with patience and dutifully assigned deadlines to me when I asked. Not only that, she made the book better with her edits.

And huge thanks to fellow novelist Dan DiStasio, from whom I learned about Vagabondage in the first place.

This novel would not exist in this form without the writers in my amazing weekly critique group, the Writers of Renown, also known as WoR. Undying gratitude to our fearless leader Karen Karbo, who was a robust champion of Emma Jean from the moment her voice first hit the page and continued that support throughout the lengthy submission process. For comments and ideas about the story that vastly improved the book, my thanks to Connie McDowell, Debbie Guyol, Dan Berne, Christine Fletcher, Laura Wood, Kevin Burke, Valerie Williamson, Art Edwards, Maura Conlon-McIver and Colleen Strohm.

Deep gratitude to the Novel Goddesses, Julie Brickman, Linda Busby Parker, Maryann Lesert, Deidre Woollard, and Katy Yocom, whose energy, support and wisdom has sustained me through many years of writing.

Thanks to all my Nashville peeps, who have been instrumental in making me consider their fair city my second home. Huge thanks to Sue and Walt Schaefer without whose home I never would have felt so welcome in Nashville and to Candace White and Keith Miller for putting me up—and putting up with me—at their house in Murfreesboro. I wrote parts of this novel at both houses, and for the comforting shelter, I am grateful. Deep gratitude for my colleagues at the Writer's Loft, especially Roy Burkhead, who hired me in the first place, and Terry Price and Rabbi Rami Shapiro, who for some crazy reason or another keep letting me return to teach.

Thanks to Mary-Suzanne Peters, who not only drove me around L.A. and introduced me to some of Emma Jean's favorite haunts, but also opens her home to me on a regular basis and offers deep friendship to boot.

To my students and clients, thanks for being so open. You teach me as much as I teach you, and prove the point that as a writer, you never have to be bored, because there's always something new to learn.

To the loyal readers of my blog, both longtime and new, I'm so grateful to your support. You've helped me learn how to put into words what I know about writing.

And finally, to my family, extended and nuclear, near and far, too many of you to list! I'm grateful to my sisters Alice and Christine, as well as to Harvey, Luke, and Lila for great food and company during our weekly Sunday Suppers. Annie, Russell, Henry, Lewis, Maggie and BGD—you make what I do worthwhile. Without you, there's really no reason to do it. And for Steve—deep gratitude for putting up with me and my writing and for your constant and steady support. I love you all so much.

Emma Jean's
BAD
Behavior

PART ONE

Chapter One

The Second-Best Moment of Her Life

Emma Jean Sullivan hated babies. She hated cute, fat, little girl babies with long eyelashes and dimpled cheeks, and she hated sturdy boy babies with button noses and comical serious expressions on their faces. She especially hated the baby whose wails were, at that precise moment, filling every cubic centimeter of air in the Woodland Hills Barnes & Noble, ruining her book signing.

Pen poised above an open novel, Emma Jean paused, cocked her head, and grimaced at the sound of the screeching tot. The screams were momentarily obscured by the hiss of the espresso machine in the store's coffee shop, but once the whine of the steam stopped, the infant's howling filled the space once again.

Emma Jean set her purple fountain pen down beside the book, on the title page of which she was carefully inscribing, *To Darlene, Here's to finding your passion!* (the *your* thickly underlined to underscore the fact that Emma Jean, of course, had already found hers) and looked up at Darlene.

"Babies are like cats," Emma Jean said. "They know I hate them, so they follow me everywhere."

Darlene gazed back at Emma Jean blankly. Perhaps the young woman had not heard her over the howls of the baby, whose screams now grew louder. How could Emma Jean be expected to converse charmingly with her fans when they couldn't hear a damn word she said?

And tonight, thank you writing gods, she had a sizable number of fans waiting to hear her delicate comments and get books autographed. Emma Jean angled her neck to check the length of the line. It snaked through *Biography,* around *New Mysteries,* and back beyond *Art.* The crowd would be more satisfying if most of its members weren't toting worn, personal copies of her four previous books. So far that evening, she'd signed dozens of her older novels, even the out-of-print ones, but very few of her latest, *The Winemaker's Wife.* No matter how hard she had worked over the last month—readings by the bushel, signings by the gallon—she couldn't nudge *Wife* onto the bestseller list. She so desperately needed the novel to sell in the manner of her previous books, what with a huge mortgage to pay, a husband with expensive tastes to support, a *life* to finance. Which was why she needed that howling baby to shut up. As long as it yowled, her fans would not be able to hear a single one of her delightful, felicitous words—words that might entice them to buy *Wife.*

The damned book reviewers certainly hadn't helped her move copies. With this release, for reasons she could not fathom, her usually rabid fans—helped along by the sweet treats she personally baked and sent them—turned savage on her. Absolutely *savage.* Emma Jean sneaked a peak at the latest review, in the *Oxford American,* which her literary escort had brought to her, although why anyone, ever in the history of the world, would think that Emma Jean would want to read such crap was beyond her. She shoved the offending magazine away. But then she peeked at it again.

Bestselling author Emma Jean Sullivan can usually be counted on to write novels that entertain all the way to the bestselling list. Not this time. With her latest release, the author's bitchy, snarky and vastly judgmental persona has finally gotten the best of her. In her most recent novel, she lends these characteristics to a horribly unappealing protagonist, making this book a thoroughly awful read. Thumbs down on this nasty mess of a novel.

The baby's howls now formed a constant staccato wall of sound, distracting Emma Jean even from the murderous rage she felt at the stinging words of the book reviewer. She turned to the two women who stood next to the table, the bookstore manager and the escort. Was the escort's name Mary or Marcy? How was she supposed to remember such things with the current cacophony in the store?

"Can't we get that baby to be quiet?"

The bookstore manager, a woman with dull, thin, brown hair and thick glasses, shrugged. "It's a free country. I can't kick someone out just because their kid is screaming. I'd have the ACLU over me like flies on poop."

Mary/Marcy leaned forward. "It's shit. The expression is flies on shit."

"I was trying to be polite," the manager said.

"To hell with polite," Emma Jean said. The baby's screams tore through her. She placed her hands on the table and rose. "If you won't deal with that baby, I'll go talk to the parent myself."

The bookstore manager scrambled to her feet. "No, no, you stay here. I'll go see what I can do."

Emma Jean sat back down. And then she had a horrible thought. The kind of behavior she had just exhibited was precisely what the reviewer had written about. Was she, perhaps, a wee bit too snarky in her daily life? Too quick to rush to judgment? But upholding the mantel of a bestselling author was a thoroughly exhausting endeavor with many busy and important details to it, so she should be granted a bit of leeway.

Emma Jean took a deep, cleansing breath to compose herself. And then a lovely idea popped into her head: perhaps she could learn to be nice. Emma Jean nodded her head decisively. Yes, indeedy, she would take non-snarkiness to a whole new level, much as she had elevated being childless to a desirable lifestyle. She would even name it: the Campaign to be Kind. She tilted her head to the exact angle she had practiced in the mirror for when meeting her public, smiled up at the next fan, and pushed the oversized plate of cookies toward her. Emma Jean always brought cookies to her book signings. That made her kind, didn't it? If she were home in Portland, she'd whip out a batch of her special peanut butter cookie recipe herself, but here in L.A., she'd had to rely on a bakery that Mary/Marcy found for her. Most of the cookies remained on the plate, seeing as how everyone in L.A. was on a diet.

Still, Emma Jean felt it vital to make the effort for the things that were important to her, and her fans definitely counted in that elite group. The others who made the cut were her students and her husband, Peter. They were the three things in life, besides writing, that Emma Jean cared about most—the holy triumvirate, her sacred cows. And, she noted to herself, she was plenty kind to the sacred cows, maybe even overly so. Her fans, after all, adored her. She turned her attention back to the ones in line.

"Society favors parents and disregards those of us who choose not to bring children into this crazy, overpopulated world," she said, dredging up a hint of a southern accent left over from her Georgia upbringing and raising her voice so it could be heard over the baby's screeches. Wait, was that being snarky or just honest? Where did one draw the line between fact and judgment?

The next three women in line nodded their heads in unison. Emma Jean watched, fascinated, as their chins bobbed up and down at precisely the same time. They were clones, arrayed in the style that, in the day and half she'd been here, Emma Jean had learned was currently ubiquitous in Los Angeles. A tan, wrinkle-free face and shoulder-length hair that fell just so were required accoutrements, with an iPhone or other smart phone and fat-free latte also requisite accessories. Tight jeans were de rigueur, as was a cute butt to put into them. And a camisole with at least a hint of cleavage was also mandatory.

Emma Jean looked down at her own V-necked tank top and yanked at the bottom of the V. She was showing more cleavage than usual, and it was all Mary/Marcy's fault, as the escort had come to pick her up early and ended up advising her on her wardrobe. "C'mon. Wear the sexy one and show some skin. Everyone in L.A. does. You'll look stodgy otherwise," Mary/Marcy had said, and Emma Jean had grudgingly agreed the top looked better on her than any other choices. Her breasts were, she was inordinately proud to admit, still quite shapely and full for her age, no doubt because she had never nursed a baby.

The infant's crying now reached a new pitch of keening desperation. Apparently the bookstore manager was not having any luck dealing with it.

"Oh Lord, I do wonder how the human race survives, don't y'all?" Emma Jean said. The three clones smiled hesitantly. One was blonde, one brunette, and one a brassy redhead that came from a bottle if Emma Jean was a day over forty. And in truth, she was eight years over forty, though her website listed her as forty-three, which was a necessary lie (so why hadn't she made herself younger still?) but a damned inconvenient one as she always had to stop and think how old she was supposed to be when she wrote about birthday celebrations on her blog or Facebook, where her fan page had thousands of followers.

"It just amazes me how we continue to procreate in the face of all evidence that it is a very bad idea," Emma Jean continued.

The blonde clone giggled. The other two nodded, their expressions very serious.

Emma Jean shook her head. "I guess I just wasn't meant to be a mama, and the good Lord knew that."

The redhead leaned toward Emma Jean, and her voluminous breasts threatened to elude the spandex of her tank. "That's what I love best about your work," she said. Emma Jean tried not to stare as a melon mound of flesh loomed dangerously above the rim of the woman's top. "You're so honest about how happy you and your husband are without children. I just read your blog post about you guys being in Paris, and it was so romantic. I love the part where he kissed you at the top of the Eiffel Tower."

"Thanks, doll," Emma Jean said. She'd liked that post, too, even if the kiss had only been a chaste peck on the cheek. It had sounded vastly passionate when she'd written about it, which was, after all, the power of the pen. "Peter and I have all we need, just the two of us. Two against the world, y'all know what I mean? He says his wine is his baby, and I say my students are my kids."

Emma Jean had borne the tragic misfortune of her infertility bravely, and after it became apparent that she and Peter would never produce a baby, she had vowed to become the standard bearer for all childless women. And so she had, writing bestselling novels and enchanting blog posts on the joys of life without children. She'd been so successful that the internationally known non-profit organization, *Choose Childlessness*, had asked her to be their spokeswoman, a task she had assumed with gusto. It took a lot of energy to uphold the stanchion of childless living, particularly when that miserable baby's screams continued to fill the air. Emma Jean, however, would persevere with the role she had been granted. She smiled up at her fan.

"I love reading about you and Peter on your blog," the brunette said. "Sometimes I wish I'd thought things through a little better before I decided to have children myself."

Emma Jean nodded, attempting to look encouraging. This was the part she liked best about book signings, the moment when complete strangers confessed their unhappiness with their children, their pets, or, most often, their husbands. She loved hearing their stories. Plus she'd learned that the more she chatted and listened to them pour forth their lives, the more likely her fans were to buy books.

The brunette leaned in closer. "How do you and Peter do it? How do you keep your marriage so vital and alive?" she asked.

"Lots and lots of sex," Emma Jean said. This was her standard response, though it hadn't been true for months. How long *had* it been? Emma Jean couldn't remember. She couldn't even remember how long it had been since she'd even *thought* about having sex with Peter.

Now the brunette's lower lip quivered ominously, and she leaned in close to whisper, "Ever since I had my last baby, it seems like my husband isn't interested in sex anymore."

"How old is your child?" Emma Jean asked.

"Six months."

"Why, darling I think it's just about the most natural thing in the world for a man and his wife to take a while to get reacquainted with each other after such a momentous occurrence. Something similar happens to one of the characters in my latest book."

"It does?"

Emma Jean nodded. "And she comes up with some dang clever ways to solve the problem, too. You should buy a book and read it; maybe it will help." Emma Jean plucked a copy of *Wife* from the towering pile on the table and opened it. "What's your name?"

"Amber."

To Amber, here's to finding your passion! Emma scrawled. Her purple fountain pen was running low on ink, so she set it on the table and picked up another. She always traveled with five or six of her special pen, the Fountaineer.

The bookstore manager had returned from her errand to quiet the baby, which had been unsuccessful, since the baby still screamed. Emma Jean reached out to the next clone in line and opened her novel to the title page, then set it up on the table, a not-so-subtle hint for Emma Jean to cut it short with Amber.

"It'll be okay, love," Emma Jean said, patting her hand in an extremely kind way if she did say so herself. Then she handed her the book, and Amber smiled gratefully, if also a bit tearily. Usually Emma Jean would have asked Amber for more details of her life's problems—after all, Emma Jean was a storyteller, and as she told her students, stories were everywhere; you just had to be open to receive them. But clearly the rabbity bookstore manager was getting nervous about the large numbers of people standing in line without buying her new book. Plus, she was unhappy about the cookies; Emma Jean could tell. She'd fussed earlier about how the crumbs might damage the towering stack of copies of *Wife* on the table. But she looked like she had never enjoyed a luscious, home-baked cookie, ever in her life. Emma Jean's credo was that one must grasp life with both hands and shake the hell out of it. The concept was so important, she'd named her blog after it—*Life, Full Tilt.*

The baby's wails reached a new crescendo, and then a door slammed, and suddenly there was silence. Like a stop-action movie, all was quiet and still. As with the sudden absence of pain, the abrupt quiet was unsettling for a moment. And then the murmurs of shoppers and the chatter of her fans in line sprang up again.

"Thank you, God," Emma Jean said. She tilted her head and smiled up at the next person in line.

Who was not a female.

Who was a male.

Who looked like Brad Pitt, especially his narrow blue eyes, friendly, but with that vague hint of fierceness behind them. There was also the short blond hair, the dark blond eyebrows, the devilish smile. Which he was currently using lavishly on her.

"But you're a man," Emma Jean said.

"I'm glad you noticed."

How could she not? My God, he was handsome. Medium height, with big, broad shoulders and a muscular chest beneath his white *Lake Tahoe* t-shirt. He cradled a large stack of books in his arms. Had the universe seen fit to reward her Campaign to be Kind already?

"It's just that most of my fans are female. Who do I sign this to?" Emma asked.

"It's for Carolina. My wife," the man answered.

She pushed one of the yellow Post-it notes she kept on hand for difficult spellings toward him. "Write it out for me."

He reached into the pocket of his black chino pants, came up empty handed. "I'll spell it."

"I'm not an auditory learner. I need to see it." She rolled her fountain pen across the table toward him. "I don't want to mess it up and make you buy a new copy."

"If that happened, I'd have to get in line all over again, and that wouldn't be so bad, would it?" He had uncapped the pen and bent to write the name on the sticky note, but he looked up at her and grinned.

Her heart unwedged itself from its customary position and did a little conga line boogie around her chest before returning to normal. Emma Jean placed the flat of her hand covering the V of her tank top to force her heart to quit dancing. The man—Carolina's husband, and no doubt she was a beauty with a name like that—bent to his task. Emma Jean stared at the crown of his head. His hair was thick and lustrous. When he was finished, he looked up and smiled at her again.

"For me, it was the best moment of my life." He pushed the pad toward her.

"What was?" Emma Jean asked, pulling the Post-it off its pad and positioning it on the title page, so that she could copy the name.

"The day my son was born. I was eavesdropping on your conversation about children, and I thought somebody should come to their defense."

Emma Jean stared into his eyes—robin's egg blue but minus the inscrutable expression most blue-eyed people carried—and imagined him at play dates or soccer games. Or whatever it was people did with kids these days.

Mary/Marcy nudged her, as if to tell her to hurry it up. But the man was still smiling down at her. Laconic. That's what she would call his smile if she were writing about him in a novel. It was the only word for it. And his eyes, with that *come hither* look that made her want to follow wherever he led. Emma Jean forced her eyes away from his, and carefully inked his wife's name onto the title page, along with the usual inscription. The espresso machine hissed and the sweet smell of steamed milk filled the air. She ripped off the Post-it note and stuck it to the table, then closed the book's cover and held it out without looking at him. She'd be okay if she didn't look at him.

"Thank you, Ms. Sullivan."

She couldn't help it; she looked at him. His eyes—those amazing blue eyes—riveted her. He took the book and added it to the top of the pile in his arms.

"You're a reader," she said.

He nodded. "It's something to do when I have a spare moment at work. I usually go through a couple books a week."

"Wow," Emma Jean said. "That's even more than I read."

"I bet you're buying this one for your wife." Mary/Marcy chose this moment to insert herself into the conversation. Emma Jean glanced at the escort, annoyed. Mary/Marcy's eyes shone as she looked at the man.

"I am, but that doesn't mean I won't read it, too." He turned the book over, glanced down at the blurbs on the back cover. "Mostly I read books about art, but I like wine, so I might dig into this one. It looks pretty good. "

Emma Jean thought about this for a moment. He read books. He was a man who read books. About art, no less. Better yet, he was a hunky man who looked just like Brad Pitt who read books. Best of all, a man who might even read *her* books.

"Have a cookie," she said. Lord, could she sound any more inane?

But he took a cookie, and a napkin, and carefully placed both on top of his pile of books. "Thanks."

"What was the second-best moment of your life?" she blurted.

The timid bookstore manager chose that moment, no doubt the first ever in her life, to assert herself. "I'm sorry sir, but if Ms. Sullivan has signed your book, I must ask you to move along. We've got a long line of readers waiting."

Emma Jean shot her a dirty look, but the handsome one shrugged and smiled his laconic smile. He raised his hand in a boyish wave, turned and walked away, biting into the cookie as he left. Emma Jean watched him—he had an adorable butt—until Mary/Marcy nudged her with an elbow, and she took the book from the next person in line.

"Could you write it to Maria?" the woman said. She was short and sported spiky hair.

To Maria, Emma Jean wrote, though the words on the page blurred. All she could see was that man, his boyish blue eyes, his shock of blond hair. How long had it been since Peter looked at her with the frank appreciation that he had exhibited?

The rest of the evening proceeded uneventfully, but her mind kept going back to him. *To Alison, here's to finding your passion!* Oops, she was so distracted she forgot to underline the *your*. Oh well, Alison would just have to live without. *To Deborah, To Susanna, To Christine*…the names rolled off her pen, an endless stream. Emma Jean smiled and nodded and signed book after book, all the while acting wonderfully, endlessly kind.

Or so she hoped. She wasn't exactly sure how kind people acted. Perhaps she could ask one of her friends for advice. Who would be wisest and most helpful on this topic? She pondered this as she scribbled autographs, her hand growing more and more tired. She thought of family members, students, and her assistant, Trish, but for the life of her, she couldn't think of any friends. Then she realized that she couldn't think of any friends because she didn't *have* any. And that probably just proved the reviewer's point, didn't it? Because people who were not snarky, bitchy, and judgmental had friends. *To Andrea*, she wrote. *To Nancy*. Well, then, she would make some. Now that she was being kind, it would be good to have some friends, wouldn't it?

Finally, she inked the last inscription. The bookstore manager had her autograph the remaining books so that she could slap a *signed by the author* sticker on them and hopefully move them faster. Was it her imagination or had the manager grown more peevish over the course of the evening, constantly harping on the disproportionate numbers of fans who brought in old copies of Emma Jean's books to sign?

It didn't help that from where she sat, she could see a huge stand-alone corrugated display of *Daughter of the Devil*. The book's author, Marielle Delany, had been a student of Emma Jean's private writing group for five years. The display featured a large photo of Marielle: an adorable pixie of a woman with a stylish short haircut wearing a floral skirt over leggings. Bless her heart; Marielle was one of her most favorite students ever, even despite Marielle's wee mean streak and tendency toward manipulation. And was the outfit she'd chosen for that photo just a bit too bohemian? No, wait. Thinking that was not nice, was it? Marielle was one of her most favorite students ever, period. And *The Devil's Daughter?* Awesome book. Huge accomplishment. Seeing as it was a lurid memoir, it was probably the only one Marielle had in her, so Emma Jean was thrilled with how well it was doing. Ecstatic, even. Over the top delighted.

Then Emma Jean had a thought. Perhaps Marielle was a good candidate to be a friend. Because the more she thought about it, the more Emma Jean thought it would be nice to have some girls to pal around with. She and Marielle could go to wine bars and bitch about their husbands, never mind that Marielle was single and gay. Well, they could go out and whine about the publishing world. Yes, that would be the ticket. Emma Jean pulled her organizer from her purse and made a note to call Marielle as soon as she returned home to Portland. She felt cheered. Perhaps having friends and her Campaign to be Kind would help her out of the dull malaise of staleness that had recently enveloped her.

Emma Jean pushed back from the table and stretched her arms out straight in front of her, then moved her neck in the roll she'd learned in yoga class, before she became a yoga slacker. Then she decided to call her husband. She opened her phone and punched the Peter button, but as usual, he didn't answer. Why did people carry cell phones if they weren't going to answer them? Was he avoiding her or just busy? Emma Jean hadn't talked to him in the two days she'd been in L.A., and she had desperately needed his emotional support, what with *Wife* not selling as well as her other novels, and the constant pressure of performing at her readings.

Emma Jean stood. The bookstore manager had wandered off and so had Mary/Marcy. She glanced around and saw them across the store, chatting by the main check out area. Emma Jean liked to keep her eye on her escort, as the thought of finding her way home alone through the canyons and freeways of L.A. terrified her. Mary/Marcy would drive her back to the motel and pick her up again the next evening for a reading in Orange County, which was apparently somewhat ominous. From the way Mary/Marcy spoke, they'd have to leave *very early* to get there on time. As far as Emma Jean could tell, one had to leave *very early* to get anywhere in L.A.

She always resisted visiting L.A., number one because she had an irrational fear of earthquakes, but number two because she hated it. Hated the palm trees, the unforgiving sun, the mad rush of the freeways. Most of all, she hated the people, all of whom were way thinner and more beautiful than she could ever hope to be. Bunch of phonies. Allegiance to one's true self was one of Emma Jean's favorite themes. So L.A. stood thoroughly in opposition to all her deeply cherished beliefs, including even things like recycling and taking public transportation, which she admitted she had a tiny bit of a problem doing herself, but *still*. Soon, she consoled herself, she'd find herself back home in Portland—rainy, green, cloud-shrouded Portland—and all would be well again. Though Portland was now her home, her public persona required allegiance to her homeland in the Deep South, Alabama: the place of her birth, and Georgia: the place she was raised, and where her heart truly lay, at least as far as her fans were concerned.

I'm just a southern girl, she sang to herself as she gathered up her fountain pens. It was a song she sang to the tune of the Queen song, "Bohemian Rhapsody." *I'm just a southern girl, living in the Wild West. Because it's so easy for me to go....*Now wait, hadn't she brought five fountain pens along? She only found four on the table.

And then suddenly, she heard a man's voice belting out the rest of the "Bohemian Rhapsody" verse. Oh God, she'd been singing out loud. She looked up. It was the handsome man from the book signing. And he was holding out the missing fountain pen.

"I pocketed it by accident."

"I...I just realized it was missing. Thank you."

"I like your words to the song better, by the way."

Emma Jean nodded. "Too bad I'm a lousy singer."

He laughed and stuck out his hand. "I'm Riley Atkinson."

"Emma Jean Sullivan." Oh, *Lord* he was handsome.

"I never got a chance to answer your question."

She cocked her head to one side, quizzically.

"The second-best moment of my life."

"Oh, right." She nodded her head vigorously, too vigorously. Her breath had got caught up in her throat and the air shimmered, forming a bubble around the two of them. The rest of the bookstore fell away, as if sheared off by an earthquake, and all she could see was Riley.

"Don't you want to hear the answer?" he asked.

She nodded, not willing to trust the words that might spill from her mouth.

"The second-best moment of my life will be when you say yes to dinner."

Chapter Two

Is She Happy Now?

Despite the blazing heat lamp beside her, Emma Jean couldn't stop shivering. She couldn't tell if it was from the damp ocean air or the proximity of Riley. He and Emma Jean sat in low deck chairs on the beach outside Paradise Cove, the ridiculously overpriced restaurant where they had eaten dinner. Fog—no, Riley called it the marine layer—from the Pacific rolled in around them.

"Sure you're warm enough?" Riley said. "Do you want to go inside?"

Tendrils of fog wafted around the heat lamp and the chairs, as the ocean crashed a few yards from where they sat. A seagull called on air that smelled of salt and fish. The mist, the heat lamps, and the torches burning every few feet gave the atmosphere an otherworldly air.

She needed to feel otherworldly now, which was why she shook her head in answer to Riley's question. She needed to convince herself she was someone other than the Emma Jean Sullivan she'd known for the last forty-eight years (forty-three as far as Riley was concerned). Because the Emma Jean Sullivan who sat beside the Pacific Ocean, her black skirt hiked up to her knees, sandals cast aside, and bare toes digging into the sand, was not someone she recognized.

Riley set his glass of wine on the umbrella-bedecked table beside her chair and stood. "I'll be right back. Don't go anywhere."

"Even if I wanted to leave, I couldn't. I don't have the least clue where I am."

"Well, that's lucky for me, isn't it?" He smiled and leaned close to her, the gold glow from the heat lamp burnishing his skin. "You're in

Malibu. Land of the uber-rich and the super-stars, who happily seem to be in short supply here tonight."

"That's good." Emma Jean smiled up at Riley. "Because I don't care about seeing any super-stars. I just want to…" She bit her lip before letting slip the rest of the sentence, *be with you.*

Riley smiled and went into the restaurant. Jesus God, what was she thinking? Where were these words coming from? And what *did* she want, really? Mostly she wanted to get drunk to squelch the feelings that rose up every time she looked in Riley's eyes. She sipped her wine, the house Cabernet, which would horrify Peter. Yet wasn't it at least partially Peter's fault that she was sitting beside the foggy Pacific, having dinner with a handsome man? After all, Peter had been ignoring her calls in her time of need. Come to think of it, he'd been ignoring her in general lately. Emma Jean sighed. Mostly what she wanted was to feel young and attractive and desirable again, the way she felt when Riley looked at her. It was unfortunate, and terribly inconvenient, that her personal moral code was rabidly anti-adultery. Because if not for her high ethical standards, she would be all over the adorable Riley.

Emma Jean glanced toward the restaurant—it sat a few feet behind her, lit up like a gaudy cruise ship—to make certain Riley wasn't yet returning and whipped out her mirror. She held the fake tortoise-shell compact up to her face. Her reflection was a little difficult to make out in the flickering glow of torchlight, but at least she could check for grievous errors.

The first thing anybody noticed about Emma Jean was her hair, her wild, blonde hair, the mass of untamable curls: her glory and her shame. Her curls were wonderful and they suited her, but sometimes she got tired of being so visible, for that was what a mass of blonde, curly hair did for you: it made you eminently observable. She held the mirror closer, like a camera zooming in. Beneath surprisingly dark and thick eyebrows, her eyes were big and hazel, close set and almond-shaped, an odd combination and one that made her striking rather than pretty. Or so she'd always thought. She gazed at herself critically. Her eyes were so large as to be nearly too big for her face (which was slender on good days, round on days she was bloated), though they did balance out the long nose which almost, but not quite, had a hook on the end of it.

Peter said her eyes gave her a mystical, ethereal look. Emma Jean held the compact out further to get an overall facial view. With age, her odd eyes were starting to overwhelm her face and give her an eccentric look she wasn't sure she liked. She pursed her lips. Maybe if they were larger, they'd balance out her eyes more. Should she consider surgery? She brought the mirror in closer. Her skin was another problem. Most women who lived in Portland had flawless skin. It rained so much their complexions were dewy and soft. Hers was pretty good for her age, but the problem was her freckles.

One minute in the sun and out they popped—and despite her best efforts to cover up, Emma Jean had spent a lot of time in the Southern California sun this trip. For the gazillionth time in her life, she cursed her father, Bob, the Fake Christian, who had passed on the ever-persistent freckles to Emma Jean. Did the make-up she'd used to cover them make her look old? She had at least a decade on Riley, after all. She heard the creak of the restaurant door behind, and then the soft swishing of footsteps in the sand. She snapped the compact shut and threw it back in her purse just as Riley re-appeared before her.

He pulled one of the deck chairs around to face her, took a sip of wine and smiled at her.

"So," Riley said. "Your husband is a wine-maker?"

Emma Jean nodded. "He is. But I don't want to talk about him."

Riley grinned. "Great. Let's talk about you, then."

But what Emma Jean wanted to talk about was Riley. She took a drink of wine and tried to hide the fact that she was staring at him. She wanted to talk about why his eyes were so blue and where they got that devilish gleam that mesmerized her. She wanted to talk about why he'd asked her out to dinner, and what he saw in her. Riley raised his eyebrows, and she realized he was waiting for her to say something.

"Um, so you said you're in aviation?" Emma Jean sipped more wine.

"I thought we were going to talk about you, not me," Riley said. And then he flashed that impish smile.

Was he actually flirting with her? It had been so long since she'd flirted with a man she wasn't sure. "Everything you need to know about me, you can read on the back of the book you bought," Emma Jean said. She experimented with crossing her leg flirtatiously and allowing her skirt to ride up a bit. Or was that sending the wrong message? She uncrossed her legs, pulled her skirt down, and then downed more wine. "Tell me about what you do in aviation."

"I'm an airplane mechanic."

Emma Jean tilted the glass up too far and had to slurp noisily to swallow the resulting rush of wine.

"What does an airplane mechanic do?"

Riley laughed. "We fix airplanes."

"Wow." Emma Jean was truly at a loss for words. She'd pegged him for a computer techie type, or an entrepreneur in some kind of murky field like finance. Like all those people who ran around saying they were in "financial planning" or "investments," and nobody could ever figure out what they actually did. But an airplane mechanic? That was real, solid, not murky. She'd never known people who worked at jobs like that. In her world, being mechanically minded meant you went to college an extra year and got a degree in engineering and went on to make buckets of money. Of course, being an engineer most often meant you were socially retarded and completely boring, so perhaps she should be grateful he wasn't like *that*.

"Do you like it?" Emma Jean asked.

Riley shrugged. "I do. I like to work with my hands. And it pays pretty well. The downside is that I work nights."

"It's nighttime now, and you're not working," she pointed out helpfully.

"I'm on vacation."

"Oh." Emma pondered this for a moment. "So where's your wife and child? Why aren't you away somewhere with your family? Don't you get free air travel?"

"I do." Riley took another drink of wine. "Of course, we have to fly standby and that sucks. But to answer your question, Carolina took Noah to see her folks in North Dakota. And I saw that you were appearing and decided to stay here and see you instead."

"You are so full of bullshit," Emma Jean teased.

"I know. Don't kill me, but the truth is I've never read a thing you've written. Clearly, though, I've been missing out. You're very popular. And your readers love you, even when you're rude to them."

"Oh God." Emma Jean clutched her heart. "Was I rude to my fans tonight? Because I adore every single one of them. Every flippin' blessed one. And the last thing I want to do is be rude to them."

"I found it charming," Riley said. "I thought it was part of your persona."

Was Emma Jean the last to know that she was such a bitch? She stuck out her lower lip in a pout. "I guess I'm not doing so well on my new campaign. I'm trying to learn to be nice to people."

Riley fell against the back of his chair and laughed, sloshing the wine in his glass like one of the waves of the nearby Pacific.

"It's not funny. I'm afraid everyone thinks I'm mean."

"You're very direct. And extremely outgoing." Riley shrugged. "Most people are scared of their shadows, so they like outgoing and direct. I know I do."

"Well, thank you." At the moment, whatever was good enough for Riley was good enough for her. He was so damn cute she couldn't stand it, the way he gazed at her with that knowing smile. She just wanted to know *everything* about him, as she would a character in one of her books. "So what are you doing on this vacation, besides lurking about bookstores?"

"Making art. I like to sculpt, too. It's my true passion, art of all kinds, and I never have enough time for it."

For God's sake. He looked like Brad Pitt, he loved books, and even though he was an airplane mechanic, he sculpted in his spare time. And he knew the exact right nice things to say to her. Emma Jean narrowed her eyes and looked at him. Maybe if she stared really hard, she'd find something wrong. Anything would do, like a huge wart with a hair growing out of it. Instead, a tendril of fog, like the tail of a ghost, drifted by. Riley looked as fresh and young and adorable as ever.

"What were you doing at the bookstore, really?"

Maybe he'd say he'd been stalking her, then she could run screaming and order a cab to get her home.

"I came to buy your book. You're one of Carolina's favorite authors. So I thought I'd buy your latest for her." He raised his eyebrows and then furrowed them. "She and I...well, you know how marriage is."

Emma Jean was pretty certain by the tone of his voice that he meant his comments about marriage ominously, but she wasn't sure and she couldn't think of any delicate way to inquire further. Oh dear Lord how she wanted to know more about his marriage, about his wife, about *him*.

"Anyway, then I saw you sitting there and heard you making those ridiculous comments about children, and I was intrigued."

"They weren't ridiculous! I have strong feelings about the joys of being childless."

Riley laughed. "And because you are so very wrong about that, I decided I wanted to meet you."

"And that's why you asked me out to dinner?" she said.

"Yes. And because I don't get to hang around with creative people very often. I thought it would be nice to hear about your life as a writer, talk about creativity and things like that." Riley finished his wine and jumped up. "It was a whim, I'll admit. And sometimes whims turn out really well, like this one. But now I need to take you home." He held a hand out to Emma Jean. She allowed him to help her up and found herself face to face with him, both of them listing a bit due to the uneven sand.

"I've had a really good time tonight." Riley leaned toward her, and she stared, fascinated, at the smooth skin of his cheeks, not a wrinkle or mole on them, despite her best efforts to find something, anything wrong. He was so damn *young*. She wanted to ask if he wore sunscreen—he must, his skin was in such good shape—but it didn't seem to be quite the right moment. He hovered closer and stared directly in her eyes. She didn't shrink away as she sometimes did when Peter came that close. His eyes looked very blue, highlighted with flecks of gold from the reflection of the heat lamps and the torches.

If she moved one millimeter, if she took a deep breath, her lips would land on his. But she wasn't going to kiss Riley Atkinson because she had an amazing, wonderful husband at home, and she also had her strong moral convictions to consider. She stayed perfectly still and stared into his eyes until he laughed and said, "Let's go."

Riley drove the way a pit bull might if dogs could operate cars—aggressive and focused. He didn't talk much while performing his NASCAR routine, which gave Emma Jean the chance to ponder. She watched him in the lights of the passing cars and pressed her lips together to keep herself from blurting out, *what do you see in an old broad like me?* Not that he saw anything. Not that he was attracted to her, or she to him. Okay that wasn't true. But even if they were wildly attracted to one another, that didn't mean that they would do anything about it. Emma Jean was nothing if not good at upholding her passionate convictions.

And her convictions about adultery were among her strongest, seeing as how her father, Bob, the Fake Christian, had committed the egregious sin with horrifying repercussions that led to Emma Jean being a semi-orphan. The fact that he was now a self-styled pastor at some ridiculous southern church made his transgressions even worse. Emma Jean sulked for a minute, thinking about how his actions had created her zealous feelings about adultery and thus prevented her from doing unmentionable things with Riley.

As if he sensed her thinking about those very things, Riley looked over at her and smiled. "I enjoyed talking about creativity this evening," Riley said. "Thanks. I never get to do that."

See? He just liked to talk about art, though for the life of her, she couldn't remember all that much conversation about it.

Riley grinned. "Especially with a beautiful, bestselling author."

And then a car cut in front of him, from out of nowhere, and Riley braked and shouted an invective at him. The other driver honked. And that is when Emma Jean had the epiphany. It must have been the noise of the horn that jarred the idea loose, as if the thought had been hovering right on the edges of her consciousness, waiting for her to catch it.

When she thought about it later, she realized that the thought had been practically jumping up and down for *months*, begging her to notice it. Because it occurred to her that maybe, just maybe, she wasn't quite as happy with Peter as she professed. Would she even have gone to dinner with Riley if she were as in love with Peter as she said? Would she be allowing Riley to drive her back to her motel? Would she be sitting in his car, at this moment, listening to Riley curse the other driver? The fact she might no longer be in love with Peter was a new idea, but one that felt right. So she wasn't happy with Peter. Was she the last to know? Was he unhappy with her, too? And was that why he was avoiding her?

But perhaps it wasn't entirely her fault that she hadn't seen these things about her marriage. Because, maybe, just maybe, if she had friends, she would have realized the unsteady state of her marriage. Wasn't that what friends did for one another? Pointed out the bad things they saw going on in each other's lives? Yes, she would definitely redouble her efforts to be kind and make friends, maybe even emailing Marielle when she got back to the hotel.

Riley exited the freeway. He seemed to know where her motel was, because he lived nearby, "up Topanga," whatever that meant. "You're sure that's where you're staying?" he said as he pulled onto Ventura Boulevard.

"Last time I checked. Unless elves came and moved my stuff while we were at the reading."

Riley navigated into the parking lot of the Aku Aku Motel, driving past the lobby and beneath a huge wood A-frame arch. "It's not the kind of place I'd expect someone like you to stay."

"Remember, darling, I'm just poor southern white trash at heart," Emma Jean said. "I'm comfortable in places like this." The motel's seediness *had* alarmed her when first she arrived, but it was clean and convenient and seemed safe enough, so she stayed. And there was also the teeny, tiny, small matter of her publisher's sudden unwillingness to put her up in a decent hotel, in the style to which she was accustomed. The less she thought about the implications of that, the better.

"I'm just a southern girl…" Riley sang.

"You mock me, but it's true," Emma Jean said. "Park here. I'm up those stairs. I'm just a poor little ole girl from a town outside Tuscaloosa, Alabama, so small if you blink you miss it."

Riley turned off the car—he drove an older model Audi—and in the glow of the parking lot light, she saw him good-naturedly roll his eyes. "The bio on the back of your book says you were raised in Atlanta."

"I was, after my Mama died. We moved there when I was four. But I was born in Eulalie, Alabama." She didn't add that she and Aunt Cleo had moved to Seattle when she was ten. Her southern roots were such an integral part of her image, she liked to let people think she'd lived in Georgia for longer than was technically true. Besides, her father still lived there, so that counted. Even though he also fell into the category of things that were better not to think about.

"Still." Riley craned his neck to peer up at the motel before flipping the switch that unlocked all the doors. "Doesn't your publisher pay for these tours? I'd think they put you up in some fancy hotel."

"They wanted to, but I insisted on coming here. It's for the sake of my next novel." That was a tiny white lie. Oh dear—was lying unkind?

Riley walked around to her side of the car and opened her door. She pulled a purple binder out of her purse and held it up. The notebook contained all the material she'd collected for the next novel, so far, as well as the few halting chapters she'd managed to churn out. Not nearly enough. Her deadline loomed. At the moment, even thinking about her blocked writing seemed preferable to pondering anything else, like what was going to happen with Riley. "It's research. For my next book, *On the Trail of Tiki*. This motel is one of the few original remaining in Tiki style."

"Whatever you say."

"Want me to tell you the plot?"

"Maybe later."

Emma Jean nervously stuffed the binder back in her bag and climbed out of the car, finding herself so close to Riley she could see the pores in his skin, lit as it was by the glow of the parking lot lights.

He smiled down at her. "I better walk you to your room."

The night air was still and warm and smelled of car exhaust and asphalt. She stared at him, uncertain. But there was nothing wrong with letting him walk her to her room, right? It was a gallant, gentlemanly thing to do. She led him up the outside staircase, directly at the top of which was her room, trying not to be conscious of how he must be staring at her ass all the way up. By the time they reached the door to her room, she was shaking so hard she couldn't get the card key to work, and Riley had to do it. Once the door was open, she turned to where he stood just outside the threshold, still holding onto it.

She didn't know what to say to him. She didn't know what to do next. "Um, thanks for dinner. I had a really good time."

And that is when he leaned down to kiss her.

Next thing she knew, they were kissing, madly, deeply, passionately, in a way she hadn't been kissed in ages. She broke away from him. Even though it was the most wonderful sensation ever, she would now tell him to stop. Except he pulled her face toward his again. And she didn't resist, couldn't resist, because it felt too good to feel his lips on hers, his tongue running along her teeth and then plunging inside her mouth.

Finally she managed to quit. "Oh God. Oh, my God."

He stepped inside the room and pulled her along with him. The door slammed behind him. She barely had time to switch on a light and toss her purse on the floor before Riley had his arms around her and his lips on her again. This was what she had been missing in life. *This.* This was what she had been looking for, though she didn't even know it. Peter never kissed her like this. No, don't think of him now. But wait, she had to think of Peter now. Just because she had realized she was no longer happy with him, it didn't give her license to commit adultery. What they were doing was a *sin,* the worst offense imaginable according to her moral code. She had to stop. Now Riley was depositing little kisses all over her face. She raised her arms to push him away and instead found her arms encircling his neck and pulling him to her, to feel his lips on hers again, his tongue inside her mouth.

Oh God. She had to stop, even if this was what she had been searching for. Even if. Emma Jean broke off the kiss and looked Riley in the eyes. "We can't do this."

"You're right." Riley took a step back and let out a huge stream of air. "Okay then."

"Thanks for dinner," Emma Jean said.

"You're welcome. And I guess...I guess I'll see you around."

But Riley didn't go anywhere. He stood there, staring at her. Emma Jean stared back. She felt her chest heaving with the pressure of her heart pounding so fast and everything looked white and shimmery around her. And then they both took a step toward each other, and he was kissing her again.

This time, it was Riley who stopped. "We can't do this." But then he pulled her to him again. His mouth on her lips, his hands on her breasts. With every ounce of strength she had, she pushed him away.

"Riley, we can't. We're both married."

He nodded, then took a deep breath. "Right. Married. I'm leaving now." He turned to go, but then pivoted back and grabbed her again, holding her close, talking into her hair. "Aren't writers supposed to live on the edge?" Riley kissed her cheek. "Don't you need to collect as many experiences as possible?"

Oh, God, she loved his logic. But she also believed desperately in monogamy. Every fiber in her being, up until now, had been against adultery. This was the moment when she could say no. And yet as she stared up at the beautiful Riley, she knew, for whatever reason, that she was not going to say no to him. That all their efforts to resist each other were going to be for naught. Because the current that ran between them was just too strong.

He leaned down, and their lips connected again, and then she let him push off her cute little blue cropped jacket and pull the low-cut tank over her head. "Oh wow," he said and buried his face in her breasts, which were encased in a black lacy bra. Riley seemed to be an expert at unhooking bras, and, suddenly, his hands were on her bare breasts and then his mouth was on them, and she'd never felt anything so wonderful.

"I want to get on the bed," Emma Jean said, in a voice she didn't recognize as her own, a low, husky voice full of lust and desire. *Stop, stop, stop*, a voice inside her head called, but it sounded distant and murky, like someone shouting through a fog, and she found it easy to ignore. And then they were on the bed, and he was pulling off her skirt and then slowly kissing her stomach, which she remembered to suck in as his mouth followed its curve. Before she knew it, he was pulling off her panties.

And then he paused for a minute.

"What are you doing?" she cried. "Keep going!"

"I can't. I don't have a condom."

"I hate condoms," Emma Jean said. Except it had been years and years since she had actually used one. At the moment, she'd do anything to feel Riley inside her, sheathed in rubber or not.

"We can't take the chance you might get pregnant." He kissed her breasts and then her mouth as he said this and then worked his way back down her body with his tongue.

"Oh God, that feels good. Don't worry. I can't get pregnant to save my life."

"Really?" Riley said, his voice muffled.

"Oh shit, don't stop," she gasped. "I'm infertile. Besides I'm too old, the odds are against me."

"You're not old," Riley said, and then he climbed on top of her.

And Riley inside her was life in a different country, maybe even a different planet. It was an entire garden in bloom, all the windows in the house open to a spring breeze, a whole room full of Christmas presents. Oh dear Lord, why didn't she know making love could feel this way?

He looked at her and laughed. "Does it feel as good to you as it does to me?"

She never took her eyes off his while she nodded yes. Ocean tides rolled in and out, vast armadas defended major cities, empires rose and fell. In his eyes, she saw it all. Babies were born, grew up, and died. All over the world, people went about their business. Emma Jean felt a part of it all. And in this instant, this connection between Riley and Emma Jean, she felt every single thing. She knew the secret. For the moment, it was all she needed to know.

Chapter Three

Sacred Cows, Tipping

Emma Jean needed a drink, now. She looked out the window as the airplane taxied along the tarmac of the Burbank airport. Christ, would they ever get airborne? She needed a drink to obliterate the memory of Riley, the feel of his skin, the touch of his hand, the softness of his lips. She needed a drink to forget that she'd spent the last five days fornicating with a man who was not her husband. Fornicating was an awful word, Emma Jean decided as she craned her neck around her seatmate, looking for a stewardess. Fornicating sounded like animals rutting. But the other f-word sounded vulgar unless it was used in the throes of passion. Adultery was a complicated business. Emma Jean sighed.

"Are you afraid of flying?" the woman in the aisle seat asked.

Until this moment, Emma Jean had been so lost in her thoughts of Riley she'd not paid any attention to her neighbor. The woman had bottle-blonde hair and smudged mascara beneath her right eye. She wore a yellow sweatshirt—Emma Jean thought she might have to kill her when she saw the teddy bears on it—and blue nylon pants with a racing stripe down each leg. Mentally reviewing the woman's outfit was discernment, not criticism, right? And Emma Jean's decision that it was hideous was certainly fact, not judgment. Wasn't it? This business of trying to be nice was almost as complex as adultery.

"Excuse me?" Emma Jean said.

"You're afraid of flying?" the woman repeated.

"Who, me? No. I fly all the time."

"Oh." The woman didn't look convinced. "It's just that you seem rather agitated. And you're clutching that little thing so hard I couldn't help but wonder."

Emma Jean unclenched her hand, revealing the plump red Buddha that now sat atop the flat of her open palm. "He's for good luck. In general, not just for flying."

The woman moved her mouth into a smile after what looked like a quick recovery from a grimace, and too late Emma Jean remembered she wasn't on a plane home to Oregon, but rather to Idaho, land of Mormons and other like-minded conservatives to whom a Buddha might be akin to the anti-Christ. Emma Jean sniffed the air, wondering about the source of the strange smell. She told her students to be precise, that specificity was the cornerstone of good description. She inhaled again, and the source of the odor occurred to her. Ketosis. It was the smell of the body feeding on itself, the smell people got when they did a strict low-carb diet. Maybe Emma Jean should ask her about it. She hadn't liked the way her stomach looked when she was naked with Riley, though she was learning—had learned, because it was over—that sex was better, way better, when you put aside concerns about how you looked naked and just *enjoyed* yourself.

"Well, I'm okay with it now, but flying used to really bother me," her seatmate said. "Had to go to a psychologist and everything."

"Oh." Emma Jean nodded.

"The counseling really helped. Now I fly all the time."

"I'm glad," Emma Jean said, though she wished the woman would stop her chatter. Emma Jean pulled the airline magazine from the seat pocket and started leafing through it, hoping she would get the hint. Usually she loved to chat with strangers, who she found a rich source of story ideas. But at the moment, all she wanted to do was think. She had so much to *process* before she saw Peter. For instance, the burning question she'd been attempting to answer the last five days: What makes a woman decide to commit adultery? Especially a chaste and moral woman like herself, for whom adultery was antithetical to everything she believed in?

Emma Jean needed that drink, damn it; even if it was just three and only lushes drank in the afternoon. Maybe she *was* a lush, or a libertine, as Riley had called her. He was no dummy, coming up with a word like that to describe her, even if he was an airplane mechanic.

She needed to forget the dull, throbbing pain she felt whenever she realized she'd never see him again, which they'd both agreed was best. "The memory of our time together will be enough," he had said. Which meant that she'd never have sex like that again. Could she live without it? She had no choice. Emma Jean had her marriage to consider, and equally important, her fans. They'd be devastated at her moral lapse, seeing as how she'd upheld the sanctity of marriage every bit as rabidly as she'd trumpeted the joys of childlessness. Plus she was known to regularly pop off against the evils of adultery. Oh, Lord, what had she done? Had the best time of her life, ever, that was what. And now it was over. She needed to forget the wonder of his touch, skin against skin, the amazing feeling of making love with him, the reality of it a constant, obsessive wonder, Riley inside her, filling her up, gazing into her eyes.

After the first night, they'd spent the whole week together. The next day Riley had gone home to check on the cats and brought back a bag of clothes. Emma Jean had dismissed Mary/Marcy—whose fault the affair was anyway, because she had insisted Emma Jean wear the top with cleavage—and allowed Riley to ferry her around. He drove better than Mary/Marcy and knew all the shortcuts. And so they'd had five days together, living in glorious sin.

But now her week of sin was over, after a wrenching goodbye at the airport, and she was left to ponder its fallout. For instance, *here* was a question: What makes a man decide to commit adultery? What kind of man would sleep with another woman when his own wife and child were out of town?

"You probably do this all the time," Emma Jean had said. "You probably make it a habit to pick up bestselling authors when their book signings bomb and they are at their lowest ebb, just to make them feel better." Then she was sorry she'd asked, not wanting to hear that yes, he did do this all the time, picking up women was routine for him, sex like this an everyday occurrence. "Oh God, do you?"

And thank you, God, or Buddha, Riley had stared into her eyes and shook his head very slowly. "Oh no," he'd said, looking infinitely sad. "You have no idea how reckless this is for me. I'm usually the soul of responsibility. How about you?"

"Who, me? Oh darling, your hands are the only ones besides Peter's to touch this woman's body since I took my marriage vows."

Any doubts she might have had about Riley's honesty were later dispelled in a thrilling manner. He'd told her how he had to leave art school and learn a trade to support Carolina's pregnancy, and still later, he'd confessed that he was certain that Noah was not his biological son.

The woman in the next seat sighed and glanced toward her. Emma Jean held the magazine up higher, pretending to read it, but in reality, she looked out the window. The plane taxied past a gigantic hangar, a parallel runway, and a cluster of odd buildings sequestered behind a chain-link fence. She peered at the hangar. Would that be where Riley worked? She was still a bit unclear on what it was that an airplane mechanic actually did.

The airplane picked up speed as it sailed down the runway, and there was that odd moment when the wheels left the ground and suddenly you realized you were flying. Emma Jean tightened her fist around her little, fat Buddha. A baby started crying a few rows back and continued even after the plane seemed to have reached its desired altitude and started leveling off. Was that the rattle of the beverage cart she heard? It was difficult to tell over the wails of the damn baby. Oh Lord, she needed a drink. Conveniently, at that moment, a stewardess walked by, holding a pillow.

"Stewardess," Emma Jean called. But she'd already passed by.

"I don't think they like to be called that anymore," her seatmate whispered conspiratorially.

"They don't?"

The woman shook her head. "It's flight attendant."

"Well, whatever they like to be called, I wish one of them would pay attention to me."

She clutched her Buddha more tightly. Was it kosher to pray to a Buddha? Maybe not if you were praying for a drink. She opened her palm and brought it up to eye level to inspect. She'd bought him at a Borders in Orange County, where she'd looked for a spirituality book that would explain the epiphany she'd had during sex with Riley, the feeling that she and everyone else in the world were all one.

She could barely even stand to say it to herself; it sounded so dopey. The Christian books seemed to have little to offer on the subject, but a quick glance at several of the Buddhist tomes convinced her she might find answers in them. At the checkout counter, she'd found the little Buddha nestled among a display of gift items. She added him to her pile of books on Zen and Buddhism, and he'd been her constant companion since.

She named him Aku Aku, after her motel, though she wasn't sure if naming a Buddha was sacrilegious or not. The original owners of the motel had known their stuff, because the name had other connotations. It had been the name of Thor Heyerdahl's second book; his first, *Kon Tiki,* was a runaway bestseller in the early fifties—Emma Jean always admired runaway bestsellers, and *Kon Tiki* was one of the five or so books she was currently reading— and had started the craze for Tiki. But beyond that, the name had deeper meaning. To the Easter Islanders, an Aku Aku was an invisible alter ego, a sort of spiritual guide. Emma Jean liked the idea of her Buddha as a spiritual guide.

Emma Jean wasn't certain the Bees—that was what she had taken to calling the Buddhists in her mind—thought anything was sacrilegious, as long as it made you happy.

The Bees had a kind of prescription for living similar to the Ten Commandments, didn't they? Emma Jean dug her current favorite book out of her bag. It was written by a Vietnamese monk named Thich Nhat Hanh, who lived in exile in France at a place—a monastery, a commune, or what?—called Plum Village. She liked his cheerful, smiling photo on the back cover and so far, she liked his straightforward explanations of the Buddhist philosophy. If the bottom ever dropped out of the novel writing market, maybe she'd move to France and become a Plum Village nun.

But, wait—oh God. Did Buddhist nuns get to have sex? Did Buddhists in general get to have sex? That might fall under the category of creating suffering, because desire for something you couldn't have—like sex with Riley—created suffering. The idea was to be happy with what you had, to not have expectations, to *be here now*. Emma Jean stared out the window at a bank of clouds. She wasn't being here now at all, was she? Because half her brain and all of her body was back with Riley. Sex with Peter she could give up, but sex with Riley she wasn't so sure about it. Though she *had* given it up, she reminded herself firmly, because she was not going to see him again, ever.

Suddenly Emma Jean became aware of the gaze of her seatmate, who nodded toward the Thich Nhat Hanh book in Emma's hand.

"You must be a Buddhist."

"I'm actually just starting to study it."

"There's a lot of that kind of thing in Sun Valley. Have you been to the Garden of Infinite Compassion yet?"

Emma Jean craned her neck to look for the flight attendant, but she seemed to have disappeared. She hit the orange call button above her. "I'm sorry." Emma placed her hands in the air in front of her, as if pushing something down. "I just really need something to drink. What were you saying?"

"The Garden of Infinite Compassion? It's got a prayer wheel blessed by the Dalai Lama. I cry every time I go."

"Actually, I've never been to Sun Valley before," Emma Jean said. "My aunt—she's really more like my mother—owns a gallery there, and I'm going up for a big opening she's having. She's been trying to get me up there forever."

"Oh, you'll love it. Gorgeous country, still mostly unspoiled. My name's Wendy, by the way."

"I'm Emma Jean. No, I think I'll hate it. I'm not much of a mountain fan. It's the ocean I love."

"Who's your aunt?" Wendy asked.

"Cleo Zelch."

"The Zelch Gallery! I know that one. I walk by it all the time on my way to work."

The stewardess, her hair blonde and poufy like the Bubble Cut Barbie that Emma Jean had adored as a little girl, appeared and leaned in to Emma Jean's seat. "Did you need something?"

Emma Jean nodded. "A drink."

"Ma'am, we're just in the process of getting the cart ready. It'll be a few minutes."

"But I'm desperate," Emma Jean said, pointing to her throat.

"I can bring you a bottle of water. I'm afraid it will be warm, but it's the best I can do."

"I was hoping for a glass of red wine," Emma said.

"Ma'am—"

Just then another stewardess appeared. This one had dark hair and rosy cheeks. "Which one of you is Emma Jean Sullivan?"

Emma Jean raised her hand. Authority figures made her feel like she was back in school again.

"Oh God, I'm so happy to meet you." The attendant leaned across Wendy, causing her to push herself back against her seat, and stuck a hand out to Emma Jean. "I've read all your books. Except for your newest one. Usually I wait until books come out in paperback. Hardbacks are *so* expensive these days."

"Well, aren't you just the sweetest thing, sugar." Emma Jean sat up straighter in her seat and took the attendant's proffered hand in both of hers. "I just love meeting fans of mine." Peter always told her she laid it on too thick, but she couldn't help it, it came naturally to her when she was meeting her public.

"I'm Rachel," the flight attendant said. "Did you have a problem, Ms. Sullivan?"

"Nothing that a little red wine won't solve."

"Oh of course, I'll bring you a glass right away."

"Thank you." Emma Jean beamed. "Oh, Rachel, wait. Could you be a love and bring me two glasses? That way it'll be less work for you."

"Good idea, Ms. Sullivan. I'll bring them right out."

Wendy regarded her curiously after Rachel and her frowning co-worker walked off. "You're an author?"

"Yep. *The Winemaker's Wife* is my latest."

"Oh man, I just read a review of that. In the *Oxford American*," Wendy said.

Wouldn't you know, Wendy had managed to get her hands on that damned review. Perhaps she could blame it for the less-than-stellar response to her L.A. book tour. Book sales at all her Southern California readings had been disappointing. She'd signed hundreds of worn copies of her older books but few of the newest release.

Having Riley to distract her had made it easy not to obsess, but now that she found herself facing a cold, hard, Riley-less world the tepid sales of *Wife* loomed large.

"I also wrote *Motherless Daughter* and *Finding Felicity*."

"Oh, I've read *Finding Felicity*. I loved that book."

"Thanks, doll." Now that Wendy was officially part of her public, she warranted the occasional *doll* or *sugar* or *darling*. And then the lovely thought occurred to her that perhaps Wendy could even become a friend. Never mind that she lived in Sun Valley, they could become pen friends. And that would count, wouldn't it? Emma Jean reached beneath her seat to find a copy of *Wife* to show her, but Wendy came up with a book first.

She held up a thick hardcover. "I just started this one. It's good. It's like, on the bestseller list or something, and it deserves to be."

Emma Jean gasped when she read the title. *Daughter of the Devil*, by Marielle Delany.

"Marielle's book is on the bestseller list?"

"You know her?"

"Very well. She's my student. And a good friend," Emma Jean added as an afterthought. Perhaps saying it would make it true. "She wrote every word of that book in my class. It's on the bestseller list?"

"Yep," Wendy said. "Just saw the list at the store when I bought it."

"On *The New York Times* list? It makes a difference, you know. These days, publishers claim it's a bestseller when it makes the list in Podunksville, Iowa."

"It was the *Times*. I know for sure. I used to work in a bookstore. Now I work part-time at the library."

Emma Jean felt like a huge weight was pushing her down into her seat, like her entire life was thudding to a halt. It wasn't fair that her own recent book tour had been a total disaster, while Marielle's book effortlessly made the bestseller list. Shouldn't her efforts to be nice have paid off a bit more by now?

"Well, bully for Marielle. Though you know…" Emma Jean paused. "Oh, no, I shouldn't say anything."

Wendy leaned forward, and her ketosis smell wafted about the row of seats. Emma Jean reminded herself not to be judgmental, even though the universe was apparently not going to see fit to reward her for it. Lovely, Wendy smelled absolutely lovely.

"What? Tell me." Wendy said.

Rachel the flight attendant, at that moment brought Emma's two glasses of wine. Wendy held one in each hand while Emma Jean found some money.

Rachel took the ten. "Thank you, Ms. Sullivan. I can't wait to read your latest."

"Call me Emma Jean. And bring me your name and address; I'll make sure you get a signed copy of it."

"Oh my God. But…I mean…oh goodness. That would be great!"

Emma Jean pulled the tray table down and took both glasses from Wendy. "Thanks, love." She took a long sip of wine and sighed with happiness.

"You were going to tell me about this book," said Wendy, hoisting Marielle's memoir in the air.

"Oh, right." She drank a bit more, which made it easy to ignore the voice in her head that was telling her to stop talking about Marielle's book. "Well, you know how they call it a memoir, which is supposed to mean it's true, right?" Too late, she remembered that Wendy worked at the library. "Oh, sorry, I didn't mean to insult your intelligence, but you'd be surprised how many times I've had to explain that to people. My first book was a memoir, you know."

Wendy nodded.

"Anyway, like I said, Marielle wrote every word of that book in my class. I have this ongoing group that I've been leading for years. So I know for a fact that much of it is simply not true. Makes a great story, but it's not a true story." Another long drink of wine, and the first glass was half full. The faster she drank it, the more of a buzz she got. And the easier it was to dismiss the mental voice that was now shrieking for her to shut up.

"It's not true?" Wendy asked. "What about the part where she watches her mother naked on the altar with all the snakes writhing around her and then they bring in the slaughtered cow and her mother drinks its blood? That part isn't true?"

Emma Jean raised her eyebrows and shook her head slowly back and forth, then reached for her glass and tossed most of the rest of it down. God, it was amazing how even the crappiest of wines made her feel better. Telling stories took a lot of mental energy, she always told Peter, whether she was at her desk or on an airplane, and expending that energy left her strangely exhausted and ebullient at the same time. It was as if she were very lightly tethered to this planet, and telling stories took her to the far end of the rope, hanging by a thread far out there in the ozone where the air was thin—very thin these days—and everything was crystal clear. Alcohol took the edges off and made things nice and blurry again.

The power of story was one of Emma Jean's favorite topics, and she pondered it a moment now. Already in her mind, she was shaping her love affair with Riley into a story, a sort of soul mates torn asunder type thing. Their story would have an overall theme of inevitability, she decided. Irresistible attraction. This attraction was so strong, so powerful—and this was the crucial part—*that the betrayal of their spouses wasn't their fault.* They *had* to give into each other. To do otherwise would be to go against the laws of nature, of God, of the Buddha. And then she had another lovely thought—perhaps her propensity for adultery had its root in genetics, seeing as how Bob, the Fake Christian had an affair that had killed her mother. That would make it *really* not her fault. Emma Jean finished her first glass of wine and plunked it down on the tray table, noticing, out of the corner of her eye, Wendy turning Marielle's book over and over in her hands, as if it had suddenly turned into an alien object.

Oh God, what had she done? She was tipping all her sacred cows, or perhaps one could say she was bulldozing right over them: betraying Peter and now betraying one of her students. And what about her Campaign to be Kind and make friends? That had flown right out the window, too. She hadn't really meant to pop off about the truthfulness of Marielle's memoir, particularly because she had decided to befriend her. They'd known each other long enough, for God's sakes. Emma Jean remembered when Marielle had first arrived in her class, a timid transplant from Ohio who had moved to Portland for the freedom its alternative culture provided. She slowly grew more confident as her writing improved. Though Marielle staunchly defended the truthfulness of her book, Emma Jean had always wondered. She'd even suggested that Marielle write it as fiction. Thus had her suspicions had long lain buried, only to be activated by the news that her student's book had reached bestseller status. While *The Winemaker's Wife* languished, so far, in obscurity, with Emma Jean in danger of not earning out her advance.

"You know, I'd still read it and everything." She handed her empty wine glass to Wendy. "Be a love and hand this to Rachel, would you?" Rachel and her counterpart were two rows ahead. Should Emma Jean ask for more wine? "Just think of it as fiction, not truth. I always tell my students that the best fiction is true, anyway."

Rachel appeared with the cart. Emma Jean asked for water and Rachel handed her a fat little bottle of it. She also winked and gave her another glass of wine. "My treat," she said, as she gave Emma Jean her name and address written on a napkin. At least Emma Jean retained one sacred cow: her fans. Emma Jean again had Wendy hold her wine glasses while she carefully stashed Rachel's address in her planner. Peter kept telling her to get an iPhone, but Emma Jean still loved the feel of pen on paper. She liked planners that looked used, that had pages wrinkled from being covered with writing, bits and pieces of arcana stuck in them, Post-it notes marking particular pages, the way hers did. Buying planners and purses was a passion of Emma Jean's. She also bought books by the truckload, and she could spend fortunes at office supply stores. The thought occurred she might soon have to curb her enthusiasms if the sales of *Wife* didn't pick up. Emma Jean squelched that thought and instead pulled out one of her purple fountain pens. She experienced a brief pang, remembering how Riley had "stolen" one from her and how returning it was what started everything. She looked up at Wendy. "If you give me your name and address, I'll send you a book, too."

It took a bit of squealing and fawning and writing of addresses to get Emma Jean's planner back in her bag, and herself sitting back upright with the two glasses which were quickly becoming one and a half on her tray table.

By the time they started the descent and Emma Jean had to give up her garbage and return her tray table to its upright position, she'd managed to down all three glasses of wine, and she and Wendy were having a fabulous discussion of Buddhism with a bit thrown in about the state of the publishing world here and there. Later, Emma Jean would regret that she couldn't remember much of what had been said as she was certain deep profundities had been uttered.

She teetered a little bit when she stood and had to grab the back of the seat in front of her, narrowly missing a handful of a woman's hair who sat there. Emma Jean's least favorite part of flying was after the plane had quit taxiing and the seat belt sign had gone off and everyone stood up waiting for the cabin door to open. Emma Jean could feel how suddenly everyone's brain was *somewhere else*.

The line in the aisle moved forward, and Emma Jean grabbed her purse from the seat where she'd hoisted it as soon as they landed and straightened from the half-bent position she'd assumed while waiting for Wendy to enter the aisle. She and Wendy hugged, Emma Jean holding her breath so as not to have to smell Wendy's lovely ketosis, and Emma promised to send her the book. "Come to the opening if you get the chance," Emma Jean said, pleased with how friendly she was being. Emma Jean slowly shuffled forward, holding her laptop in front of her to fit between the seats. She hated flying coach, but this plane was so small—a direct flight from Burbank to the Hailey airport, which was tiny, according to Peter—that it had no first class. At the front of the plane, she followed the same routine with Rachel that she had with Wendy, but at least she didn't have to hold her nose, as Rachel smelled good, fresh and young and fruity.

But when Emma Jean stepped into the doorway of the airplane, she stopped dead. The plane was so small its open door formed the steps down to the tarmac. In Burbank, they had wheeled a rickety chrome ramp up to the plane for embarkation, but here there were only the narrow steps carved into the door and Emma Jean had to grab the edge of the door to steady herself. She felt an instantaneous sensation of pitching forward, falling, and her head was dizzy and it sounded like deep inside her brain a doorbell was ringing over and over. But as she stared out the door of the plane, she knew these sensations were not from the alcohol.

Was it fate? Would the Bees call it karma? (But if so, hadn't her recent behavior earned her bad karma, not good?) Later, looking back, Emma Jean would wonder if it was God's way of offering up a balm for the trials to come, except then she'd also remember that she, as a somewhat practicing Buddhist, did not believe in God.

"Oh dear Lord, why didn't anyone ever tell me?"

Because, as she looked out the door of the plane to the mountain landscape, for the second time in a week, Emma Jean Sullivan fell in love.

Chapter Four
The Solace of Falling in Love

Emma Jean walked backward across the tarmac all the way from the airplane, inhaling the scenery. Oh God, the blue sky! The mountains so cozy and comforting! The clean, fresh air! The airport was in Hailey, a few miles down the road from Ketchum and situated in a half-mile wide valley with brown mountains crowning it on either side, some covered with groves of trees. They were pines and firs and maybe aspens. She'd have to get a book and figure it all out. Emma Jean wanted to breathe in every aspect of this new world, to allow it to fill her up the way that Riley did. But first she had to find her husband.

She quickened her step, opened the door to the small airport, and stepped inside a miniscule waiting area that was one big room with a few rows of ratty seats. At one end were the check-in windows, and at the other was baggage claim. And in the middle of it, there stood Peter: his once sandy blond hair now graying and his hairline rapidly receding, his brown eyes hidden behind glasses, his khaki pants a little too baggy. Peter looked boyish, but not in the way Riley looked boyish, because Riley was still so damn young. Peter looked boyish in an absent-minded professor kind of way, like his brain hadn't aged at the same rate as his body.

He had his hands in his pockets, and he rocked from toe to heel as he stared at the bulletin board. She felt a sudden rush of love for him, like a mother seeing her child again. Maybe everything would be okay. Maybe she'd fall back in love with her husband. Peter was, after all, the man she'd been married to for the last fifteen years, the man she had built a comfortable life with. For most of those years, things had been pretty good, so perhaps they'd get through this recent rough patch readily. Maybe she'd be able to forget Riley quickly and easily. At the moment, Peter looked appealing the same way her old slippers did after a long day interacting with her fans. Emma Jean launched herself at him just as he caught sight of her.

"Hi, darling."

She flung her arms around her husband's neck. He smelled vaguely of something fermenting. He felt solid and real, and now that she was hanging onto his body, old. His body didn't feel the least bit boyish. Peter felt old as in established and loyal and steady, not old as in fuddy-duddy, though, let's be honest, he did act a bit old man-ish at times. But that was a good thing, Emma Jean hastened to tell herself, remembering her vow to be kind.

Peter took a step back and placed his hand at her waist, to steady both of them. He sniffed, then held her at arm's length and looked at her suspiciously.

"You're drunk," he said.

"It was a long flight," Emma Jean said.

"It was only two hours."

"Well, it was crowded. And the stewardess—"

"They don't like to be called that anymore."

"Oh Jesus. From your lips to Wendy's mouth. Or Wendy's mouth to your lips. Or whatever the expression is. The flight attendant had read my books and so she gave me wine."

"Emma Jean. Flight attendants do not just give you wine."

"Rachel did."

"What kind of wine are they serving on planes these days?"

Emma Jean opened her mouth but realized she didn't have a clue what she'd been drinking. "Um…"

"You're impossible." Peter shook his head, then patted her on the shoulder and separated himself from the arm's length embrace. "Baggage claim's over here. Let's get going, I need to get back and make sure the wine is set up." Peter glanced at his watch. "The opening starts in half an hour."

"Half an hour?" Emma Jean screeched. "I thought I'd have time to relax first."

"Your plane was late, honey. And nobody but you would think it a good idea to get drunk on your way to a reading."

"I'm doing a reading?" Emma Jean ran to catch up with Peter, who strode ahead of her toward an area at the end of the room where an airline employee was off-loading bags. Emma Jean regarded him with interest. He wore a vest with bright, reflective orange and yellow stripes on it. Did Riley wear vests like that when he worked among aircraft?

"Didn't Cleo tell you anything?"

Emma Jean shook her head, but when Peter turned to grab her luggage, she bit her lip. She hadn't answered many calls during the time she'd spent with Riley. Come to think of it, Aunt Cleo *had* phoned several times. And Emma Jean hadn't listened to messages, either. Normally, Emma Jean prided herself on her professionalism. Well, she never would have drunk all the wine if she'd known she was going to be expected to perform.

While Peter hoisted her bags from the slanted metal shelf that served as the claim area, Emma Jean turned on her phone and nearly immediately it rang. Caller ID listed Riley's number. She pressed a hand to her heart to stop it from dancing. Oh God, she wanted to hear his voice. But just then Peter turned toward her. She pushed the silence button.

"Who was that?" Peter said.

The best lies have an element of truth in them. Or so Emma Jean had once written in a novel. And, plus, wasn't it better for her Campaign to be Kind if she were partially honest? "Oh, it was this airplane mechanic I met at—"

But Peter was already gone, headed out toward the door. So much for charming him with the truth. Emma Jean bent to pull the handle up on her suitcase and follow him. Outside the air felt clear and fresh on her face and it smelled like grass and dirt and sunshine and water. But her inhalation seemed to stop at her neck, like she couldn't quite get any air into her lungs. It made her feel even more lightheaded than she already was from the wine.

"Damn, it's hard to breathe here," Emma Jean said.

"High altitude. It's worse when you fly direct. If you drive, you have more time to get acclimated."

Peter had arrived in Sun Valley the night before, because he liked to be the one in control, the one to make arrangements and scout the lay of the land. Emma Jean acceded to Peter's needs along these lines, because she knew he did it in reaction to her greater success. It was also one of the best things about him. Peter could be counted on to take excellent, wonderful care of details at such times and she was grateful. It was a very manly trait, and if there was one thing she believed strongly in, it was the importance of not stripping him of his manliness, the way some husbands of successful women were. She *hated* unmanly men. Riley was nothing if not manly.

Speaking of whom, she wondered if he'd left a message. And then she marveled for a moment that he had called, despite her dramatic vow never to see him again, despite the fact she had clutched her bosom and told him not to contact her. She loved a man who didn't follow orders, at least when she wasn't married to him. She wanted to see if he'd left a message but checking her phone would be too obvious and so instead she climbed into the rental car.

And oh, bless Peter's heart, there sitting on the console was a bottle of her special Vitamin Water, the kind she always wanted to fortify herself with before a reading. Truly he was the best, most thoughtful husband ever, Riley or no Riley.

As soon as she got her seatbelt on, her phone rang again, causing her heart to catapult. But it wasn't Riley this time, it was her father. She pressed the button to ignore the call.

"Who was it?" Peter asked, as he backed out of the parking space.

"Bob, the Fake Christian."

"Again? Shouldn't you talk to the poor guy once in a while? He is your father, after all. It's actually impressive how often he calls, seeing as how you never answer. The man is determined, you've got to give him that."

"So what if he's determined? He's an evil, adulterous bastard, and I don't care if I ever speak to him again," Emma Jean said. "His immoral actions killed my mother. Why should I want to talk to him?"

"Okay, okay," Peter said.

Emma Jean opened the windows wide to let the wind blow through the car, hoping that it ruffled her hair in an attractive manner. Then she had an unpleasant thought. She herself was an immoral adulterer, just like her father. While on the one hand, it was nice to blame her actions on genetics, on the other hand, *she* was no better than her father, the man she had spurned for actions very much like her own. But could she help it if adultery ran in her blood, if the propensity to stray was part of her DNA? Looked at from that angle, succumbing to Riley was practically inevitable. Even so, she must hew to a higher standard than Bob, and that was the very reason why, she reminded herself, that she and Riley had agreed they must never see each other or contact each other again. The very reason why she would ignore the fact that Riley had just called, despite that she could feel her heart bursting with yearning to hear his voice.

She would now ignore such thoughts and be in the moment, viewing the luscious scenery. They drove along a stretch where ranches lined both sides of the road. The sky was clear and cobalt, a deep blue in the gathering twilight, deeper than she'd ever seen it. Must be from the high altitude, though she wasn't certain. She hadn't spent much time in the mountains, preferring the solace of the sea.

"I can't believe this place. I'm so in love with it. Why haven't I been here before?"

Peter cleared his throat. He was a throat clearer and a cougher and a nose-blower. "I believe your Aunt Cleo has been trying to get you up here for about the last two years or so."

"Oh." She had indeed resisted her aunt's pleas to come see the "new" gallery in Ketchum for the entire two years Cleo had owned it. Why, she couldn't say, except now she wondered if it was because somewhere deep inside, she had known she would fall in love with the place. And falling in love implied responsibility, didn't it? If you loved something, you had to take care of it. You had to spend time with it and learn about it and then it became part of you and if you couldn't have it, you were sad. It was what the Bees would call forming an attachment, an expectation. So did that mean the Bees thought falling in love was bad?

"Emma Jean, listen. We have to talk."

"Oh, I know darling, I have so much to tell you." And so much she *couldn't* tell him. "Guess what? I've been studying Buddhism."

"Emma Jean. Unless you're writing or reading, you can barely sit still to carry on a conversation. How are you going to meditate?"

Meditation was one of the drawbacks of Buddhism, she had to admit. While the philosophy behind the religion attracted her, the actual practice of it—sitting for hours in zazen on a special pillow—completely freaked her out. But then the way Riley's face looked when he was inside her popped into her mind. And she remembered how she felt the first time, when suddenly she understood that everyone was connected. For one fleeting moment, she'd known it with all her heart and soul. She wanted to know that always.

"I do needlepoint," she said. "That requires sitting still."

"Oh, Emma Jean," he said and shook his head sadly, as if she had been a misbehaving child who had disappointed him. "We need to talk about more than your latest whim."

"It's not a *whim*. It's a passion."

"Really. We have to talk."

It wasn't like Peter to be so insistent. Oh God, what did he want to talk about? Usually when he made serious pronouncements such as this, when he wanted to *talk*, it turned out to be something fairly trivial, like the time he wanted to buy a new car, or when he was going to be working long hours during crush and he wanted to make sure she was okay with it. But never before had she had something to hide. Suddenly Emma Jean felt the heart-stopping burden of carrying a secret. What if he had found out about Riley?

"Oh, darling—" Emma Jean fumbled for the right words to indicate her *extreme* interest in talking to him but also the terrible *inconvenience* of talking to him at this precise moment. She was about to pull out one of her trumps, one of the ironclad excuses that never failed: *I'm going to do a reading and I need this time to prepare mentally.* This trump had many permutations, and all were imminently usable. *I'm on deadline, sweetheart.* Or, *I've got to prepare for my class.* All were linked to her career, and since her career was the more lucrative and successful and enabled him to take a lesser-paid job, to follow *his* passion, every one of her trumps usually shut him up immediately.

"I know, I know, you have a reading," Peter said.

What was he going on about now? Oops, that would be, what was her wonderful husband talking about? Emma Jean lectured herself sternly. He was her beloved Peter, as comfy as her old chenille bathrobe. And he was very, very good at arranging things for her, a fact that she was very, very grateful for. Among other things. There were many, many other things that she adored about her husband and she would ponder them later, after her reading. Perhaps she would even make a list.

"I understand you need time to prepare for your appearance, Emma Jean, but you and I need to talk. You've been gone for a week, and I tried to call you repeatedly, but you didn't answer, which is why I am forced to tell you about my new business now."

Traffic in front of them slowed to a crawl, and the scenery changed from fields and ranches to houses with a few small buildings interspersed. The buildings and condos got denser and suddenly they were in the middle of town.

"Oh, what an adorable place!" Emma Jean cried. Nearly all the buildings were constructed of wood and river rock, or in charming chalet style. It was like the quintessential image of a mountain town, miniature in scale, with cute little stores bedecked with strings of lights that were just blinking on and lavish flower baskets hanging from lampposts.

"Emma Jean, pay attention. I'm trying to tell you something. I'm starting my own winery. Sullivan Wines." He turned down a side street, past a ski shop and a pizza parlor and Emma Jean peered out the window at the mountain that loomed over Ketchum, with its ski runs cut through swaths of trees.

"Oh, I love it here darling, it is absolutely wonderful. God, I can't believe we've not been here before." And then suddenly Emma Jean processed Peter's words. "Wait, what? What did you just say?"

"Here we are," Peter said as he pulled into a head-in spot in front of a modern-looking building. It featured a large picture window through which she could see people milling about, and a small courtyard beside the entrance filled with modern sculpture. An elegant sign above the door read, *Zelch Gallery*.

"What did you just say?"

"I'm starting my own winery. Sullivan Wines. You know it's what I've always wanted to do."

"Now? You're starting a winery now?"

Emma Jean stared at Peter with her mouth open, in a highly unattractive manner, no doubt. What the hell was this about? Peter had talked about starting his own winery for years, God knows sometimes it was all he talked about, but starting a winery took money, and he had none. As a matter of fact, he relied quite heavily on *her* money. And let's be honest, he did like to spend her money quite a bit. But she'd be damned if she'd go to the poor house financing a winery. She might well be her on her way there even without a damn winery to fund. Anyway, when would he have time to make his own wine? Wasn't he busy enough already, what with his winemaking job?

"There's no time like the present," Peter said. "Did you know that more millionaires get their start during recessions than at any other time?"

A tic on Peter's cheek pulsed as he leaned forward to turn off the engine. Back when she had first met Peter, she had liked his self-help and psychobabble proclamations, especially because he'd just returned from studying at Esalen and everything he said sounded so *wise*. But back then, he'd also been a handsome young attorney who impressed her with his knowledge of wine, a solid, steady provider—until suddenly he'd gotten the crazy idea to turn his hobby into a profession and gone off to study viticulture.

"And what about your job at Canyon Creek?" Emma Jean asked.

But Peter was already out of the car and heading toward the door of the gallery. She scrambled to follow him, her head suddenly pounding with the start of a hangover. Too much was going on, the torturous departure from Riley, the long plane ride, and now this. Peter driveling on about his new winery. She couldn't handle it, didn't want to deal with it, wanted life to be as simple as it had been in L.A. the past week.

And then the molecules in the air rearranged themselves as a tornado of turquoise and green flew out the door, and she was in her dear Aunt Cleo's arms.

"Oh baby, I've missed you! God it's good you're here! How are you? Let me see you." Cleo held her at arm's length, and Emma Jean smiled at her outfit. It was as blue as the sky, with green and yellow trim, and she couldn't quite figure out what it was—caftan? Dress? Poncho and skirt? Sari? Yards of glittery silk swathed her aunt and it crinkled and sparkled whenever she moved, as she was moving now to pat Emma Jean's cheek and look more closely at her.

"Sun Valley is wonderful," Emma Jean murmured.

She was used to her aunt's inspections and submitted to them cheerfully. It gave her a chance to feast her eyes on the woman who had raised her from the time she was four. In the fading twilight, Cleo's hair wasn't quite as garishly red as Emma Jean knew it would be in daylight, and her make-up not quite as heavy-handed. Even taking into account the too-ruddy cheeks and the heavy kohl beneath her eyes, Aunt Cleo, at almost eighty, looked fabulous, skinny as one of the decorative lampposts. Why oh why hadn't Emma Jean gotten the thin gene?

Her mother, Claire, had struggled with her weight, Aunt Cleo had told her once. Emma Jean had waited eagerly for more details, but none were forthcoming. She'd learned not to ask Cleo for information about her mother, Cleo's sister, who had died so young. Sometimes Cleo offered up bits of biography like tiny jewels, and the best thing to do was be very, very quiet and hope she threw out more, because asking was a sure way to clam her up. For years as a child, Cleo told her a story called *The One True Story of Your Mother*. The catch being that every week or so the so-called true story changed. Once her mother was a fairy princess called back to her homeland. The next week she'd be a mermaid, the next a Russian ballerina who couldn't stay in the United States. Emma Jean was positive that her beginnings as a writer lay in Aunt Cleo's fanciful stories about Emma Jean's dead mother.

Now Cleo glanced from Emma Jean to look around, and Emma Jean knew she was locating Peter, who had gone on ahead into the gallery. "What have you been doing?" Cleo hissed in a loud whisper. "You look different. Something's different."

"Oh, Aunt Cleo," Emma Jean said. She'd just known that her aunt would recognize the subtle difference in her. Now all the pent-up tension of the last week overwhelmed Emma Jean, and she sagged against her aunt. "I've been bad."

Aunt Cleo looked at her closely again. "You don't get that glow from being bad. It's love. You've fallen in love, haven't you?"

"Not exactly. I've committed adultery, just like my depraved bastard of a father. It's all so awful I can't stand it, but—"

Cleo shook her head and grasped Emma Jean tightly to her boney chest. "No buts, darling, love is never bad. It's an immutable law of the universe that love can only be a force for good."

Emma Jean hoped her aunt was correct. But what if it wasn't love she felt for Riley? What if it was just lust? Was that only a force for good?

"I don't know if it's love or not," Emma Jean said into her aunt's chest. "But I've vowed never to see him again because it's so very wrong."

She hoped that her aunt would propound another sweeping maxim about love that would make her feel better, but just then, she heard someone calling her name from inside the gallery. One of the blurry faces came into view. Marielle. What was she doing here? Had half the population of the known universe decided to attend Aunt Cleo's opening?

"Oh, God," Emma Jean said, remembering what she'd said about Marielle to Wendy on the airplane. "I've been trying so hard to be nice, and I totally blew it. I just don't come by niceness naturally."

"Of course you don't; you're my niece," Cleo said.

Emma Jean glanced inside again. Her one-time future best friend waved cheerfully. "I wasn't just bad; I was petty."

Cleo patted Emma Jean's cheek. "Pettiness, at least, is something that can be transformed with generosity. Love is a force of nature, granted capriciously by the universe, and thus it must always be welcomed and never spurned. We'll talk more later. C'mon, your public waits."

Chapter Five

Generosity is Its Own Reward

"Everybody, she's here." Aunt Cleo swept into the gallery, a rustle of flashing color. "I'd like you all to welcome my niece, the one and only Emma Jean Sullivan."

There was a wee smattering of applause from within. Emma Jean took a deep breath. "Generosity," she murmured to herself. "No expectations. Breathe. And for God's sake, be nice. Marielle is your friend." She stepped inside the gallery and saw, to her surprise, quite a large crowd, most of them clustered by the table holding wine and appetizers, which was presumably why the clapping had been so light, because people had been focused on refreshments, not her. Immediately inside the door, beneath a huge otherworldly oil painting, stood Julia Williams, Peter's grown daughter, a somewhat otherworldly creature herself. Well, otherworldly if other worlds featured beings who kept their heads lowered and skittered about like hamsters, with faces pinched and beady-eyed.

But wait, what was this? Tonight, Julia held her head high and looked directly at Emma Jean. She was even smiling. She wore, as always, a floral print dress, but with brightly colored flowers on it, not the dull pastels and shapeless sacks she usually favored. It was fitted, the bodice skimming her waist and breasts—breasts? Emma Jean didn't even know her stepdaughter had breasts.

"Wow. You look wonderful," Emma Jean said, and she didn't even have to force the words out, because it was true. She was so pleased with her spontaneous kindness that she went a step further. "I love your dress."

"Oh, thank you, Emma Jean, and hi! Isn't this the most exciting night ever? God, what with Marielle and Daddy's news, it's just…it's just overwhelming."

Emma Jean had managed to forget Peter's news in the crush of seeing Aunt Cleo, and now she scowled at the memory of her dastardly husband planning to open a business without telling her. But Julia didn't seem to notice. She appeared overcome with emotion, so overcome that she grabbed Emma Jean's shoulders and hugged her tight. Emma Jean hugged her stepdaughter back, feeling a flush rise on her cheeks, made worse by the fact that they were currently crushed against Julia's flowered bodice.

Julia talking about "Daddy's news" meant that everyone apparently knew about his new business except her. Could she help it if she'd been a bit *busy* the past week, earning a living and all that? Emma Jean pulled away from her stepdaughter but Julia held her tight. Emma Jean patted the young woman on her shoulder to indicate not only the warmth she felt for her, but also that it was now time to end the uncharacteristically effusive hug. Julia had been fourteen when Emma Jean married Peter, and everyone knew it was impossible to form a decent bond with a teenager. Her stepdaughter had spent only the occasional weekend and holiday with them, then she'd gone off to college, and then she'd married, all of which suited Emma Jean just fine.

The person she really liked was Julia's husband, Connor. He ran an online business selling rare books, and that alone would be enough for Emma Jean to adore him. But he also had a confidence and a rakish charm that Emma Jean admired in young men. She and Connor had spent many an evening drinking wine and talking about books. Even though Julia worked at a brick and mortar bookstore, she rarely joined in.

Finally Emma Jean managed to extricate herself from her stepdaughter's embrace. "Where's Connor?"

Julia assumed an expression Emma Jean had last seen on the face of her dead guinea pig lying pathetically in a bed of wood chips in the corner of its cage. "Didn't Daddy tell you? He said he would call you while you were in L.A. and tell you."

Call number five thousand that she hadn't answered. Jesus, why did the world have to choose the one week out of the entire forty-eight years she had existed on this planet that she had chosen to have an illicit affair for everything to happen?

At that moment, Marielle slid in beside Julia, clutching her arm possessively. Julia's visage took on the look of a radiant fish. Could fish be radiant? Well, she looked dewy, like a fish that had just been pulled from water. It was faintly reminiscent of an expression of Peter's that Emma Jean disliked, one where he opened and closed his mouth like a sturgeon looking for food.

"Hey, Emma Jean," Marielle said. "Great review in the *Oxford American*."

"Isn't Marielle's news just so exciting?" Julia crowed.

Marielle pulled Julia closer and kissed her on the cheek, a kiss that turned into something more when Julia turned toward her and the lips of the two women met. It was also a kiss that took a fair amount of maneuvering, as the elfin Marielle had to stand on tiptoes to reach Julia's mouth.

Emma Jean bit her own lip. Marielle and Julia were together? Would Julia be so stupid, so hamster-ish, as to choose Marielle over Connor? Not that Emma Jean had anything against same-sex unions. She never could understand what the fuss was about. If you liked someone, who cared what gender anyone was? Her head pounded. She needed more wine to ease her burgeoning hangover. Perhaps it would help her to think less snarky thoughts, too, which she was finding very difficult in this trying situation. Emma Jean took a step sideways toward the food and beverage table. But then the two women quit kissing and looked at her expectantly. Generosity. Breathe. Be kind, even though this latest development probably derailed her plan to become best friends with Marielle.

"Well. I'm happy for you two," Emma Jean said.

"Thanks, Emma Jean," Julia said. "And isn't it exciting about the book?"

Julia meant Marielle's book, the very book that Emma Jean had just spent hours confessing wasn't true, no doubt. "Number one on *The New York Times* bestseller list. Wow."

"*Devils' Daughter* is number one?" Emma Jean's voice sounded somewhere between a shout and a squeak.

Marielle and Julia both wore grins on their faces, and Julia nodded her head up and down vigorously.

Not a single one of Emma Jean's books had reached number one on the bestseller list. Ever. Her books had flirted with the top spot and gotten tantalizing close. But never, ever had any of them reached number one. Emma Jean wanted to reach out and slap Marielle to turn that grin into a grimace. But the Bees would definitely not approve of such behavior. And her own Campaign to be Kind would not allow it either. "Marielle, you are brilliant. Number one. Wow! A student of mine on the bestseller list. *You* should be reading here tonight, not me."

"Oh, but I am. Right after you," Marielle said.

Wait. What? Had Marielle said she was reading *after* Emma Jean? Being first at a reading was akin to being the opener at a rock concert, the act nobody remembered because they came first, before the real stars of the show. Emma Jean had not flown all the way to this remote town, ripping herself from the arms of her lover, to be a warm-up act. Emma Jean would find Aunt Cleo and have her rearrange things.

Except that just then Aunt Cleo was walking to a wood dais. And now she was asking Julia to come to the stage to make introductions, and Julia was going on and on, some *dither* about the teacher and the student and how tonight they had a special opportunity to witness not only the birth of a new star in Marielle Delany but also to hear how the words of the teacher had influenced the student. Then Julia was calling her name and people were clapping and all she had time to do was pull Aku Aku from her purse for luck and walk to the front of the room.

Emma Jean set the Buddha on the dais, then took a deep breath, looked around the room, smiled at her audience, and began reading: *Carolyn Marie Peterson expected to accomplish many things in life, but becoming a winemaker's wife was not one of them. In truth, being a wife had not been high on her list of goals. Until the day she met Stewart. Or, more to the point, until the day she first tasted his wine.*

Emma Jean paused in her reading to glance at her audience. They were smiling and nodding appreciatively. She had them hooked with the first paragraph, as she had hooked other audiences so many times before. Let Marielle try to top this reading. This was what Emma Jean did, what she'd been doing for years. Just let anybody try to usurp her throne.

When she finished—to wild applause, she was happy to note— she found a place near the rear of the crowd and listened to Marielle. She had to admit, the girl had flair. Of course, Emma Jean herself was in no small part responsible for that flair, having, during the last five years, coached and edited and critiqued every damn word Marielle was currently reading. Emma Jean had mentored her on other matters as well, recommending that she move from a crappy apartment in Beaverton, the worst of all suburbs, to the hip part of town Marielle now lived in. She'd advised her on decorating, given her books and magazines to read, told her about television shows and movies. When Marielle had first arrived from Ohio, she was a shy, little mouse obsessed with writing down her story, and it was Emma Jean who admonished Marielle that the best writers got out and lived life so that they had something to write about. Apparently Marielle had taken her advice to heart.

All of a sudden, life seemed terribly complex. Her poor, stunted novel that she was going to have to *scramble* to get in on time, Marielle and Julia together, Marielle's book on the bestseller list and her own barely selling, Peter starting a business without telling her a thing about it. Emma Jean thought about Riley, and her mind settled and eased, like finally finding a comfortable position after tossing and turning in bed. Now she began to understand why people had affairs. They were like oases for the mind. Thinking about Riley was a place she could go to, a refuge when things got complex. Suddenly she longed for the simple purity of her time with him. The simple luxury of sex. She figured now was a good time to check to see if he had left a message.

Emma Jean edged toward the wine, which was, thank God, very close to the door. She needed a drink and some fresh air. But Peter stood at one end of the table, surrounded by his usual wine groupies, who secretly Emma Jean thought were the most annoying people on earth. She liked wine, yes she did, but she saw no reason to blab on and on about the subtle nuances of it. And, oh dear Lord, it would only be getting worse, if Peter were going to start his own business. Luckily, he was so absorbed in his role as wine guru that he didn't notice her. She grabbed a glass of wine from the table and skirted a group of jeans-clad patrons who seemed rapt at Marielle's words. Frankly, Emma Jean had never thought the book was *that* interesting. Weren't satanic cults a bit overdone?

Just as she was about to sidle out the door, Emma Jean felt a tug on the hem of her jacket. She assumed she'd caught it on something and jerked herself free. But then she felt the tug again. Emma Jean turned around and found herself gazing at the oddest-looking child she'd ever seen. She was a girl about ten or eleven, though Lord knew Emma Jean was terrible at guessing the ages of children. She had a head of blonde, curly hair, much like Emma Jean's own, though one half of the girl's head looked like someone had gone at it with nail scissors. Or a hatchet. She had long, skinny legs with scabby knees beneath jean shorts that looked as someone had hacked off the hems in a fit of rage, and she wore a dirty blue tee and a white crocheted scarf wrapped around her neck a gazillion times. As Emma Jean stared at her, the girl grabbed an end of the scarf and twirled it.

"Aren't you dying of heat exhaustion with that thing on?" Emma Jean asked.

"It's stylish. My mother says you have to suffer to be beautiful. Here—you forgot something."

The girl extended her tightly closed fist and then opened it. Atop her palm sat Aku Aku.

"Oh my God, I forgot him on the dais, didn't I? Why bless your curly-haired little heart. Thank you darling." Emma Jean took the Buddha from the girl and impulsively enfolded her in a hug. "Thank you. I would have hated to lose him."

The girl was the first to step away from the embrace then stood staring at her. Emma Jean stared back. The girl's bizarre looks were strangely compelling. Her features were too large for her face, and overall, she appeared unfinished, like a cake that hadn't baked long enough. Someday, when her features set and she grew into them, she'd be a stunner. For now, though, she was simply odd.

"I thought your reading was vastly superior to this one," she said.

Well, this was more like it. Emma Jean lifted her chin in a preen. But wait, what kind of child used words like that? Emma Jean looked at the girl suspiciously. "How old are you?"

"Aren't you going to thank me for the compliment? I'm twelve."

"Thank you. I appreciate it. But what are you doing here? Aren't twelve-year-olds supposed to be off playing video games or kicking soccer balls around or something wholesome like that?"

"Not me. I'm going to be a writer. I figure it's never too early to start." The girl stuck out her hand. "Ava Cameron."

"Nice to meet you, Ava."

"So, since you're a bona-fide author and all, I have a few questions to ask you," Ava said.

Oh Lord, she did not need this tonight. She just did not have the energy to be nice. All she wanted was to slip away and think about Riley. Check to see if he'd left a message. Get to her laptop and see if there were any emails from him.

"Number one, how much do you write a day?"

Emma Jean belted down half her wine and poured herself more. "Darling, I so appreciate each and every one of my fans, even young ones, like you, but if I don't get some fresh air, I am going to die. Simply die."

"That's okay. I'll follow you."

Emma Jean saw an opening in the crowd that would allow her out the door and darted out it. She sighed with happiness to breathe the fresh air again. In the cool evening, the mountain loomed above the town like a friendly giant. Emma Jean stared at it. She'd never been a skier. She was a southern girl, after all, and the south didn't have much in the way of mountains. But now the thought intrigued her. The mountain was comforting and gazing at it helped her to relax. She sat on the low wall that surrounded the courtyard and rolled her neck to ease the kinks out. But then she felt a presence. And there was Ava again, standing in front of her.

"Number two," Ava said. "What kind of advice do you have for someone like me, who yearns to be a writer?"

Who was this girl? Emma Jean cast a suspicious eye on her. "Aren't you a little young to be reading my books?"

"Oh I haven't read any of them yet. But I will. I just heard of you. My foster mother said she met you and that you were really nice and you wouldn't mind talking to me."

"And, who, pray tell, is your foster mother?"

"Her name's Wendy. She's the librarian. My real mother lives in L.A. She's so beautiful that men stop in their tracks when they see her. She's a model. She's earning money to reunite us."

Did all twelve-year-olds talk like this? Somehow she didn't think so. Emma Jean would just as soon that Ava—precocious and gifted as she was—perform her talented and gifted act with someone else.

"There you are!" Wendy's distinctive smell wafted before her as she climbed the steps to the gallery courtyard. Lovely, Emma Jean reminded herself, Wendy smelled *lovely*. "Oh, she's probably driving you to distraction, isn't she? Ava, it's time to go home."

"But Emma Jean hasn't had a chance to answer any of my questions yet," Ava said, picking up one end of her scarf, throwing it over her shoulder, then tossing her head just so.

There was something positively sweet and comical about the girl's attempts to be sophisticated. "I write as much as I can every day, and my advice to you is to do the same. And read. Read all the time."

"You don't have to tell Ava to read. That's all she ever does," Wendy said.

"Nothing better to do," Ava said.

Wendy shook her head. "All these gorgeous summer days, I try to shoo her out to play but all she wants to do is read."

"Better than playing with a bunch of ass-clown kids," Ava said.

"Ava! Watch your language. Now scoot your butt to the van. Simon's waiting. I'll be right there."

Ava rolled her eyes but gave Emma Jean a resigned wave and ran down the front steps and across the street to a blue mini-van.

"Simon's my son," Wendy said. "He's just learning how to drive."

Emma Jean nodded, trying to show interest and concern, despite her tiredness. Wendy was a fan, and she *cared* deeply about all her fans. It was just that it had been *such* a long day, and she was *so* tired, and she *so* needed to see if Riley had emailed her, even if he wasn't supposed to, and she, of course, would not be emailing him back. She forced herself to be kind and polite.

"I didn't realize you had children," Emma Jean said.

"Yep," Wendy said. "Just the one boy of my own, but I take in foster kids. God didn't see fit to allow me to bear more children, so I just gathered up some that were in need." She leaned in close to Emma Jean. "That Ava is a handful. She's why I was in L.A., actually. I was searching for her mother."

"What happened to her? Ava said she was a model."

Wendy snorted. "Of the sort that models everything, if you catch my drift. But nobody knows where she is at the moment. She's seems to have gone missing."

"Well, I hope you find her," Emma Jean said.

"Me, too. I better get going. Thank you for everything."

"You're welcome," Emma Jean said, heaving an enormous sigh of relief after Wendy strode off. How did people cope with children, day in, day out, hour to hour? She would simply drop from exhaustion if she had to deal with kids. But, thank the good Lord above, that was not ever going to be an issue she would need to worry about.

Emma Jean pulled out her phone to check to see if Riley had left a message. Nope, nothing. She hit the button for the mail utility. No emails, either.

"There you are, darling. We've been looking for you." Aunt Cleo lurched out the door, holding a wine glass high in the air. Emma regarded her with suspicion. Was Cleo drunk? She rarely lost control of herself. She was outrageous and outgoing and outré, always, but never drunk, or stoned, or anything but pure, unadulterated Cleo. But Emma Jean had no time to wonder further because Cleo pulled her inside, then Marielle and Julia were clustering around her, and Peter, too, who was wearing a variant of the fish face that she detested.

"We're toasting to success!" Cleo said. "Your success, Emma Jean—which of course we've all come to expect; you do it so well and so routinely—and our new star, Marielle!"

She *hated* the way Cleo kept referring to Marielle as a "new star." For Christ's sake, wasn't she laying it on a bit thick? And she hated Marielle's smirk, too. She hadn't realized her former student's favorite expression was a smirk. No, it must be a new affectation because if Marielle had smirked in Emma Jean's classes, she would have kicked her out, Campaign to be Kind or not. She hated smugness and smirking above all else. It wasn't as if she was desperate for students, either; she had a waiting list a mile long of people who wanted into her classes precisely because Emma Jean had a reputation for turning out students with publishable manuscripts. But most of all, Emma Jean hated trying to be nice, which clearly she was failing miserably at because it was way harder than she had ever imagined.

Marielle and Julia held their wine glasses high, Marielle holding hers in her left hand and Julia holding hers in her right, which enabled them to have their free arms wrapped around each other.

"To Emma Jean and Marielle," everyone yelled.

And then Julia piped up. "And let's not forget Daddy. We need to toast to him, too."

"To Peter!" Marielle said.

Emma Jean raised her glass, offered a strained smile and whispered to Peter under her breath. "I can't believe you told every goddamn person on the planet about your plans except me."

"It came together quickly, darling," Peter said quietly. "The investors are lined up, ready to go, and I didn't want to miss this chance. Anyway, I tried to call you a million times."

"To Daddy!" Marielle said. "You're going to be such a huge success!"

"To my son-in-law!" Aunt Cleo said.

"Is it my fault I have to make a living?" Emma Jean hissed. "And speaking of which, what about your job at Canyon Creek? You never answered my question."

"I'm not planning on quitting my job, don't worry, that is unless—"

The rest of his sentence was drowned out in a wave of yells and cheering.

"To Peter!"

"To Marielle!"

"To Emma Jean!"

Emma Jean set down her glass. Suddenly, she no longer wanted any more wine. She felt the activity, the energy and the excitement swirling around her, and all she wanted to do was be alone. She was tired, so deeply, deeply, tired. She stared at the people who surrounded her, the people she supposedly loved and knew best, and realized she didn't really know any of them. Then an image of Riley swam into her head, and she recognized what she really wanted was the one thing she couldn't have—more time with him.

Chapter Six

Her Life, Upside Down

"Bye, darling."

Three months later, Emma Jean stood on her front porch and waved as Peter backed down their long, gravel driveway on his way to work. She winced as he clipped the edge of an August-tired rose bush but then put a smile back on her face. "I can't wait to see you later!"

Should she remind him that her private writing class was meeting at the winery to celebrate a student getting a story published? No, he'd just forget anyway. Poor man, they'd been working him so hard at Canyon Creek, it was no wonder he couldn't remember things. Besides, this way she could surprise him. She was making her special southern pineapple upside down cake, and it was one of his favorites, right up there next to coconut cake and key lime pie. Emma Jean clutched at the cotton of her dress as it billowed in the late summer wind and imagined how happy Peter would be that afternoon when he came into the tasting room and found a piece of cake waiting for him. And not only a piece of cake, but also Emma Jean, presiding gracefully over her class, she even more delectable than the cake. She would need to change out of her current attire: a longish, white Mexican wedding-style dress which struck just the right note for a day spent at home writing but would not be appropriate for conducting her fiction writing class. No, she needed to wear something alluring for Peter, something with a bit of cleavage, perhaps.

"Could you lay it on any thicker?" Trish, Emma Jean's assistant, had appeared at the bottom of the front steps, carrying a plastic bag from Fred Meyer, the local grocery store.

"Oh dear God, you scared me half to death. Where did you come from?"

Trish pointed to her little, red Toyota, which Emma Jean now saw was parked in the space behind where Peter's car had been. "You were so busy with the adoring housewife act you didn't notice that I was pulling up as he was leaving."

Emma Jean held the door open for her assistant and followed her into the house. "It's not an act! I worship my husband!'

Trish hung her purse on the hall coat tree and cast a stink eye at Emma Jean. "And I'm the Pope's secretary."

Emma Jean thought Trish could at least come up with a more original cliché and was about to say so, but Trish had already walked halfway down the long hall, toward the back of the house. Emma Jean padded after her, her bare feet luxuriating in the deep plush of the red Oriental carpet runner. She admired the way the magenta of her newly manicured toes matched one of the subtler hues in the rug. Emma Jean felt it was important to maintain good grooming habits, particularly when there were men involved. Perhaps she could wear her sexy silver, strappy sandals to the winery later and go for some toe cleavage also.

Emma Jean joined Trish in her office. It was a large room on the ground floor, with space for Emma Jean's oversized desk and a work area for Trish. It also held one of three fireplaces in the house, which Emma Jean loved to light on cold days, and was located across the hall from the spacious kitchen, with its stainless steel appliances, cherry cabinets and marble countertops. The kitchen opened onto Emma Jean's favorite place, the family room, where a soft red couch sat beside a massive stone fireplace.

The house was one of the best things about her success as a novelist. It was a new home built to look like a Victorian farmhouse on a large lot in northeast Portland, where few newly built homes existed. Emma Jean liked old, historic houses, but she also liked the convenience and cleanliness that new homes afforded, so she had been thrilled to find a place that combined the two. It was the first house she had ever had that had completely and totally felt like home to her, and she never, ever wanted to live anywhere else.

"Did you and the Worshipped One have a good dinner last night?" Trish asked. She had settled herself in the ergonomically correct computer chair in front of her computer, and had already opened Emma Jean's website email inbox.

"Dinner? Oh no, that didn't work out. Peter got home late from his meeting with the investors, so I just grabbed a bite by myself."

"But I thought you had a big romantic night out planned," Trish said.

"Oh darling, you know how it is—"

"I'm not your public, Emma Jean. Quit with the darling business, already."

Emma Jean did have a bit of a tendency to lapse into her public persona when feeling defensive or uncertain. She shot Trish what she hoped was a withering look. "As I was saying before I was so rudely interrupted, I feel it is my duty as a loving wife to be tolerant when Peter's busy schedule keeps him from getting home on time."

"Oh, Jesus, Emma Jean, you are just one piece of work."

"Thanks for the deep psychological insight, *Patty*."

Trish's full name was Patricia Sexton, but she got annoyed if anyone called her anything other than Trish. Sometimes Emma Jean called her Patty just to bug her because there were so few things that riled Trish. Of course, Trish's ability to remain calm was one of the things Emma Jean cherished most about her and why she desperately needed her assistance several days a week.

Trish was dark-haired and pretty in an all American, girl-next-door kind of way: calm, focused and consistently cheerful—all traits Emma Jean admired greatly but couldn't seem to muster up herself. Even though Emma Jean adored her fans and was deeply grateful for each and every one of them, she got dreadfully tired of answering email: *Dear Fan, thank you so much for your wonderful comments on my latest book. It means so much to me that you would take the time to write,* blah, blah, blah—but Trish seemed to have an endless supply of energy and good humor for such things. When first Emma Jean had met Trish, she had mistaken this quality for superficiality, but during the two years of her employment, she'd learned such was not the case. Trish had a quick mind and pondered issues deeply.

"Earth to Emma Jean," Trish said.

Oh Lord, she'd done it again, gone off in a brain fart. Emma Jean was desperately afraid that she'd started menopause. There were the brain fogs, the tiredness, the nausea, and most obviously, the lack of a period. For years, she'd thought she'd be happy about menopause, but now that Riley had come on the scene, she was less than thrilled. Menopause meant she was old. And it would be damned difficult to explain to Riley, seeing as how as far as he knew, she was forty-three, not forty-eight. Dangerously close to forty-nine, truth be told.

"We were discussing your new novel—"

"We were?"

"—or more specifically, the lack thereof. You need to write at least 1,000 words today."

"Which I will now do," Emma Jean said. She would prove to Trish how productive she could be. She opened the file for the chapter she was working on, but she couldn't seem to focus on the words on the monitor. The smell of the pineapple upside down cake baking in the oven was making her feel a little nauseated, for one thing. Maybe she needed some inspiration from the Wiccans. Lately she had been reading about magic and paganism. She loved the way the Wiccans thought everything was connected, how magic was thought made tangible. She reached for her latest book on the subject, which was on spell casting. That was it; she could perform a ritual for focus.

"Put that book down. You're writing," Trish said.

Such was the downfall of having an assistant, always nosing into her business. "I was pondering a spell for inspiration."

"Forget inspiration. Just put words on the page. You've not made any progress on that novel. Besides, I thought you were studying Buddhism, not magic."

"Oh I'm still totally into Buddhism. I just figure a little spell casting can't hurt anyone. Now quit bothering me; I need to write. I could get so much more done if you didn't constantly interrupt."

She ignored the way Trish shook her head and returned her focus to the computer screen. The novel should have been going better than it was, seeing as how the book held themes dear to her heart. The story centered on a lonely, disaffected, middle-aged woman who was swept into a transcendent adventure. Natalie, the heroine, searched for original Tiki-style locations across the country, and her quest ended up transforming her on a deep personal level. *All* of Emma Jean's heroines changed dramatically on a deep level, except Emma Jean couldn't seem to find the key to Natalie's personal revolution. Maybe Natalie could stay at a seedy Tiki motel in the Valley and have a wild sexual affair. Emma Jean perked up at the thought. There could be themes of heartbreak, betrayal, longing, and…love. Yes, love. Natalie could fall in love, or at least mad lust.

Did Emma Jean even know the difference between love and lust? She suspected that what she felt for Riley was lust, and what she felt for Peter was love, but she wasn't sure. She tried to remember back to the time when she'd first met Peter. He'd been pouring wine at a holiday event at the historical society, and she was one of a group of writers who was supposed to sign books for hordes of eager readers. The hordes came in a trickle, and Emma Jean and the other writers imbibed large quantities of Peter's wine to pass the time. She'd brought Peter home, she remembered, and he'd spent the night at her apartment in Northwest Portland, the one with the shiny hardwood floors and arched doorways. But how did she feel when she first laid eyes on him? Had her heart flip-flopped the way it did when she first saw Riley? She couldn't recall, and wouldn't you think she'd remember if it had?

Emma Jean pushed her chair back and looked toward Trish. "Have you ever fallen in love?"

"Don't talk to me; you're writing." Trish remained with her back to Emma Jean.

"I'm brainstorming ideas for Natalie, and I need your input."

"I can't hear you," Trish said in a sing-songy voice.

"C'mon, Trish, honest, I really need to know. Have you ever fallen in love?"

Trish wheeled around in her chair, and even from across the room, Emma Jean was surprised at the darkness of her expression. "Yes, I've fallen in love. It was a while ago, and it was wonderful and awful at the same time. Eventually the awfulness outstripped the wonderfulness, and so it ended. Does that answer your question?"

"But don't you want to feel that wonderfulness again?"

Trish shrugged. "The enticement of it fades. And besides, it was incredibly distracting and time consuming." She gestured toward Emma Jean. "Case in point, the way you are sighing like a teenager. I don't have time for that; I have goals, Emma Jean."

"I have goals, too," Emma Jean sniffed.

"Such as?"

Emma Jean was taken aback by the question. Trish was her well-paid assistant; she should be intimately familiar with her every objective.

"Honestly, I want to know, Emma Jean. The way you've been acting lately, with all the heavy sighing and procrastinating, I'm just not sure."

Emma Jean waggled her head in an imitation of Trish's manner. "I want *Wife* to sell well, and I want the damn Tiki book to be written. And it would be nice if it hit the bestseller list when it's released."

"Hmmm," Trish said. "And that's all? What about your personal goals?"

"I want to quit feeling like crap and lose the weight that I've put on in the past three months. And…" Emma Jean paused and thought. She wanted desperately to see Riley again and to have fabulous sex with him. But she didn't think Trish wanted to hear that. "What about you, Trish? What do you want?"

"I want a hugely successful career with more clients than I know what to do with." Trish was studying to be therapist and would be finishing her Master's alarmingly soon, at which point she would no doubt leave Emma Jean's employment.

"I still think you should take my writing class. I won't even charge you for it—think of the value," Emma Jean said. She had been hoping she could entice Trish to hang around a while longer with this offer.

"I've told you a million times, it's counseling that is my calling. I don't want to get waylaid from what I know to be my life's work," Trish said. "Which is also why I do not need to worry about falling in love."

Emma Jean admired this trait, as she herself believed to the depths of her being that everyone on the planet had a calling, a life's work, a reason they had been put here. She believed that much of the world's unhappiness, at least in the developed countries, came from people's inability to commit to their calling, or even to identify it in the first place, and consequently had always been deeply grateful that she had always *known* she was to be a novelist.

"And," Trish said, "we have work to do. So let's get to it."

Emma Jean turned back to her desk and grabbed the colorful spiral notebook in which she made notes for the novel. She scribbled a couple lines about the discussion on love. And that was a good enough start that she could traipse on over to Amazon and check things out. This was a habit that she limited herself to indulging once a day. Okay, okay, sometimes she did it twice. Okay, so yesterday she had done it three times. Emma Jean clicked on the page for *Devil's Daughter*. Holy crap, Marielle's book was still in the top ten. Even though she could barely stand to look, she clicked over to the page for *The Winemaker's Wife*. Emma Jean shielded her eyes until the page fully loaded.

Her rankings hadn't changed, and any way she tried to put a spin on it, having a book ranked number 3,548 in sales was not a good thing. And what was this—her reader reviews warranted only three stars? Jesus, had her fans joined the ranks of regular reviewers in savaging her? She scrolled quickly through them. Most of them were five stars, with the odd four and three star thrown in. It was the solitary clunker review with only one star that really brought the total down. *Avid Reader from Salem, Massachusetts. This book leaves a sour taste in my mouth, like wine that's gone bad.* Jesus Christ, what about the book made Avid Reader such a bitch? But here was a review that looked interesting from someone named "Book a Week." *Pity the poor Winemaker's Wife whose marriage is as stale as old bread. Reading about this mired-in-the-past couple is about as interesting as watching concrete set.* Emma Jean scratched her head, puzzled. She had used her marriage to Peter as a model for the couple in the novel.

"Since you're not writing, listen to this," Trish said.

"I'm writing." Trish's bitchiness was making her very cranky. "I just committed a stellar plot idea to paper. What trivial matter are you interrupting my genius for?"

"Okay, you ready?" Trish said, peering across the room toward Emma Jean's desk. "Oh for Christ's sake, quit checking your sales figures and listen to me."

Emma Jean folded her hands contritely in her lap. "I'm listening."

"It's an email from someone named Ava Cameron. Here it is. 'Dear Ms. Sullivan, I have to do a report for my English class. It's supposed to be on a dead author but I talked the teacher into letting me write about you, even though you're still alive. At least I hope so, ha, ha, ha. I've read all your books now but I still have questions, so if you could write me back I'd appreciate it.' Do you want to hear the list of questions?"

Emma Jean shook her head no.

"Who's Ava Cameron?"

"I don't know," Emma Jean said. "Oh wait, it was that girl. Wendy's foster daughter. The odd one. I met Wendy on the plane to Sun Valley and then she brought Ava to the opening. After my reading, Ava followed me around and peppered me with questions."

"I think this one requires a personal response."

"Can't you just send her the standard thank you fan letter and attach a bio or something? If I respond to her, she'll hound me forever."

Trish shook her head.

"Oh, Jesus God," Emma Jean said. "Okay, I'll do it first thing tomorrow."

Emma Jean didn't want to think about the odd child she'd met in Sun Valley because thinking about her would lead straight to thinking about Ava's mother, Wendy. The very same person to whom Emma Jean had so lustily confessed her idea that Marielle's so-called memoir was a made-up fantasy. She'd felt so guilty about her behavior, seeing as how she and Marielle were going to be friends and all, that she'd actually tracked down the number of the public library in Ketchum and called Wendy. Fat lot of good that had done. When Emma Jean explained to Wendy that she wanted to backtrack on her comments the wee-est bit, Wendy had helpfully said she had just finished writing up a piece about the controversy for the library newsletter.

"I've got another one. From a reporter. For *Vanity Fair*," Trish said. Emma Jean spun around in her chair. "A *Vanity Fair* reporter?"

Trish nodded. "Requesting an interview."

"Well say yes, for God's sake." Now wasn't this a cheering thought? Perhaps they wanted to do a profile of her. Only the biggest and best authors got profiled in *Vanity Fair*. Well, sometimes they wrote about obscure ones nobody had ever heard of, but that's because the reporter was sleeping with them or something. Anyway, wow. She'd endure another month of menopausal misery for a shot at *Vanity Fair*.

"Already taken care of. There's two more. One from your father."

"Delete that one."

Trish turned around in her chair. "Remind me again why you've been carrying on this unreasonable personal vendetta against him for the past two years?"

"Because I found out he killed my mother. Duh."

"I thought she was killed while running with the bulls in Pamplona."

"Yes, she was." Emma Jean spoke slowly, as if explaining something to a child. "But she fled to Spain after learning about Bob the Fake Christian's adultery. Ergo, he killed her."

Trish shook her head. "But you've always said you barely remember your mother, and that Aunt Cleo was the best stand-in mother a girl could have. So I've never really understood your moral outrage over your father."

Emma Jean sighed heavily. Hot therapist Trish would make if she couldn't even understand the impact of the most profound incident in Emma Jean's life. She'd even written her first book about it, and *Tales of a Motherless Daughter* had shot right to the bestseller list. "It's like this: He denied me a shot at what could have been. Just think of how different my life might have been if my mother had lived."

"Looks like you have a pretty good life to me," Trish said.

"Women who are not motherless just don't understand," Emma Jean said.

"Whatever you say, Emma Jean." Trish turned back to her computer. "Oh, wow, he's going to be in Sun Valley."

"Why are you reading his email? I told you to delete it. What's he going to be doing in Sun Valley?"

"Visiting Cleo, apparently."

"That's odd. Maybe he's got one of his fake Christian conferences there or something."

"Fake Christian?" Trish said.

"I don't care what anybody says, that man is not a Christian. How can you call yourself a Christian when you are a conniving adulterer?"

"We do need to delve more deeply into this, Emma Jean," Trish said. "Has it occurred to you that there are parallels between your father's actions and your own?"

Emma Jean often regretted the day she had confessed her affair to Trish, though even if she hadn't fessed up, Trish would probably have wormed it out of her. It had been shortly after Emma Jean returned home from the trip to L.A. and Sun Valley. Trish had caught Emma Jean furtively talking to Riley and guessed immediately. Only after Emma Jean had extracted a solemn and sacred vow from Trish that she would never divulge what she knew, did Emma Jean fill her in on the details.

"Yes, it has. I have realized that my affair with Riley could not be helped, since it is in my genes. Alas, I have also decided that I do not wish to be in anyway like my father. Thus, I have sworn never to see Riley again," Emma Jean said.

Trish muttered something under her breath.

"What?" Emma Jean said. She should never have told Trish about the affair.

"Nothing."

"Who's the other email from? You said there were two."

"It's from Aunt Cleo."

"She still gets my addresses confused, doesn't she? No matter how many times I try to explain to her to use my personal mail, she just can't quite get it." Emma Jean felt cheered at the thought of her aunt. At least not all of her family members were deadbeats like her father. At least she had one fabulous relative.

"Hey, let's give her the benefit of the doubt. She's almost eighty, after all."

"I know. I hope I got her longevity gene. It would only be fair, since I didn't get her thin gene. Read it to me."

"'Darling,'" Trish began, "Fall is in the air here today and I wouldn't be surprised if we soon have our first snow. You must return some time after the snow has fallen; you'd love it. Come to think of it, you should be over here this fall. At any rate, I have a question for you. Whatever happened with your young man in L.A.? I haven't had a chance to ask you how things are going with him. Also, I wanted to ask you about his art. Is he someone I should know about? There's so much going on in the L.A. art scene these days, it's hard to keep track. I'd hate to think I'd missed anybody important. Oh love, I do so hope everything is going well with you, XOXO, Aunt Cleo."

Trish swiveled in her chair to face Emma Jean again. "You didn't tell me Riley was an artist. I thought he was an airplane mechanic."

Emma Jean pulled at her lip. "I'm not actually sure how much of an artist he is. It's one of the things I've been trying to find out."

"Apparently Cleo thinks he's quite the artist."

"I may have given her that impression." She hadn't had a lot of time to talk to Cleo about Riley, but in the short while they spent discussing him, Emma Jean had spun out quite a nice story about his character arc. It wasn't a lie, exactly, more like a slight embellishment. She had cast him as a man striving mightily to be more, striving to create metal art in his spare time. Such ambition fit in so nicely with the way she liked people to be. And, let's face it; quirky artist was just a wee bit more glamorous than airplane mechanic. Ah well, the universe seemed to be a trickster when it assigned lovers, and Emma Jean was fine with Riley being an airplane mechanic. She was just *fine* with it. And it didn't matter anyway, because she was done being an adulteress.

Though she had to admit, every time she learned something new about Riley, she pouted at her decision to lead an adultery-free life. Because Riley was hopelessly, endlessly fascinating to her. In the days and weeks since she had returned home from her fateful trip to L.A., she and Riley had begun a deep email correspondence, in which they wrote of all things dear to their hearts. The exchange was personal, profound, and yes, vastly spiritual. And so, despite the lack of physical contact, Emma Jean had realized that the relationship was perfect, just perfect, the way it now stood, with the two of them sharing long, passionate emails, though committed to never seeing each other again. She had decided that as long as she didn't instigate contact, it was okay. Because when Riley wrote or called her, it would be rude—some might even say unkind—not to answer.

And so between Riley's emails and a wee bit of sleuthing on Facebook, Emma Jean had learned all manner of fascinating things about him. For instance, he had been an only child who adored his mother beyond all reason. Somebody had once told her that Mama's boys made the best men and that apparently was true, because clearly Riley was the best man ever. She thrilled to hear that sometimes on breaks from work he read scientific papers on spiders. Riley had an insane fascination with spiders. Hated snakes, but liked spiders, whereas Emma Jean was just the opposite. Now wasn't that interesting? And also, Riley loved to cook and often prepared elaborate Italian meals when he was off work. Could you even believe how cute that was? If there was anything Emma Jean appreciated, it was a man who *did* things. Unlike Peter, who mostly sat and read industry magazines when he was home.

"So what kind of art does he do?" Trish asked.

Emma Jean had almost forgotten Trish, so caught up was she in thoughts of Riley, and she could tell by the way Trish said *art* that Trish did not believe Riley was an artist at all. Which was baloney, because in his most recent email, Riley had called himself *a slave to the artistic impulse, be it my own or another artist's,* a direct nod to his interest in art history.

And then her phone rang. It was at moments like this that Emma Jean believed in God, because the ringing phone saved her from more explanation to Trish. But then if she believed in God, did that mean she could still be a Buddhist?

"Aren't you going to answer the damn thing?" Trish said.

Oh wonder of wonders, it was Riley. She started to press talk, but then she remembered that Trish disapproved of Emma Jean taking his calls. Oh Lord, she wanted to talk to him. Maybe she would learn some fascinating new tidbit about him. But she would remain firm in her resolve. She pressed the ignore option.

Emma Jean sighed heavily and turned to Trish. "I would like you to appreciate how strong I am. Note that I did not answer the phone, despite the fact that it was my wildly attractive L.A. lover. Is it just me, or does that cake smell God-awful? Maybe the butter was bad or something. It's making me want to retch."

Just then her phone dinged, a signal that she'd received a text message.

"That thing is so noisy," Trish said.

Emma Jean's heart pounded as she opened the text message inbox on her phone. Oh yes! It was a text from Riley!

Here's how I spent Noah's story time at Barnes & Noble today. I miss you!

He'd sent a photo that showed the end cap of a bookshelf at the Barnes & Noble—prime territory that publishers paid dearly for—with her books arranged with the covers facing out on all of the shelves. And another one showing how he had put a whole stack of them on one of the display tables. Oh wasn't he a doll! And wasn't she just the luckiest person alive! The thought of Riley making love to her made her insides quiver. But then she remembered her solemn vow never to see him again, to rise to the level of her chaste, virtuous self, and the thought made her groan in agony.

"What are you moaning about?" Trish said.

"Nothing."

Trish crossed the room in two long strides and grabbed the phone from Emma Jean. She glanced at the photo Riley had sent and then handed the cell back. "You told me you're not contacting him."

"Can I help it if he texts me with adorable messages?"

Trish stood close to Emma Jean—too close, it was one of Trish's tragic flaws that she didn't understand the concept of personal space—tapping her pen to her lips and staring at Emma Jean.

"Stop it."

"I'm just looking at you."

"You're looking at me that *way* you have. That judgmental way.

When you dragged it out of me about Riley, you promised you wouldn't be judgmental," Emma Jean reminded.

"Far be it from me to be judgmental about the woman who pretends to adore her husband while getting teenage mushy about her lover."

"I'm not pretending to adore Peter! I do adore him! My affair with Riley is totally and completely limited to emails and the occasional phone call. Thus, it has revitalized my marriage. I swear, if Peter knew about it, he'd thank me, things have been so good between us."

"When was the last time the two of you had dinner together?"

Emma Jean knotted her brows to think. But wait, she was the one in charge here, not Trish. She didn't have to answer. It didn't mean a damn thing that Peter was gone most of the day and night. Their brief moments together were golden, absolutely golden.

"Uh-huh," Trish said. "And when was the last time you had sex with Peter?"

"Why are you asking me these stupid questions? You're supposed to be working *for* me, not against me."

"Because I have a feeling it's important. Answer me."

"I can't imagine why. But Peter and I had sex a couple times after Sun Valley. I wanted to see if...if there was a difference."

"And it's been how long since you were in L.A.?"

"Almost three months."

"Open this," Trish said, pushing the plastic Fred Meyer bag toward her.

Emma Jean sighed. There'd be no peace until she did as Trish asked. She reached inside and pulled out a box. At first she thought it was hair dye. Emma Jean felt her curls. Did her blonde locks need a touch-up? But when she looked at the box, it wasn't hair dye at all.

It was a home pregnancy test.

Chapter Seven

She Hated Surprises

Somewhere deep inside her, one door—for some reason it was large, and metal—clanged shut and another one opened. She wasn't going through menopause; she was pregnant. She clutched her neck. Could it be true? And if it were true, *was* it Riley's baby? Could it be even remotely possible that she was carrying Riley's baby? Or was there any chance at all that it was Peter's? All of the questions flitted through her mind like fireflies on a Georgia summer evening. But then she shook her head. There was no way she could be pregnant.

Emma Jean looked up at Trish. "I don't need this."

"I think maybe you do."

Emma Jean shook her head again, this time decisively, and set the pregnancy test on the long table beside her computer. "I can't get pregnant. Peter and I tried and tried when we first got married and never had any luck at all. I'm infertile."

"Are you sure?"

Emma Jean nodded.

"Did you go to the doctor about it?"

"No. Because it was obvious that I was the problem. Peter had sired Julia, after all. Besides, then we decided we didn't want children. Having each other was more than enough. So you can just return your pregnancy test to Fred Meyer."

Trish shrugged. "Some people like living in denial. But in this case, the truth will out in a very obvious way soon enough."

Emma Jean turned back to her computer. She cast a surreptitious glance at Trish and then felt her stomach. Was it just the teensiest bit bigger? Maybe. But then that could be from the food she'd been downing. She'd been alone so much in the evening, with Peter meeting with his investors after working all day at Canyon Creek, and she'd filled the hours with eating, since she always seemed to be ravenous. But that didn't mean she was pregnant. It was just her newly awakened sexual appetite, which she was sating with food, since she couldn't satisfy it with Riley. And the fact that she had awakened two mornings ago and run straight to the bathroom to vomit meant nothing. Not one thing.

And if she *were* pregnant, what then? What would she do with a baby? She *hated* babies. Emma Jean heard the oven buzzer ring and pushed back from her desk. Even though the smell of the cake baking made her want to vomit, that did not mean she was pregnant. Bravely she walked into the kitchen to remove the cake from the oven.

Emma Jean opened the oven door a bit and peeked in. The cake was done to perfection, its top—which would soon be its bottom—an even golden brown. She grabbed two oven mitts from a hook on the wall and carefully pulled out the cake, setting it on the rack she'd placed on the counter. After it had cooled a little, she'd flip it over onto a serving plate to reveal its crown of glazed pineapple. Emma Jean was nothing if not an expert baker, specializing in recipes from her southern girlhood. Peter would be so happy. He loved her pineapple upside-down cake.

How would Peter react if she were pregnant? If she had her own bun in the oven, so to speak? She paused for a moment to laugh at her own joke, but then realized it didn't seem very funny. And, oh God, what about Riley? What if it *was* his baby? And how would she ever know? Emma Jean stared at the cake and decided that the whole thing was ridiculous. Trish was delusional. She was not pregnant because she could not get pregnant. Period. Plus, she was too old. Yes, that was it. She was too damn old to get pregnant. The odds of a middle-aged woman like herself getting knocked up were tiny.

Emma Jean marched into her office. "I've decided that you are nuts, Trish. There is no way on God's green earth that I am preg—"

She stopped herself mid-sentence, because for some unknown reason Trish was conversing with a scruffy-looking hobo in her office. Now what would a homeless person be doing in her home?

"Hello, Emma Jean," he said.

Emma Jean peered at the man. Oh dear Lord, it was Connor. Connor, Julia's poor cuckolded soon-to-be-ex-husband, and he looked like a sad, bedraggled basset hound. *Oh how awful,* Emma Jean thought. Previously, Julia had been the unattractive depressive, while Connor held himself erect and always looked handsome and alert.

"Look who's here," Trish said. "Connor found some books of yours and dropped by to return them."

"Oh, darling, Connor, how are you doing?" Emma Jean said, after she'd extricated herself from the obligatory hug, during which, she had to say, Connor felt as soft and floppy as a rag doll.

"Lousy," he said.

"I'm so sorry," Emma Jean said.

"Me too," Trish said. "Julia's decision was a shock to us all."

Connor nodded his thanks to each of them and then his gaze wandered about the office while he seemed momentarily at a loss for words. His gaze fell on the altar Emma Jean had arranged beside her desk. It held Aku Aku, her lucky Buddha, who sat beside an incense holder with a long stick of incense in it. She never lit it because Peter started coughing when she did, and Trish said it made the house smell like cat pee. Emma Jean herself hated the smell of incense, but didn't it seem the sort of thing you should have on an altar? She also put a tiny cobalt blue vase on the altar, and filled it with fresh flowers regularly. Connor seemed impressed with the altar, so impressed he couldn't stop staring at it.

Trish cleared her throat. Emma Jean looked at her, and Trish furrowed her eyebrows and nodded her head toward Connor, who had now reached out a long finger to touch Aku Aku.

"How's business, Connor?" Emma Jean asked. It seemed a safe topic, because Connor sold rare books over the Internet, and he and Emma Jean had spent many a pleasant evening discussing books and the overall state of the world together.

Connor lifted his eyes from the altar and glanced at Emma Jean. Then he shrugged. "I don't know. Okay, I guess." He dropped his gaze again. Well, Aku Aku was a compelling icon, and the altar was artfully arranged, if Emma Jean did say so herself. But then she realized that he was no longer staring at the altar. His head had shifted a bit and now he was looking directly at the pregnancy test. Just as with Aku Aku, his hand reached out to touch it. That would not do. It would not do at all. Emma Jean searched her mind desperately for a way to distract him.

"Hey, I've been meaning to ask you," Emma Jean said. "Have you ever run across that first edition of *Kon Tiki* I was looking for?"

Connor didn't move, and it was difficult to tell where his gaze fell, the altar or the pregnancy test. Why did they have to make the damn box so big and colorful?

"You and I talked about it a couple months ago," Emma Jean said, even though she was pretty sure they hadn't. No response for several long moments.

Finally he raised his head, a confused look on his face. "I can't remember. Maybe I saw it in a stack last week." He brought his finger to his mouth, bit on a nail absently, then shook himself. "Can't recall. Things have kinda gotten away from me since Julia left."

And now he was staring at the pregnancy test again. Oh Lord, this time she absolutely *had* to divert his attention.

"If it's because you are disorganized, we can help you with that. Trish is, like, the best organizer, ever, aren't you Trish? Tell you what. I'll lend her to you. Ouch." Trish kicked her, flippin' kicked her; could you even believe that?

"I don't know," Connor said. He still seemed to be staring at the pregnancy test. Emma Jean edged toward it, thinking she could casually shove it behind the altar. And then he looked up and smiled the sweetest rueful smile that was positively Riley-like in its charm. "Actually, that might help if you wouldn't mind. I hate to admit it, but I probably could use some assistance."

Trish wore a forced smile as Emma Jean stepped out of kicking range and in front of the pregnancy test.

"This is good," Connor said. "This will be helpful. I'm glad I came. I was afraid you wouldn't want to see me."

"Oh, you're always welcome here," Emma Jean said. "I love talking books with you."

Connor nodded. "I'll be back then." He turned to Trish. "And if you did have time to help me, I'd be much obliged. I'll pay you, of course."

Trish ushered Connor out, and Emma Jean ignored the dirty looks she kept shooting her way. Emma Jean was pleased with herself. She'd always been so fond of Connor, and this way, she truly was helping him. Plus, maybe Trish could get some good scoop on Julia and Marielle. Sometimes it seemed that all the universe needed a gentle nudge in the correct direction, and then everything fell into place. She smiled and bowed at Aku Aku.

On the drive out to the winery, Emma Jean felt magnanimous and content, thanks in no small part to the brilliant ploy she'd used to save her bacon with Connor. As part of her thanks to the universe, Emma Jean asked Trish to remind her to be nice to Marielle, who would be visiting the class to tell them about her travels for her book.

"Oh that'll go over big," Trish said. "Like you ever pay attention to anything I say." Trish was behind the wheel of Emma Jean's Acura SUV, having insisted she drive after Emma Jean nearly sideswiped a car while looking at a text she hoped was from Riley.

"I'm serious," Emma Jean said. "Being friends with Marielle is part of my Campaign to be Kind. Can I help it if she annoys me at times?"

"Which is no doubt why your efforts to be friends with her have not been successful," Trish pointed out.

"That's not true." Emma Jean pulled the seatbelt away from her chest—she hated the manner in which seatbelts tightened across you so you couldn't breathe—and pondered. "Well, if you won't tell me when I'm being bitchy, maybe you can tell me how to be nice. I mean, I try. But then the wrong thing just comes out. Maybe because I'm just saying what I think."

Trish signaled to pull off the freeway and glanced over at Emma Jean. "You might start by trying to be curious and open instead of judgmental of yourself and others."

"I don't judge myself!" Emma Jean said. The nerve of her assistant sometimes galled Emma Jean. Absolutely galled her.

"Maybe not," Trish said. "But generally people who are judgmental of others are first judging themselves harshly."

Could she help it if her Campaign to be Kind and make friends had gotten derailed by her obsession with Riley? Emma Jean sighed. She looked out the window the rest of the way to the winery and practiced being open and curious, even though she had driven this way a million times before and there was not a blessed thing to be curious about.

"Are you ready for me to begin?" the young woman asked. Her name was Amy, and she wore brown hair pulled back in a ponytail and had shiny spots on her forehead and cheeks that Emma Jean always wanted to dab with powder.

Emma Jean sat at the head of the big, heavy, oak table in the tasting room at Canyon Creek Vineyards and arranged a half smile on her face. That was something she learned from reading Thich Nhat Hanh, the half smile. He meant it as a way to emanate serenity, as a means to calm, but in this situation, it allowed Emma Jean to pretend she was listening to her student read a chapter about drug addiction, which could use, to put it delicately, a lot of work.

Emma Jean tried to listen to Amy read, but she'd been distracted all session. Honestly, between the pregnancy test, Riley's text, and seeing Connor, her brain was awhirl. This was her ongoing advanced writing class, and they were celebrating Amy's recent publication with this special party. Amy had gotten a story accepted by a prestigious literary magazine, which wasn't the same thing as getting a book contract, God knew, but Emma Jean believed fervently in celebrating every student success, no matter how small. So she'd had Trish call and make arrangements for the class to meet at the tasting room as a special treat. And she'd made her special pineapple upside-down cake, of course.

And of course, it was especially lovely having Marielle among them, and Emma Jean had already smiled, nodded and been remarkably open and curious about her former student and current friend. She had been, dare she say it, *kind*, even when Marielle had shown off the vast collection of pens she bought in each city of her book tour—awful, garish things like you'd find in a souvenir shop or airport gift stall.

Now Emma Jean looked around the tasting room, trying to be open and curious, as if she were seeing it for the very first time. It had bleached woodwork with white walls draped with tapestries woven with various grape-harvesting scenes. At one end of the room, a large wood hutch held a variety of items marketed by Canyon Creek—glasses with the company name and logo etched on it, a line of specialty olive oils, tablecloths in the same pattern as the tapestries hanging on the walls, coasters made from cork, and several books on wine and food. Peter had been associated with Canyon Creek for nearly ten years, and he had made a good name for himself, his Pinots and Chardonnays consistently winning taste tests and awards. The massive table they all sat around was covered with wine bottles in varying states of fullness, as well as water pitchers and glasses.

Speaking of Peter, where was he? Emma Jean hadn't quite managed to pull off the planned cleavage, neither breast nor toe, because they ended up being so rushed after the Connor interruption. But still, she'd put on a lightweight sweater and jewelry that lent a successful writerly air to her overall outfit, and she felt that Peter would be impressed. Amy finished her reading and looked up at Emma Jean expectantly. Emma Jean regarded her student. She didn't have the least clue what Amy had just read. She looked around the rest of the faces at the table—four women and two men—and smiled brightly. "What do we think? Who has comments?"

Paul Chapman, the older of the two men in the class, raised his hand. "I think Amy did a good job of showing the pain of her protagonist's addiction."

Trish, bless her heart and dear God don't ever let her quit, seemed to understand immediately that Emma Jean was lost. She stood to pour more wine. When she refilled Amy's glass, she swooped in and picked up Amy's manuscript, then deposited it in front of Emma Jean. She loved her students, every single one of them, beyond all reason. It was just that this particular evening she was so *distracted*.

Paul could be relied upon to launch into a long boring digression about a fellow student's writing that rarely spoke to any salient points but rather simply rehashed what the story had been about. Usually he drove Emma Jean to distraction, and she just about always interrupted him mid-spiel, but tonight he was a savior. She ignored the surprised looks on the other student's faces and the smile of delight on Paul's as she allowed him to run on.

Emma Jean reached for her wine glass and then made her hand veer to pick up her water glass instead. Not that she believed that she was pregnant, but wasn't drinking alcohol verboten when you were with child? Just then a redheaded woman poked her head into the door of the tasting room.

"Oh, sorry, I didn't realize anyone was using this room," Katie said.

"Hi, Katie," Emma Jean said, glad for the interruption. Katie was one of the employees who poured wine and coordinated special events for Canyon Creek.

"Oh, Emma Jean, it's you! It is so good to see you, I was afraid you wouldn't be coming out here anymore."

"Darling, you'll never get rid of me," Emma Jean said, even as she wondered why Katie would think such a thing.

"Well that's great. I always enjoy seeing you so much. Hey, I've got a tour group that wants to see the tasting room. It's our only access to the viewing deck outside."

"Well, bring 'em on through, darling," Emma Jean said. The leap back to her public persona cheered her.

The door opened wide and Katie walked in, motioning her group, a large mixed bunch of mostly middle-aged men and women, to follow her. "This is our tasting room," Katie said. "Open to the public and for special events, like this one. Emma Jean Sullivan—I'm sure many of you have heard of her—is holding her writing class here."

The group smiled and nodded. "I've read all your books," one of the women said. Unfortunately, she was short and dumpy, plain as a scoop of vanilla ice cream. Emma Jean hated when that happened. She preferred her target reader to be perky and stylish, like the L.A. clones. Emma Jean beamed a smile at the frumpy one anyway. A fan was a fan, and God love 'em all. Then she smiled at the rest of the group.

"Oh, I wish I had a book you could sign," the frumpy one said. She had a head of tight curls, which had to have been permed—

Emma Jean didn't know people still got perms—and for some reason the name Poodle Head leapt into Emma's mind.

"Come to one of my signings," Emma Jean said. She smiled in what she fancied was a kind, bestselling novelist-to-acolyte sort of way, emphasis on the kind part. "I'm doing a lot of them right now for the new book."

Trish piped up. "There's one at Powell's next week."

"Oh, goody." Poodle Head clapped her hands together. "I'll try to come."

Emma Jean beamed at her munificently, a queen bestowing blessings on her subject. It was so easy to connect with people; she was always advising those who expressed awe at her facility with strangers. All you had to do was be willing to engage.

"Let's walk on through to the viewing area," Katie said to her group. "There's a deck out here, and you can watch the winemaking from it. This is an interesting time of year, because the grapes will soon be harvested and brought in to be processed. We call it crush."

Katie shepherded the group out onto the deck, and through the large windows, Emma Jean could see her lining them up along the railing so they could watch the trucks deliver loads of grapes. Then Katie popped her head back in.

"Can I interrupt you one more time?" the young woman asked.

"Of course," Emma Jean said, always happy for a chance to show how gracious she could be to her students, who rarely got to see her out in public.

"Do you know if Peter is going to be coming around any time soon? Because I lent him a book, and I'd really like to get it back. I mean, I know it's no big deal, but I have this thing about lending out books, and—"

"But he's here today, Katie. You can probably catch him in his office."

She watched, puzzled, as the expression on Katie's face change from earnest explainer to panicked deer. "Um, okay. I guess I'll just go look for him, then," Katie said, and then she made a funny face, skewing her lips in a way that told Emma Jean something was up.

And just then, a tall, bald man from Katie's group stepped back into the room. "Do you expect any big changes with this new winemaker you've been telling us about?"

"Um, sir, if you'd step out onto the deck, I could answer your questions where we won't be bothering the class," Katie said.

But now all of Emma Jean's systems were on red alert. "New winemaker? What are you talking about? Katie, what's going on?"

Katie dropped her head forward. "He hasn't told you, has he?"

"Told me what?"

"Peter hasn't worked here in over a month, Emma Jean."

She was having difficulty processing what Katie said. Peter hadn't worked at Canyon Creek in a month? Emma Jean felt like her brain was suspended in a vat of mud.

The balding man helpfully held up a glossy Canyon Creek brochure. "The new winemaker's name is Pascal LeMonde."

"Let me see that." Emma Jean rose from her seat, crossed the room in two long strides, and snatched the brochure from the man's hand. She pulled the glasses she wore on a beaded chain around her neck to her eyes. *Pascal LeMonde became only the third winemaker at Canyon Creek this past August*, Emma Jean read. The words didn't make sense. She read them again. *Pascal LeMonde became only the third winemaker at Canyon Creek Vineyards this past August, succeeding Peter Sullivan.* Emma Jean shook her head to clear it and tried reading again. The words remained the same.

"This can't be right," Emma Jean said. Suddenly she was hyper aware of everything in the room, as if it were frozen in time: the faint smell of wood and fermented grapes, Amy's cloying perfume, the way every single one of her students was staring at her, as was every man and woman in the wine tour. She raised her eyes from the brochure and looked around at everyone.

"I'm so sorry, Emma Jean," Katie said. "You might find Peter at his office in town."

"He has an office in town?" Emma Jean shrieked. Why did she not know any of this?

"Um, it's a very small one," Katie said. "Or so I've heard. I've not actually seen it myself."

"But it's an office! One that I don't know about! One that costs money!"

And suddenly everything clicked into place. Why Peter seemed always to be gone, no matter what time of the day or night. *Because he didn't want to have to see her, and tell her the truth.* Why the business section was always mysteriously missing from the paper. *Because he didn't want her to read the news of the appointment of Pascal Lemon, or whatever in the hell his name was.* Why he smiled and nodded and said, "Great, things are going great, the crush is good this year," whenever she asked him about his day at work. *Because there was no day at work.*

Emma Jean looked up, looked at the expectant faces of her students: Amy, her shiny spots glowing under the chandelier crafted from wine glasses and bottles, Dean and Paul, their smug, superior looks for once taken over by surprise. And Marielle—was that a smirk on her face? The rest of them all stared at her with their mouths in various stages of openness. And then she looked at the wine tasters, the rest of whom had shuffled back in the door: Katie, as sweet and girl-next-door as they came, currently wincing and ringing her hands, and Poodle Head and the Gawky One.

Slowly—magnificently even—Emma Jean looked at every one of them. "Class dismissed," she said through clenched jaw. Then she smiled at all of them and thought to herself, *I'll have his head on a platter for breakfast and his gonads as an appetizer for lunch.*

Chapter Eight
If They Could See Her Now

Emma Jean sank into the hot, sudsy water. She leaned her head against the plastic, air-filled pillow that attached to the bathtub with three little suction cups and sighed deeply as the steaming water lapped around her body. She closed her eyes, so as not to be able to see the tiny strip of paper lying on the counter across the room. Then she opened them again. The strip was like a flashing beacon from a far distant universe, compelling her to stare at it.

The small bit of paper was blue. Deep blue, bright blue, *blue* blue. A blue that indicated a positive result on the pregnancy test. Emma Jean had peed in a cup, stuck the test strip in it, stood there and watched it turn positive. She'd been stunned at how quickly the test turned blue, how blue a blue it was, how final. How *positive*. And no matter how many times she repeated the test—this was her fifth effort—it turned blue every time. Every flippin' time.

Emma Jean took a deep breath to center herself.

Then she burst into tears.

Pregnant. She was pregnant. Oh dear God, how had she gotten to this point? Pregnant at age forty-eight with one of the baby's potential fathers living thousands of miles away with his wife and other child, and the other a lying, shiftless, unemployed winemaker, who, by the way, was at this very second out apartment-hunting because Emma Jean had told him *she could not live with him anymore*, ever, or at least not at this moment. Her book—the topic of which said shiftless husband had suggested to her, let us not forget—was tanking. *Tanking.* Her Amazon rankings were slipping, even as Marielle's stayed consistently in the top ten. The flippin' top ten.

And Trish, her loyal assistant, had announced yesterday that she'd be leaving her job at the end of the year—only three short months away.

The thought of Trish leaving made the tears run stronger down her face. Just because Trish was getting her Master's in Counseling, it didn't mean she actually had to work in the field, did it? Couldn't she just continue practicing her psychological theories on Emma Jean? And to think, Emma Jean had been planning an extra-special surprise party for Trish, the day after commencement, catered and everything.

She'd even written a blog post on it, and her fans had begun responding with all sorts of helpful ideas for the party. Oh God, her fans. What would happen when they learned she was pregnant? Her reputation would be utterly and completely trashed. Her entire image—her brand, if you will—was built on a platform of baby hating. Her fans would desert her in droves once they found out.

She scooped a handful of bubbles into the air and blew them across the length of the tub. Maybe she just wouldn't tell her fans. She could have a baby in secret, couldn't she? No, but wait. That would be untruthful, and the angels wouldn't like that. Angels sent out only peace, love, and other virtuous qualities. Emma Jean suspected they liked it best when humans did, too. She was only beginning to learn about angel lore, though, so she wasn't sure. Plus she was a bit shaky when it came to virtue these days. Oh, Lord how she needed some angel wisdom now, on every aspect of her life.

It was a cool morning in late September, with the frosty nip of fall officially in the air, and she'd lit votives in glass holders and other candles all around the perimeter of the tub. Aku Aku sat majestically nestled in the cluster of candles, the one bright spot in Emma Jean's life.

What was she going to do with a baby? Emma Jean closed her eyes and tried to picture how it would be. An image of the baby sleeping peacefully in a bassinette next to Emma Jean as she wrote arose in her mind. That wasn't so bad. She took a breath, just like the Bees told her. The baby was older now, crawling, then walking, and Emma Jean had to keep getting up from her desk to chase it. And then the baby was a toddler, and Emma Jean was taking it to a playgroup and all the other mothers were twenty years younger and thin. Her eyes flew open.

She couldn't do this. How in the world was she going to deal with a baby, let alone the pregnancy that would produce the baby? After only a few weeks of pregnancy—or more to the point *knowing* about the pregnancy—she was already set to cash it in. She felt bloated, nauseated, dizzy and scared. What were her options? Her mind ran to the obvious solutions in such a situation. Adoption. *Don't be silly*, she told herself, *that was for teenagers or drug addicts*. She could never allow the flesh of her flesh to be raised by strangers. Well, there was the other "A" option, then—abortion. Emma Jean scooted lower in the tub, attempting to get the bath water to cover her burgeoning stomach, and frowned. Abortion seemed desperate, the alternative of last resort, and she suspected it wasn't something the angels would approve.

Maybe she would just miscarry. Didn't old women like her miscarry all the time? Maybe if she grasped the lesson the universe had meant her to learn with the unexpected pregnancy, the angels would let nature take its course and she would lose the baby. Suddenly she remembered a scene from an old Margaret Drabble novel, in which the heroine took a hot bath and drank vodka, which was supposed to induce a miscarriage. But she didn't have any vodka at the moment, and she was too tired to climb out of the bathtub and get some.

So what *could* she do, seeing as how she was alone in the world and everyone hated her? A spa. She could encamp to a spa and enjoy the rest of her pregnancy in luxury and comfort. Emma Jean pictured herself in a white robe, sipping water after a massage, except how would she lie on her stomach with a baby in it? Perhaps a spa wasn't the best idea. Besides, they were expensive, and what with the way her indolent husband was spending money, she was broke. Well, how about a long journey? She could take a pilgrimage to India. Emma Jean imagined herself atop a camel—wait, were there camels in India or had her mental images gotten scrambled? Whatever kind of animals India featured, she realized it was also hot and dirty, and she didn't especially want to have her baby in a Hindu temple.

There was simply no solution. She couldn't do this. How was she going to do this? She was too old and set in her ways. She'd be dealing with a child in her dotage. It was too late for her to deal with a child—a baby, no less.

She and Peter had tried and tried to get pregnant, back when she was still young and theoretically fertile, back before she had decided she hated babies. Truth be told, she'd begun hating babies because she couldn't have one herself, because what was the use of loving something you couldn't have? She'd lain awake nights and sobbed over her inability to get pregnant. She remembered the last time they'd tried, ten years ago now. Emma Jean had been certain, absolutely certain, that this time would be the charm. She'd taken her temperature, tracked when she was most likely to be fertile, and she and Peter had then had sex as often as possible on those days. Afterwards, she had lain in bed with her hips propped on a pile of pillows. All the books said you should put your legs over your head, but Emma Jean felt that was taking it a bit too far. Besides, her stomach got in the way. So she lay there with her hips propped up and Peter brought her tea and lay beside her and read her poetry and the latest reviews of her book, which, back then had been *Finding Felicity*, and it had been climbing the bestseller charts.

Two weeks later, she'd gone to the bathroom and found a spot of red on her panties. And that was the precise moment she started hating babies. Hating them with all her heart and all her soul. She'd burst out of the bathroom and into the bedroom, where Peter was lying on the bed watching something inane on TV.

"Darling!"

"Huh?"

"It's official. We are *not* going to be parents. Ever." She climbed onto the bed, lay down beside Peter, and picked up his arm so that she could wrap it around her shoulders. "I am sick and tired of working so hard to have a baby. It's time we forgot about it and focused on us."

"You started your period, didn't you?" Peter asked.

Emma Jean nodded. She'd felt a tear slip from her eye, but she blinked it back bravely. She would now embrace her role as a childless woman. She would now glory in it. She would exalt it, in a way it had never been exalted before. If the good Lord saw fit to make her barren, she would make the most of the situation and become a beacon for all the other child-less women on the planet.

Now Emma Jean felt new tears forming. She and Peter had done the child-less marriage thing gloriously for years. So when had it changed? Where had they gone wrong? Because when Emma Jean thought about those days of Peter bringing her tea and reading her poetry, she realized it hadn't been like that between them in a long, long time. Peter never read her poetry anymore. He hadn't read one of her books in years, let alone a review. And he didn't bring her flowers, either. Wasn't that an old song? Emma Jean played the tune in her head. It had been some sort of dreadful duet, but now it seemed the perfect soundtrack to her disintegrating marriage. Despite the glossy picture she'd tried to paint for Trish, her marriage was a sham. She never even saw Peter anymore. And now she'd be seeing him even less.

The thought made more tears run down her face. She could not even believe what that lying, two-timing bastard had done. Quit his job at Canyon Creek back in *July* and then not bothered to tell her until she found out in the most humiliating of ways.

On the day, one week ago now, that she had learned of his betrayal, he hadn't arrived home until nearly midnight. By then Emma Jean was even angrier than she had been at the winery. She'd called his cell repeatedly with no answer, and when she'd tried to leave a message, a recorded voice came on saying his mailbox was full. In some ways Peter was so together, so cautious and anal as to drive her crazy, but in other ways, the important ways, like dealing with messages and keeping things tidy and staying organized, he was awful.

And it was then she'd gotten the idea to go through the bills, which was an eye-opener. Bills for the office rental in Dundee— the small town that was the epicenter of the wine industry—bills for office furniture, for a computer, for electricity, and water. Jesus! Another month of this and she wouldn't be able to afford the hot water she was currently lying in.

When Peter had finally walked in that night, Emma Jean was sitting on the couch in the cozy area off the kitchen, next to the huge stone fireplace that she loved to light. She'd been too pissed off to read that night, and so she was just staring at the Duraflame log fire.

"Hey, love," he said, tossing his briefcase to its usual spot beside an old oak chest. "What are you doing up? Lately you're always in bed when I get home."

It was true. Emma Jean used to be one of those people who could make do on three or four hours of sleep a night, a trait all her friends envied and one she sometimes wrote about on her blog just to read the admiring and envious comments that ensued. But no way in hell could she even last to midnight these days. The past few weeks, she'd been in bed, fast asleep, by ten.

"I waited up to see you," Emma Jean said.

"That's sweet." Peter walked across the room and planted a kiss on her forehead, then plopped down on the couch beside her. It was a wonderful couch, one of Emma Jean's favorite pieces of furniture ever, red velvet, soft and smooshy. She'd found beautiful pillows in rich jewel toned tapestry fabrics and striped silks to toss on it.

"I'm not sweet. I've never been sweet. I hate being called sweet. And my motive for sitting up to talk to you is nowhere near being sweet."

"Whoa there." Peter pulled his head back and held out his hands in front of him, as if pushing her away. "Down girl. What in the hell has gotten into you?"

Emma Jean looked into her husband's eyes and knew that no matter how much bravado he was attempting to evince, Peter understood exactly what was coming. She could see the files opening and closing in his mind, see him pondering options, stories, and excuses. She wasn't going to make this easy for him. So Emma Jean had gone to L.A. and had an affair. Okay, that was bad; she admitted it, but it wasn't like it was premeditated. She just hadn't been able to resist Riley in all his adorableness. But Peter—Peter had planned to start his own wine company, then quit his job two months ago and not told her. He had laid plans that affected their marriage without consulting her.

Emma Jean threw one of the glossy Canyon Creek brochures at him. Unfortunately, the brochure was so light, it fluttered to the ground in a pathetic way. "I'm talking about the fact that you quit your job in July and didn't bother to mention it to me."

"August."

"What?"

"Technically, I didn't quit it until August."

"Oh for Christ's sakes, Peter, that's a minor point at the moment. July, August, it doesn't really matter. What matters is that you've quit. First of all, you start your own winery without telling me, and now you've quit your job without so much as a word about it."

Peter dipped his head down and back up in a gesture she used to find endearing but which now made her want to scream. Then he smiled. "I just did what you taught me, Emma Jean, proceeding on the theory that it is better to ask forgiveness than permission."

Correction. He no longer made her want to scream, he made her want to kill him. Good thing she didn't want to have her baby in jail, or who knows what she might do. Peter seemingly mistook her silence for encouragement and blathered on.

"I wanted to surprise you when I had something tangible to show for myself. I was trying to create something wonderful for our marriage. For us. For *you*."

"Oh that's a good one." Emma Jean uncurled her legs out from under her and sat forward. "You quit your job, leaving me as the sole bread winner, which, let us not forget, has always been the case, and now you tell me you're doing it for me, for our marriage? That's rich."

"Don't you see?" Peter moved toward her, until he was hovering alarmingly close. "This is my chance. I saw opportunity and I grabbed it, instead of letting it pass me by. It's my chance to be able to support you for a change. And frankly, it's all I got. I'm tired of being emasculated by you. Something's got to change."

"Emasculated? Since when are you emasculated? Seems to me you never had a problem happily spending my money before you started reading the dictionary. Or wherever you learned such a big word."

"Stop it, Emma Jean. Quit being a bitch and listen to me."

"Maybe if you quit calling me names I could think straight enough to. I'm not a bitch. I'm your meal ticket." She scooted sideways on the couch so as to get away from him. Unfortunately, he followed, stepping around the coffee table.

"Calm down for a minute and listen. I want to be able to take care of you. I want to make lots of money and keep you in the lifestyle that you love. But I can't do that working for somebody else. Nobody gets rich working for somebody else. It's rule one of creating wealth. You've got to have your own business these days."

"But, Peter, how do you think you're going to get rich running your own winery? That's a money pit if there ever was one. Jesus."

"Honey, it's all I know. Winemaking is all I know."

"Oh for Christ's sake, don't be so melodramatic. You know the law. You were an attorney before you studied viticulture."

"You think I should go back to the law?" Peter said.

Emma Jean shrugged. "Why not? You could make good money and do wine on the side."

"Oh, honey. You know I'm never going to make it as an attorney. That's another rule of wealth gathering. You've got to do something you love. If you hate it, you won't have the passion to put your all into it."

Emma Jean shook her head. "What get rich quick book have you been reading now?"

Peter waved his hand and sat down next to her on the couch. "I really want this, Emma Jean. I want it bad." He took her hand in his and looked into her eyes. "It's because of my father, you know?"

Emma Jean jerked her hand away from his. "What in the hell does your father have to do with this?"

Peter sighed dramatically, laying it on a bit too thick, Emma Jean thought. "I've told you about my Dad. How he slaved away as a postal clerk for years. How he always told me not to follow in his footsteps, to work for myself." Now Peter affected a particularly soulful look. "My father worked in misery for years, counting the days until retirement. And then he died. I don't want that to happen to me, Emma Jean. I didn't listen to my father's advice for years, because I was too afraid. But the time is right for me now."

Emma Jean was so impressed with Peter's story of his motivating impulse, even though she'd heard it before, in a less dramatic form, that she'd not even protested his long speech. And because he had pulled the story card on her, she probably would have left it at that, backed down, given him another chance. Except that then he went too far. Peter stuck his lower lip out, raised his eyebrows and opened his eyes wide, in a pleading gesture that made him look like an ugly little schoolboy, a pathetic dog, an oversized rat. It was his fish face, the same one his daughter Julia made, the one that made her want to slap both of them.

"Father or no, you betrayed my trust, Peter. And I can't handle that right now. Maybe if things were going better for me..." Emma Jean shook her head. "I'm so stressed out about *The Winemaker's Wife*. I'm so stressed about *everything*. I just can't handle it. I think you should move out."

"Move out? Emma Jean, no. I'm not going to move out; I live here. This is my home."

"Technically, its mine," Emma Jean said. She stood and walked to the refrigerator, refilled her water glass from the exterior spigot. "Seeing as how I pay the mortgage."

"Come on, Emma Jean, you've always said that what's mine is yours, that we are building our financial future together."

"That was before you decided to gamble everything on a winery. You need to leave, Peter. Now. Tonight. I'm sick of looking at you."

"For Christ's sake, it's midnight!"

"You should have thought about that before you took these impulsive actions. You should have realized there would be consequences, Peter, and if having to find a hotel at midnight is one of them, it's a damn small price to pay."

"No," Peter said. "This is bullshit."

Emma Jean took the last sip of water in the bottom of her glass, then raised it high above her head and threw it. The glass smashed against the stone fireplace with a satisfying crash. Regretfully, she wasn't sure how Peter reacted, because she left the room without a backward glance. All she knew was that he'd slept in the guest room that night and left the next day.

He was now living in a hotel room in downtown Portland, as he told her in repeated messages and constant emails. Christ, between Peter and Riley her inbox filled with messages every day. Which, in the case of Riley, was not a bad thing. *I just bought a book on the life of Krishnamurti*, his most recent email had read. *I think you'd really like this guy's brand of spirituality.* Oh, Riley was the most interesting human in the world, but he lived far, far away, and anyway he would probably no longer want to write her when she got fat and ugly due to being pregnant.

Emma Jean sat up in the bathtub and turned the faucet on to pull in more hot water. And now, she had to admit it to herself, she was wondering if she had made the wrong decision about kicking Peter out. She kind of missed him, the way he did little things for her. Well, maybe it wasn't so much that she *missed* him—after all, he had been gone most of the last few months from morning until night—it was just that she hated being alone.

The funny thing was, she'd always thought she loved it. She loved being alone long hours during the day while she wrote, loved being up late in the quiet house working on her blog. What she hadn't realized was how much she counted on Peter to arrive home. So she could quit being alone and tell him all about her day. She wondered what it would be like having Riley come home to her and she smiled, thinking about it. Then she remembered he'd be coming home in the morning, exhausted, wanting to fall into bed just as she was ready to get up.

The hell part of it was that she still desired Riley something fierce. She lusted for Riley's touch, for the way he clutched her breasts and bit her shoulder when he was entering her from behind. She still wanted to look in his eyes and see him laugh when he touched her, wanted to feel every inch of him inside her, the way he *filled* her up, and not just sexually, but filled a void she hadn't even known was there.

The longing for Riley that overtook her at times threatened to swallow her up completely. It was what the Bees called having an expectation, and of course the fact that her expectation couldn't be satisfied caused her all manner of pain and anxiety. But wasn't living in the Buddhist way just a wee bit dull? Never wanting anything, just accepting things as they were? Desire rules the world, Emma Jean always told her students. She didn't think she'd ever understood that quite so fully as she did now. Better, perhaps, to stick with the angel lore. So far, as far as she could tell, the angels approved of just about anything. Now that was a theory of life Emma Jean could embrace.

Someone knocked on the bathroom door and then it opened a crack. "Emma Jean? Are you in there?" It was Trish. All Emma Jean could see of her was the crown of her dark head.

"Come in," Emma Jean said, suddenly flooded with relief that she wasn't alone, that there was still someone in the world who loved her, even if that someone, Trish, was also about to betray her by leaving her employ for another job.

Trish opened the door wide and came in the bathroom. She looked darling, like she always did, more so lately as her graduation date approached, her eyes bright and shiny, and her expression always so interested in the world. Curious and open, you might even say. Emma Jean had to admit, she'd make a fabulous therapist.

"Could you bring me some vodka, please?" Emma Jean said.

"Of course I'm not going to bring you vodka, you're pregnant."

"But that's the point." Emma Jean sat forward and reached for her glass of water, which she'd stationed on the side of the tub.

Trish strode across the room in one long stride and snatched the glass from Emma Jean's hand.

"What are you doing?" Emma Jean reached for it at the same time, knocking Aku Aku off into the tub, but managing to wrest the glass from Trish's grasp. "Hey, watch out for Aku Aku."

"You shouldn't be drinking vodka, Emma Jean."

"It's just water." Emma Jean pulled Aku Aku from the water. He was covered with bubbles. Emma Jean sat him in her hand. "He looks cute this way, don't you think?"

Trish sat on the toilet, crossed her leg, and glared at Emma Jean. "What is all this about?"

Emma Jean pointed her finger toward the pregnancy test on the counter, then covered her eyes and sank back into the bubbles. She sensed movement, but before she could react, Trish had put her hand in the bathtub and pulled the plug. She handed a towel to Emma Jean.

"What are you doing?" Emma Jean said. "I want my bath." She reached to flip the lever to stop up the tub again but Trish covered it with her hand.

"C'mon, get out. We've got an appointment."

"I don't feel like having an appointment. I hate everybody and everybody hates me, so what's the point?"

"The point is, you've consistently refused to believe that you are pregnant, despite numerous pregnancy test results to the contrary. Not only that, you've refused my efforts to get you to the doctor for prenatal care, and so obviously you don't want this baby—"

"That is the only true thing you've said all day," Emma Jean interrupted.

"—And so we are going to deal with it once and for all, like adults. Okay?"

Emma Jean took the towel from Trish and nodded, feeling slightly light headed, which must have been from standing up so quickly after lying in the hot water for so long. The idea of dealing with the baby—somehow, someway—was vastly appealing, like opening all the windows in her house at the same time.

"And how, pray tell, are we going to do this?" Emma Jean asked.

"I've made an appointment at the doctor's. For an abortion."

Emma Jean slumped against the bathroom wall.

Trish was right. There really wasn't any other choice. She had mulled every single damn option, and having an abortion was the only that made any sense. She would simply have to buck up and deal with this latest travail, as bravely as she always did.

Emma Jean wasn't exactly sure how one dressed for an abortion, but for the sake of comfort, she chose grey cotton yoga pants and her favorite writing sweater. Perhaps not the height of style, given the holes in the sweater and that spot she couldn't get out on the front, but it would have to do. She stuffed a tote bag with books, her journal, and her spiral devoted to *On the Trail of Tiki,* for the two-hour stay Trish had told her she'd have in the recovery room.

Trish drove to the doctor's office situated on the other side of town, across the river and at the base of the West Hills. Emma Jean gazed out the window; her hand placed on her stomach, and imagined how courageous she appeared, despite the fact that Trish seemed unimpressed with her bravado.

"We're here," Trish said. "I'm going to pull over in front and let you out while I go park."

And that was when Emma Jean saw him.

The man sat on the sidewalk in a lawn chair, holding a sign that said, *Stop the Killing Now*, which featured a picture of a bloody fetus. Emma Jean stared at him with her mouth hanging open, repulsed. He had dirty, matted grey hair, a long beard, with crooked teeth and a pair of glasses held together by a safety pin on one side. But then she made an effort to view him in an open and curious manner, just as Trish had advised her, and suddenly his appearance spoke to Emma Jean as someone who had made sacrifices for his cause. She didn't believe in his cause, obviously, but clearly he had given up cleanliness, decent clothes, maybe even a home for his beliefs. Passion of this magnitude fascinated Emma Jean, more so recently, with her experiences with Riley. Of course, it was that very same passion that brought her here, to this abortion clinic, and she wasn't at all sure what that signified.

But suddenly she remembered something from the day she had met Riley. "It was the best day of my life," he had said of Noah's birth. If Emma Jean had this baby, would its birth be the best day of her life? How would she ever know if she went through with the abortion? And what else might she miss?

"This is when you exit the car so I can go park," Trish said. "Oh, for God's sake, quit staring at that man. And whatever you do, don't look at his sign."

But even as Emma Jean watched the man, he put the sign with the photo of the bloody fetus down and reached for another one.

"Don't look, Emma Jean, please?" Trish said.

Slowly the man lifted the new sign, and Emma Jean, watched, mesmerized. And then...oh could it be? She stared at his new sign in awe. In absolute, profound amazement. Because, even though she could scarcely believe it, the new sign featured an image of an angel. Yes, an angel.

Emma Jean could barely breathe.

"Well, at least the angel sign isn't quite so bad," Trish said. "Go ahead and hop out now, and I'll meet you as soon as I park."

Emma Jean pulled her gaze from the protestor to Trish. Once, not so very long ago, Trish, too, had been a baby. A precious baby, full of the angelic spirit that got scrubbed out of people as they grew up in the harsh reality of the heathen world. Emma Jean looked back at the dirty protestor. Oh, wasn't that photo on his sign so gorgeous? And *he* had been an angelic baby, too. Suddenly, Emma Jean experienced a moment nearly as profound as the first time she'd felt Riley inside her. For one brief and all too fleeting instant, she grasped it. She couldn't even exactly say what *it* was, because that knowledge was part of the moment that was now gone. All she knew was that *it* was deeply profound, and encapsulated every mystery of life.

"A clear omen," Emma Jean murmured.

"Yeah, an omen I'm going to get a ticket if you don't get out of this car," Trish said.

Emma Jean smiled beatifically at Trish and hoped the angels appreciated how very patient she was with her assistant's mortal urge to hurry. The world suddenly looked soft and hazy, as if she was seeing everything through a lovely silver veil. Perhaps pregnancy would not be so bad after all, if only because it seemed to be having the lovely effect of increasing her spiritual aptitude. She was, it seemed highly likely, now having epiphanies for two.

Dimly, she heard a car horn honking.

"Emma Jean, get out of the car," Trish said. "There's a delivery truck that needs this spot."

Slowly, majestically, Emma Jean shook her head. "I won't do it. There is no way on God's green earth that I am going to abort the blessed baby inside me and deprive it of life on this gorgeous planet. Take me home."

Never was Emma Jean so happy to see her wonderful home. The wonder of the decision she'd made reverberated within her as Trish pulled up the long drive, past the gazebo covered in rose bushes, currently not in bloom, but lush green and pretty just the same, and the herb garden she'd planted when they moved in. That had been a fleeting passion; she'd not been gardening much the past few years. Maybe that's what she needed, to take up gardening again, her hands in the loamy soil, insects flying by, the sun warming her back as she dug in the dirt. Well, maybe next spring. She could set the baby in a little infant seat beside her.

But—what was this? Peter's car was pulled up to the hedge, his traditional parking place. Emma Jean and Trish glanced at each other.

"The bastard knows he's not supposed to be here when I'm not here," Emma Jean said. "What's he doing?"

Trish pulled into the spot next to Peter's Mercedes SUV and turned off the ignition. "Don't you think you're being just a wee bit hard on him?"

"How can I trust him after what he did?"

Trish sat back in the seat, holding the keys from one finger. "Not to be moralistic or judgmental here, but don't you think he could say the same if he knew about you and Riley?"

"But what Peter did has long-term consequences for our life together. What I did was just have a brief fling with Riley." Emma Jean squashed firmly the thought of the amorous email he'd sent her that morning, three months after the "brief" fling.

Trish looked pointedly at Emma Jean's stomach. "I think it's safe to say your brief fling might have at least one long-term consequence."

"Oh come on, Trish," Emma Jean said. "You know this baby has to be Peter's."

"Uh-huh. You have sex with one man for years and never get pregnant, but as soon as you hook up with Riley, boom, you're pregnant. I'd say the odds are pretty good it's his. And by the way, have you considered his role in this little drama?"

"What do you mean?" Emma Jean clutched her stomach and tried to decide if she felt ill from the pregnancy, though luckily much of the morning sickness seemed to be subsiding, or from what Trish was saying.

"Don't you think you need to tell him what's going on?"

Emma Jean stared at Trish, stricken. In truth, the thought had not occurred to her. Riley had Carolina and Noah, and clearly their affair was just a fun fling and was about nothing more than great sex, so why should she tell him about the baby? The truth of the matter was that she was terrified Riley would quit sending her his profound, adorable emails if she told him. And he'd probably quit calling, too. Then she'd never get to talk to him, since it was against her moral code to call him. It was different when he called her and she sometimes answered the phone by accident. Or when she accidentally responded to his emails.

"Oh God, Emma Jean, you blow me away sometimes. C'mon, let's go see what Peter is doing here."

Emma Jean felt like her feet were encased in concrete blocks as she trudged up the front steps. She dreaded confronting Peter. Slowly she turned, step-by-step, inch-by-inch what was that old saying from? She and her best friend Lucy used to say it, back when they were little girls in Atlanta, what seemed like a light year ago now. Didn't Joan Baez sing something about light years in *Diamond and Rust,* surely one of the best love songs ever?

Emma Jean stopped on the second step from the top, humming the tune.

"You're stalling," Trish said. "What?"

"*Diamonds and Rust.* Joan Baez song. Peter and I always loved it." Emma Jean hummed a few more bars of the song. "I felt that way about Peter for so long, Trish. What went wrong?" She sighed. "And it's so much more sad and romantic, knowing that it's about Bob Dylan and their doomed love affair. Of course, then I think Joan Baez became a lesbian, didn't she?"

"I thought it was a Judas Priest song," Trish said.

"Oh Lord, how old are you, ten? Joan Baez probably wrote the lyrics when Judas Priest was about two."

"It's not one guy, Emma Jean. Judas Priest is a heavy metal band."

"Well what are they doing singing a Joan Baez song?"

"Oh for God's sake, come on." Trish yanked on Emma Jean's arm, pulling her up the last step. Emma Jean watched her benevolently. Even in anger, Trish was beautiful, young, fresh, and dewy. Emma Jean couldn't tell if it was just Trish or that the entire world looked different after her latest epiphany.

Trish opened the door and stopped. "Um, Emma Jean? I think maybe you better go first."

"Why?" Emma Jean stepped inside after Trish. Candles, flickering in the breeze from the draft of the open door, sat on the hall table. Clusters of them sat on the low coffee table, too.

"Look down," Trish said.

The parquet floor of the entry hall was strewn with pink and red rose petals. Peter knew how she loved roses. Dear, adorable, Peter. The man she'd kicked out a week ago. Suddenly she wanted to see him more than anything.

"Peter? Peter?" she called.

"I'll catch up with you tomorrow," Trish said. Dimly Emma Jean heard the front door close behind her assistant, but she didn't turn to look because she was running down the hall, which seemed to be covered with more petals, their quantity getting thicker and thicker as she proceeded. The back of the house was all dark, except for the room to the right, the family room off the kitchen, Emma Jean's favorite room, the one with the big stone fireplace where she liked to curl up and read on the smooshy red couch, the very same room from which she had ordered Peter to move out.

And there on the coffee table fashioned from an old sea navy chest were more candles, a huge bouquet of red roses in a tall crystal vase, and, could it be—her favorite dessert, coconut cake, hopefully purchased from the Fremont Bakery, which was the only place in the world Emma Jean had found that could bake a coconut cake that even came close to Aunt Cleo's.

"Oh God," Emma Jean said, because there on the smooshy red couch sat Peter, his face alternately lit and shadowed by the candles, despite the fact there was still a bit of light in the sky, which shone through the windows behind him.

"Emma Jean," Peter said. "I love you."

She dropped her bag in the door to the family room and ran to Peter, dropping to her knees on the rug and putting her head in his lap. She couldn't believe how happy she was to see him, because now she would no longer be alone. "Oh God, Peter, I love you, too. I never knew how much I missed you until I walked in the front door."

Peter stroked her hair. "I want to come home, baby. I want to prove to you how big a success I can be on my own. And more than that; I want to be here for you, and for us. I know I've been gone a lot lately, and that I've been distant, too. But that's all over. I'm here for you, baby, starting right now."

Emma Jean hugged her husband's knees, pressing her nose against the denim of his jeans and inhaling the clean laundry smell of them. She'd missed that smell, oh Lord how she'd missed it. And how she had missed Peter. What had she been thinking, to kick him out like that? Blame it on hormones. But it wasn't too late, now was it? Oh God, she was the luckiest person in the world.

"Oh darling, I'm so happy. I know we can make it work. Just come home, Peter."

He kissed her on the head. "I was hoping you'd say that. I brought my bag, just in case. Shall we cut the cake?"

Emma Jean scooted up so she was perched on the edge of the couch, her heart pounding with joy. Peter brought plates and utensils from the kitchen and set them on the table. Just before he started cutting the cake, he looked up at her, and then he pursed his lips together in his fish face. Emma Jean tried not to focus on the sudden overwhelming sense of disappointment that flooded her as she watched her husband, newly returned to the fold, plunge a knife through the coconut frosting.

Chapter Nine
The Windmills of Her Mind

There were few things in life that Emma Jean loved more than a road trip, but offering to drive the leg after lunch had been a mistake. She could barely keep her eyes open.

"Onions," Peter said out of the blue, pointing to the truck, which was a flat bed, full of vegetables that were clearly onions.

"Uh-huh," Emma Jean said. She glanced over at her husband. He'd been pointing things out like this, in one-word descriptions, ever since lunch. Was he attempting to be ironically funny? Or was he really that desperately boring and she'd just never noticed before? Honestly, she was trying her best to keep the fires of her marriage stoked and burning white-hot, but there was only so much one woman could do.

They were on their way to Walla Walla, a small wine town in Washington, for a romantic getaway. As an added bonus, Emma Jean had decided this madcap escape from the world would be the perfect time to tell Peter about the baby. But so far, the silence between them felt so awkward she'd not had a chance to announce her news. She believed firmly not only in the power of presentation, but also in the art of timing. And clearly driving through the rolling brown hills along the Columbia River, fighting drowsiness, was not the stellar moment to share her good tidings.

Another worry niggled at the corner of her brain as she drove. On the way out of town, Peter had insisted on stopping at Marielle and Julia's apartment, to pick up a travel guide he'd lent them. Why they needed this guide when they'd been to Walla Walla a million times before was beyond Emma Jean, but Peter kept insisting it had vital information on new wineries in it. So Emma Jean refrained from sighing heavily—being nice to Peter was an integral part of her kindness campaign—and cheerfully went along.

But was it her imagination, or had Marielle been distant, even churlish? She had been at the apartment alone—the very same charming apartment Emma Jean had helped her to find—and didn't seem particularly thrilled to see them arrive unannounced at her door. Maybe it was because she looked completely disheveled in her gray sweat pants and baggy old T-shirt imprinted with the name *Oberlin* on it. "You caught me in the middle of writing," Marielle said, and then Emma Jean understood the decrepit clothing and wild hair. But even when Emma Jean had thrust a plate of freshly baked peanut butter cookies at her, Marielle had not budged from her crankiness. "Oh, cookies. Well, I'm not eating sugar at the moment but maybe Julia will like them."

When Peter went looking for the travel guide, Emma Jean had made small talk, correction, *attempted* to make small talk with a concrete-faced Marielle, while glancing surreptitiously about the apartment, which she'd not been to recently. Hadn't Marielle learned anything about design from Emma Jean? She was disappointed to see that it was decorated in rust belt retro, all bland shapes of tan. No, she corrected herself, the apartment was done up in subtle earth tones, particularly lovely if you liked the color of dirt.

As soon as Peter found the travel guide, which now sat on the car console, Marielle had waved a limp goodbye and retreated to her office, leaving them to show themselves out. But Emma Jean had no more time to ponder what had crawled down Marielle's throat and died, because now Peter spoke again.

"Trees," Peter said, pointing to an orchard.

Emma Jean's stomach gurgled as she signaled and pulled into the left lane to pass a truck. Perhaps they were playing that game of finding something that started with every letter of the alphabet, and Emma Jean had not been paying attention when it was announced.

"And look, there is a truck full of pumpkins."

But no, now they were back to P, and wasn't one of the rules that you did it in alphabetical order? So there wasn't a game, it was just Peter, being boring. Honestly, there was no other way to put it.

This getaway had been his idea, and he'd sold it to her as a chance to celebrate the demise of their short-lived separation, to re-establish themselves as a couple. At first she hadn't wanted to spend money for a weekend at some godforsaken town in the middle of a bunch of wheat fields. But then Trish had arranged a reading for her at the bookstore and she'd rallied. Surely the residents of Walla Walla would be fans, seeing as how it sat smack dab in the center of wine country. Emma Jean envisioned long lines of people—some of them with their fingers stained purple from working with the grapes—standing in line for her to sign *Winemaker's Wife*. And Peter, flush with the knowledge of his impending fatherhood, gazing at her—and the throngs of fans—adoringly.

She hadn't quite found the right time to tell him about the baby because they never talked. In the old days, they'd talk for hours, going over every aspect of their lives. Now though, despite her noble efforts to adore him and revitalize the marriage, they didn't have much to say to each other. In a strange way, she felt like she knew much more about Riley and his life on a day-to-day basis, even though she and Riley rarely talked, either. But Emma Jean was learning that email could be an intimate medium.

Every night if there was a lull at work, Riley would write her a letter, telling her his thoughts and impressions about the world. And oh, what marvelous impressions they were! Riley had profound thoughts on everything from the environment—*We must care for it to ensure that our grandchildren know what trees are, and real ones, not ones grown in a lab somewhere or simulated on a computer*—to the internet—*Someday, people will be uploading the contents of their brains to it, and then we truly will have a world brain. Plus, we'll finally achieve immortality.* How she loved sharing thoughts and ideas with Riley!

But the one thing that Emma Jean wanted to talk about with both Riley and Peter was the one thing she couldn't yet mention. It was mostly all she wanted to think about, too. That was, of course, her pregnancy. She was carrying a baby, an amazing life force within. Being pregnant was the most wondrous thing in the world. She couldn't believe she had almost let Trish convince her to get rid of it. Honestly, how off base could Trish be?

Emma Jean felt like she was connected to every other woman who had ever had a baby, and at the same time, like she was doing something that nobody had ever done before. She'd taken to calling the baby Claire, after her mother, because she was certain it was a girl. But she couldn't tell Peter any of that, because he didn't yet know she was pregnant.

Emma Jean left the freeway and turned north onto a two-lane road that soon led through a tiny town.

"Here we are on the outskirts of lovely Irrigon," Peter intoned. "The Irrigon suburbs."

Emma Jean smiled weakly.

"Ah. And the Irrigon Mini-Mart now has espresso."

Emma Jean sped past. Well, twenty-five miles an hour wasn't exactly speeding, but the cops in these small towns were bears about the speed limit.

"You missed it, hon. They have Pepsi products also, just in case."

She shifted in her seat, to allow her stomach more room behind the wheel. She should have had a salad, which at least wouldn't have felt like a chunk of granite lodged in her gut. At least she assumed that she was feeling her lunch, but maybe the baby was big enough to feel inside now. She pondered for a moment and then shook her head. She didn't think so. She'd ask the doctor when she saw him for the first time next week. She had so many questions. Emma Jean had been reading up on childbirth and was fascinated with everything about it. She kept her books in her office so that Peter wouldn't see them, and if he did, she could say they were research.

Oh God, she had to tell him.

Maybe she could tell him at dinner. Peter had made reservations at one of the new restaurants that had recently sprung up due to Walla Walla's burgeoning status as a chic wine destination. Dear Lord, how much was this little getaway going to cost her? All of a sudden Emma Jean worried about money in a way she hadn't in years, because now she had another person's future to think about: Claire, the wondrous life force within.

Emma Jean needed to ensure that her daughter would enjoy a happy, harmonious, and abundant home. Abundance was her new watchword. The three different books she was reading about it assured her that it was her divine birthright and there was no need to feel guilty. Abundance was a spiritual path, she was pleased to learn. Riley had assured her this was so in one of his recent emails. So now she just needed to finish the book that would boost her abundance and give her another payment on her advance. She was far behind on writing *Tiki*. She had a December 31 deadline, and so far, she had all of three chapters done. She really had to buckle down, seeing as how it was now October, and time didn't seem to be slowing down any. Lord knew that *Wife* still wasn't selling, despite the mantras she'd learned to repeat every day.

I am a bestselling author. My book is selling millions of copies. You were always supposed to state the things you wanted in the present, as if you already had them, but this worried Emma Jean. Might not the universe get the wee-est bit confused? After all, *Finding Felicity* had been a huge best seller. And all of her other books had at least cracked the list. So when she said she was a bestselling author, it was technically true. Or it had been true once. Would the universe be able to figure out she was stating things positively and in the present about *Winemaker's Wife*?

Emma Jean sighed. Spirituality was so confusing for a new seeker like herself. She wished she could discuss it with Peter, but he'd not been the least bit interested the few times she had broached the subject. Not like Riley, who, during one of the phone calls he had managed to sneak in, had told her that personally, he liked Taoism, and she might want to investigate that. After they'd hung up, he'd sent her a list of his favorite titles on the subject, and she now had a new collection of books coming from Amazon and couldn't wait to dig in.

Past Irrigon, they drove through Umatilla, a much bigger town with a deserted feel to it. It took her a minute to notice that Peter had ceased his running commentary. She'd become so used to getting lost in her thoughts when she was with him.

Peter had his head back against the seat and it looked like he had fallen asleep, but when she looked at him, he murmured, "I think I'm going to close my eyes for a minute. I'm not going to sleep, just close my eyes."

Peter always said that, like it was against the law to sleep. Within a few minutes, he was snoring. But she didn't mind, because the landscape had narrowed and the road ran between the broad Columbia River on the left and rocky cliffs on the right. Emma Jean loved this stretch of road, as the long, brown hills on the far side of the river fascinated her, and the river itself was a siren that sang to her soul always. Driving through vast landscapes like this allowed Emma Jean to think, always had, ever since she was a little girl and she and Aunt Cleo would drive back and forth from Atlanta to Mobile, where the remnants of her family had lived.

Sometimes Emma Jean thought that's when she had become a writer, making up stories in her mind on those drives through the lush, green south. She had always loved the motion of the car, and the sense of the world passing by. She pushed the Explorer through a curve and up a hill. And her thoughts turned again to her pregnancy. The one thing this pregnancy had done was make her think about her own mother.

Strange how Emma Jean had never obsessed over her parents, as she knew other orphans did. Maybe it was because Aunt Cleo had always been so good about filling the empty spaces of her life—with art, with laughter, with houses full of people and light and energy. Cleo had been larger than life, and she'd pushed Emma Jean to think beyond the ordinary, too.

"Anything worth doing is worth overdoing," Cleo always said.

Emma Jean embraced this motto for herself early on, after a rough patch around the age of thirteen when her deepest desire in the world had been to be like all the other girls. The issue had come to a head when Cleo had encouraged Emma Jean to present a play she had written and the other girls—the ones she so desperately wanted to be friends with—had laughed at her, saying it was a stupid way to spend time; they wanted to go to the mall to buy make-up.

But Cleo had pointed out that those girls all looked the same, dressed the same, and acted the same (much like the L.A. clones, Emma Jean remembered). "Do you think your poor, dead Mama wanted you to grow up to be just like everyone else?"

Emma Jean wasn't so sure. From what little she had gleaned about her mother, she gathered that Claire had been the meek and mild sidekick to Cleo's wild, extravagant personality. But now she wondered anew. Because a meek and mild woman would not dash off to Spain to run with the bulls. Would she? Why hadn't Emma Jean pondered these issues previously? In truth, she remembered very little of Claire. Every once in a while, a whiff of roses carried her back to a hazy memory of a blonde in a billowy cotton dress, but the memory faded before she could grasp hold of it. No, in Emma Jean's mind, her mother existed mostly as the heroine of an adventure story.

And, what a story! One of the few females to dare to run with the bulls at Pamplona, the event made legendary by Ernest Hemingway, let alone die doing it. If she had to have a dead mother, Emma Jean was at least grateful her mother had died in a fabulous way. The chapters devoted to Claire's death in *Tales of a Motherless Daughter* had garnered ecstatic critical reviews (*vivid reportage by a writer at the top of her powers*) and avid admiration from her fans (*Your mother's tragic death was so stunningly written I felt I was there*).

Claire's death was a distant, wavering event in Emma Jean's life, an iconic moment she'd not really had to suffer much over. And Cleo had been such an extraordinary stand-in mother, Emma Jean's life had continued seamlessly. Until the day fifteen years ago when she'd been helping Cleo clean out her basement. Emma Jean had found a box of mementos, including a letter from one of Cleo's friends who had repeated the sordid story of Bob's affair and Claire's flight to Europe.

So there it was. Her father was not only an evil adulterer, he was also a killer. Emma Jean sniffled a bit, thinking of how unfortunate it was that she had inherited Bob's adultery genes. Oh dear Lord, would she be passing on the same predisposition to her baby? Maybe Peter's genes would be stronger and take precedence or whatever the biological term would be. After Emma Jean had learned that her father was a cold-blooded murderer, she had cut off all contact with him. Not that they had been terribly close beforehand. The fact that Bob had given over custody of her to Cleo so very easily had always rankled. Nevertheless, despite Emma Jean's best efforts to keep her distance, he had continued to call her and email her in the years since, more so after he had gotten religion and become a pastor at some stupid southern church. And Emma Jean had continued to ignore him.

Now she wished her mother was still alive so she could ask her questions about *her* pregnancy. Had she felt this strange mixture of elation and dread? Had she walked the planet feeling like a completely different person than she'd been four months earlier?

Peter shifted and snored as Emma Jean leaned into the curve that followed the junction to Walla Walla and headed the car east, through the miles of wheat fields. Emma Jean glanced at Peter. If he woke up right now, she decided, she would tell him about the baby immediately. She'd tell him she was pregnant, and they could discuss it all the way to Walla Walla; they'd laugh and he'd be excited and then maybe she'd feel like herself again.

But he didn't wake up. Instead she stared at the wheat fields and then, there suddenly came into view, windmills, tall and graceful, long lines of them snaking along the crest of all the ridges to the southeast—they must be gargantuan because even from far away, they looked huge. Up close, they must be unbelievable. This was one of Emma Jean's favorite parts of the trip—when the windmills came into view. The first time Peter had brought her up here, she'd gasped in delight when she caught site of the windmills. It had been the early days of their relationship, and she had been entranced with him and the whole winemaking thing.

When first she had met Peter, she had thought him perfect precisely because he fit her idea, gleaned from years of Cleo's insistence on non-conformity, of the unconventional man. Peter wasn't like all the rest of the earnest young men who wanted to date her. After all, how many men quit their jobs as successful attorneys in order to study wine? It was the most romantic thing ever, and it fit Emma Jean's idea of how her husband should be perfectly.

It was so unfortunate that Peter's image had worn thin, brittle enough to snap, even. As if he had sensed her thoughts about him, Peter stirred. Then he fell back asleep. Emma Jean thought about how much she used to love waking up beside him, listening to his plans for his day at the winery. His career—and their life together—had seemed vastly glamorous, a grand adventure, even if he himself had been a bit on the dull side. She glanced at her husband, whose head now lolled against the window. A snort escaped him, and he rolled his head so it hung forward against his chest.

When had she grown disgusted with him, rather than charmed? When had adoration turned to boredom? The road funneled through a minuscule town, and Emma Jean braked to slow down. The change in movement must have reached somewhere into the depths of Peter's psyche, and just as the car traced a path between several wineries, he woke up.

"Oh, wait, Emma Jean, I want to taste the new Cabs here. Pull in," he said, pointing to the winery situated in an old schoolhouse.

"What timing, darling."

"I have a sixth sense about things, even in my sleep," Peter said.

Except for the fact that your wife is pregnant, Emma Jean thought, as they got out of the car. And now the moment to tell him had passed yet again.

Chapter Ten
Fancy Meeting You Here

The Walla Walla reading was a bust. There was simply no other way to describe it.

Emma Jean had enjoyed visiting this particular bookstore in the past, but as a customer, she was able to ignore the tables of tacky gift ideas, and most particularly, the large displays of fantasy role-playing games in the back. As an author, that turned out to be impossible, because they set her up beside a table full of gaming accessories. Some of those accessories turned out to be human teenage boys, who were having a club meeting which mostly involved yelling loud epithets at each other.

About a dozen chairs had been arranged for her reading. Two people showed up. Since there was no microphone, Emma Jean was forced to shout her reading in order to be heard over the noise of her neighbors. When she had finished, both the people in the audience left without so much as a glance or a smile.

For the next hour, Emma Jean sat at a table with her hands folded neatly between stacks of *The Winemaker's Wife* and the plate of scrumptious home-baked peanut butter cookies, which she periodically had to shield from raids of the game-playing boys. They'd eaten half her supply during a trip to the bathroom. She smiled as people walked by and even said hello and worked on making her eyes twinkle, but nobody stopped. She repeated her mantra over and over. *I am a bestselling author.* But apparently the universe did not see fit to make her a bestselling author in Walla Walla. The one time it looked as if a customer was approaching her, the gaming boys chose for a particularly loud outburst. Her potential fan fled.

"I just don't understand it," the manager said, swallowing a last bite of cookie as they returned a stack of *Wife* to a display upfront. "I thought the signing would attract a huge crowd, what with the topic and all. Maybe it hit too close to home. Maybe none of the local wine people want to read about wine."

Maybe the wine people were just all illiterate and too focused on their damn grapes, Emma Jean thought darkly. Emma Jean thanked the young woman for her efforts and left the bookstore. But outside in the crisp autumn air, the thought of going back to a stuffy, empty hotel room was unappealing. Peter had gone to visit wineries, and Lord only knew how long that could take. Perhaps a walk was in order.

Since she was on foot, she would take a stroll and forget the disappointment of the book signing by plotting how to tell Peter about the pregnancy. Emma Jean wandered along Main Street through downtown, a pleasant stroll past wine shops and delis with patrons sitting at sidewalk tables, coffee shops and boutiques. After a few blocks, she veered to the right, past a brewpub where she and Peter had eaten several times, heading toward the campus of the small, private liberal arts college that, besides the wineries, was the other primary reason for the town's existence.

She perched on a stone bench beneath a huge, old oak. Perhaps being surrounded by the accumulation of years of knowledge would jar loose an idea as to how to tell Peter. He seemed so self-contained lately, and she hadn't figured out how to unsnap the lid that kept all his thoughts and emotions inside. Had he always been this way? Most definitely not, because she wouldn't have married somebody who acted so distant, would she? Emma Jean remembered long walks through this very campus on other visits to Walla Walla, when they had talked about everything from politics to wine to literature. Why, it was not far from this very location that Peter had given her the idea for *The Winemaker's Wife*. Fat lot of good it had done her, but still.

She watched co-eds walk by and tried to imagine being the parent of a college-age child. Someday, perhaps, she would be sitting in this very same spot waiting for Claire. She and Peter would sit beneath the tree, arms entwined, gazing at each other adoringly while they waited for their daughter. Emma Jean took a deep breath, pleased with her vision, when it was interrupted by a shout. A group of young men, loud and boisterous, walked by. One of them was blond-haired, with a devilish grin. He reminded her of someone. Oh dear God, he looked just like Riley.

Emma Jean clutched her heart. How she missed him! How she yearned for his sweet, young energy, his enthusiasm, his interest in life, and of course, her. Emma Jean sighed. Peter just didn't have a jolly personality. However, she had made her choice, and she would stick with it no matter how difficult the journey turned out to be. A noble choice it was, given how that she loved Riley so much. It was the correct spiritual choice, too. And when she thought about it, staying with Peter was also the kind choice. Still and all, she pulled her phone from her purse and looked at it with longing. Perhaps if she sent strong mental messages, Riley would call her, and then she could accidentally answer it. She cupped the phone in her hand and stared it, furrowing her eyebrows and nodding her head to encourage the brain waves.

And then the phone rang.

Emma Jean shrieked in joy, startling a cute blonde co-ed walking by. But when she looked at the caller display, she didn't recognize the number. Maybe it was Riley calling from work. Except it was too early for him to be there yet. Well maybe his phone broke, and he was so desperate to talk to her he stopped at a phone booth. Did phone booths still exist? On the other hand, it could be Angela or someone from the publishing world offering her a fabulous surprise, like a special book tour or the chance to be a featured author on a cruise to Jamaica. Emma Jean pressed talk, certain she would hear her lover, or someone nearly as exciting, on the other end of the line.

"Hello daughter."

"What?" Emma Jean couldn't quite grasp who was calling.

"It's your father, Bob."

"Oh." She'd been so certain it was someone terribly exciting calling and instead, it was just the Evil Adulterer and Fake Christian.

"You may be wondering why I'm calling."

"Then again, I may not be," Emma Jean said. "Because, you see, I really don't care."

Long silence.

"Can you speed it up, Bob? I'm a little busy at the moment."

He didn't need to know that she was lolling about on a college campus. But the less said to Bob about anything—herself, her life, the world situation, the price of tea in China—the better.

"Well, it's like this. You didn't answer my email so I got your number from Cleo. I want to see you, Emma Jean. It's been several years."

"I don't think so. I don't consort with adulterous murderers."

"There's something we need to talk about. Something that impacts you directly."

Emma Jean scowled. She had to admit to the tiniest twinge of curiosity, but she had made a sacred vow to not be interested in anything Bob said, ever. Then she had an awful thought. Did her Campaign to be Kind have to include Bob? Surely not, at least not on this phone call. That was something she'd have to build up to, being nice to Bob. "Ask me if I care. No, don't. Because I don't care. Nothing that you do influences me."

There was a bit of a silence, and then Bob cleared his throat. "I know we've had our differences, Emma Jean, but this truly is important. I'm going to be in Sun Valley until next week. Cleo said it was a short plane ride over there and that maybe you'd come."

"Cleo was wrong. She may be willing to see you, but I'm not in the mood. So how about we just agree to meet later, okay? Like in another life later."

Emma Jean pushed the red button on her phone to end the call. Then she closed her eyes, lifted her face to the sun and attempted to meditate, to ease the stress of her father's phone call. She couldn't even remember when the last time was that she had seen him. She didn't *want* to remember. Why was he suddenly trying to worm his way back into her life? And didn't it seem like he had been in Sun Valley for an inordinate amount of time? Emma Jean sighed. This had been such a stressful day, what with the failed book signing, her inability to tell Peter about the pregnancy, and her stupid father calling. Emma Jean was pretty sure stress wasn't good for the baby. She needed to relax, just like all the books said. She breathed in and out, slowly, evenly, peacefully.

* * *

That night, Emma Jean dressed for dinner carefully, donning an outfit she knew Peter would like, black skirt with a long slit up it so he could see her legs, and a low-cut, form-fitting top. She felt buoyed by the scene she'd written that afternoon on campus—seven pages in purple ink, a scene in which Natalie met the owner of an original Tiki bar and convinced him to sell her some of his wares. The words had flowed from her pen after she'd awakened herself with a loud snort and realized she was curled up on the campus bench sound asleep.

Now she felt refreshed and ready to charm Peter with her news. Emma Jean was taking the jacket that matched her outfit off the hangar—she was feeling way too tubby *not* to wear a jacket—when her cell phone rang. She was surprised to hear the voice of Julia, Peter's daughter on the phone.

"Hi, darling, do you want to talk to your father?"

"Oh no, I called to talk to you," Julia said.

"Really?"

Emma Jean sat on the edge of the bed and looked out the window, gazing at the wheat fields, which undulated just beyond the edge of town. It was October, so the wheat would have been harvested by now, right? Even though she'd been born in a small town, agriculture was a vast mystery to her, and she was embarrassed to admit her ignorance, especially around Peter, who considered winemaking a sort of gentlemen's farming.

"I *need* to talk to you," Julia said. There was an urgency in her voice that made Emma Jean feel guilty, she wasn't sure why. "Oh, thanks for the cookies, by the way."

Emma Jean was pleased that her little gesture had not gone unappreciated after all. "Glad you liked them. Now, what can I do for you, doll?"

"It's about Marielle," Julia whispered.

Oh God. So she hadn't imagined it. Something *was* wrong with Marielle. She knew it. In a strange way, this thought pleased her. Because this was the kind of thing that friends would intuit, wasn't it? And since Emma Jean had sensed Marielle's bad mood from the minute she'd answered the door, probably because she was studiously practicing being open and curious. This meant they were friends now. Didn't it?

"What is going on with Marielle, darling?" Emma Jean said.

"Well, it seems like you know so much about relationships and stuff, so I wanted to ask you..."

Julia thought she knew a lot about relationships? Wow, she was flattered. Perhaps she had watched the way Emma Jean and Peter had always meshed and admired their togetherness.

"I mean, you write about them in your books and everything..."

Oh. That was different. Just as good, probably better, but different. It required a different mindset, a different mode of advice giving.

"What can I help you with, Julia?"

"Well, I, er, I was wondering if it is normal for things to cool down. I mean, we've been seeing each other a few months. And it's been three months since I left Connor to live with Marielle. And it just seems like...I was reading this article...it seems like things should still be hot and heavy between us."

"But they're not?" Emma Jean asked.

"Well, I, um, don't know. Maybe I'm overreacting. But it seems like Marielle is always distracted these days. And she never has time for me anymore. She doesn't put me first, I guess. It's always the book, the book, the book."

Emma Jean waggled her head and imitated the words silently: *the book, the book, the book*. She hated that damned book. *Devil's Daughter*, my ass. But wait. Was it bad to hate a friend's book? Was it bad to envy a friend's success? Being a friend was nearly as complicated as being a spiritual seeker. "Honey," she said to Julia, "this is an important time for Marielle. The months around when the book comes out are crazy. And you only get one chance to take advantage of it. So I'm sure it's not about you. She's just trying to get in every bit of publicity that she can."

"You think?" Julia said.

"I know," Emma Jean said. "I've been there myself many times."

"Well, that's why I thought you'd be the one to ask for advice. I guess it makes sense. And there's that whole other thing that's going on now."

Peter came out of the bathroom, fastening the cuffs of his shirt. He pointed to the phone and mimed asking who is it? Emma Jean held up a finger to indicate she'd tell him in a minute.

"Oh darling, you young people are just so busy and have so many things going on, I can't keep track of them. Remind me what you're talking about."

"It's the thing with her book. You know, the reporter that started investigating whether it was true or not."

Emma Jean sat up straighter on the bed. A reporter was investigating whether Marielle's book was true or not?

"Honey, I've been so deeply engrossed in writing Tiki, that I'm guilty of staying out of touch. Catch me up."

"Well, it's some *Vanity Fair* reporter. And at first Marielle was really excited—"

"Rightfully so."

God, *Vanity Fair*? Emma Jean would sell the rights to her first book for a profile in *Vanity Fair*. And now Marielle got one out of the blue? It wasn't, well, *fair*. But wait. Trish had said something about a *Vanity Fair* reporter contacting her to interview Emma Jean. What had ever happened with that? She'd have to call Trish and find out. If Marielle was going to be in *Vanity Fair*, Emma Jean wanted to be, too.

"But then the reporter started asking all these questions about this detail and the documentation for that incident, and Marielle got nervous. She says it's like the reporter doesn't believe a word she says."

Of course, Emma Jean thought—tried hard not to think—but thought it anyway, if there was no problem with Marielle's truth telling, she would have no reason to be nervous. Still and all, she felt for Julia, truly she did what with Marielle so distracted with the book and the reporters at the time Julia had left the adorable Connor for her.

"Huh," Emma Jean said. "It sounds like normal reporter-type stuff to me. Reporters always act that way around their subjects."

"Oh no, I think this is different. For real, Emma Jean. This reporter said she read a story about it in a newspaper somewhere."

Emma Jean rubbed her temples. She'd cut out caffeine, since all the pregnancy books said to, and sometimes the lack of it gave her a headache. Like now, when she was trying to follow what Julia was saying.

"But that doesn't mean anything," Emma Jean said.

"This was an interview in a paper in some podunk town. Utah or somewhere. The person who was interviewed said she had it on good authority that half of the stuff that happened in the book was made-up. A flat out lie. Wait, we've got the article. The *Vanity Fair* reporter brought it with her."

Emma Jean fell back on the bed. A newspaper in some podunk town somewhere? Wendy's face, on the day Emma Jean had first met her on the airplane, swam into her mind's eye. Oh God, Emma Jean had been so drunk that day on the plane—what, exactly, had she said to that woman?

"It's from the Hailey, Idaho newspaper. A column that the local librarian writes. Her name is Wendy Harper."

How on earth had a *Vanity Fair* reporter gotten wind of an article published in the Hailey newspaper? And furthermore, why had Wendy thought she needed to write a *newspaper* column based on what Emma Jean had told her? When Emma Jean had called her, Wendy mentioned writing an article for the library newsletter, but nothing about the town newspaper. Anyway, the story was, for all intents and purposes, just hearsay, for God's sakes.

"And she goes on and on about how she'd had it on good authority that the book couldn't possibly be true."

"Why, pray tell, why is a *Vanity Fa*ir reporter paying the least bit of attention to something the librarian of a tiny town wrote about Marielle's book? That's ludicrous."

"Because this Wendy person goes through some of the incidents in Marielle's book and dissects them, and crosschecks the historical dates and all that. Oh, listen, Emma Jean, I hear Marielle's car. I better go. I don't want her to know I'm talking about her."

"Julia? I think it'll all be okay, darling. Just give Marielle the space she needs right now, and she'll appreciate you even more."

"Thanks, Emma Jean."

"Love you, darling."

"What did you say?" Julia asked.

Emma Jean had to stop and ponder. "I said..." God had she actually uttered the words? She was getting soft in her old age. It must be the pregnancy hormones. "I said...love you."

There was a long stretch of silence through the phone. Finally, Julia spoke. "Thank you, Emma Jean. I love you, too."

Peter was looking at her quizzically. "That was Julia?" he asked. He was combing his hair so that it lay flat behind his ears, and minimized the effect of his bald spot. Not quite a comb over but almost. He wore a light blue shirt tucked into taupe slacks, and they were cut so well that they fell from his waist to his cuff in one admirable line.

Suddenly Emma Jean felt a rush of love for her husband. Maybe it was a reaction to the stress of the failed book signing and Julia's phone call, but he suddenly looked very appealing. She got up from the bed and flung herself at him. The comb he held in his hand fell to the dresser as he put his arms around her.

She kissed him on the cheek, and then rested her own cheek against his crisp blue shirt. "She needed to talk girl talk."

"She never talks girl talk with you."

"She does now. Maybe because it's all girls involved." Emma Jean started laughing at her own joke until she realized that Peter didn't get it. She broke away from his embrace, patting her hands on his chest. "Don't worry, baby, she'll be fine. Are you ready for dinner?"

Emma Jean looked at her husband with resolve. She would tell him about the baby tonight. She nodded her head decisively. Yes, she would.

The restaurant was spacious, with brick walls and tables with white cloths topped with softly glowing candles. They ordered bruschetta, because Emma Jean was famished, and at the last minute, she also requested fried wontons. Soon she'd be able to get a job at Goodyear, to fill in as their blimp. But she couldn't help it; she wanted to eat everything, especially now that her brief bout with morning sickness seemed to be subsiding. She sipped water, even though Peter had poured her a glass of Chardonnay.

Peter smiled at her from across the table. "This is nice."

Emma Jean nodded in agreement.

"I'm so glad it worked out. It's so much more fun to come up here with you."

"Mmmmm," Emma Jean said. Should she tell him now or wait until he'd finished his first glass of wine?

"Life is so much better with you than alone, darling," he was saying. "It's just too bad the book signing was scheduled at the same time as my appointment to look at the equipment. You would have loved the winery."

"Hmmmm," Emma Jean murmured. Wait, what was he talking about? This was supposed to be a romantic getaway for the two of them, not a looking-at-equipment trip.

"Remind me where you went today?"

"Out to Jim's place. He's got one of those wineries in the industrial park by the airport. And let me tell you, he's got a good buy on that variable frequency destemmer-crusher."

Emma Jean's hand snaked across the table toward the wine, and at the last minute, she forced it to veer toward the water. She slugged a huge gulp of it down. Peter would have come up here whether or not she had agreed to come along. He wasn't interested in romance; he was interested in winery equipment. And here she had suffered through a miserable afternoon with the role-playing teenagers just for his sake.

"Is that what you've been doing all afternoon, looking at crap for your winery? I thought there was some special tasting you'd been invited to."

"That came afterward. Emma Jean, listen, I got a great deal on it and the guy who's selling it said he'd move it down to Portland for me for free. There was only one catch."

Emma Jean groaned. She hated catches.

"Just this once, I had to put it on the card. I tried to call you, but you didn't pick up."

"Of course I didn't pick up, I was at a book signing!" Never mind that there was nobody to sign books for and she'd purposely ignored his call because she'd felt too upset to talk.

"I know, and I want to hear all about it. There were other people coming to see the equipment, sweetie; I had to jump fast."

Emma Jean sighed. Perhaps a few thousand was a small price to pay. It would make him happy and then he'd be in a good mood when she told him about the baby. She sipped water and smiled sweetly at him.

"Okay, darling, it's no big deal." Now she would steer the conversation to safer topics, and then after a brief lull, she would tell him her news.

"There's something I wanted to ask you about, Emma Jean."

Emma Jean felt her stomach knot and her head began to pound. Did he suspect about Riley? She took a bite of bruschetta. "Oh, this is just so delicious, have some more, darling. What are you going to order for dinner?"

"The trout. This is important, Emma Jean. I want to talk to you about refinancing the house."

"Wait, what? Refinancing? Are you crazy? Why would we do a thing like that?"

"It's just…it's just that I've had a minor setback. One of the investors backed out. And with the economy so uncertain…it's just harder." Peter raised his hands in front of him earnestly. "Nothing for you to worry about; I don't want you to think twice about it. But I'm so close to being completely set up, it would be a shame to stop now. So I thought if we refinanced, I could pull some money out for the winery and maybe you could use a little to do some things, too. We could fix up the basement the way you've always wanted to."

Fixing up the basement was the farthest thing from her mind, as was refinancing the house. Plus, Peter had lied to her. He had billed this weekend as a romantic escape, and the whole time, all he'd wanted to do was buy equipment.

"That way we will both be happy," Peter said. He smiled at her as he drank his wine.

"I am not going to be happy with you playing Russian roulette with our financial security and spending my money right and left, ever," Emma Jean said. To say nothing of endangering Claire's abundance, which was her birthright, according to all the books.

"I thought it was our money," Peter said.

"It is our money. It's just that we need to discuss how we spend it together." Suddenly Emma Jean had an awful thought. She was just as bad as Peter, withholding information of vital importance, like the little nugget that she happened to be pregnant. Although it was a personal matter, her body was her own. Wasn't it? Nonetheless, she had to tell him. She had to tell him now.

"Darling, I have news, too, and—"

"Well, look who's here. It's the guy we were just talking about. Peter Sullivan. How the hell are you?"

"Hey." Peter looked up at the two men who had stopped at their table and stood to shake their hands. Well dressed in khakis and crisp shirts, the men looked like brothers. Emma Jean glanced from one to the other, trying to ascertain if they were related.

"This is my wife, Emma Jean Sullivan," Peter was saying. She rose halfway from her chair to shake hands and sat again. "And this is John and Randy Chapman, Emma Jean; they run the Rainshadow Winery south of town. Good to see you guys."

"Hey there, little lady, it's nice to meet you." John Chapman—at least she thought it was John—smiled at Emma Jean. "We've been trying to get your husband to move back up here and work for us, especially after Canyon Creek treated him like crap."

"Yesiree," Randy said, "we were taking bets on who would get fired after that debacle with the Pinot, but Jesus, we never dreamed it would be Peter."

Fired? He'd gotten fired? Emma Jean ratcheted her head to glare at Peter, who was studiously ignoring her, smiling at John. The way Emma Jean had heard the story, Peter had left Canyon Creek voluntarily, because he had investors lined up for his own winery. But now a different picture began to emerge, and she could just follow its blurry outlines: He'd decided to start Sullivan Wines and lined up investors *because* he was going to lose his job, not vice versa.

Peter continued to ignore her, and worse, he even chuckled. "I prefer to think of it as creative differences."

John and Randy both laughed as if that was the funniest thing anyone had ever said.

"We've always got room for a winemaker of his talents in this region, especially one who comes with such a pretty little lady attached," John said.

"I'm ready anytime," Peter said. "All I've got to do is convince Emma Jean."

"You two should move on up here," Randy said. He turned toward Emma Jean and now she noticed that he had particularly long eyelashes for a man, which didn't seem fair at all. "After all, you can write your little books anywhere."

Should she kill Randy, John, or Peter first? Emma Jean smiled up at the two brothers. "True. But I get to choose where I want to write those little books, because coincidentally those little books are what are paying for this dinner. And everything else in our lives."

Randy didn't miss a beat. "She's a feisty one. I can see why you like her, Peter, yesiree I can."

"Oh Christ," Emma Jean muttered under her breath.

"Hey, are you guys here for dinner?" Peter said. "Why don't you join us?"

Emma Jean kicked him under the table. Peter looked at her quizzically.

"Oh, Peter, darling, do you think that's a good idea? I was really looking forward to our romantic dinner together."

"We don't want to interrupt your romance," Randy said, winking at Peter.

"Don't worry about that," Peter said. "Our entire relationship is one long romantic adventure. We'd love to have you sit with us."

Was it Peter describing their relationship as a long romantic adventure, when in reality it was a dull, boring slog? Or was it the smug look on both John and Randy's faces? Emma Jean wasn't sure what riled her so strongly that she knocked a glass of water over. Water pooled in the plate of bruschetta, spread across the white tablecloth, and dripped onto the floor, pieces of her marriage relentlessly ebbing away with it. A waiter rushed over to deal with the mess, and as they jumped up to avoid the spill, Emma Jean whispered to Peter.

"I have something important to tell you tonight," she hissed.

"Just tell me now, honey, then we can go sit with Randy and John."

"But it's an exciting surprise," Emma Jean cried. Her voice came out high-pitched and shrill. Standing across the table from them, John and Randy smiled.

"Go ahead and set it up for four people," John said to the waiter. "Is that okay, guys?"

"What do you say, Emma Jean?" Peter said. He held his wine glass in one hand and a white cloth napkin in the other.

Most likely it was Peter's wholesale unwillingness to do what she wanted, and his utter refusal to listen to her that made her blurt. And blurt she did. She needed Peter to know, and she needed him to know, now.

"I can't keep it a secret any longer, Peter. I have to tell you." Emma Jean took a deep breath. "Guess what, darling, I'm pregnant."

Peter was taking a drink of wine at the precise moment that Emma Jean made her announcement. He spit some of it out, dribbles of red spewing onto the newly cleaned table, and slammed his wine glass down hard.

"Yesiree, that's some exciting news," Randy said. "Even more reason to celebrate."

But Peter's face looked anything but celebratory. Probably it was because of the way she had chosen to announce it. But she had felt like a rubber band being stretched taut, so taut that she felt she would snap if she didn't let the secret out. Peter's expression now looked like that of an angry god about to hurl lightning bolts at her.

Emma Jean winced. "I guess I should have waited to tell you. But I was so excited to tell you and...darling, what is it?"

"Are you sure, Emma Jean?"

She nodded.

"You're sure it's not that other thing. You know, the change or whatever it's called?"

Emma Jean shook her head. "I'm certain, darling. I took the pregnancy test five times to be sure. Isn't it the most wonderful news ever?"

Across the table, Randy raised his glass. "A toast! A toast to Emma Jean's pregnancy." He looked at Peter and winked. "How about that Viagra, huh? Something must be working right for you two."

John raised his glass then, too. And dimly, Emma Jean was aware that other diners had begun to raise their glasses, too. She pulled her attention from Peter's face and looked around the room. At every table, people smiled towards her. Most of them had their glasses raised and several were on their feet. Cheering ensued.

She looked back at Peter. "I know you think I'm too old for this, but I'm not. I'm not, darling! And I'm so excited. And also, my whole baby-hating platform? I'll figure something out. I'll talk to Angela, and we'll find a way to deal with it."

But no matter what she said, the expression on Peter's face did not change. She heard the clink of glasses around her.

"I'm sorry. I'm sorry, Peter. I know better than to spring things on you. But isn't it just amazing? Oh my God, Peter, I'm so excited. After all these years, I'm pregnant. We're going to have a baby."

"To babies!" someone shouted.

"To new life and new beginnings!"

"Hip, hip, hooray!"

Emma Jean shot a cautious smile and nodded at the crowd. She saw John and Randy with glasses held high. And now everyone in the restaurant seemed to be standing, with glasses raised. Even the waiters had set down their trays and stood, watching and clapping. It was the exact type of scene she would normally appreciate so very much, were it not for the increasingly surly look on Peter's face.

Peter ignored them all, staring at Emma Jean. Finally, he grabbed her arm. "We've got to talk."

"That's what I've been saying all evening," she reminded him.

Peter pulled her back to a spot next to the wait station, out of earshot of John and Randy. His hand where it clutched her elbow hurt. She tried to shake it off but he held on. His face was murderous in a way she'd never before seen.

All the spiritual books said to meet anger with calm, so Emma Jean tried the cheerful approach one more time. "Isn't it the best news ever?"

"Actually, it's not," Peter said. His eyes had darkened to two smoldering black dots. Emma Jean took a step back, but Peter followed. Her shoulders pressed against the wall beside an emergency exit door.

The tornadic expression on his face and his burning black eyes made her nervous, very nervous. And why was he saying the baby wasn't good news? She didn't know what to do but press forward. "But, darling, it's what we've always wanted. We're going to have a baby together!"

Peter shook his head. "You're going to have a baby, Emma Jean, not we. I had a vasectomy years ago."

Then he threw his napkin down and strode from the restaurant, leaving Emma Jean to stare, open-mouthed, as diners looked quizzically after Peter and the door banged shut behind him.

Chapter Eleven
She Loves L.A.

Emma Jean leaned her head against the window of the airplane and gazed at the mountains as the plane made its descent to the Burbank airport. She closed her eyes for a moment to give thanks that her hellish journey was nearly over. Pretty much all of the spirituality books talked about how important gratitude was. Well, she was definitely grateful to be away from her monstrous beast of a husband. What an atrocious brute he had turned out to be. Emma Jean pressed the back of her hand to her forehead, thinking about the horror of it all.

The trip had cost a fortune, and even though she was totally broke, thanks mostly to her lousy lout of a husband, she had willingly paid it. She would have done anything to get herself to L.A., now that she knew Riley was the father of her child. Oh, could you even believe it! That adorable, wonderful man had spilled his seed inside her, and together, they had created a wondrous new life. Emma Jean smiled to herself, thinking how cute the baby would be. And how utterly adorable Riley would be as a father. Wait, he already was a father. But she never got to see him being fatherly, so his relationship with Noah had never seemed fully real to her and thus it didn't count.

The plane met the runway and Emma Jean pushed her hand against the seat in front of her as the pilot hit the brakes. She was so very close to seeing Riley, she felt consumed with excitement. Let's face it, she'd been pretending about Peter since she had met Riley anyway. Emma Jean had tried her best, her very best, to mend the fissures in her marriage, but she'd had so little to work with, seeing as how Peter was a lying, betraying bastard, no better than her father. She'd only stayed with him because it had seemed so difficult to unravel their lives together—the *Childlessness by Choice* co-chairmanship for one thing (though let's face it, Emma Jean had done all the work), and their romantic image her fans so loved for another. So wasn't she the luckiest woman in the world now that she was free to join her one true love, Riley?

And even though he had sounded the wee-est bit hesitant on the phone, she was certain that he'd be his usual passionate self once they were together again. Their phone conversation had been unsatisfactorily brief, due to the fact that Carolina was home and Riley had to hide in the bathroom to take her call.

"I'm coming to L.A. tomorrow, Riley, because I have something very important to discuss with you," she'd said.

"O-kay," Riley said, drawing out the "K" as if he were thinking deep thoughts about it. "I guess that will work. Actually, I need to talk to you, too."

After she had hung up she had tried her best to put a positive spin on the ominous sound in his voice until she decided it was just Riley worried about his fading marriage to Carolina, and also how he would find large amounts of time to spend with Emma Jean. Her mood improved as she called the Aku Aku to reserve a room (the very same one!), rented a car, and took a cab to the airport. The closer she got to Riley, the better she felt. She took this as a sign that she had imagined his hesitancy. Her latest spirituality book, one she'd bought at the Walla Walla bookstore during a lull in the signing, assured her that it was of utmost importance to heed signs, symbols, and omens.

Emma Jean looked for some sort of positive omen as she gathered her belongings to exit the plane. A phone call from Riley welcoming her to L.A. would be a fabulous sign, but despite the fact that she checked and rechecked her cell to make sure it was on, it didn't ring. Outside, she took her sweater off while she waited for her luggage. The baggage claim area was outside, and it was hot. Didn't they know it was October, and things were supposed to be cooling down? But she had to admit the warm air on her skin felt good. It had been grey and rainy and abnormally cold when she left Walla Walla, or maybe the chill had come from the sudden and complete disintegration of her marriage.

She didn't want to think about it, but her mind didn't seem to want to obey her. Emma Jean kept remembering how Randy and John had scattered like cockroaches and how she had picked up her purse and with as much dignity as she could muster, and left the restaurant in search of Peter. Back at the hotel, she'd found him in the ornate lobby bar, which was all burgundy velvet and gold brocade, and mostly empty of people. He sat on a high stool at a massive polished wood bar, a glass of red wine and a shot of bourbon in front of him. She watched him as she walked toward him. His shoulders were slumped and his head hung low on his neck, like a bruised apple ready to be picked.

"Peter."

At first he didn't look at her.

"Peter," she said again.

And then he turned, and the expression on his face was grotesquely twisted, a combination of anger and pain. Emma Jean clutched at her stomach with remorse. But then she remembered—he had betrayed her long before she had even thought of doing it to him. Suddenly all she desired was to be done with him.

"I just wanted to let you know I'm leaving. I'm catching a flight to Seattle in the morning and from there to L.A."

"So you can see your lover?" he sneered, then took a large gulp, finished his shot of whiskey and signaled to the bartender for another. Then he sipped his wine, ignoring her.

Emma Jean's stomach roiled at the combination of alcohol. "The bellman is moving my things to another room." She paused for a moment. What did one say when one's marriage was ending, suddenly, precipitously, and irrevocably? "I'll let you know when I get back from L.A. so you can be out of the house."

Peter turned on his bar stool. "What if I don't want to move out of the house?"

"Oh you'll move out alright," Emma Jean said. "After the stunt you pulled, there's no way you'll ever live in that house again. I can't believe you had a vasectomy and never bothered to tell me."

"Because I knew you'd freak out," he said.

"Ya think?"

"You've been fucking some other man," Peter said.

Emma Jean winced at how very graphic the f-word sounded coming from his mouth. "When did you have it?"

Peter sipped his wine. Emma Jean could see his reflection in the mirror behind the bar, and if she had to pick a way to describe him, beside horrific bastardly betrayer, it would be confused.

"Look at me. When did you have the vasectomy?"

He sighed, but still didn't face her. "Shortly after we were married."

"Oh, for God's sakes. And you never bothered to tell me that little detail when I was wondering why in the hell I couldn't get pregnant?"

"It was just...easier without children," Peter said.

"So that time we went to Napa and toured all the wineries and tried all weekend to get pregnant, you'd had a vasectomy."

Peter didn't answer. The bartender brought him his shot glass, and he downed it.

"Oh God, I can't believe you," Emma Jean said. "And that time we were at the beach? And we had sex, and afterwards I had my ass propped up on all those pillows and you were bringing me chocolate and tea so I wouldn't have to move? You told me that the sperm would have a better chance of reaching the egg that way. Jesus, Peter. You mean you'd had the vasectomy then?"

He hadn't moved an inch, not one inch and Emma Jean knew his silence was more damning than anything he could say.

"And you let me think the whole damn thing was my fault. You let me believe there was something wrong with me," Emma Jean said. Her feet hurt and she desperately wanted to sit down but the only place available was the bar stool and that would be uncomfortably close to Peter.

"Then you decided you hated children," Peter said, turning towards her. "So what's the big deal? This way, we never had to worry about it. Until you decided to go fuck some other man."

She really wished he would stop saying that vulgar word. She signaled the bartender and asked for a glass of water.

"Why? Why did you do it, Emma Jean?"

"I think the proper question here is why did *you* do it?" she said.

"Here you go, ma'am," the bartender said, placing a glass of water on the bar. Emma Jean smiled her thanks and downed half the glass.

"Why did I do it?" Peter continued. "I had my reasons. But nothing gives you the right to commit adultery." Peter's angry Zeus look had been replaced by a pleading expression now, and the thick lock of hair that was always out of place fell down across his forehead as he stared down at her.

"People have affairs all the time, Peter. What they do not do is have vasectomies without telling their wives." She drank the rest of the water, leaning over the bar to reach it, and then slammed the glass down. It was too damn bad she couldn't have a drink. A *drink* drink with alcohol in it.

"You're not the only one who gets to be angry, Emma Jean. How do you think I feel?" Peter said.

"I'll tell you what I think." Emma Jean stepped close to him. "I think you are the biggest bastard on the face of the planet. I started an affair three months ago. Only three flippin' months ago, Peter! You've been lying to me for twelve years. I've been living with a lie for the entire time I've been married."

"It's too goddamned bad that Cleo had to spoil you rotten," Peter said.

"Oh, now it's Cleo's fault that you had to have a vasectomy and lie about it for the entire length of our marriage?"

"You are still Cleo's spoiled and selfish princess, Emma Jean. You still do whatever the hell you want, whenever you want. Even if it means fucking someone you aren't married to."

At the end of the bar, the bartender was watching them as he wiped glasses, no doubt due to their raised voices. Emma Jean made an effort to lower hers.

"That's not true," she said. "And by the way, when did you get to be the arbiter of all things moral?"

"Honey, I—"

"Don't call me honey," Emma Jean snarled.

Peter leaned closer to her, so close she could see the smooth skin on his baby-face cheeks, marred only by a couple broken blood vessels, a recent addition, Emma Jean realized. He'd been drinking too much, and at this rate, his baby face would be wizening quickly. She took a half step back, running into one of the barstools. He placed his hand on her elbow. She shook it off.

"You should consider the consequences of your actions. You never consider anybody but yourself, just like Cleo's little princess," Peter said.

"Stop with the goddamn psychobabble!" Emma Jean said. "I'm not a princess, I'm a grown woman and I write best-selling novels and let me just remind you that the afore-mentioned books are what keep this boat afloat. So don't give me this crap about how spoiled and selfish I am. You want selfish? I'll show you selfish. How about I cut you off and let you finance that damn winery on your own? You and your precious investors who I'm beginning to suspect never existed in the first place."

"Oh, Emma Jean." Peter raised his hands in front of him in a conciliatory motion. "That's not the point."

"Then how about we just do that, then? If it's not the point, then let's just do it. No more money for your business. Ever. And you can explain to me what the point is while you're sitting on the floor of your empty winery."

"The point is that your selfishness led you to seek out unattached sex."

"What make you think its un—" Emma Jean stopped herself. "It's a little late for your concern now." She pressed her cold water glass to her forehead to ease her tension. "Wait, you know what? You just successfully turned this whole conversation around. Now it's all about me, it's all my fault. Like your actions had nothing to do with it."

Peter shrugged. "I thought we were happy together. I was happy. You're the one who rocked the boat."

Emma Jean shook her head sadly. "You rocked the boat years ago, Peter, when you got that vasectomy. And that started a ripple that turned into a tidal wave."

"Spare me the tortured metaphors."

Peter drank the rest of the wine in his glass in one fell swoop, wiped his mouth on the back of his hand and looked once again at Emma Jean. "You want to know the real reason I had that vasectomy?"

"I'm all ears."

He signaled the waiter for another glass of wine. No wonder he had broken blood vessels all over his face. The man was a veritable drinking machine.

"I got the vasectomy because I couldn't handle having another child."

"Duh," Emma Jean said.

"Seeing as how I already had two."

Emma Jean stared at him. Was he choosing this moment to confess to her that there was another mini-Peter running loose in the world? "You only have one child."

He shook his head. He set his wine glass down, held up two fingers and then pointed at her. "You. You were the other child. I had my hands full dealing with you."

Emma Jean slapped him. Then she turned on her heel and walked from the bar.

The clunk of bags hitting metal brought her back to the present, to the baggage area of the Burbank airport, and thank God, because who wanted to dwell on a horrible scene like the one with Peter?

Emma Jean saw her bag come down the chute—it was black, like every other suitcase on the planet, but Aunt Cleo had given her orange and red tassels to tie around the handle—and moved to pull it off the roundabout. But just as she stepped toward the carousel, she felt something. Whatever it was made her stumble. It felt like the earth had moved, and she'd heard a noise, like a train roaring far, far away. She looked around. Nobody else seemed to have felt a thing. The other passengers stood, talking on cell phones, talking to each other, watching for their luggage.

Emma Jean pulled her suitcase off the carousel, struggling a bit. It was heavy, as she was incapable of packing light and had long ago given up trying. Was it possible that she'd just felt a minor earthquake? The one thing that she was truly terrified of—even more than L.A. traffic—was earthquakes. Emma Jean expected the earth to remain solid and steady beneath her feet. The few times she'd experienced earthquakes in Portland, and they'd been minor ones, it had jarred her sense of security for weeks on end.

But, never mind, because here she was in L.A., ready to see Riley, the most adorable human alive, and the father of her child. And she figured she could also use the time to work on *Tiki*, despite the recent traumas in her life. It did seem unfair that she was still expected to produce words of her usual sterling quality when she had so much trouble to contend with. However, she would persevere. Emma Jean squared her shoulders. She was a professional. She would set aside her personal tragedy and put the drama on the page. She'd hoped that Angela or her publicist could set up a reading or a workshop or something while she was in L.A., but that hadn't happened, mainly because neither of them deigned to return her calls. Anyway, she needed to write. She had a December 31 deadline looming and her erstwhile book did not in any way resemble a novel. A niggle of fear corseted her heart. What if she couldn't finish the novel?

As Emma Jean pulled her suitcase inside the terminal to the rental car area, she scanned her mind for ideas. Well, she knew how to do needlepoint. Maybe she could teach herself how to paint canvases. But as far as Emma could tell, needlepoint was not a particularly popular hobby at the moment, not like knitting, which everyone and their aunt, including Trish, seemed to be doing. Besides, painting was one of those things that always appealed to her, an activity she could totally envision herself doing until she actually did it—at which time she couldn't wait to be finished. So scratch that career idea.

Maybe she could write erotica, she thought as she took her place in the line at the rental car desk. She could read her finished pieces out loud to Riley and he could tell her if they aroused him or not. At the thought of Riley, she stationed her suitcase so it wouldn't fall over and pulled her cell from her purse. He'd told her not to call him, because it was too risky that Carolina might be around, that he would call her. But he hadn't called. She opened the flip on the phone one more time just to make sure, then stuck it in the pocket of her jeans where she would feel it vibrate before it actually rang. Sometimes it got buried in her purse, and she didn't hear it.

But the phone didn't ring the entire time she was in line for the car—could somebody please explain to her why, in this day and age, it took so long to rent a car? Renting a car and getting a new cell phone could be used as methods of torture. She entertained herself by watching the people around her. One woman in particular, with brunette hair teased into a full style dangerously reminiscent of the eighties, seemed to be watching Emma Jean, too. The woman wore a deep turquoise blue blazer over a white tee shirt and jeans, a good look for airplane travel, Emma Jean decided. Yes, the woman was definitely staring at her. Emma Jean stood a bit straighter, sucked in her stomach, and gazed into the distance as if thinking profound thoughts about her next novel.

"Ma'am? It's your turn." The man behind her nudged her, and Emma Jean was so startled she forgot to thank him in her gracious manner before walking up to the counter. She handed the clerk her credit card and stood there through the interminable paperwork. The clerk ran her card and then got a funny look on her face. Emma Jean knew that look. It was the look people got when they recognized the name, when it finally clicked that the reason her name was so familiar was because it graced the cover of the novel they'd just read. Emma Jean arranged her benign novelist smile on her face.

"I'm sorry, Ms. Sullivan, but this card isn't going through," the clerk said.

"What?" Emma Jean squawked.

The clerk, a sweet-faced young blonde, placed the gold card on the counter. "It's been declined. I'll need another form of payment."

Emma Jean stood at the counter with her mouth open, despite how witless it no doubt made her look. Jesus God. Last time she'd checked the balance on that card, there'd been thousands of available credit. She fished another card from her wallet and handed it over. "Use this one. I don't know why the other one's not working, but this one should."

Could she be more humiliated? She looked around to see if the people in line behind her had noticed the snafu. Didn't appear so, they were all lost in their own worlds of boredom and impatience, talking on cell phones, or perusing newspapers. Except for the woman in the blue blazer, who stood nearby, watching Emma Jean, head cocked to one side, as if straining to listen to... something. Was she trying to hear Emma Jean's conversation with the clerk?

Well, to hell with her. Emma Jean turned back to watch the clerk run the second card. That was a relatively new one, a card that accrued airline miles and so far only she had a card from that account, not Peter. But Peter shared cards with her on all the other accounts. They'd always combined finances. Peter. The flippin' winery. The variable frequency drive destemmer-crusher he'd been looking at. The no-good bastard. That would be why the card didn't work, because he'd run it up to its credit limit. He was probably still in Walla Walla, gaily charging equipment on her card.

She reached for her phone to call him and yell at him, even though he was the last person on earth she wanted to talk to. Still, she needed to put him in his place and make sure he didn't spend every penny of hers before she could start divorce proceedings. But just then the cute, little clerk handed her papers to sign, and thank you God, the keys to the rental.

"Thanks, doll, and sorry for that little snafu," Emma Jean said. She turned to head for the parking lot to find her car, cell phone in hand, dialing Peter as she walked, only to find her path blocked by the woman in blue.

"Emma Jean Sullivan?" The brunette thrust her hand at Emma Jean and didn't give her a chance to answer. "I'm Sally Marx, from *Vanity Fair*."

Well wasn't this a lovely surprise? Emma Jean pressed the red button to end her call to Peter.

"It's so nice to meet you," Emma Jean said, taking the reporter's hand, and grasping it firmly, despite the fact it felt oily and sweaty. So *that's* why Sally had been staring at her, she'd been taking in details of Emma Jean's look for the article, no doubt. Oh God, did she look fat? And did her outfit look acceptable? She hadn't dressed with a reporter in mind that morning; she'd dressed with comfort on the airplane in mind. *And* she'd dressed with Riley in mind—she wore a loose white top, one that had a plunging neckline with lots of cleavage and also, conveniently, covered the fact that the top button on her jeans no longer buttoned and was held together with a safety pin. But with luck, the gauzy top would add to the ethereal look she strived for on her book covers.

And, double oh God, had Sally heard the transaction with the rental car clerk? It would most decidedly *not* look good to have a scene where her credit card was declined in a *Vanity Fair* article.

"Isn't it a wonderful coincidence to run into each other at the airport?" Sally said, "Your agent told me you'd be in L.A. and I've been planning to call you, but here you are instead. Fabulous!"

Sally's patter was just vague enough that Emma Jean couldn't quite grasp her intentions. Had she come to L.A. just to find Emma Jean? Was she planning to call her just because she wanted to be friends? And why hadn't Angela mentioned Sally?

"Fabulous!" Emma Jean agreed. "Are you the same VF reporter who was requesting an interview with me a month or so ago?"

"Oh, I am, I am, and your wonderful assistant got back with me so promptly, that was fabulous, too, but this story is unbelievable, it's taken on a life of its own, practically, and it's taken me longer than anticipated to get back to you." Sally finished this spiel breathlessly, paused, cocked her head—what was it with this gesture of hers—and smiled at Emma Jean.

Was Emma Jean missing something? As far as she knew, no story about her had taken on a life of its own, unless, oh God, it couldn't be true, somehow news of her pregnancy had gotten out. Quell disaster that would be, what with *Wife* tanking and Emma Jean struggling valiantly to maintain her child-less image on her blog.

"Refresh my memory. What's the angle of your story?"

"Oh, it's about Marielle Delany and how not a word of *Devil's Daughter* is true. Not one word, as far as I can tell. But I'm so eager to get your take on it, seeing as how she wrote the book in your class and all."

Emma Jean imagined snakes slithering out of the woman's mouth, nasty, poisonous, venomous ones. "The *Vanity Fair* story is about Marielle?"

Sally Marx nodded. "So when can we get together? I'm here for a couple weeks, looking into contemporary Southern California satanic cults, how about you?"

"You want to interview me about Marielle?"

Sally nodded.

Emma Jean stared at the reporter for a long time. From afar she'd looked youngish, but up close Emma Jean could see where Sally had artfully made herself up for that illusion. In truth, Sally Marx was probably close to Emma Jean's age. Finally, Emma Jean surprised herself. Whereas once she would—had, for that matter—sell her soul and Marielle's, too, for a shot at a story in *Vanity Fair*, she was now a more fully evolved being. A *kind* being, who was, she reminded herself, now friends with the story subject in question. As such, she simply couldn't sell Marielle out again.

Emma Jean shook her head. "No can do, Sally, sorry."

And then Emma Jean turned on her heel and walked away, her bag with the orange and red tassels on the handle trailing behind her, determined to shed the bad karma of the Burbank airport and turn her attention to the glorious future.

Chapter Twelve

Did the Earth Move For You, Too?

Was the way this trip started a bad omen? Once Emma Jean got into the rental car, she worried, then tried furiously not to think about it. The Law of Attraction stated that what you thought about, you got more of, according to the book she was reading, so if you thought about bad things, then you got more of the same. Ditto with positive things. Thus she tried her best to take her mind off her miserable husband and the gall of that *Vanity Fair* reporter, which both fell into the category of bad things, and she certainly didn't want more of that. Even so, she was desperate to call Peter and tell him exactly what she thought of him maxing out the credit card, but first she had to negotiate her way out of the airport parking lot and try to figure out how to get to the freeway.

Peter saved her the trouble of phoning him, because he called as she pulled out onto the broad street that fronted the airport. Emma Jean took this as a sign that the Law of Attraction worked. But, she was even angrier with Peter when she answered because she'd wanted the call to be from Riley.

"You bastard!" she screamed into the phone.

"I was hoping you'd have cooled off enough by now to talk like a sane person," he said.

"Where are you?" Emma Jean demanded. "In Walla Walla, spending my money? Because my credit card wouldn't work when I tried to use it just now. I can't handle this, Peter, I just can't. I need to be able to concentrate in order to write and your behavior is just stressing me out totally."

"I'm not the one who fu—"

"Don't say that vulgar word."

"Fucked another man," Peter said. "Perhaps you could have thought about the possibility of getting pregnant before you had unprotected sex with someone."

"I was under the impression I had nothing to worry about, seeing as how I was never able to get pregnant all those times you and I tried."

"It is not my fault that you had an affair," Peter said. "You made your bed, go lie in it. So to speak."

"Can't you even come up with something original to say?"

"I was taught by a master of the cliché."

That was just not fair. She strived diligently and strenuously to come up with original ways to say things, and he knew it. He used to help her with it. One night early in their relationship, they had sat up late, drinking wine, and made a list of common clichés, along with ways to freshen them. She had used that list as a reference point ever since, and even *The New York Times* had noted how unusually unique her clichés were, commenting on the way she'd used *as solid as a bowling ball* instead of *as solid as a rock*. Emma Jean shook her head. Where had the lovely man who had helped her with clichés gone? Of course, even back then, he was a lying, betraying bastard; she just hadn't known it. Speaking of lying, she had another thought.

"You lied to me about your job, too, Peter. You told me you quit and in reality you were fired."

"If that asshole who owns Canyon Creek knew what he was doing, there wouldn't have been a problem."

Emma Jean sighed. "I'm hanging up now, Peter. Don't spend any more of my money. Wait, where are you?"

"On my way home from Walla Walla."

"And where are you planning to stay in Portland?"

"At our home, Emma Jean. I own half the place, my name is on the deed, and unless you file a restraining order against me—which no judge in his right mind would allow—you cannot deny me my legal right to stay there."

It was her house, even if his name was on the title, because she had earned the money to buy it, found it, and decorated every damn inch of it. She loved that house with every fiber of her being. Emma Jean wished she knew more about the law, so she could come up with some meaningful retort, but Peter had her trumped there. It wasn't fair, seeing as how he used to be an attorney.

"But it's my income that covers the mortgage payments." It was the best she could do.

"Emma Jean—"

"Oops, there's another call coming in, I've got to go. You'll be hearing from my lawyer soon."

She pushed the end button on her husband. She'd made up the part about another call coming in, even though she wished it were true. Since the Law of Attraction worked when she thought about Peter, she needed to think positive thoughts about Riley calling. God, could you even believe how deceitful Peter was? Now he was going to be ensconced in the house and truthfully, she was quite sure that he was right—she had no legal means to evict him. What was the old saying? Possession was nine-tenths of the law. Emma Jean sighed and laid her cell on the center console of the SUV, where she'd be sure to hear its vibration and could grab it in plenty of time, even if she was distracted by L.A. freeway traffic, which she was. By God, these people drove fast and they wove in and out of the lanes of traffic as if there were no other cars on the road but themselves.

"Shit," she said, as a gold Mercedes nearly clipped the front left bumper of her Explorer. At least she had a big, honking SUV, which made her feel somewhat protected. She was maneuvering to the right hand lane—wasn't it the Ventura Boulevard exit she was supposed to take?—when the phone actually did start vibrating and then she swerved as she reached to pick it up. A blue Acura honked, and she almost dropped the phone, but thank God she executed a complicated save on both the call and the vehicle while managing to take the exit and answer the phone at the same time.

"Are you here?"

Oh God, it was Riley, and he had never sounded sexier.

"Oh darling, it's so good to hear your voice. I am here. Almost to the motel. Where are you? Are you coming to see me?"

"I'll meet you there."

"How soon?"

"Let's say 2 to 2:30, somewhere in that range. I'll call you when I'm close."

Emma Jean now remembered that nobody in L.A. ever gave you a precise arrival time, but rather a range of possibilities. Precision was impossible in a town where you could run into a traffic jam at 3 o'clock in the morning.

"I can't wait to see you," Emma Jean said.

"Are you ready to be really bad?" Riley said.

Oh God, how she loved him! "I am! I am so ready, darling!"

"I'll see you soon," Riley said, and his voice was low and husky.

Emma Jean was about to hang up but then Riley spoke again. "And Emma Jean? We need to talk, too."

"I love talking to you, Riley."

After they hung up, she realized that the way he said *talk* sounded vaguely ominous. But, never mind, because she was almost to the motel. She drove down Ventura Boulevard with its shiny new strip mall featuring Starbucks, Rite Aid, Vons, some ghastly theme restaurant, and acres of cars. On one side of the street sat Jerry's Famous Deli, where she and Riley had eaten several times, despite the fact Emma Jean was deeply suspicious of anyplace that had the word famous in its name when she'd never heard of it. On the other side of Ventura, it was a different century. There were dilapidated old storefronts: a carpet store that had been going out of business last time she was here and still was, a bridal gown store, a liquor outlet, news stand, small restaurants and motels, including the Aku Aku.

As she pulled beneath the Polynesian style A-frame of the Aku Aku motel into the parking lot, talked to the guy in the motel office about the warm weather and the possibility of Santa Ana winds, got the key for room 239, and pulled her suitcase up the long flight of steps to the second floor, her excitement grew, a tingling inside her at the thought of seeing Riley. Emma Jean forgot about Peter spending her money faster than she could earn it and the insipid *Vanity Fair* reporter. Instead she thought about seeing Riley, about flinging herself into his arms for the first time, about feeling him kiss her, about feeling his touch. She couldn't believe she would be in his arms again in just a matter of minutes. She couldn't wait to see him.

But when he wasn't there by 2:30, she got tired of perching delicately on the side of the bed and started unpacking. She set up her computer on the little table by the sliding glass door, pulled out her stack of books and placed them neatly beside her laptop, found Aku Aku, the Buddha, happy to be back to the place of his namesake, and set him up, too. She pulled out her crystals—the angels recommended you work with them, and Emma Jean was quite excited about this new practice. So far, she had citrine for creativity and pregnancy and she thought she might look for a crystal store in L.A., so she could buy a rose quartz crystal for love.

And then she waited. And waited some more. Her insides sparkled and bubbled, thinking how it would be when her phone rang and then she heard the knock on the door, but the minutes dragged by without a single sound. Soon she began to feel a bit like she was the last person on the planet, and after more minutes went by, she couldn't take it anymore. She was simply too antsy to stay inside the dingy, little room. Emma Jean grabbed her cell phone and room key and went outside to distract herself with a stroll through the grounds of the Aku Aku. Well, maybe "grounds" was too grandiose a word for the place. Okay, seedy would work as a description, too. But it didn't matter because she was open to everything and anything, as part of her Campaign to be Kind and non-judgmental.

But even outside, all she could think about was Riley, how great it had been to hear his voice and know they were in the very same city, how wonderful it would feel to have his arms around her, how adorably cute he would look when first she saw him. And then she envisioned how his face would appear when she announced her news, how excited he would be. And maybe, just maybe, the time would be right for them to declare their love for each other.

Because she was beginning to suspect that she might actually be in love with him. Certainly she hadn't felt this way about Peter at any time during the last few years. And even when she wracked her brain, she couldn't think of a time when she had felt this overwhelming excitement about Peter. Riley was such a different kind of man than

Peter, she thought as she strolled the corridor of the motel. He had a lot of chi running through him. All the best people did, and it expressed itself through some sort of passion, whether that was writing, painting, winemaking, or sex. It was Emma Jean's particular theory that people with a lot of chi needed a creative outlet or the chi didn't get released into the world, and it circulated and stagnated inside you and caused internal pressure that made you feel like you might explode. Sex was a good expression of it, but it wasn't enough.

Although Emma Jean had to admit that certain kinds of sex were about as good an expression of the creative spirit as you could get. Adultery was thrilling, no doubt about it. Women didn't do murder, unless they killed their kids in a fit of psychosis or were aiding and abetting a man in his plots. So the one way left for them to act out against society was adultery. And it was particularly true in her case, since she had raised marriage and the exaltation of it to an art form, celebrated with gusto in all her novels.

Having an affair was exciting in a way that marriage wasn't. It made her feel young and alive. She continued down the corridor and took a right, where an iron gate led to the pool area. Emma Jean went through it, thinking maybe she'd bask in the sun for a while. The air felt warm on her skin and she could work on her tan and think more profound, non-judgmental thoughts while waiting for Riley to call. The far end the pool house featured another tall A-frame for its roof, continuing the Polynesian theme. Emma Jean looked around, trying to decide where to sit.

One person sat by the pool, a woman wearing a blue bikini and a huge head of brunette hair. She was sitting with her back to Emma Jean, but something in the set of her shoulders looked familiar. Oh Jesus God, no, it was that *Vanity Fair* reporter. What was her name? Sally Marx. What was she doing at the Aku Aku? Emma Jean knew the answer to the question as soon as she asked it. Sally was lying in wait to talk to her, to trap her into incriminating comments about Marielle. But she wouldn't get Emma Jean to talk, no she wouldn't. It wasn't fair that the story wasn't about her. And besides, the whole *Vanity Fair* article on Marielle would never have happened if it weren't for Emma Jean in the first place, so that made it doubly unfair.

Emma Jean scurried back to her room before Sally could see her. Back at the motel room, the bubbles inside her burst and she felt her first pang of fear. What if Riley didn't call? What if Carolina had phoned and he needed to go home to her? What if he ended up not having time for Emma Jean? She would die, she would just die if that happened. Emma Jean perched on the bed and told herself to buck up. If Riley didn't come, she decided, she would find something to do on her own. She would not be one of those women who sat around waiting for her lover. She was a sophisticated world traveler, and so she certainly could master the freeways of L.A. She would go find that bookstore where she had first met Riley. Looking at books *always* cheered her up. And afterward, she would find a nice little place to have dinner.

In the meantime, she would do what normal people did at such times and call a friend for support. Yes, she would call Marielle. But then the thought occurred that she couldn't exactly tell Marielle that she was sitting in a seedy motel, afraid her lover might not call. Wow, having friends entailed a deep level of trust, if one had to confess things like affairs, didn't it? Emma Jean nodded her head, pleased with her epiphany. She would ponder how best to present the story of Riley to Marielle so that they could digest every little detail of it together. But in the meantime, another thought occurred to her. If she called Marielle, the phone would be tied up when Riley called. Emma Jean still hadn't mastered switching from one call to another on her phone and always ended up hanging up on people.

And then her phone trilled. She fumbled for the talk button when she saw it was Riley. Thank God she hadn't called Marielle!

"Oh, darling, where are you?" Emma Jean said.

"At your door."

Emma Jean ran, lightly, she hoped, across the room, pausing only momentarily to check her reflection in the mirror—cheeks a bit more bowling ball-ish than she might like, but after all she was *pregnant,* and four months gone at that, so what could you expect?—and her wild blonde hair did balance the chipmunk cheeks out.

She opened the door, and there he was.

Later, she would swear that sparks had shot from him and electrified her, that the angels had directed glorious streams of light to illuminate him, his amazing wonderfulness. Riley! She couldn't believe him, how fabulous he was, how much she loved him.

"Hey," he said and smiled. All she could do at the moment was *be* in his presence, drink him in: not as tall as she remembered him, but it felt wonderful when he took her in his arms. There was a line from an old Boz Scaggs song that Emma Jean had always loved. It was about a dance through the cosmos and she'd always wanted to experience it. Thank the gods, she had with Riley, who stood before her, looking smug as a snake that had just swallowed a mongoose, or whatever it was that snakes swallowed

He kissed her and she responded desperately, fiercely, wanting him to be closer, to give her more, to kiss her deeper, and she pressed her lips more firmly against his, moved her tongue deeper, felt for his crotch. He broke away and pushed her gently toward the bed.

"I don't have a lot of time," Riley said, and Emma Jean only had one single solitary second to feel disappointed because he was ripping her shirt off her, cupping his hands beneath the lacey purple bra she had bought new, just for him. "Your breasts are bigger than I remember them," Riley said, nuzzling her chin, licking her neck and then moving his tongue and his lips further, down her cleavage, even as his hands undid her bra snaps and the sudden cool air on her nipples was quickly replaced with Riley's tongue.

Emma Jean was pulling his belt out, fumbling for the snaps on his jeans, needing to feel his bare skin against hers, needing to feel him inside her. Oh God, she loved him so much! And she loved the way he made love to her, like a dancer, slow and sweet at first and then faster, dropping back down to a rhythm somewhere in between, every once in a while looking away with a smile on his face as if he heard a distant song then turning back to her and grinning, his eyes alive and twinkling. Honestly it was the only way to describe them: they twinkled. Emma Jean never wanted to look away from them; she saw the world reflected back to her in his eyes, felt the universe in his touch. He climaxed turbulently, ardently, crying out, like he'd just seen the face of God, and that brought her to climax also.

Afterward they lay on the bed, with Riley's arms wrapped around her, Emma Jean feeling safe and enclosed by his touch, which currently was focused on him stroking her hair. "Mmmmmm," Emma Jean said, drowsy, happy, content to stay like this forever. She wondered, in passing, if this would be a good time to tell him about the baby. But then they would have to discuss serious issues, and right now, all she wanted to do was lie here in his arms.

Moments later, Riley glanced at his watch and groaned. "I didn't realize it was so late. I've got to meet Carolina. Crap, and I was hoping we'd have time to talk."

"I know, darling. I want to talk to you, too," Emma Jean said. "I've got exciting news."

"It's going to have to wait," Riley said. "You're going to be here for a few days, aren't you? I've got to get going."

She took it as a good sign that he didn't move. Even his words about leaving didn't puncture her happy post-coital mood. The air conditioner blasted cold air on her naked body, and Emma Jean pulled the covers up around them and curled into a fetal position next to him.

"I want to go back to that place you took me the first night we met," Emma Jean said. She had just realized that the restaurant would be the perfect place to tell Riley that he was going to be a father.

"Hmmm," Riley said, sounding very sleepy.

Emma Jean poked him. "Wouldn't that be fun?"

"Paradise Cove? Yeah, I like that spot, too. But I can't do dinner. I have to work."

"Call in sick," Emma Jean said, half playfully, just to float the idea. Wouldn't airplane mechanics have generous sick day allowances, the way teachers did? He'd have to relinquish a sick day, which might be a problem later when it was time for his family to vacation, but shouldn't he be willing to sacrifice a little for her? After all, she was paying for the motel, she flew all the way down to see him, and all he had to do was show up, pull his pants down, and have fabulous sex.

"Wish I could." Riley planted a kiss on her forehead, broke away from her, and hopped up. "But what would Carolina say when I arrived home at midnight after having dinner with you?"

She listened to the shower running and the sounds of Riley grabbing a towel from the rack to dry himself, then rolled over onto her side, propping herself with her elbow when he came back into the room to get dressed.

"You wouldn't go home. You'd stay here with me, silly."

"Hmmmm. That would be nice, wouldn't it?"

And then the earth moved, hard, like someone had hit the motel with a truck, slammed into and rocked it on its foundation, except of course they were on the second floor, Jesus Christ, because now the motel rocked the other way, the bed and the entire room was shaking and someone was screaming, and she was trying to sit up but the damn bed was rocking back and forth violently like a horrible carnival ride. When she managed to sit up, she scootched to the edge of the bed—all she could think of was fleeing, heading for the door, she couldn't remember for the life of her what you were supposed to do at a time like this.

She needed to get out of this room even if she was naked as the day she was born. But as she neared the edge of the bed, the shaking intensified—dear Lord was that even possible?—and instead of gaining a foothold on the floor, her entire body flew from the bed to the floor where she landed, hard, on her back, and where things besides herself seemed to be falling through the air, like her computer—damn, did she have a backup of the novel somewhere? The lamp from the bedside table and one of the chairs sailed past. Outside, she heard glass shattering and the sound of a million car alarms going off and then as if one last act of God, the stack of books she had so carefully placed beside her computer, fell onto the floor, and one of them—the heavy dictionary she'd insisted on bringing with her, in spite of its heft—landed hard on her stomach, one of its corners gouging her belly button, before it landed smack on top of her. Another one fell on top of it with a thud.

And then, suddenly, all was still and quiet again.

But Emma Jean couldn't seem to lift herself from the floor. Nor could she move her hands. Oh God, her stomach. The baby. She tried to move her arm to push the books off herself, but she couldn't. The lamp had fallen and pinned her arm to the floor and her other hand seemed to be wedged beneath the computer. Not that either of them were that heavy, it was just that she felt so dazed.

"Noah," Riley said, as if in a dream. And then, to her, "Are you okay? You're okay aren't you?" but he didn't seem to be making a move to help her, because he had his cell phone out and was dialing.

"I can't get through," he said.

"Quit fussing with your phone and help me out here. I'm stuck," Emma Jean said.

Riley glanced at her briefly, punched buttons on his phone again. "I've got to find Noah."

Emma Jean pulled her arm out from beneath the lamp and it clattered the rest of the way to the floor. She used her free hand to yank the other one from beneath the computer and was able to push the books off of her and sit up a little more.

Riley continued to play with his cell phone and took two strides across the room to slash open the drapes over the sliding glass door.

"I'm naked," Emma Jean yelled.

"Put some clothes on, babe. We've got to go see what's going on. I've got to get home."

"For the love of God, look at me, Riley! Quit fussing with your phone and give me a hand up."

"Oh God, I'm sorry." Finally he seemed to focus. Riley knelt beside her. "Are you okay? Sorry, Emma Jean, I've just got to find out if Noah is okay. He is terrified of earthquakes."

"Like I'm not."

Riley moved the books to clear an area for her to stand up. "Jesus, this thing is heavy," he said as he lifted the dictionary and then offered her a hand up.

The book was indeed heavy, and it had landed smack on her stomach. Did something like this cause women to miscarry? Oh Jesus God, she didn't know. But as she stood, she felt the faintest flutter inside.

"Oh my God," Emma Jean said. She leaned against the wall and clutched her stomach.

"Are you okay?" Riley said.

Emma Jean stared at her stomach. There it was again. Another flutter, like wings beating inside her. She clutched her stomach. "Oh Jesus," she said. "Wow."

"What—" Riley sat back on his knees, looking up at her. "What's wrong?"

Slowly, Emma Jean shook her head. She rubbed her hand back and forth on her stomach and felt a slow smile spread across her face. Her baby, the wondrous life force within, had moved. It must have been the violence of the earthquake that caused it, the sudden fluttering, the dawning of life. Emma Jean pressed harder on her stomach. Oh my God, her baby was alive! Not that she had ever doubted it, but suddenly the baby felt real to her. Alive. A living, growing thing inside her that she had created.

"I hope it's nothing serious, because it is going to be hell getting you to a hospital. Although I don't think it was that bad of a quake." Suddenly Riley stopped talking and looked at her more closely. "Hey, you're smiling, that must mean it's not too bad."

"It's the first time I've ever felt her," Emma Jean said.

"Felt what?" Riley said. And then understanding dawned on his face. "Oh God. Emma Jean, are you...no. You're pregnant?"

She bit her lip and nodded.

"Is it mine?"

She nodded again. "It's yours alright. Peter had a vasectomy years ago that he never bothered to tell me about."

"For real?"

"Yes. Which is why I have left the lying, conniving bastard to his own devices."

Riley looked at her, shook his head, and then started laughing. "You're pregnant. That's amazing, Emma Jean. You're pregnant?"

"I really, truly am." She felt cheered by the fact that Riley appeared not to have noticed the extra weight she was already carrying.

"Damn. When's it due?"

"April or May probably. I'm not sure yet. I've got another doctor's appointment next week."

"Oh, you're going to love it. Having a baby is amazing, you'll see."

The room shook again, and Emma Jean clutched the bedpost.

"Aftershock," Riley said. As soon as the shaking stopped, he stood and started throwing on his clothes.

"You're not leaving."

"I gotta go."

"But I just told you I was pregnant."

"I know, babe." He stuck a foot in his untied shoe and did a funny little hopping motion in order to reach his other shoe. "It's a lot to process. Especially now, when I've got to find Noah."

"You're going to leave me here alone?"

"I've got to find Noah. He'll be crying his head off."

"What if there are more aftershocks?"

He had his pants and his shoes on now and was fishing his shirt from beneath the pile of books. Emma Jean heard running along the corridor outside and those damn car alarms were still shrieking. There were horns honking, too, and every once in a while a shout.

"I've got to go." She noticed a dead look now. There was definitely no twinkling.

"Don't you care about me? Don't you care about our baby?"

"I do, actually. More than you know. But right now, I need to find out about my son."

"Riley, wait."

Emma Jean followed him to the door then remembered she was naked and ran back for her robe. By the time she got outside, he was already down the hall. The sight of him walking away panicked her.

"Riley!"

He paused and turned.

"Don't leave me!"

He took a step toward her, wrapped her in his muscular arms and hugged her tight. Then he kissed her head, released her, and gave her a tiny little push back. "Gotta go, babe."

The earth shook again as he started down the metal staircase, which was intact, but now slanted to one side.

"Riley!" she called after him.

But Riley never turned around.

Suddenly all her fears turned into one huge tide of anger.

"Fuck you!" she yelled. "I'm never going to see you again. And I'll never let you see the baby. Ever! You'll be sorry you left me like this, because it is the last time you will see me. I mean it, Riley."

Riley kept walking and turned the corner out of her sight without so much as a wave. She wasn't even certain if he'd heard her. She stood on the balcony, clutching the iron railing, and stared out over the view. In the near distance, there were high rises that seemed intact, though when she looked closer, she saw broken windows. Sirens wailed and out on Ventura Boulevard, traffic seemed to be gridlocked, like everyone in the world was racing home at once. In the parking lot, there were a few areas where the asphalt had buckled, but otherwise little in the way of damage or debris.

Now she noticed other people carefully navigating the stairs: a woman with a small boy clinging to her neck, an older man standing at the bottom, holding out his arms to the woman to get her to relinquish the child so she could walk down more easily. And someone with big black hair who looked vaguely familiar was actually walking up them.

It was Sally Marx.

"Are you okay, Emma Jean?" the reporter said once she got to the top.

Emma Jean stared at her. She looked like she'd had five people help her get dressed and don make-up, every hair in place, her black suit impeccable. How did this woman survive an earthquake looking like this? And what was she doing here? Too late, Emma Jean recalled seeing Sally lounging at the pool.

"I heard you yelling and came to see if I could help," Sally continued.

Sally's eyes darted from Emma Jean's face to her body. Emma Jean realized she was standing there with the flimsy silk gold robe open, allowing Sally, and the whole damn world for that matter, to see her naked body beneath. Emma Jean pulled the robe closed and hastily belted it. The thought occurred to her that she probably looked awful. She'd not had a chance to fix her hair and make-up after making love with Riley, thanks to the earthquake, and she probably had black mascara smeared all down her cheeks.

"I'm fine," Emma Jean said.

"That was a trip, wasn't it?" Sally gestured toward the parking lot. "I was getting in my car for an appointment when it started. Damn. Crazy shit. I've never been through an earthquake before; we don't get them in New York."

Sally stopped and glanced pointedly at Emma Jean's stomach. Emma Jean placed her hands defensively over it and wondered if Sally had heard her yelling about the baby. Great, this was just great. Riley rushed off to find his son leaving her stranded in her hour of need, and now a reporter for *Vanity Fair* might know she was pregnant. But suddenly, she didn't care. Because all she wanted was to go home, to leave L.A.

"So hey, is there anything I can do for you? My appointment got cancelled. We could go have a glass of wine, take the edge off, you know? Or you could have a soda or water or something."

"I don't think so, Sally." Emma Jean slowly shook her head. "I am getting the hell out of here."

"That might be a bit difficult, given the situation," Sally said.

"I don't care. I'm going."

Emma Jean turned and walked away, back toward her room.

"Are you sure you don't need help getting back to your room?" Sally called.

Emma Jean ignored her. Too damn bad if Sally guessed she was pregnant. It didn't matter, because she was going home now. Home to gray, gloomy Portland, where there were only tiny, little earthquakes every once in a blue moon. Home to her wonderful house, which sheltered her in time of need. She could light a fire and curl up by the fireplace on the red, smooshy couch in the family room and all would be well.

Back in the motel room, she grabbed her phone and dialed the airlines to change her ticket. After several failed attempts to get through, she put the phone on speaker mode, and set it on the bed so it could ring while she was packing. She threw on her clothes and started piling books in her travel bag. And then as she packed her crystals, it hit her. She couldn't go home. She couldn't go home to Portland because Peter, her lying, conniving, lout of a husband was going to be at the house. At her beautiful, wonderful, sheltering house. For all intents and purposes, she had no home. She was alone, with nowhere to go. Oh, the trauma of it all was nearly unbearable!

Emma Jean plopped down on the edge of the bed, hard, beside the phone. Vaguely, she could still hear it ringing. She stared open-mouthed at the motel pool out the back window, where it looked like people were resuming their sunbathing, as if everything was normal. But nothing was normal in Emma Jean's world, and it wouldn't be, ever again. Suddenly she heard a male voice.

"Hello? May I help you?"

For a minute she thought it was Riley, returned after all. She clutched at her heart. Oh, she knew he'd be back! Wasn't he the most wonderful man in the whole world?

Then the voice said, "This is customer service, can I help you?"

Crap, it wasn't Riley. But the voice seemed to have jarred something out of her consciousness, because suddenly Emma Jean knew what to do. She held the phone to her ear.

"You sure enough can help me, darling. You can't believe how glad I am to have finally gotten through to you. I need to book a flight and get the hell out of here."

PART TWO

Chapter Thirteen
Her Good Behavior

Emma Jean adjusted the piece of rose quartz so it caught the sunlight—according to all her crystal books, sunlight cleansed and recharged crystals—moving it closer to Aku Aku. One of the many good things about Sun Valley was, well, the sun. Even in mid-October, with the leaves turning and already falling off the trees, the sun shone nearly every day. It was definitely chilly—at night it got bitterly cold, in a bone-chilling manner which Emma Jean was not used to—and Aunt Cleo told her the snow would soon fly, but for now the sun and the fresh mountain air felt mighty good.

She pushed her chair away from the desk in the main room of the Zelch Gallery. From here, she could watch the front door to see if anyone came in, which happened rarely, as this was what the locals called slack, when there were no tourists in town. The season started in earnest on Thanksgiving, when the ski lifts opened, and people swarmed the hotels, condos, and restaurants, but until then, the town was blessedly quiet and anonymous. She babysat the gallery a few days a week, to give Lynette, the only other employee, some days off. It was the least she could do for Aunt Cleo, who had welcomed Emma Jean home with few questions asked and been thoroughly pampering her since her arrival.

She stood and walked to the front window, from which she could see Mt. Baldy looming above the stores and buildings on the other side of the street. She loved looking at the mountain. She loved *being* in the mountains, a thing that surprised her no end, as she had always been an ocean girl, a lover of sun and sea and sand. If one were homeless, the mountains were a good place to land, and she was happy here for the time being. If one could call oneself happy after one had made a complete mess of one's life.

The phone rang, jarring her out of her reverie, and she walked back over to the desk to answer it. "Zelch Gallery," she said, in her best, crisp, efficient voice. The caller wanted information on gallery hours and the name of the artist currently showing, and Emma Jean happily provided them. It felt good to be useful and productive, especially since she wasn't getting any writing done, even though she set up her laptop and all her notes for *Tiki* on the gallery desk.

But never mind, because the most important thing was maintaining serenity for little Claire, the wondrous life force within her. And after the chaos of L.A., Sun Valley felt calm and peaceful. Very Zen, like in the book she was reading, or trying to, Zen writing being somewhat austere and boring to her mind. But even boring was good, after what she had been through. Emma Jean squared her shoulders as she looked out at the mountain and pondered the last week.

She'd been skittish as the Mexican jumping beans Aunt Cleo used to buy her as a kid until she'd gotten to the Burbank airport, and the constant aftershocks didn't help. Never in all her life had she been so happy to see her fabulous aunt as the night Cleo had picked her up at the Sun Valley airport. Wrapped in a long, knitted geometric shawl in black, white and red, and sporting shiny silver eye shadow and henna-colored hair, Cleo had enfolded Emma Jean in a hug of wool and love. For a moment, all seemed right with the world, and Emma Jean could forget everything that had happened to her. Then Cleo held Emma Jean at arm's length and cocked an eyebrow quizzically as she inspected her.

"So you really are pregnant," Cleo had said.

"Oh God, do I look that bad?" Emma Jean's hands flew to her face.

"You don't look bad; you look beautiful, honey. It's just that you are starting to show—your face and your stomach both look a bit rounder."

"I look like crap, don't I? I know I look like crap. Of course, after what I've been through I deserve to look like crap."

"Far from it. You look great. You have that pregnancy glow, darling," Cleo said.

Secretly Emma Jean was pleased with the compliment, though she wondered if she could believe Cleo's opinion, since Cleo always said nice things about her. She stowed her luggage in the back of Cleo's car and stationed herself in the passenger seat, exhaling a long sigh of relief that yet another torturous journey was over.

Cleo got in the car, placed her hands on the steering wheel, and pursed her lips as she gazed at Emma Jean.

"C'mon, Aunt Cleo, can't we get going? It has been one hell of a long day, and I could eat three horses, seeing as how all they feed you on the damn plane is peanuts."

"I think pregnancy suits you," Aunt Cleo said. "I'm damned pleased you didn't go through with the abortion, darling. I didn't know it until now, but I've always wanted to be a grandmother."

And then she had driven Emma Jean to Cristina's, one of the best restaurants in town, for a scrumptious meal.

But welcoming as Cleo had been, Emma Jean had also felt a strange sense of distance from her aunt that she'd not been able to figure out. Ever since that first night back, it had almost seemed as if Cleo was avoiding her. For one thing, Cleo spent most of her time holed up in her home office, often on the phone, from the murmurs Emma Jean heard through the closed door. For another, Cleo went out for dinner every night, leaving Emma Jean at home to fend for herself.

"Who are you meeting?" Emma Jean had asked the night before.

"Oh, clients," Cleo said airily.

But Emma Jean spent long days in the gallery with nary a client dropping in, certainly not anyone with enough money to warrant being wined and dined, so where was Cleo dredging up clients to meet with? Anyway, Emma Jean didn't mind, truly she didn't; she was so glad to be away from both Peter and Riley, unreliable, ungrateful bastards that they both were.

They had both been hounding her. Even though usually she would have been thrilled with all the attention, at the moment, she just didn't care. She was tired of men and trying to figure them out. She didn't have a clue what either one of them wanted. Peter sounded surprisingly conciliatory when she listened to the messages he left on her cell, but she figured he was just worried about money. After all, their joint back accounts were dwindling fast, a fact of which she was reminded every time she visited the ATM.

And Riley—oh, God, Riley. He was harder not to care about, she had to admit, seeing as how being with him in L.A. had reaffirmed that she was desperately in love with him. But she couldn't even believe how callously he had treated her after the terror of barely surviving the earthquake. Then, to add insult to injury, he'd left a message that she'd found the night she arrived in Sun Valley, telling her how sorry he was, that he hoped she was okay, he was at work, it was crazy, Carolina and Noah were fine, and he wanted to see her again tomorrow. He'd make more time, take her out to dinner, call in sick, whatever she wanted. Emma Jean had listened to the message and then pressed save. She'd clutched the cell to her heart, like a crystal pressed against her chakra, then closed her eyes and worried. What had she done? Had she left too hastily? But Riley had *abandoned* her to her fate that day. And since then, his messages had been much more prosaic, with him saying cryptically that they needed to talk. Well, to hell with him. She'd been plenty ready to talk when she was in L.A., but he was the one who had to go rushing off to find his son.

Being mad at both Peter and Riley made her latest spiritual project much easier. She was doing penance. It was penance for her bad behavior. She wasn't exactly sure what form it was taking beyond removing herself from the real world and living in the bubble of Sun Valley, but she was hoping that was enough, along with praying fervently every night for her sins to be absolved. She'd looked up penance on Wikipedia and learned that it often involved public humiliation, which she prayed to God she would not have to endure. Even though she didn't understand the full picture of penance, she was pretty sure that refusing Peter and Riley's calls was at the very least earning her some points with the big guy in Heaven, or wherever he hung out.

Working at the gallery was also part of the penance. Enduring long stretches of boredom was surely good for racking up some bonus points with God. Plus the penance project seemed easier, at the moment, then her friend project, which she had so far failed miserably at. Well, maybe if she did penance then she could make friends. The sound of the gallery phone startled her back to the present. It turned out to be Aunt Cleo, as usual, who went through her ten-time daily routine of asking Emma Jean how she was doing, the only visible aspect of her concern. At least Aunt Cleo's ministrations were easier to deal with than Trish's, who kept calling and asking if Emma Jean wanted to *talk*. Emma Jean could tell from the way Trish said *talk*, that she was meant *talk* talk, delving deeply into the roots of her current predicament, which Emma Jean simply couldn't handle at the moment. After cooing for a few minutes, Aunt Cleo asked her to go upstairs and bring down a stack of brochures that she'd run by and pick up later.

"Don't forget I have that doctor's appointment at one," Emma Jean said.

"I'll be there, darling; I promise. And we'll plan to talk later, okay, baby? We have so many things to talk about."

Emma Jean hung up. Working at the gallery was a bit like babysitting because Aunt Cleo was nearby—usually off running errands or doing paperwork at the condo—should real customers or any problems appear. She decided to go find the brochures. The pregnancy hormones were making her forgetful, though in her case, it was just as likely to be caused by impending old age.

She pushed herself away from the desk and carefully walked up a spiral, wrought iron staircase—why Cleo thought that such a thing was a good idea was beyond Emma Jean—to an office in the rear of the second floor. Against the back wall of the office was a row of file cabinets and along one side was a long table that looked as if it were used for mailings and the like. Emma Jean found a box of brochures, two stacks of them in an open-topped cardboard box, and tucked them under her arm in order to be able to hold onto the rail of the spiral staircase. It was even more awkward to walk down the stairs than it was to trudge up them, and now that she felt so fiercely protective of little baby Claire, she lived in fear of falling.

Just as she reached the bottom stair, a voice startled her.

"Hi," it said.

Emma Jean grabbed for the rail, dropped the box and the brochures scattered across the floor. "Jesus God, you scared me half to death."

She looked to see who her visitor was and saw it was a young girl.

"Remember me?" the girl said. "I'm Ava. My Mom is Wendy, and she works at the library, and usually I hang out there but I've read all the books so I thought I'd come here instead."

Emma Jean stared at Ava, remembering now the girl's strange, oversized features and odd demeanor. At least, Emma Jean thought her demeanor odd, but for all she knew, Ava was a normal twelve-year-old. Though Emma Jean was fairly certain most twelve-year-old girls did not wear all black, and layer upon layer of it the way Ava did. Shouldn't she be wearing a shirt that spelled out *princess* in glitter or a cute, little flowered dress or something? Ava wore black shoes, black tights, and a black dress and had a black scarf tied at her neck, all of which contrasted with her blonde curls.

But then Emma Jean realized what Ava had just said. "You've read all the books in the library?"

Ava nodded. "Well, maybe not exactly all of them. But all the ones I'm interested in."

"Wow." Emma Jean looked closer at Ava. She had a sweep of freckles across her nose and cheeks and a broad, solid forehead. *Full of brains*, Aunt Cleo would say. "What do you read?"

"Wendy—she's not my real Mom; she's my foster Mom—always says I should stick to the young adult section, but I've read all those. So, last time I checked out *Gone with the Wind*."

"*Gone with the Wind*. That was the first adult novel I ever read," Emma Jean said. "Girls still read that?"

"I do. Probably none of the other girls in my class do, but that's because they're stupid. I've read all your books now, too." Ava, with her hands clasped behind her back, had a funny way of swaying back and forth from foot to foot as she talked.

"Your mother lets you read my books? They're a bit on the mature side."

"She's my foster mother. She can't tell me what to do."

"I hate to break it to you, darling, but your foster mother can indeed tell you what to do."

"Aren't you going to pick up the papers you dropped?" Ava asked.

Emma Jean knelt awkwardly to gather the brochures while Ava watched.

"You could help, you know."

Ava pushed three brochures toward Emma Jean with her black-shoed foot, leaving a fan of dust on the top one. "When my real mother comes back for me, I'll listen to whatever she says. She's beautiful."

"Refresh my memory." Emma Jean looked up at Ava. "Where is your real mother?"

"In L.A. She's modeling to make money for us."

Ah, yes, Emma Jean recalled Wendy referring to the mother's modeling in a way that made her think porn was involved.

"She's coming back to get me really soon. She just needs to make a little more money. Then we're going to get a house here. Actually, it'll probably be more like a mansion."

"That's good, sweetie." Emma Jean finished gathering the brochures and stuffed them back in the box, then rose awkwardly to walk into the front room, Ava following. This would be when she could gently ease Ava away. Tell her she had to work on her novel or something. The girl fell silent for a minute—thank you, God—and the sounds of the gallery stereo system filled the room. Lucinda Williams. Not exactly art-buying music, but Emma Jean liked it and few people came in anyway. She just needed to remember to change it back to classical before Aunt Cleo arrived.

"I love Lucinda Williams," Ava said.

"Who are *you*? Aren't you supposed to love Miley Cyrus?"

"She's for stupid girls."

"Like the ones you go to school with?" Emma Jean sat down at the desk and punched a key on her laptop to bring it back to life. She'd open her *Tiki* file and then inform the child that she had very serious matters to which she needed to attend.

"Uh-huh." Ava nodded, and her blonde curls bobbed.

"Hey, wait," Emma Jean said. "Shouldn't you be in school right now?" Emma Jean looked at her watch. Almost twelve-thirty, which she should have known by the way her stomach was growling.

"I get out early."

"Why, pray tell?"

Ava walked closer to the desk and picked up the binder where Emma Jean kept all her notes for *Tiki*. "So, as you know, I'm going to be a writer when I grow up, and—"

Just then, Emma Jean's phone rang. Before she could reach for it, Ava grabbed it.

"Hello."

Emma Jean made a noise of outrage in the back of her throat and held her hands out as if to strangle Ava. But the girl turned away.

"Oh no, this is Ava." Emma Jean heard. "I'm her newest student. And assistant. Who are you?"

Emma Jean lunged for Ava, who held the phone out and smiled sweetly. "It's Riley. Your *friend*."

Emma Jean rolled her eyes and grabbed the phone.

"I didn't know you'd hired an assistant," Riley said.

Ava stood in front of the desk, hands clasped in front of her, swaying back and forth, watching Emma Jean intently.

Emma Jean sighed. "Can you hang on a minute?" she said to Riley.

She covered the phone and looked pointedly at Ava, who raised her hands. "I'm going, I'm going. I'll be back for my first writing lesson."

Emma Jean watched Ava walk out the door, stooping to pick up—what? She strained to see. A heavy, worn library book, *Gone with the Wind*, no doubt, and some sort of pink, glittery bag that was completely out of sync with the all black ensemble she was wearing. She made sure the glass door was closed behind Ava before she went back to Riley. "Okay, sorry, I'm back."

"What was that all about?"

"Oh, it's just this girl. A bit of a pest." Emma Jean realized that hearing Riley's voice was making her heart pound double time. Even if his behavior had gravely disappointed her, it was absolutely wonderful to hear him on the phone. After all, he was the love of her life. Her love for Riley was so vast, so astoundingly deep, that she hadn't even realized how lacking her love for Peter had been. And so she couldn't stop the rush of words that came out next. "How are you, darling? I miss you so much I can barely stand it. What's going on?"

"You miss me because you don't take my calls. If that girl hadn't picked up, you wouldn't have taken it, would you?"

Could she help it if she was busy doing penance?

"I'm trying to be good, Riley."

"Isn't it a little late for that?"

"You could be more supportive," Emma Jean said. "Here I am, stuck in this godforsaken mountain town all alone except for Aunt Cleo."

"You wrote me you loved Sun Valley," Riley said. "That it was the only place where the chi matched the life force chi of the baby and that it was where you needed to be."

Oh, right. There was the one email she had allowed herself to answer. It had seemed important to let the father of her baby know where she was holing up, though she may have gone on just a wee bit longer than was technically necessary.

"But I didn't call to argue, Emma Jean. I called because we need to talk."

There was that ominous tone in his voice once again. He said *talk* in the deep tones of a television announcer, and she didn't like the sound of it at all. She racked her brain for something to tell him to keep the conversation light and came up alarmingly short, seeing as how she did very little these days.

"But first tell me about the baby. Is everything going okay?"

"She's fine. And I'm going—"

"It's a girl? You didn't tell me that. Wow! A daughter. Awesome."

"I don't know for sure. I feel like it's a girl, though. Her energy is amazing. She's very profound. I've got a doctor's appointment this afternoon."

"Are you sure they have decent medical care in that little Podunk town?" Riley asked.

"The doctor delivered Demi Moore's baby when she lived up here, so that ought to be good enough for you." His L.A. provincialism annoyed her. Then she had a thought. "You should come up here and see for yourself what it's like. It's very sophisticated, being a world-class resort and all. Lots of movie stars have houses up here."

"You know how hard it would be for me to get away," Riley said. "Emma Jean—"

But even if she was royally pissed at him, the idea of showing Riley Sun Valley was appealing. He could come to the doctor with her at her next appointment, and they could check out the birthing rooms at the hospital together. "No, seriously, you should think about it. I mean, c'mon, Riley, you get to fly for free."

Emma Jean saw a flash of black outside and noticed Ava loitering by the low wall that fronted the sculpture courtyard in front of the gallery. At least she was far enough away not to eavesdrop on the conversation.

"I can't leave Carolina to deal with Noah. Emma Jean, we need—"

"Why not?"

"What am I supposed to tell her, that I'm taking a vacation to see my lover?"

"If you really wanted to see me, you'd figure out a way," Emma Jean said. It would be okay, penance-wise, for *him* to come see *her*. Then she could say she simply couldn't stop him. "I am carrying your child, after all."

"You should move back to civilization. I'm still not convinced about the quality of prenatal care."

"I've moved to Sun Valley, Riley, since every human being in my life with the exception of Trish, who I pay, has deserted or betrayed me," Emma Jean said. More movement outside, and she watched as Ava wandered off down the block. Good. Maybe she was going back to the library.

"Anyway, Dr. Gilbert will be fine," she continued. "He does prenatal care for all the stars when they are staying up here. They already know me in the office, cause they've never had a pregnant woman over the age of 45."

"I thought you were 43."

"Oh darn, I've got to go; someone's here."

"There's nobody there, Emma Jean. You're just trying to get off the phone. Listen, we've really got to talk, baby."

And then a man dressed all in shades of brown, with a head of long silver hair pulled into a ponytail, walked by the gallery window, hesitated, and then strolled in.

"I really do need to go; somebody just came in, Riley. I'll talk to you soon, okay?" She pressed end before he could protest or start in again about needing to talk. But then she regretted her haste because after she had hung up she realized that he had said, "I love you," as he signed off.

Jesus God, he told her he loved her and she had almost missed it. When had he ever said *I love you* to her before? Oh God, when he said things like, that it made her crazy. Made it so *damn hard* to be contrite and do her penance. Christ, the world hinged on timing. Why didn't any of the religious traditions teach you about that? Riley hadn't seemed that interested in spending time with her when she'd been in L.A. Now that she was far away, and unavailable, he was telling her that he loved her.

This just proved her point—it was better not to talk to him, better not to get her hopes up that something real could happen between them. Because the truth of the matter was, she did want something real with Riley. She watched the pony-tailed man meander out the door. Sharing the searing experience of the earthquake had bonded her to Riley irrevocably. Half the motive for avoiding him was to protect herself, though doing penance was really, truly the other half. She didn't want to have a half-assed relationship with anyone any more. The more distance Emma Jean got from Peter, the more she realized how separate their lives had become over the last couple of years. She didn't want that anymore. She wanted all or nothing.

But she didn't have time to worry about it now, because, oh crap, it was time to leave for her doctor's appointment, and Aunt Cleo was nowhere in sight. There was no choice but to lock up the gallery and get going.

Chapter Fourteen

Her Baby!

Emma Jean stepped outside and pulled the door shut behind her. The weakening sun warmed her skin, but there was a mountain chill in the air that made her shiver and pull her sweater tighter around her burgeoning waist. Then Emma Jean realized she'd forgotten to set the alarm, a task that she hated because she lived in fear that she was going to punch the wrong number and call the police by accident. Not that it mattered—truth be told the town could use some excitement—except that too many false alarms and Cleo had to start paying. Now *that*, Emma Jean could understand, since she herself seemed to be paying for two households, her own and Peter's. Trish kept telling her she needed to cut Peter off, but for some unknown reason, she hadn't been able to do that yet. As Emma Jean fumbled with the gallery lock, she had an epiphany. Paying Peter's bills was part of her penance! After all, the man had no means of support other than Emma Jean, even if he was about to drive her to the poorhouse. Which he was because last time she'd gone to the ATM, there'd only been a few hundred dollars left in it, and she'd had to transfer money from savings.

By the time she went back in and set the alarm and got the front door locked, she was already five minutes late for her doctor's appointment and she wasn't even on the road yet. So this made her even less thrilled to see Ava loitering on the front bumper of her car, a rental Explorer that she would soon have to turn in because it was costing her a fortune.

"Oh for God's sakes, I thought you went back to the library," Emma Jean said.

Ava shook her head. She was carrying her book. "I needed caffeine so I went to the coffee shop and started my novel."

"Coffee stunts your growth. I'm pretty sure you're too young for it, but I don't have time to discuss it because I'm late. I'll see you later, okay?" Emma Jean headed toward the car door, using the keyless remote to open the SUV.

But before she could get the key in the ignition, Ava slid into the front seat.

"What are you doing?" Emma Jean said. "I told you, I'm late."

"Where are you going?" Ava said as she buckled her seatbelt.

"To the doctor."

"Are you sick?" Ava asked, her eyebrows knotting together.

"No, I'm not sick, but I'm going to be if you don't get out of the car."

"Pregnant, huh?"

"Oh for God's sake," Emma Jean said. "Just get out."

"Let me come with you. You're already late," Ava pointed out.

Emma Jean wished she had more experience coping with children so she'd know how to deal with Ava at this moment. Peter's daughter Julia had been a little older when she and Peter married, but Julia lived with Peter's ex and only came to stay with them every other weekend. Emma Jean had tried and tried to be a stepmother to Julia, but Peter and the girl had such a tight bond she could never find any room between them. Polite distance had worked best. But this Ava did not seem to understand polite distance, or any other kind of distance for that matter. And neither kindness nor directness seemed to have any impact on her.

"Okay," Emma Jean said. "Since you appear to not be getting out of the car, I'll drop you at the library on the way."

"No!" Ava yelled.

"Why not? I thought you liked hanging out there. You can't loiter on the street all afternoon."

Ava shook her head. "Don't make me go there."

Emma Jean put her seat belt on and backed out of the parking space. "But that's where your mother is."

"She's my foster mother." Ava folded her hands in her lap and cast her head down. "And I'll get in big trouble if you drop me off. I might even get deported."

"You can't get deported, darling; you're a citizen. We're stuck with you. Why…oh I get it. You're cutting school. You don't get out early; you're supposed to be in class."

Emma Jean steered the SUV down the deserted Sun Valley street. Ava kept her head down and wouldn't look at her.

"Am I right? I'm right; I know I am. Jesus, now I'm aiding and abetting the delinquency of a minor."

"You shouldn't swear," Ava said. Now she was looking at Emma Jean, her brows pressed together in a tight knot.

"And you shouldn't cut school."

"I hate school," Ava said. "Everyone is stupid. I think I should be home-schooled, but Wendy won't let me."

Emma Jean sighed. This was why she disliked children, because they made everything so damn complicated. She glanced at her watch. Ten after. "Okay, here's the deal. You can come to the doctor's office with me. But you have to call your mother and tell her what's going on."

"I do?"

Emma Jean nodded as she turned onto Ketchum's main street, which turned into the highway to Hailey a few blocks south. "Poor Wendy is probably frantic with worry while you've been lollygagging about town."

"She's not."

Emma Jean handed Ava her cell. "Call her."

"I've got my own." Ava pulled a phone out of her glittery pink bag, sighed heavily and punched a couple buttons.

It turned out that Ava was right—Wendy *wasn't* terribly worried, even though the school had called to tell her that Ava was absent yet again. Emma Jean learned this after Ava had a protracted conversation with Wendy and then handed Emma Jean the phone.

"She wants to talk to you."

Apparently Ava's truancy was a common occurrence, and Wendy had spies all throughout town that informed her of Ava's whereabouts.

Most often when she cut school, she spent her afternoons at the coffee shop, reading.

"But don't tell her I know that," Wendy said. "This way I can let her think she's getting away with something and keep an eye on her at the same time. She does her homework and seems to be about two grades ahead at school, so we give her some slack."

"I don't envy you," Emma Jean said.

"You have no idea. You'll have to let me know if she's starting to bother you too much. Now that you're at the gallery, I fear she'll be dropping in on you all the time."

Wasn't that a cheery thought?

The doctor's office was an odd combination of cutesy baby décor and mountain rustic: heavy wood chairs beside matching tables piled with parenting magazines and bright plastic toys; wallpaper and trim in pastel pinks and blues yet the wall art was carved wood or fabricated metal pieces depicting trees, lakes, streams, even the stray moose and bear. But Emma Jean didn't have time to wonder who on earth had thought such a design scheme would work, because the nurse called her right in.

She turned to check on Ava, but the girl had already stationed herself on one of the rustic chairs and buried her head in *Gone with the Wind*.

It turned out that Dr. Gilbert was an ancient, rounded man who looked like a wizened forest elf, and at first, Emma Jean wondered if the medical care would indeed be adequate. But then she remembered about Demi Moore.

"So, what was it like delivering a huge movie star's baby?" Emma Jean asked as Dr. Gilbert placed his stethoscope on her chest.

He grunted in reply. Emma Jean looked around the examination room, wondering if perhaps there might be a signed photograph of the star and whatever her husband's name was, tactfully placed. But she saw nothing. Perhaps the good doctor was just humble.

"I bet she looked gorgeous her entire pregnancy and didn't gain any weight at all, right?" Emma Jean said.

Dr. Gilbert looked up at her, and his demeanor called to mind an exasperated scientist. "What are you talking about?"

"Demi Moore. You delivered her baby, right? That's what I read on the Internet. It's one of the reasons I chose you. Because, you know, the baby's father lives in L.A. and all, and so I thought he'd feel good about the connection."

Dr. Gilbert looked at her blankly, and Emma Jean felt the need to explain the nimble leaps her mind sometimes made.

"You know, L.A., Hollywood, famous movie stars, Demi Moore." Still he didn't respond.

"Oh, I get it. You're protecting her privacy, right? That works. That's good, actually. Because, you know, I'm famous in some circles, too, and I'd really appreciate it if word of my pregnancy did not sneak out."

And just then light dawned on Dr. Gilbert's face, and it was like the sun rising over the desert. Emma Jean prepared her famous novelist expression on her face, even though she was now lying on her back with her legs in the stirrups. But what the doctor said had nothing to do with either her or Demi Moore.

"I need to get something from the other room," he said. "I seem to have mislaid the box of gloves." And he left her lying there on the examining table with her feet in the stirrups, her legs spread wide. She forgot about Demi and tried to scooch herself to a more comfortable position to no avail. Emma Jean sighed. Having a baby was definitely not for sissies. She'd had no idea, nada, nienta, none at all. Clearly she had vastly underestimated the rigors of pregnancy and motherhood in her years-long rant against babies. It was hard emotionally, too. She now missed her mother keenly. How she wished her mother had not fled the Fake Christian's adultery and met her demise at the horns of a bull. Because she yearned to be able to ask her mother questions about what it had been like when she was pregnant with Emma Jean. Had she felt the same paradox of uniqueness and connectedness? The same odd pain in her lower back every time she rolled over? The same deep profundity when the baby moved?

The night before, at Aunt Cleo's condo, Emma Jean had asked Cleo questions about her mother and how it had been when she was pregnant. But Cleo had answered every question with a noncommittal "hmmm" or an "I don't really remember, dear." Yes, her aunt was in her seventies and entitled to some memory loss, but Emma Jean was beginning to suspect also that Cleo was avoiding the whole topic. Emma Jean was also starting to believe that, despite all of Cleo's pampering, her aunt was, for some reason, extremely uncomfortable with Emma Jean's pregnancy.

The door opened, and Dr. Gilbert had bustled back in. In what Emma Jean felt was an unnecessarily leisurely fashion, given that she was lying with the cold air tickling her nether parts, he scrubbed his hands and pulled on the recalcitrant rubber gloves.

"My partner delivered her baby," he said.

It took her a minute to figure out what he was talking about. Demi! He was talking about Demi!

"And after that, he upped and moved to Hollywood." Dr Gilbert shook his head, which Emma Jean sensed rather than saw. She could feel how very upset he was about his partner's move but she wanted to learn more. Had his partner moved to Hollywood on account of having delivered Demi's baby? Had he become so star-struck that he had no other choice? Perhaps he had become Demi's private doctor? Wouldn't that be a good story to tell Riley? And it would immediately dissolve all his fears about the quality of her care. But then Emma Jean felt the cold speculum inside her, and the doctor was pressing on her stomach, and she couldn't think of anything except how uncomfortable she was.

"Everything looks good," Dr. Gilbert said. "Have my nurse make you an appointment for an ultrasound. We need to pinpoint the baby's exact age."

"Wait," Emma Jean said. "That's it? But I wanted to discuss *things*. Is it possible to do a water birth anywhere in the Wood River Valley? And I've been doing some reading. What do you think about finding a doula? And then the other thing is that I thought an herbalist might help some of my discomfort. Can you make any recommendations along those lines?"

Dr. Gilbert fixed her with a baleful stare. "You have a lot to learn, don't you?"

"Oh, I do, I do," Emma Jean said. "I've read every book I can find. I want to learn everything."

"Talk to the nurse about the ultrasound," Dr. Gilbert said, and then he shuffled out the door.

In the waiting room, she suppressed her disappointment as she stood at the nurse's window and conferred about appointments. The nurse gave her a wad of brochures on nutrition and exercise as well as information on childbirth services in the area. Emma Jean couldn't wait to get home and look through it all. Just as she was turning to go, she remembered Ava.

But the waiting room was empty. No Ava. Only a young woman with a distended stomach who looked like she was about to deliver on the spot.

"Where did she go?" Emma Jean said.

"Oh, you mean your granddaughter?"

Emma Jean fixed the woman with what she hoped was a meaningful stink eye. But the woman just smiled. "She's something. She said to tell you she'd be outside. She needed some fresh air."

Outside, she found Ava deeply engrossed in conversation with a woman who looked vaguely familiar. Oh, for flippin' sake, it was Sally Marx. Erstwhile *Vanity Fair* reporter who wanted to wage a smear campaign against Marielle. Was this woman relentless or what? Why couldn't she get what she needed about Marielle somewhere else?

And she was sitting right beneath the sign that said: Dr. Gilbert, ob-gyn. She and Ava sat side by side on the low brick wall that ran parallel to the parking lot. Emma Jean bit her lip and remembered Sally staring pointedly at her stomach right after the earthquake. In the rush of events that had followed, she'd forgotten all about it. Lord, she didn't need Sally Marx to know about and blab her pregnancy to the world. Emma Jean hadn't quite figured out how to break the news of her pregnancy to her fans yet.

Emma Jean crouched behind some kind of shrubby mountain pine and watched Ava speak animatedly to Sally Marx. When Ava glanced her way, Emma Jean pointed to Sally and then toward the parking lot, and sank back down behind the bush, hoping Ava would get the hint, say goodbye to Sally Marx, and head for the car. Instead, Ava waved, and Sally looked in Emma Jean's direction at the exact moment she was crouching back down again.

"Did you lose something?" Sally called.

Emma Jean rolled her eyes and brushed bark dust off the hem of her pants and walked over to them, assuming a dignified demeanor. Sally took her hand and said, "The last time we met, we'd both just survived an earthquake. That was wild, wasn't it?"

"It was wild alright," Emma Jean said. She shook Sally's hand, dropped it quickly, and then turned to Ava. "Come on, darling, I've got to get back to the gallery."

"Oh, Ava and I have just been having the best chat," Sally said. She was wearing a puffy, white, down jacket and ultra-slim jeans over spiked heels. Emma Jean looked more closely at Sally's face. Something about it looked different, and she watched, fascinated, as the woman's features turned grotesque.

"Ava told me all about how she's your new assistant and how the timing is just perfect, because you're going to need lots of help once the baby comes," Sally said. "Can I assume that the handsome young man I saw leaving your motel room is the lucky father?"

"You leave him out of this," Emma Jean said.

"I can't guarantee that. I'm a journalist. We write about whoever strikes our fancy. One tiny question, though, Emma Jean. Where does your husband, the winemaker, fit into all of this?"

Sally's face had taken on an especially unsettling expression. Emma Jean figured out what was different—the woman's mouth moved, but nothing else in her face did. She'd been Botoxed. And even though Emma Jean tried her best to think kind thoughts, all that came to mind was that Sally now looked like a clown.

"It's none of your goddamned business. C'mon, Ava, we've got to get going."

Ava hopped down off the wall and ran to Emma Jean. "Bye, Mrs. Marx."

Sally called after them as they were a few yards away. "I'm starting to think that I'm writing about the wrong author," she said.

Emma Jean couldn't help it. She paused and glanced back.

"Seems like your secrets may be even more fascinating than Marielle's," Sally said.

Emma Jean hustled Ava into the car and peeled out of the parking lot, hoping some noxious fumes would overcome Sally and send her into a coma that could only be treated at a hospital far, far away.

Chapter Fifteen

Kick Her When She's Down

Emma Jean slid her credit card back in her wallet and picked her decaf, non-fat latte up off the counter at the Mountain Karma coffee shop. She was living on credit cards these days, and trying her best not to think about it. Aunt Cleo had said she could use the gallery credit card if she needed to and pay her back later, but she hadn't seemed to be able to find it. Besides, that just wouldn't feel right. Emma Jean had earned her living by the word since she was a young woman, and one way or another, she'd continue. She set her coffee down on a table in the back room, where she'd arranged her laptop. A fire glowed in a river rock fireplace next to her, taking the chill off the cold October morning. If she weren't so damned depressed, it would be a cheery, cozy place to sit.

But she was feeling blue. Doing penance was no fun; there was just no two ways about it. She loved Sun Valley, yes she did, but it had a remote feel, more so now that Aunt Cleo had flown the coop. More to the point, she'd flown to Seattle, to tend some crisis at her other gallery.

"No, you can't leave me," Emma Jean said when Cleo told her the news. "I can't handle the gallery alone. And besides, I need you for emotional support in this trying time. Why do you have to go?"

Cleo had patted Emma Jean on her cheek. "Don't be so dramatic, darling; you'll be fine. I must go. Eloise has upped and quit on us. Lynette is here. You'll be fine."

Emma Jean made a scoffing noise. "Like she's any help. That woman deigns to put in an appearance about once a week if I'm lucky. Can't your Seattle staff cope without you?"

Emma Jean had been sitting, wrapped in a brightly colored, hand-knit afghan, on the back deck of Cleo's condo beside a pot of geraniums. Cleo had just brought her a cup of hot tea, which she now sipped.

"Oh, but Eloise is vital to the day-to-day operations of the gallery. Absolutely vital. Without her, they are unmoored." Cleo sank onto the deck chair, her purple and magenta caftan fluttering around her. "Seattle's not like Sun Valley, darling. That location is always busy, and sometimes, they simply can't handle it."

Emma Jean gazed at Cleo. Something in the tone of her voice sounded funny. She was also fidgeting, fingering the chiffon of her get-up, rattling the ice cubes in her glass of bourbon.

"You're staring at me," Cleo said and then belted the rest of her drink.

"I *am* staring at you, because you are acting weird. What is going on with you, Aunt Cleo?"

Cleo's glass thunked on the table. "I haven't the faintest idea what you are talking about. Nothing is going on except a crisis with my employees."

"Are you leaving because of me?"

"I need another drink." Cleo rose and kissed Emma Jean on the head as she passed. "Contrary to popular opinion, darling, the world does not revolve around you."

Even so, Emma Jean hadn't gotten over the feeling that Cleo wanted distance from her. Now, in the coffee shop, she stared at the fire and wondered why Cleo was acting so oddly. Cleo had abandoned her to face all of her issues, all alone, in this remote, cold town. Ah well. Emma Jean would cope somehow; she always did.

She clicked over to her website and decided to check on her blog. Perhaps reading a few comments from adoring fans might cheer her up. Yes, that was the ticket. Reminding herself of her incredible fan base always, always made her happy. But wait, what was this? A nasty comment about her pregnancy?

Emma Jean stared at the computer screen and read a comment attached to her post titled, *It Is Beautiful Up Here In the Mountains*, in which she had waxed poetic about her writing retreat in Idaho, which was how she was billing it to her fans. *Burn Emma Jean Sullivan Novels* was the subject line. *I read your stupid novels and they helped me decide it was okay to be childless. Now you're having a baby. Meanwhile, I'm old and alone. It's your fault I'm miserable! I'm burning all your books. Right now, even!!!* And another one: *Thanks to you I decided it was okay not to get pregnant, and now I hear that you are having a baby and I could just cry. Thanks to you, I've missed my chance. Thanks to you, I'm stuck with nobody to take care of me in my old age. I'll never read another one of your novels again.*

Had she written a blog post in her sleep wherein she confessed her pregnancy? Oh God, it had to have been Sally Marx's doing. But where and how? Emma Jean scrolled down further, through the dozens of comments. Ah, thank you Kristin, who had written *I must have missed something. What are you guys talking about? Emma Jean Sullivan would never, ever betray us by getting pregnant.* Well, that last part wasn't so good, but at least she could follow the link the next commenter provided and find the source of this vicious rumor.

Could she handle this by calling it a vicious rumor? That might work, except for the wee small problem that it was true. Emma Jean waited for the site to load and there it was—Sally Marx writing an essay about her time in the beautiful mountain town of Sun Valley, where she happened to keep running into the pregnant baby-hating novelist Emma Jean Sullivan. It wasn't just some rinky-dink website either, it was *Salon*.

Oh God, the public humiliation part of her penance was coming true. What should she do now? Calling Riley was the first thing that came to mind, but it was 10 o'clock in the morning, nine his time, and he'd still be asleep. But perhaps she could email him. And maybe if she opened her inbox, she'd have a message from him. And that might help the double time pounding of her heart.

But instead, it made her heart pound triple time. Because her inbox flooded with dozens more angry emails, with subject lines like *I'm boycotting Emma Jean Sullivan novels*. She watched them swamp her inbox, like the cavalry marching to war, then opened one and scanned it. Apparently her fan club site, run by the dumpy but loyal Margaret, had gotten hold of the news and was trumpeting it all over the place.

Emma Jean turned her computer off, slammed the laptop shut and scooted back from the table so fiercely the only other customer in the room looked up from the book he was reading.

"Everything okay?" he said. He was one of those tan, fit, and handsome ski-boys that hung out everywhere in town.

"I'm just late for work," Emma Jean said, which was technically true, since she was supposed to have opened the gallery fifteen minutes ago. And, oh crap, the Hemingway Festival started this week and Cleo had told her to expect a few more customers than usual.

She trudged the two blocks to the gallery feeling like her head was going to explode, even though the air was crisp and clean and the day was sunny. Little Claire seemed to echo her thoughts and started a jerky little rumba inside her. Breathe, she told herself. She paused in front of the gallery and stared at Mt. Baldy, which never failed to calm her. But just as she was taking a deep, cleansing breath, the way the Taoists did, a group of tourists walked up. Damn Hemingway Festival.

But at least there were four of them, an older couple and a young one, maybe mother and father and daughter and son-in-law, or vice-versa, and they were more interested in conversing with each other than talking to her. She set up her laptop on the front desk with the view of the mountain. Should she pop Riley an email and let him know what was going on? She should call Angela, her agent, for sure, even though the woman never deigned to take her calls any more.

Out of the corner of her eye, she noted yet more customers walking through the door. Why did the gallery have to get busy on this day of all days, for God's sake, when she needed time to *think*, and decide what to do? And then one of the customers from the first group—the cute young woman—walked up to the desk.

"Excuse me? I have a question about an artist? He's a sculptor? Just starting out? I saw some of his work at a group show in L.A. and I've been looking for more ever since." She looked down at a piece of paper with a name written on it, and looked back up. "His name is Riley Atkinson."

Emma Jean dropped her purple fountain pen on the floor, and the young woman bent to pick it up.

"Here you go," she said, and handed the pen back to Emma Jean. "He does, like, big, monumental pieces in metal."

"Oh," Emma Jean said. She stared at the girl, who had short, black, spiky hair and wore big hoop earrings that swayed every time she moved her head, which seemed to be a lot.

"So I guess you haven't heard of him, then," she said.

"No," Emma Jean said. "No, sorry, I haven't."

It was terrible for her karma to lie, and she was no doubt setting the cause of her penance back by leaps, to say nothing of her Campaign to be Kind, but she couldn't help it. She was just so shocked. Riley, an artist in a group show? He talked about his interest in art constantly. He talked about his interest in art history and how he wished he had time to make art, emphasis on the wishing part. And she knew he'd spent a year at art school. (*Where my brain exploded with all the possibilities life holds*, he'd written in an email.) But Emma Jean had thought that Riley's interest in art was theoretical. Being an airplane mechanic vaguely interested in art and being an artist good enough to have shows were two very different things. It made him into a whole different person, one she wasn't sure she knew. Really, how well did she know him? Long, glorious emails were one thing, but truly *knowing* a person took more. And shouldn't she *know* the father of her baby in more than the biblical sense?

Emma Jean grabbed her phone. She didn't care what time it was in L.A., or if Riley were asleep, or if Carolina was home. She had to talk to him, now. But then the spiky-haired girl wafted by, looking at paintings, and Emma Jean realized she couldn't very well call Riley when she had just told the girl she didn't know him. Besides, it wouldn't look good to be hollering into a cell phone while people looked at art.

And so she waited. She waited while the initial group of tourists meandered about—didn't these people have anything better to do? She waited while more people came and went. She waited and tried to concentrate on something, anything other than the fact that the world now knew she was pregnant and that Riley was...what was he? Well, he was less than honest with her.

But should she be mad at him because he had been less than honest with her in a *good* way? After all, Riley being an artist was a good thing. But shouldn't her lover want to share every bit of his life with her? They could have been having delicate conversations about marketing art, for instance. Emma Jean pouted at the thought of what they'd missed. And then she remembered the larger issue, that Sally Marx had outed her pregnancy, and the world now knew she was not who she said she was and that she would never, ever sell another novel as long as lived.

The afternoon wore on, as her brain made a constant Riley—artist—pregnancy loop worthy of a roller coaster. She downloaded emails a couple times but that just made her feel worse, as they were all from angry fans. Oh Lord, what was she going to do? Her fans hated her. Her career was finished. Done, finito, vamoosed. Her husband was spending what little money she had left. And now it turned out she couldn't even seek solace in thoughts of her lover, because she didn't know who in the hell he was. Finally, the small stream of customers abated, and Emma Jean punched Riley's number into her cell phone.

"Hey, I was just going to try to call you. We need to talk, baby."

"You bet we need to talk," Emma Jean said. "Why didn't you bother to tell me you were a good enough artist to be in a show?"

"Whoa, hold up there. What are you talking about?"

"I'm talking about the fact that you've been lying to me."

"I have never lied to you, Emma Jean, and I never will. I told you I was an artist the first night we met. And I've continually expressed my interest in it in multiple emails."

"You told me you were interested in art. There's a difference."

"In your mind, maybe. What is this about, anyway? Why are you asking me about my art now? You've never shown the least bit of interest."

"How was I supposed to show interest when I barely even knew about it?" Emma Jean watched a man walk by on the sidewalk in front of the gallery and pause to look in the window. She willed him not to come in, and miraculously he turned away.

"Look, it's no big deal. I do metal sculpture. I told you that. I've had my work in a couple group shows, and that is it. Now, listen, Emma Jean—"

"Oh God."

"What?" Riley said.

She held the phone down at her side and stared at the massive painting that was featured on the front gallery wall. She had just had the most horrible thought ever.

"Are you okay? " Riley was shouting into the phone.

"I don't think so."

"Oh God, is it the baby? Hang up and call 911."

"It's not the baby, it's you. It's you, Riley! You used me! You used me because you had read all about me, and you knew that Aunt Cleo ran a gallery and you thought maybe she could give you a show. Admit it, Riley. That's the only reason you even came to the stupid book signing."

"Whoa there, Emma Jean. Calm down, okay? I don't even know what you are talking about."

"The book signing! When we met! You made it look all so casual—"

"Because it was," Riley said. "I came to it to buy Carolina your book. Which she loved, by the way."

"—when really you had it all planned, and you only came to seduce me to get to Aunt Cleo."

"How do you come up with this shit? Jesus, Emma Jean, you make it sound like I set out on purpose to use you."

"But you did! Admit it! God, could I be more humiliated? I wish I'd never laid eyes on you."

"I didn't know you had an aunt who ran a gallery when I came to the signing that night. What does it matter? It's not like I've been bugging her to give me a show. I've never talked to her in my life. Calm down, would you?"

"How can I, when all my lover is interested in is his flippin' career!"

"Listen to me. I wasn't on a mission to seduce you to get to your aunt that night at the bookstore."

"Really?" Emma Jean said, desperately wanting to believe him.

"Honest. Scout's honor."

"You were a boy scout?"

"No, but it always sounds good. Emma Jean, we need to talk."

"I know." She sighed. "It's awful, Riley, the whole world now knows."

"What are you talking about?"

A young couple of the tan and Nordic type walked by and Emma Jean held her breath until they cleared the gallery entrance without turning in. "About me being pregnant. Everyone knows. My fans, the fan club. My inbox is going crazy. So's my blog. It's awful, darling, just awful."

"And how did this happen?"

"Sally Marx. She's a *Vanity Fair* reporter who's been sniffing around."

There was a long silence. "My name didn't come up, did it?"

"Oh for God's sakes, Riley! Is that all you can think about? Jesus, here I am in my hour of need and all you are worried about is whether you are implicated or not. I am appalled. Shocked and appalled."

"Oh, baby, don't go there."

"Don't oh baby me," Emma Jean said. "Your lack of support for me in this trying time is truly stunning. I just don't know what to think."

"Emma Jean—"

"I just wonder if I should even be talking to you. Honestly, Riley. I've been trying to be good and not take your calls—"

"You called me—"

"And maybe it's better if I don't talk to you. I mean, this clearly is just not working. I'm so distraught, and you are so not there for me."

Emma Jean heard Riley draw a long, ragged breath. "Honey, this isn't easy for me to say, but I have to say it."

Oh God, she did not like the tone of his voice, even if he did call her honey.

"I think we need to take a break."

"Like a break from this phone call, right? Can you talk later?"

"No, Emma Jean. I mean a break from our relationship."

Emma Jean groped with her hand behind her to pull the chair so that she could sit without toppling over. When she'd said it was better if she didn't talk to him, she'd still wanted him to be available, for Christ's sakes.

"You mean like taking a *break* break? Like breaking up?"

"Yes."

He couldn't mean this. "But I'm carrying your baby."

"I know. And I am going to do everything I can to support and help you with it. But it isn't right. Our relationship isn't right. I'm married to Carolina, and I need to see if she and I can make it work. I can't do that as long as I'm in a relationship with you."

"But I thought you didn't like her very much," Emma Jean said.

"I don't. But I did once, and maybe I can get back to that place. I have to try, for Noah's sake."

"What about Claire's sake?"

"I told you. I'll support you in every way I can. I just can't be in a relationship with you right now. Believe me, baby, this is the last thing on earth I want to do. I've been trying to do it for weeks—ever since before you came to L.A., actually—but I just couldn't bring myself to. But now's the time. I'm so sorry, Emma Jean, but it's over."

"You're ending it? You're ending the flippin' relationship? But I'm in love with you!" Emma Jean shrieked.

"That's the hell part of it," Riley said. "I'm in love with you, too."

Which was when she pushed the red button on her phone and threw it across the room, where it landed by the gallery's front door. She sat for a long time, waiting for the tears to come. But they never did. She just felt empty. She stared at Mt. Baldy, at the huge, brilliantly colored painting hanging on the wall, at the front sidewalk. No more Riley in her life. No more of his touch, of his laugh, of the way he looked at her sideways when he was teasing her. No more avoiding his phone calls until she couldn't take it anymore and then hearing his voice like salve on all her wounds.

Across the room, her phone rang. At least it still worked, though what did it matter, since Riley would no longer be calling her? It was probably just an angry fan, or Margaret, her fan club president. She ignored it. Then it started ringing again. Sighing, Emma Jean got up. But by the time she'd walked across the room, it had stopped ringing.

Not that it mattered, but she checked to see who had called. Maybe it was Riley, calling to say he was wrong? Maybe he was calling back to tell her he had reconsidered and was leaving Carolina that very second to come flying to her side. But when she picked up the phone, caller ID read *Angela Devine Lit* and then trailed off. Flippin' A! Angela calling her at long last! How many times had Emma Jean placed a call to her with unique and unusual promotional ideas for *Winemaker's Wife,* only to be told that Angela was busy?

And she hadn't left a message. Oh well, she wouldn't have been able to put on a perky face for Angela anyway. Lord, could anything else go wrong today? She was doing her penance for her sin of adultery, that was all there was to it. Though the penance was more like severe punishment, and even that didn't begin to define it. Something more along the lines of devastated or destroyed or annihilated would be more fitting. Because how could she live without Riley? How could she endure it?

Emma Jean paced the gallery, phone in hand. Here she was, all alone in this godforsaken mountain town, without a single person she could talk to or confide in. Stuck tending a gallery for a bunch of yahoo tourists, she might add. Oh, to see a friendly face right now. Or hear a friendly voice. But wait. She could call Marielle. Because that was exactly what friends did in times of need—they called each other. She wouldn't be able to tell her about Riley, which was a drawback, but she could say she was just having a bad day and needed a friend to cheer her up.

Emma Jean picked up her phone, one side of which was now dented, and scrolled through looking for the number. When finally she found it, she pressed the button and smiled in anticipation. Yes, calling her friend Marielle would be just the ticket.

"Hello?"

It wasn't Marielle, but Julia, which Emma Jean hadn't counted on. Still and all, she persevered, chatted with Julia for the requisite minute, and then asked for Marielle.

"Oh, she's not here, Emma Jean. She's in New York, appearing on a bunch of TV shows. *Good Morning America* and *The Today Show.* And *The View.* That one is airing tomorrow; you should watch it."

It was all Emma Jean could do to not throw the phone again. She made appropriate impressed noises and got off the phone quickly. Then she sat and stared at it, dejected. Everybody else in the entire world had a thriving career except for her. But, wait. She could call Trish! Wasn't that what assistants were for? Plus, now that Trish was no longer going to be her assistant, maybe she could be Emma Jean's friend. She was always kind to Trish, wasn't she? Except for those rare moments when she called Trish Patty, which Trish hated. But Emma Jean would even be willing to stop that now. She punched her number into the phone, remembering too late that Trish's psychological evaluations generally bugged the hell out of her. But she needed some solace now, and even the annoying psychological version would do.

"Why hello Emma Jean, how are you today?"

Perhaps this had been a terrible miscalculation. Trish sounded abnormally perky.

"Awful. I'm lousy, I'm miserable, I'm wretched."

"Oh, I'm so sorry. Do tell what's wrong."

And Emma Jean did tell her, even though Trish did not sound the least bit sorry. When she was done relaying her story there was a moment of silence.

"So? What should I do?" Emma Jean demanded.

"I hate to break it to you, but I don't see that there is much you can do," Trish said. "The news of the pregnancy was bound to come out sooner or later. And Riley...well, Riley is just doing the right thing."

"But I don't want him to be right unless it involves me!" Emma Jean wailed.

"Don't you want him to be a good man? To be all that he can be? He is doing something incredibly difficult, Emma Jean, particularly because it's you he loves. Don't ask him to be less than he is."

She should never have called Trish. Emma Jean had to admit the woman had a point; it just wasn't what she wanted to hear.

"Oh, just a minute," Trish said. "Come in!"

"Who's there?" Emma Jean said.

"Connor."

"Connor? As in my stepdaughter Julia's husband?"

"Your stepdaughter Julia's soon-to-be-ex-husband."

"What's he doing there?"

But all Emma Jean heard was a giggle.

"Trish? Are you there?"

"Sorry, I'm back."

"What is going on?" Emma Jean demanded.

"I've been helping Connor organize his business." There was another giggle, this one lower and throatier and carrying a definite hint of sexual tension. "Remember when he came over that day and you suggested it?"

Vaguely she recalled the day. "Is that all you're doing?"

"Well, not exactly."

Emma Jean heard a deep voice in the background, and then Trish laughed again. Had she ever heard her assistant laugh so much? She didn't think so. "You two are together, aren't you?"

"Uh, yes, you could say that."

Clearly Trish was completely distracted by Connor tickling her or kissing her or doing God knows what else. "Listen, Trish, I'll let you go and have your fun now," Emma Jean said. "Don't mind me, even if I am in my hour of need."

"I'll call you later," Trish said. "And quit worrying; everything will be fine."

Worrying was a bit too nice of a word to describe how she felt, which was even worse now that it appeared everyone in the whole world was in love, except for her. No, double worse, she was in love and loved back but she couldn't be with said lover. Could her life get any more pathetic?

"You call this art?" a deep voice boomed.

Yes, apparently life could get worse. A man and a woman had entered the gallery, both dressed in jeans and brand new hiking boots. The woman wore a white down vest that made her look like the Michelin man, and her husband wore a bandanna tied around his neck. Oh, Lord. Emma Jean moved her mouth in what she thought was a smile but she wasn't sure, because she wasn't sure she would ever really know how to smile again. But Emma Jean was well versed in Aunt Cleo's School of Selling Art, which was basically to treat everyone graciously and with kindness, i.e., as if they had money. And even though her heart was breaking, she would attempt to be helpful and kind.

Then a glorious thought burst through the gloom that surrounded her. Selling a painting would earn her a commission. Cleo had gone on and on about that, in what Emma Jean thought was an attempt to make babysitting the gallery more palatable. And now that her checking account was empty, and she was living on credit, the thought made her perk up. Not only that, selling a painting would make Cleo happy, and that might go a long ways toward breaking down the strange wall that had grown up between them.

And so Emma Jean smiled and nodded and answered their questions about art and artists and tried her best to be charming, doing a very good job of it, if she did say so herself. But despite her valiant efforts, she simply could not get the couple—their names were Patty and Ray—to commit. Ray wanted more information on the artist, a resume, and a list of places he'd shown, more specifics on the materials he used to assemble his work, everything short of an actual birth certificate, as far as Emma Jean could tell. "It's how he made his millions," Patty had whispered loudly before they left. "He's always very, very careful about any transaction."

"Damn right," Ray had boomed.

Emma Jean promised to find and assemble the information for them. After they left, she was almost sorry, because as long as they were in the gallery, it forced her to think about other things. Immediately her mind turned again to Riley, and then to the tragedy of her turncoat fans. What she really needed at this precise moment was a drink. Oh Lord how she needed a drink. Emma Jean stood in the middle of the floor of the gallery and had an epiphany—God was definitely a man, because if God were a woman, she would have arranged it so that females could drink during pregnancy. A female God would *so* have made it okay to drink.

Chapter Sixteen

Her Price is Wrong

"Please, Lynette, I'm so desperate I don't know what to do," Emma Jean said into her cell phone. She was standing in the kitchen of Aunt Cleo's condo, drinking herbal tea and trying to convince the gallery's so-called employee to open for her, because she felt awful. Just awful. She'd spent a sleepless night tossing and turning with Claire kicking once in a while for emphasis. All she could think, over and over again, was no Riley, no Riley, no Riley, no. The chorus to this verse was no career, no career, no career, no. And finally, no friends or fans, no friends or fans, no. Sleeplessness was not good for pregnant women, she was learning. It was *especially* not good for old, pregnant women.

Lynette was simpering on and on about some terribly important thing she had to do in Twin Falls, a two-hour drive away, and as far as Emma Jean could tell, that terribly important thing mostly meant going shopping. Emma Jean stared out the window as she listened. Aunt Cleo's condo was located near the Sun Valley resort, a mile or so away from the actual town of Ketchum. From the kitchen, Emma Jean had a view of Dollar Mountain, the place where the bunny slope ski runs were located. Dollar Mountain looked like a 3-D postcard, with the ski lifts zigzagging across its flanks, the roofs of Elkhorn Village at its base lit by the morning sun.

The kitchen itself, like the rest of the condo, was seventies style. Plain oak cabinets outlined a gold refrigerator on top of which were stacked cereal and granola boxes. Formica countertops and a nondescript brown floor morphed into white walls and a tan carpet in the rest of the place. But the walls were covered in amazing art by Cleo's favorite artists and small sculptural pieces of glass or metal sat in bookshelves and on podiums. Between the art and the views of the mountains, it didn't really matter what the bones of the place looked like, though Cleo talked often of updating it.

And at the moment, Emma Jean didn't care one whit about Cleo's condo or Lynette's excuses. She was tired and upset, and she would give anything, maybe even her unborn baby, for a cup of strong caffeinated French Roast coffee. She was going to need something to get her through this day, seeing as how Lynette couldn't deign to actually do her job. Emma Jean's phone started beeping, signaling another call coming in, about the time that Lynette was launching into a description of the lingerie she needed to purchase. Emma Jean said goodbye in a manner far more gracious than Lynette deserved. Apparently there was a God after all, because it was Angela, her agent.

For once, Angela was trying hard to reach Emma Jean. Was it to inform her that *Wife* had suddenly hit the bestseller list? Or better, that Oprah had chosen it?

"Angela, hello, how *are* you?" Emma Jean hoped that her delicate emphasis on the word *are* conveyed just the right tone of intimacy.

"Oh, hello, this is Inga. May I speak with Emma Jean, please?"

"Inga? Inga? Who the hell are you? I thought it was Angela calling."

"I am Inga, calling on behalf of Angela," Inga said, in a stilted vaguely Russian sounding voice. But wasn't Inga a Scandinavian name?

"Well, now you've reached me, you can put Angela on the line," Emma Jean said. "I'll hold."

"Angela is busy."

"C'mon, Inga, Angela is never too busy for me. Put her on."

"Is busy," Inga said. "I will tell you her message."

Is busy? What the hell was this? Was Angela running some kind of halfway house for Slavic refugees? Maybe she'd changed careers and not bothered to tell Emma Jean and that was why Angela refused her calls.

"Says you must talk to Sally Marx."

"What?" Emma Jean was so busy with her image of buxom blonde Angela cavorting in the midst of the Serbian émigrés that it took her a minute to track.

"Is good for publicity. Angela says frankly, you need any kind of publicity you can get at the moment," Inga added helpfully.

"Listen, clearly you don't know anything about publicity. I mean, I hate to be rude, Inga, but you can barely speak the language. So just put Angela on, and we'll get all this cleared up."

"Angela says give Sally an interview. Explain to her about baby."

"I'm supposed to sell out my close friend Marielle?" Emma Jean ignored the little voice inside that said she'd already done this. "And talk to Sally Marx about the baby when she has already blabbed about it to the whole flippin' world? I'm supposed to happily talk to the woman who has made my life a living hell? Sell out myself *and* Marielle? I don't think so, Inga. And you can tell Angela that, okay? In case you don't know the correct American vernacular, its fu—" Emma Jean stopped herself just in time. Lord, what was she thinking, about to tell Angela to fuck off? She took a deep breath. *Be Zen*, she ordered herself.

"Inga, doll, do me a favor. Just tell Angela that she and I need to discuss this issue personally, okay?"

"Is good. I will do."

"And can I give you a little tip while I have you on the phone? In this country we. Do. Not. Begin. Sentences. With. The. Word. Is. That's all. Thanks, doll."

Emma Jean pushed the red end button and blew a long stream of air out. Oh God, she felt like crap. And still she had to go open the gallery and sit there and be nice all day, without benefit of caffeine. And now she had to add Angela to her list of worries. But then Emma Jean had a lovely thought. Maybe she could find the information for Ray and Patricia and manage to sell a painting. Yes, that was the ticket. She would throw her overwhelming feelings of sadness and misery into doing something positive. She would sell Ray on the damn painting, yes she would, which would make Aunt Cleo happy and replenish her bank account, all in one fell swoop. She managed to get herself out the door on that invigorating thought.

Emma Jean parked her car near the gallery. No more rental car for her; she was now driving Cleo's sturdy Volvo. She walked the two blocks to Mountain Karma for her daily cup of decaf, thus getting at least a little bit of exercise. Small houses and buildings housed a variety of shops and restaurants, and most of them were decorated with white lights that hadn't yet been turned off for the day. Sun Valley was a sleepy town this time of year, and it didn't wake up until mid-morning. The day had suddenly turned cloudy and the air felt very, very cold as she walked. Emma Jean wondered if it would snow. Maybe a blizzard would blow in, and she wouldn't have to worry about the gallery.

There was no time to linger at the café, as Emma Jean's phone conversations had made her late. Outside Mountain Karma, a fairly long flight of steps led back to the street, and Emma Jean carefully made her way down them, balancing her messenger bag over her shoulder and her coffee cup in hand. At the bottom of the stairs, she nearly collided with someone and had to hold her coffee out in order to keep from spilling it.

The person she had nearly run into was a man, a tall, handsome, older man. Emma Jean stepped back and squinted up at him. He seemed vaguely familiar, with his full head of silver hair and impeccable dress—neatly pressed jeans with a white shirt tucked into them beneath a dark leather jacket and a wool scarf wrapped around his neck. She kept staring at him, and suddenly it came to her—he was Bob Barker, the former host of *The Price is Right*. Emma Jean knew lots of celebrities had houses in the valley, and Aunt Cleo had pointed out the spreads of Clint Eastwood and Tom Hanks, but she didn't know that Bob Barker came here, too.

"Hello, Emma Jean."

Wow, Bob Barker knew her name! Maybe he'd read her books. He took a step closer to her, and suddenly it all became clear. This man wasn't Bob Barker at all. He was *Bob* Bob, her father Bob, the Fake Christian, Bob, the evil adulterer.

"Dad?" said Emma Jean. Then she winced. He might be her damned father biologically, but she had made a sacred vow not to call him by that name. How long had it been since she'd seen him? At least two years, maybe three. And the last time they'd been together had been mercifully brief, at the funeral of a cousin. "What are you doing here?"

"Visiting Cleo," Bob said. He looked at her expectantly. "I was planning to stop by the gallery to see you, so isn't it a nice surprise that we've run into each other here?"

Emma Jean shifted her heavy bag on her shoulder. "You missed Aunt Cleo. She left a couple days ago. But I bet you could catch a flight to Seattle this afternoon if you hurry. And it's a good thing you didn't come by the gallery because I'm terribly busy when I'm there."

"I know she's gone." Bob shook his head. Not a hair moved, even with the breeze that had brought the clouds in. He wouldn't use hairspray, would he? "I'm planning to stick around here a few days anyway."

Emma Jean was having a hard time connecting the dots. "Why are you here if you knew she was gone?"

Bob waved his hand and turned toward the front window. He took a deep, exaggerated breath. "The mountain air is invigorating, don't you think?"

"The mountain air is damn cold," Emma Jean said. "Now, if you'll excuse me, I have to go open the gallery."

But Bob didn't move. Despite herself, Emma Jean stared at her father. His skin was surprisingly smooth and deeply tanned for his age—he had to be at least as old as Cleo. Maybe he'd had Botox or plastic surgery. Or maybe it was just good genes. Hopefully, that boded well for her. When Emma Jean quit staring at his skin, she looked to his eyes and was surprised what she saw there—intense sadness and longing. For what?

Maybe it was the pregnancy hormones, but suddenly she knew the answer. *For her.* Emma Jean shivered and grabbed the stair railing for support, as suddenly she felt light-headed.

"I'll come with you," Bob said. "I've helped Cleo open before."

"Why'd they let you out of Alabama? Did the auto parts store go down the tubes? And I thought you were running some fake church in Eulalie on the weekends."

"Preaching has always been my avocation, Emma Jean. The auto parts business is my vocation. But I've sold my stores to return to my true love and study theology. I've got a couple months before I begin classes, so I came here. To see Cleo."

"But she's not here, remember?"

"I am here for other reasons, also."

He still had that look of longing in his eyes. And the more he talked, the more she felt the soothing cadences of his speech with its vague southern accent wrapping around her. Like marshmallows melting in hot chocolate. Or more to the point, like sugar in the ghastly sweet tea all southerners seemed to prefer. She found her heart pounding. Emma Jean stepped out of the way of a Mountain Karma customer.

"And what was the other reason?"

"Why, to see you, of course."

Emma Jean stared up at her father, the man whose adultery genes she had apparently inherited.

"We have a saying at our church," Bob continued. "God wants you to be his best friend. That's how I feel about you, Emma Jean. If I can't be your father, I want to at least be your friend."

"You know, Bob, all this churchy stuff kind of rubs me the wrong way, seeing as how you killed my mother. What do your parishioners think of that?"

Bob put his hands in front of him as if hushing a noisy congregation. "Do we have to have the same argument every time we talk? You know your mother died running with the bulls."

"We don't always have the same argument. How can we? We never talk. And my mother fled to Spain and met a horrible death after she learned you'd been cheating on her. So yes, you did kill her. And now I'm really cold and I'm going to leave."

"Oh, Emma Jean." Bob shook his head sadly and then ran a hand through his thick silver hair. "You of all people should know that stories are never that simple."

The man had no scruples. Now he was playing the story card on her. She had to admit she was just the teeniest bit curious about his side of the story but she wasn't going to bite. No, she was not. Emma Jean started to step away from him but something about the look in his eyes stopped her. Bob was going to be little Claire's grandfather. And wouldn't it be good for Claire to know him?

"I pray for your soul every night," Bob said. "I pray that God will help you to seek forgiveness and accept me back into your life."

"If you'll excuse me, Bob. I have work to do."

"Are you working on your next novel while you babysit the gallery?"

Emma Jean shot him what she hoped was a withering look. "I never speak about my work before it's published."

Bob nodded. "I can respect that. It's how I always felt about writing sermons."

Damn it, she wished he'd quit bringing up things about religion that interested her. She would love to hear how one went about writing a sermon. She was such a babe in the spiritual woods she had absolutely no clue, how one would impart religious knowledge in such a way as to make people want to adhere to it.

"I've really got to get to work now," Emma Jean said.

"Would you like a ride to the gallery?"

Emma Jean shook her head. "No, the walk is good for me, thanks."

Bob nodded and then did a funny thing with his hand, half wave, half salute. "I don't give up easily, Emma Jean. I am one very determined man."

She pondered Bob as she walked past the cute, little dress shop she would visit one day when she wasn't the size of a sumo wrestler. All that crap about forgiveness when he was responsible for the pain of her childhood, not having a mother. She well remembered the day she had learned the truth about her father being an evil, adulterous bastard. The letter from Cleo's friend had been in the box of mementos that Emma Jean had been glancing through after finding it in an office she was helping Cleo organize. She hadn't meant to snoop, but as always, she couldn't help it, she was drawn by the power of the written word. It didn't lay out full details, but enough for Emma Jean to catch the drift and later she'd questioned Cleo to learn more. Cleo had stonewalled, of course, but Emma Jean had managed to construct a basic outline of events in her head.

Her poor, dear, mother Claire had learned about Bob's adultery when she had walked in on him and his malicious, deceitful paramour. Desperate and destroyed, Claire had fled the house in a panic: what would she do now, with a small child to raise? How could she ever appear in public again without feeling shame? How would she ever be able to handle this catastrophe? And then, gloriously, her mother had hit upon an idea—she would flee to Europe. It was tragic and romantic and Emma Jean loved the story, despite it encompassing her own abandonment, because it proved her mother was a woman of verve and élan.

At least those were the thoughts Emma Jean had constructed for her in various scenarios throughout the years. She'd written a variation of that theme in her memoir. No matter what, though, they always ended the same tragic way, with her mother meeting her demise at the horns of a bull. Was she thinking about Emma Jean as she gasped her last breath? Or was Claire remembering the horrible betrayal of her husband?

The hell part of it was that Emma Jean had had a good relationship with Bob before she had learned the truth about his ways. He hadn't been able to raise her as a child, because he had to make a living, and besides everyone knew that fathers made lousy sole caretakers. Anyway, Bob had been attentive, sending money and presents, and visiting often, even after she and Cleo moved to Seattle. She had to admit that she sometimes missed it. Okay, sometimes she missed *him*. And it was the tiniest bit thrilling to see him and hear about his church. Emma Jean shook her head. No, she couldn't allow such thoughts to enter her head. He was the bastard who had caused her mother's death.

She was pondering these profound issues when she drew up even with the gallery and saw a knot of customers clustered by the front door, waiting for her to open. Oh, for Christ's sake. Couldn't the world just leave her alone? She had so much to think about, besides even her father. There was the loss of Riley, and her career, and the fact that, as far as she could tell, besides her father, everyone in the whole world hated her, including all of her fans and her agent. Here she was in hiding, trying to do penance and the world simply wouldn't let her. Plus she wanted to search for information on the art to encourage Ray to buy a piece. Emma Jean sighed, smiled and nodded at the customers, and unlocked the door.

There was a steady stream of customers all morning. Finally, toward late morning, there was a lull. She wondered if she could get away with locking the door and sneaking upstairs. But then the phone rang. Let them leave a message, she decided. The gallery had no caller ID and Emma Jean hated not knowing who was calling. She ignored it and headed toward the spiral staircase. No sooner had it quit ringing when it started again. She ignored it again. And it started ringing again.

What if it was Angela, calling to tell her the phone call with Inga had been a terrible mistake? What if it was Riley, calling to tell her he was at the airport that very minute and she needed to come pick him up? She lunged for the phone, said "Zelch Gallery, this is Emma Jean," in her crisp, efficient, art gallery voice, and realized as she heard an unfamiliar voice on the other end that neither Angela nor Riley had the gallery phone number.

"Hello? Yes? This is Betsy at the Hemingway school and we need you to come pick up Ava right away."

Chapter Seventeen
Mean Girls

Emma Jean pulled Cleo's sturdy Volvo into a *Driver Remain at Wheel* spot in the parking lot of the Hemingway School and cut the engine. She angled her head so she could see the one-story school that looked like any other elementary school in the world save for its location near the base of the mountain. Emma Jean took a deep breath, opened her car door, and closed it again. Took another deep breath and this time managed to open the door and climbed—lumbered was starting to be a better word to describe how she moved—out of the car.

As she walked toward the front door, she was overtaken by a line of schoolchildren and their teacher, apparently returning from recess, despite the cold. Emma Jean paused to let them pass. The boys jumped, scrambled, and punched each other while the girls chattered and whispered. And when they caught sight of her, they chattered and whispered more, and nudged and pointed as well. Jesus, this was what she hated and feared about small children, or even large children—their open curiosity. Not knowing what else to do, Emma Jean smiled and waved, as she would with a group of adults. To her surprise, a couple of the children smiled and waved back, and the teacher did, too.

This wasn't so bad. Maybe she could handle it after all. It wasn't so much the thought of Ava herself that bothered her; it was the idea of being *responsible* for her. Having Ava stowaway on a visit to the doctor's office was one thing. But being the adult in charge of keeping her out of trouble was quite another.

*　*　*

When the secretary had called at the gallery, Emma Jean's first thought had been to say the woman had the wrong number.

"Are you sure it's me you want?" Emma Jean had said.

"Yes, it is. You're Emma Jean Sullivan, right? Could you please come get Ava right now?"

"Um, excuse me? You want me to come pick her up? What about Wendy?"

"She's in Twin Falls." Apparently the entire population of Sun Valley was in Twin Falls that day.

"Isn't there a foster dad in the picture?"

"He works up in Stanley, and he's out in the woods at the moment. That's why Wendy put your name down as the second emergency contact. Ava insisted you were the only other person she'd go with should the eventuality arise. And now it has arisen."

"Is she sick or something? I'm not very good with sick people." Emma Jean had no interest in spending the rest of her day tending an ill Ava. She had no interest in spending the rest of her day with a *well* Ava. Not that the girl wasn't charming in her way, but Jesus God, the child was exhausting.

"Oh, would that she were. Not to wish harm on her, but maybe a minor illness would slow her down. No, Ava is being expelled."

"She's what?"

"She's being expelled."

"I didn't know you could do that for middle school kids. What on earth did she do?"

A long sigh came through the phone. "It would take too long to tell you the whole story. Let's just say she attacked another student. It'll be a miracle if the other family doesn't press charges."

"Oh, Lord," Emma Jean said. "I'll be right there."

And so she had pulled on her heavy wool coat, the one that no longer buttoned over her stomach, her gloves, scarf, and hat and looked up the address of the school on the Internet. Since she was on the computer anyway, she took a brief glance at all three of her email inboxes, just on the off chance that Riley had emailed her, which of course was not the case. But there were still dozens of messages from disgruntled fans coming in, and those had taken a few minutes to download before she could put the computer to sleep and leave.

Inside the school, the halls were lined with children's artwork, and a pile of coats and mittens spilled out of a wood box, atop which was a sign saying *Lost and Found*. A large bulletin board was plastered with flyers for school events and notices of volunteer opportunities and a big black arrow directed all visitors, even parents, to sign in at the office.

A woman sat behind a reception desk and sighed when Emma Jean identified herself. "We thought you'd never get here."

It hadn't taken her that long to arrive, Emma Jean thought. "I hurried."

The woman softened, then identified herself as Betsy, the one who had called, and told her that the other secretary—Emma Jean was surprised the school was big enough to warrant two of them—had just taken Ava to the bathroom.

"Isn't she old enough to go alone?" Emma Jean said.

"Are you kidding? After what she did, we're not letting her out of our sight," Betsy said.

"What exactly happened?"

"Somebody said something that Ava took issue with, and she went after them. Screaming, hitting, biting. Can't get a lot of information out of her about what the other kid said. She can be very stubborn when she wants to."

"Tell me about it. That child has feet of concrete."

"Let me go check and see what is taking so long. I'll be right back." Betsy got up, and Emma Jean watched her walk away. She was overweight but one of those women for whom the moniker "pleasingly plump" had been invented, because she was nicely proportioned and moved gracefully so that on her the extra weight looked like something to be desired, not obsessed over.

Emma Jean glanced around the office while Betsy was gone, and her eyes fell on a large student painting with bright hues, simple shapes, and heavy use of paint curling the edges of the paper. She had a sudden flash of memory, herself at age nine, being called into the office at Margaret Mitchell school in Atlanta, and fearing the worst, only to be told that her painting had been chosen to hang in the school office for a month. Aunt Cleo had been so proud, so certain her beloved niece would become an artist, but instead it was words that had snared her.

"Here we are." Betsy re-entered the office, a scraggly-haired Ava and a mousy woman, presumably the other secretary, in tow. Ava wore a variation of her usual black outfit, this time with a black and white striped shirt over the skirt, along with a black cardigan with a rip in it. A smear of dirt muddied her black tights on one leg, and both of her black Converse were halfway tied and somewhat askew. She glanced at Emma Jean sullenly and then looked away.

"It wasn't my fault," Ava said.

"Why hello to you, too," Emma Jean said.

"Those girls are so stupid they should be arrested," Ava said.

"It's so nice to see you, even under these difficult circumstances. And thank you so much for picking me up, even though I'm sure you have better things to do, like work on your book," Emma Jean said.

Ava rolled her eyes. "You can still write. I'll go to the coffee shop."

"Oh no you won't," Betsy said. "Your days of lollygagging at the coffee shop are over."

Emma Jean *had* been thinking that she would dispatch Ava to the coffee shop as soon as it was politely possible. But she smiled brightly and grabbed Ava's hand. "Come along, darling. Let's go."

Ava snatched her hand away. "Don't call me darling."

Emma Jean shook her head and laughed silently. She had to admit that sometimes Ava reminded her alarmingly of herself.

Ava stonewalled on the drive back to the gallery. No matter what clever way Emma Jean found to ask her about the incident, she only said, "It wasn't my fault," or "Those girls are dumb."

"This is sure going to be a fun afternoon, isn't it?" Emma Jean said as she unlocked the door to the gallery.

Ava shot her a scathing look that could crumble mountains and went ahead of her into the gallery. She plopped down into the corner, next to the fireplace, pulled a spiral notebook and pen out of her backpack, and began writing. Emma Jean turned the gas fireplace on and hovered for a minute. She was uncertain how one treated a child who had just been expelled from school.

"Is there anything I can get you?"

Ava shook her head without looking up and kept writing. Emma Jean applauded the girl's instincts to turn her anger, or whatever it was, to the page. She left Ava to her writing and opened her computer. Perhaps she would do some writing, also. If only she could concentrate on her book, which had proven to be impossible the past few days, what with the weight of events pressing on her. And there was no point in checking email, since there would be nothing from Riley and about five thousand messages from angry fans.

Now of course, when she wished for customers to arrive, there weren't any. The gallery was silent, but for the scratching of Ava's pen across the page. Lord, Emma Jean would love to be able to write as fluently as Ava. She used to do that, all the time. What had happened? Life had happened. Recent events in her life were just the tiniest bit distracting. The next half-hour wore on. By the sound of it, Ava got tons of writing done. Emma Jean spent it reading the latest gossip blogs from Hollywood. After getting thoroughly caught up on the latest celebrity news, she had an epiphany. She walked around the art-hung partition to where Ava sat, still madly writing.

"Hey, do me a favor would you?" Emma Jean said. "How about you move your base of operations up front, where you can keep watch for anybody coming in? I've got some business to attend to upstairs."

Ava shot her another paint-curdling look and took her own sweet time getting up and arranging herself at the desk where Emma Jean usually sat. Emma Jean took it as a good sign that there were no more heavy sighs or disgruntled looks forthcoming. "Just holler if someone comes in, okay?" she said, and scooted off to the stairs before Ava could complain about the arrangement.

Upstairs, Emma Jean blew out a long stream of air in relief. She opened the door to the storeroom, turned on the light, and did a little happy freedom dance. Lord, how did parents do it? How did they deal with recalcitrant children, day in, day out? She'd gone crazy in minutes. But for the moment, she was free.

Now, how to find what she was looking for? A bank of file cabinets sat against the rear wall. The artist's name was Eliot Hartley, and so she looked for the *H* file drawer, pleased with her deductive brilliance. Within seconds, she found a bulging file filled with every bit of information Ray and Patty could want. She tucked the file under her arm and went to close the file drawer, which is when she saw it: a file labeled, in a convoluted Aunt Cleo sort of way, *Her Mother, The One True Story of.*

Oh, God. *The One True Story of Her Mother* was the endless story Aunt Cleo had told her nearly every night as a child. Emma Jean pulled the file out. It was a manila folder, soft with age, and it bulged with pieces of thin, crinkly paper and old newspaper clippings.

Emma Jean picked up a sheaf of onionskin—my God, onionskin, she'd forgotten it existed—paper, three sheets fastened together by a rusty paperclip. It seemed to be notes that Cleo had typed up.

Emma Jean read:

1. Mother was a fairy princess who disappeared when the wicked witch cast a spell on her. Even now, she is struggling to find a way to return to her darling daughter.

2. Mother was a freedom fighter in another country who has been called away to fight for the poor. She missed her daughter terribly but cannot be spared from her duties because she is the best warrior.

3. Mother is a doctor, immunizing the poor, who works in the deepest interior of the African jungle.

4. Mother is a nun with special powers who people come from all over the world to visit.

5. Mother is a teacher in a poor, remote village in Mexico.

At the bottom were several handwritten notations, apparently ideas Aunt Cleo had had and not had time to type up: *Snow queen in Iceland, Eskimo princess, Lucia Queen who must help Santa every year, Cowgirl who can't leave her animals.* Looking at the list was like finding a box of old dolls. She remembered every story, the words on the paper releasing long-dormant memories. Wow. What a lot of work Aunt Cleo had put into these stories.

Emma Jean looked at the second sheet of paper. And sat back in her chair, her mouth hanging open. Because there, typed out, was the whole story of her mother's death, the details of Claire running with the bulls every bit as vivid as Emma Jean remembered from when Cleo told her. But here the story of the bulls—the real one true story of her mother—sat along with all the concocted tales Cleo had come up with through the years. Should Emma Jean read anything into that? She pondered for a moment and then shook her head. No, of course not.

She opened the folder again, but the rest of it seemed to be full of faded newspaper clippings, that were, as far as Emma Jean could tell, inspiration for some of the stories that Cleo had made up. But now her curiosity was stoked, and she went back to the file cabinet to look for more. Divining Cleo's odd style of filing took some work, but eventually she hit upon a series of files labeled with her mother's name. Most of them seemed to contain mementos and scrapbook-type items, and Emma Jean pulled them out so that she could look at them more thoroughly later. At the very back of the file drawer, almost, but not quite hidden was a file labeled, *Her Death, Details of.*

The very first item in it was her mother's death certificate. Emma Jean was about to set it aside with the other things she's found when the line reading *Cause of Death* caught her eye. Because typed neatly in the box were the words *allergic reaction*. What? This didn't make any sense. Her mother died at the horns of a bull.

"I don't understand," she said. "This makes no sense."

"What doesn't?"

Emma Jean startled and looked up.

Ava stood at the door. In her interest in her mother's papers, Emma Jean had momentarily forgotten about the girl.

"I'm hungry," Ava said. "I never got to eat lunch."

"We'll deal with that in just a minute," Emma Jean said.

"I'm hungry now."

"I'm in the middle of something."

"You're just sitting there looking at a bunch of stupid old stuff."

"It's not stupid, it's about my family."

"Oh." Ava perched on the edge of the long work table and peered at the clippings and papers in the file. "This is ancient."

"Uh-huh." Emma Jean answered absently. She stared at the death certificate, trying to make sense of it. Her mother had died at the horns of a bull, not from an allergic reaction. She was certain of it. Emma Jean stared at the paper, but no matter how long she looked at it, it still didn't make any sense. Finally, she thought to look further in the folder. Next up she found a toxicology report from a lab in Atlanta. Unfortunately, she couldn't read it, because it looked as if someone had spilled water or coffee on it, blurring the words beyond legibility.

This was not at all the story that Aunt Cleo had told her. And furthermore, dying from an allergic reaction was incredibly lame. Emma Jean did the only thing she could think to do—she reached for her phone and dialed Cleo's number.

"Oh for crap's sake, I am dying of hunger here, and you are making a phone call?" Ava said.

Emma Jean pointed at Ava. "If you ever want to eat again, you'll be quiet for a minute." But it didn't matter, because of course Cleo didn't pick up. She tried the Seattle gallery, and nobody there knew where she was. So she called Cleo's cell again and left a message saying she had questions about her mother's death, and she needed to speak to her immediately.

"Your mother died?" Ava said when Emma Jean hung up. Apparently a mother's death trumped hunger.

"Uh-huh."

"What's this?" Ava said. She had her finger on the onionskin sheets of paper on which Cleo had typed up stories.

"It's a list of story ideas," Emma Jean explained. And then she told Ava how Aunt Cleo had told her the never-ending tale of *The One True Story of Her Mother*.

"But didn't you want to know the truth about your mother?"

"I thought I did know the truth," Emma Jean said. "Aunt Cleo made all this stuff up to make sure I felt okay about it. But I'm beginning to think she made up what I thought was the truth, also."

"Oh," Ava said and fell silent. She had a very high, wide forehead and Emma Jean could practically see her little brain processing.

After a few moments, she spoke again. "Weren't you sad you didn't have your mother?"

Emma Jean shook her head. "Not really. That sounds terrible, I guess, but remember, I was really little when my mother died. I missed her at first, I think. But I always had Aunt Cleo. And she was about the best mother you could imagine."

Ava looked at the sheets of onionskin paper, her brow furrowed. "What about your father?"

"Now that is an entirely different subject," Emma Jean said. She pointed at Ava. "You, however, get points for being brilliant, because perhaps good ole Bob the evil adulterer could answer some of my questions."

Emma Jean reached for her phone.

"Are you going to call him?"

"Oh shit," Emma Jean said. "I can't. I don't have his number." She had fended off all of Cleo's attempts to give her Bob's number, even going so far as to erase it from her cell after that time he'd called her in when she was in Walla Walla.

"You're not supposed to swear around me," Ava said. "Can we go get pizza now?"

The pizza parlor was deserted, seeing as how it was just 3 o'clock, too late for the lunch rush and too early for dinner. They ordered a large combination, which Emma Jean put on her credit card, as always, and sat in the corner at a rickety wood table beneath a glowing beer sign. Emma Jean tried not to think about how much she liked beer with pizza. She was getting lots of practice trying not to think of things she liked that she couldn't have, like Riley, and a bestselling novel, and avid fans. And let us not forget friends. Instead she sipped her water. She had tucked the file in her purse and brought it with her and while they waited for the pizza she got it out again.

Ava sighed heavily, and Emma Jean dug in her wallet, pulled out quarters, and sent her to the game room. Then she looked at the rest of the papers in the file. Next up was a typed piece of paper, correspondence from an attorney who was apparently settling her mother's estate, of which, apparently, there was not much to settle, a few household items and that was about it. Lucky for Emma Jean, there'd been an insurance policy which she had inherited when she came of age—it had helped her through the lean early writing years. She wished she hadn't gone through all of it back when she was helping Peter get started in the wine industry, as the money would have come in handy now. But those papers were it for the file.

On a whim, Emma Jean had shoved the folders full of mementos in her messenger bag and now she pulled them out, certain there had to be more clues to her mother's death somewhere. She leafed through odds and ends of her mother's life, ticket stubs and matchbook covers and girlish notes, most of which had bits of tape on them, as if they had been pulled out of a scrapbook. Normally, she'd have been fascinated with this find, were she not on the hunt for important information. Finally, she hit pay dirt, a yellowing newspaper clipping that had accidentally gotten stuck to the back of a theater program written in Spanish. It was so brittle and faded that Emma Jean could barely read it, and indeed, there was no headline or dateline or photo along with it, only one brief paragraph of type.

Eulalie resident Claire Marie Zelch died in Spain last week, according to the American Embassy in Madrid. Zelch, 25, was visiting Pamplona, Spain for the annual Running of the Bulls, when she suffered an allergic reaction to a dinner of shellfish. Zelch went into anaphylactic shock and died. Funeral arrangements are pending, according to the family.

Emma Jean read the paragraph over and over again. The words fed into her brain, but she couldn't seem to make sense of them. Her mother had died from eating shellfish, not at the horns of a bull. Wow. Emma Jean pulled her phone from her bag, and punched in Cleo's number again. This time she left a more heated message, saying she really needed to talk, now.

She glanced around for Ava and saw that she was still engrossed at the video game arcade, then pulled the next paper out of the file. It was a small sheet, maybe eight inches by four, and decorated around its border with purple and red roses. A faint whiff of some sweet perfume wafted up to her nostrils. Emma Jean beheld the paper with a sense of wonder. She remembered when you could buy stationery like that in little pads that came with matching envelopes. God, people wrote letters once, too, back in the days before email.

The letter was undated, but the handwriting was neat, round, and even. It was only two paragraphs long, and it was signed, Camilla. That would be Emma Jean's grandmother, Aunt Cleo and Claire's mother. Emma Jean read the letter:

Darling Cleo,
Like your namesake, you are strong and clever and you will figure out how to deal with the challenge of raising a daughter. For Emma Jean is your daughter now, well and truly, and you must think of her as nothing less.
As for what to tell her about her mother, first of all wait until she asks. Someday, you may want to tell her the truth but you will have to decide that when the time comes.
Just do your best and you'll both be fine.
Your loving mother,
Camilla

Emma Jean leaned her head back against the chair and tried to think. Suddenly Emma Jean wished she knew more about her mother. More to the point, she wished she had wanted to know more. Her memories of her mother had always been shadowy and dim. She'd been interested in her, but not obsessed. She cringed to think of it now, but she hadn't missed her mother much as a child. Search her mind as she might, she simply couldn't remember spending that much time with her mother. After all, as she had explained to Ava, she had been mighty young when her mother died.

And, Aunt Cleo had always seemed parent enough to stand in for her missing mother and father. As was the childhood she'd given Emma Jean—openings at the art gallery, festive dinners in downtown Seattle, sophisticated urban events galore. And then they'd drive home, to their house at Three Tree Point above Puget Sound, and Emma Jean could kick off her shoes and run barefoot down the old Indian trail to the water's edge, where the sound of the gentle waves—more like the waves of the Gulf Coast than the Pacific Ocean—always lulled her and set her imagination free. She watched sunsets from the beach, took long walks along the sand or the road or down the Indian trail, and she'd worked out childhood and teenage problems that way as well.

If she'd suffered, or had a terrible childhood, perhaps she would have spent long days pining to know her mother. But she hadn't. Besides, her mother had died in such a romantic and dashing manner. Or so she had thought. She picked up her phone to call Cleo again, but just then she heard shouting and turned to find its source.

Which, unfortunately, happened to be Ava.

She stood with her back to the bank of video games, her feet planted like a pug dog and her fists raised like a pugilist. Two young girls faced her, hands on their hips, head tilted in the universal teenage stance of disdain. As Emma Jean approached, she studied them. They both wore low-slung tight jeans and cute, sparkly T-shirts. One of them had a white leather bag strapped over her shoulder. The other was wearing pink shoes. These girls fit Emma Jean's image of contemporary pre-teens, and they were without a doubt a couple of the "stupid girls" that Ava always complained about.

"So you're going to fight again?" one of the girls said.

"Maybe this time you'll get sent away from more than just school," the other said.

"You quit saying bad things about my mother," Ava said.

One of the girls was taller than Ava by at least a head. She looked down and curled a lip in the utter disdain only a young girl could effect. "I heard she was a porn star."

"My Mom said she's a meth head," the shorter one said.

"It's for sure that she's not a famous model," the tall one said.

"She is too!" Ava shouted.

"You're so pathetic," the tall one said. "You are not even worth our time."

They spun as one and turned to sashay off, banging out the side door and onto the street, laughing as the door slammed behind them.

"You'll see," Ava shouted after them. "You'll see when she gets here. She's beautiful! And she's making tons of money for us!"

"Hey, hey," Emma Jean said. "What is going on here?"

Ava turned, took one look at Emma Jean, and the fierce look on her face crumpled. She did, too, her entire body sagging. Emma Jean caught her just before she would have fallen to the floor. Ava's body was wracked by sobs, and all Emma Jean could hold her, smelling her faint vanilla odor until her crying eased.

Finally Emma Jean got her back to the table, where the pizza had long since arrived, forced her to drink water and got a few bites of pizza in her.

"I hate them," Ava said.

"I can see why," Emma Jean agreed. "But why do you even bother with them? Clearly they are beneath you, so why worry about it?" She was probably not winning any saintly points for pointing out the general bitchiness of the other girls, but Emma Jean didn't care. They had been horrible, mean ogres, and she didn't want Ava to think that their behavior was the norm.

"Because they were making fun of my mother."

"I got that much," Emma Jean said.

"All the girls do. They say I'm going to end up a crack-head porn star just like her."

"Oh honey," Emma Jean said. "Is that what you were fighting about at school today?"

Ava nodded, and sniffled and snorted back another sob. Emma Jean handed her a napkin. "Drink more water."

"You know what, though?" Ava set the water glass down and stared at Emma Jean. "Sometimes I'm afraid they are right."

Emma Jean stood, skirted the table and took the chair next to Ava, where she could reach to put her arm around the girl. "Now that really pisses me off. You are a smart, funny, talented girl, and you are going to grow up to be a kick-ass writer. Those girls are going to be pumping out babies by the time they are sixteen. Their looks will be gone by twenty—and you'll just be coming into yours. Best of all, by then, you'll have forgotten they exist."

Ava stared into Emma Jean's eyes as if searching for the answer to life. "You really think so?"

"Absolutely." Emma Jean nodded her chin emphatically. And despite that, Emma Jean thought, Ava would remember those girls with hatred forever. "I know so. They don't make 'em like you very often, darling. Oh God, I'm sorry, I forgot. I'm not supposed to call you that."

Ava picked a piece of pepperoni off the pizza and popped it in her mouth. "I guess you can if you want."

"I'll only do it once in a while. You think we ought to call Wendy now and see if she's home?"

"I guess. I wish she wouldn't come home, though. Then I could stay with you."

The thought made Emma Jean nearly collapse with exhaustion right then and there in the pizza parlor. She flopped back against her chair.

"I knew you wouldn't want me to," Ava said.

And then Emma Jean surprised herself by kissing Ava on the cheek and telling her that maybe it could happen some other day.

Chapter Eighteen
Her Methods of Engagement

Emma Jean sat in the weak, late-autumn sun on the deck of the condo with the laptop on her, well, lap. The pink quartz crystal and Aku Aku rested on the cedar table beside her, and she had wrapped herself in one of the afghans Cleo kept in a basket by the back door to ward off the mountain chill. Over the last couple of days, Emma Jean had exhausted herself doing Internet searches to find out more about her mother's death and finally had given up, seeing as how she hadn't found anything. Zero, zip, nada. Calling Cleo hadn't yielded any info, either, because her aunt was still not answering her calls. Emma Jean couldn't recall a time ever in her life when she and Cleo had gone so long without talking to each other, so now she knew for certain that Cleo was avoiding her. What she didn't know was why.

Shouldn't it be the other way around? Shouldn't Emma Jean be in a royal snit, avoiding Aunt Cleo? After all, it was she, Emma Jean Sullivan, whose backstory had suddenly and irrevocably been altered. For God's sake—or Buddha's, she still couldn't decide which—she was the one who had just had her whole life story yanked out from beneath her. Her mother, dead at 25 of shellfish poisoning, not from being gored by a bull.

But at least she'd found something to distract her from her questions about her mother's death. Too bad it wasn't a good distraction, like Riley calling her. She shrugged the afghan off her shoulders, as she was getting warmer by the minute, fueled by a consuming anger. Little Claire was doing somersaults in response to her mood. Surely this anger wasn't good for the baby, which was why Emma Jean was dispelling it onto the page, writing a scathing letter to her fan club president, Margaret.

The woman had the utter gall to write Emma Jean suggesting that she owed her fans an explanation about her pregnancy, "after so many of us have followed you in your decision to remain childless and now feel betrayed." Explain her pregnancy? How about this? First you find a wildly attractive man who looks just like Brad Pitt and then you go have wildly wonderful sex with him. That was about as much explanation as she could muster. And furthermore, the thought of the wildly attractive man who had impregnated and then abandoned her made her want to weep. Perhaps deep sadness was a better emotion for poor little Claire to absorb than burning anger.

She finished the message to Margaret and pressed send. Then Emma Jean stood, trying to shake off her confusion, anger and despair. *Breathe,* she told herself. *Commune with the mountains. Pretend you are a Tibetan lama looking at the Himalayans. At least admire the damn scenery.* She gazed at Dollar Mountain, solid and benign in the sunshine, appreciating that the mountains felt secure, enfolding, and cozy.

And quiet. Dear God, it was quiet in the mountains. It was quiet here in a way she'd never experienced before, like a giant down comforter had been pulled over the world to muffle all sound. You could breathe the quiet. You could inhabit it. You could *smell* it, and quiet smelled like pine needles, loamy earth, and a cool mountain stream.

At the moment, the quiet made her want to scream. What she wouldn't give for the traffic on Ventura Boulevard outside her room at the Aku. For Riley to call and beg her forgiveness, which she would offer after making him grovel for a while. Oh, who was she kidding, it would take her about one second to welcome Riley back into her life. She missed him so much it hurt, deep in her stomach, a pain like she'd never known before.

Sun Valley was not only quiet, it was remote. And being in a remote, godforsaken town when you were pregnant and friendless and all alone because your lover and your aunt and everyone else you had ever known had deserted you was not much fun. In truth, she'd been forced to give up her attempts to call Cleo, because she'd had to turn off her phone. Every once in a while—far more often than Emma Jean would have thought possible—an enterprising, childless fan somehow managed to find her number, and it was just so unpleasant to listen to their tirades. And every time she logged onto her email, more hate mail came through.

Not that turning off her phone or refusing to check email made much difference. When she did turn on her phone, the only messages she heard besides the ones from the angry fans were sniveling ones from Peter. Nothing from Riley, nothing from Angela, nothing from Cleo. Nothing from anybody she loved or who loved her. Emma Jean stuck her lower lip out in a pout. Perhaps therein lay the problem—everybody hated her, including Margaret, erstwhile fan club president. Well, if Margaret didn't hate her now, she would soon, once she read Emma Jean's email.

Oh God, what had she done? Now that she'd sent her nasty tirade to Margaret, she felt worse, not better. She remembered that Margaret had a propensity for sharing Emma Jean's personal emails on the fan club website. And besides that, she had failed miserably in her Campaign to be Kind, because emailing venomous letters was not nice. Not nice at all. Well, it was too late now. Emma Jean stared at the scenery and wondered what to do next. Life in retreat was also the wee-est bit boring, particularly since she had all but given up on pretending to write.

She'd convinced Lynette to take over the gallery for a few days, especially since despite her best efforts, Ray and Pat had failed to purchase a painting, but now even talking to clients sounded better than hanging out at the condo, stewing. God, she was tired of being fat and alone. At least once she had the baby, she could go on a strict diet and exercise regimen. But what good would it do if she was still alone and there was nobody around to admire her svelte body? She'd seen her retreat from the world as part of her penance for her bad behavior, but fat lot of good hiding from the world did. So maybe retreating wasn't the answer. Engagement, that was the ticket. Yesiree. Yes, indeedy. Engagement. She would now interact with the world. She would insert herself into the middle of things. She would walk into town and go shopping. That would make her feel like her old self. And maybe, just maybe, she would even turn her phone back on—the ultimate act of engagement. Before she could change her mind, hiding being somewhat addictive, she donned walking shoes and a warm wool sweater, and pulled her messenger bag over her shoulder.

It was a beautiful afternoon, chilly even though the sun shone. The thin air of the high altitude made the sky bluer than she'd ever seen it before, bluer than it was in Portland after a spring rain, way bluer than it ever was in L.A. Emma Jean headed down Sun Valley Road, past the resort. In front of her lay the foothills of the Sawtooth mountain range, some of them covered with firs and pines and patches of Aspens which you could identify by their brilliant yellows. Baldy was the most obvious of the mountains, with its clear-cut ski runs alternating with swathes of green trees. The little town of Ketchum lay nestled beneath it, like a storybook village.

Since the point was to be spontaneous and *engage,* she was walking without a preconceived destination, but as she ambled along, she had an inspiration. She would go to the bookstore. A new book or two would be just the thing to cheer her up. Perhaps a volume on Hinduism? Lately, she was pained to admit, the Bees bored her. She'd gotten the Dalai Lama's latest book and hadn't been able to get into it. Everyone said he was such a good writer, and she revered the man, but she did not agree. Sometimes it sounded like he talking to a bunch of little kids.

The bookstore was a cramped affair full of shelves and tables brimming with books and because of this, it was one of Emma Jean's favorite places ever. She forced herself to calmly browse the *New Releases* and *Staff Picks* before making a beeline for the *S* section of Fiction and Literature. Unfortunately, it appeared there were still three copies of *Winemaker's Wife* on the shelf, the exact number there had been two weeks earlier, the last time she was in. They sat next to a series of gaudy historical romances, so it was no wonder they weren't selling. She pulled one copy of *Wife* out and set it face out, so the casual browser might notice it.

Then she had another thought. She looked around. The store was empty, save for the perky little clerk who sat behind piles of books and papers at the front desk, absorbed in something on the computer screen. Emma Jean left the one copy of *Wife* face out on the shelf, grabbed the other two, and then sauntered to the big display table up front. She turned her head this way and that, as if she were pondering the titles laid out on the table. She touched one pile of books, picked up a volume from a different pile, all the while making room for the two copies of *Wife*. She was so absorbed in her project that she startled when the cute little clerk said, "Can I help you?"

Emma Jean looked up. The young woman was standing right beside her. She was yet another one of the athletic types that formed one stratum of the social sandwich in Ketchum, tanned and toned and just itching for the ski season to start, you could tell.

"I was just..." Emma Jean paused. This was usually the moment when she switched on her Emma Jean Sullivan, famous novelist routine. But at that moment, she stood there looking pregnant and very un-authorish. And beyond that, she simply didn't have it in her to go through her usual routine. "I was just wondering if you had books on Indian religion?"

"Oh, we've got a whole section." The woman turned. Emma Jean quickly set her two copies of *Wife* in the space she'd created on the table and then followed the clerk. Unfortunately, though she found two tomes on Hinduism and a book about New Thought religion that she desperately wanted, when she attempted to purchase them, her credit card would not go through.

"Oh, that silly husband of mine always forgets to pay the bills on time," Emma Jean chirped. "Here, use this one." She handed the clerk her most recent credit card, the one Peter didn't know about, the one she'd been hanging onto for emergencies only. Well, this was a book emergency.

As she left the bookstore, her messenger bag now laden with books that she felt guilty for buying, she wondered how much credit she had left on that card. Because, that credit basically constituted all the money she had in the world. She had to get back to work on *Tiki*. She desperately needed the next payment on the advance. But, oh Lord, she was so far away from having an acceptable manuscript ready it wasn't even funny. Perhaps she should just walk back to the condo and get to work. No, she told herself firmly. She could write that evening. She was in town to engage. And she'd be nice while she was at it, and earn some points for her penance project.

As proof of her willingness to participate in the world, she sacrificed her potential sanity and turned her phone on. Emma Jean squared her shoulders, feeling very brave. Then she immediately stuffed her cell back in her bag, where odds were good she wouldn't hear it, but still. At least she had turned it on. That counted, didn't it?

She headed back up Sun Valley Road with the vague idea that she would find some more shops to visit. She wouldn't buy; she would just look. But once she started walking, she regretted all her purchases even more. The books were heavy, and carrying them caused the intermittent pregnancy pain in her lower back to flare up. Emma Jean suddenly felt exhausted from her trudge with the books. She forgot over and over again that Claire, the wondrous life force within her, also wondrously zapped her energy. She hoped she had enough oomph left to shuffle the mile back up to the condo, but at the moment, she wasn't sure. She felt like a marionette that had gone slack on its strings. A block away, she spied a building that housed both shops and a coffee shop. Perfect. She could sit for a bit with a cup of tea and then glance at the boutiques before she headed home.

The coffee shop was located in the lower level of an arcade-like building. The interior was warm and dark after the glare of the high-altitude sun, and the smell of coffee and the hiss of espresso greeted her. Emma Jean blinked her eyes to get things in focus. After the second time she closed and opened them, she saw that the shops on the first floor surrounded an open area dotted with tables and chairs. They were all empty save for one, at which sat Ava.

"Oh my God," Emma Jean said and rushed toward the girl. Had it only been three days since they'd eaten at the pizza parlor? It seemed like three years. She ran up to Ava, who was lolling, there was no other word for it, on a metal chair, and gave her a huge hug.

"Darling, how are you?"

Ava wiggled out of Emma Jean's hug. "You haven't been at the gallery. And I tried to call you but you never answer."

"Oh, I'm so sorry, but I've had my phone off." She eased herself into a chair and stretched her legs out in front of her.

Ava continued to stare at her as if what Emma Jean just said made no sense.

"I've been writing," Emma Jean said, even though her writing constituted an email to Margaret. But nothing she said seemed to be flying with Ava.

Just then, her phone began to ring.

"I thought you had it turned off," Ava said.

"I did! I just turned it back on a minute ago. It's been off for days before this."

The phone continued its cheery bleating.

"Aren't you going to answer it?" Ava said.

Emma Jean was eager to prove to Ava that she would answer the phone in the future, on the off chance Ava might want to call her, so she punched talk without looking at who was calling.

"Will wonders never cease? She actually answers her phone once in a while."

Peter. About the last person on earth she wanted to hear from. Oh, Lord, this was why engaging with the world could be so damn difficult.

"What do you want, Peter?"

Ava cocked her head to one side quizzically as she listened to Emma Jean and toyed with a pink mug full of geegaws that sat on the table.

"Just the opportunity to speak with my darling wife."

Was Peter drunk? Emma Jean glanced at her watch. Not yet 3 p.m., and it would be an hour earlier back in Portland, assuming that was where he was calling from.

"Where are you?"

"Do you really care, Emma Jean?"

Emma Jean blew out a long stream of air. "Honestly, Peter, at this precise moment, no, I don't. Because I happen to be exhausted, and you are only making me more so."

Ava now sat upright in her chair, pushed herself back from the table, and raised her hand in a wave.

"Wait, don't leave, I want to talk to you," Emma Jean said.

Ava sighed heavily. "But you're busy talking to someone else."

"Are you talking to me?" Peter asked. Then he cleared his throat.

"Hang on one second, Peter." Emma Jean covered the phone with one hand and dug into her bag with the other. She handed Ava a twenty-dollar bill. "Go get me a decaf latte, okay? And buy yourself a cookie or whatever you want with the rest of the money."

Ava shrugged, took the money, and walked off toward the coffee shop.

"Okay, I'm back, Peter. But could you make it snappy? I need to talk to Ava when she gets back."

"Who is Ava?"

"Nobody that you know, just a girl I met here who I happen to adore."

"You hate children."

"I'm carrying one inside me, Peter. It's a little late for me to hate children."

"A baby is different than a child who you are famously bad at dealing with, as I recall. You could never deal with Julia."

"Maybe you never gave me the chance," Emma Jean shot back. "Maybe you were so busy convincing me I didn't want a baby that I never got to establish a relationship with her." She'd never actually thought of this before, but as she said, she realized that there could be a lot of truth in the idea.

"I didn't call you to talk about children," Peter said. "I called to talk about us."

"I'd rather talk about children." Emma Jean watched as Ava stood at the counter in the coffee shop, ordering. "Because, honestly, Peter? There is no us."

"Exactly. Which is why I've been talking to real estate agents about putting the house on the market. It's a good time, Emma Jean. The market is rebounding like crazy."

"You mean my house? You want to put my house on the market?"

"It's our house. My name is on the title."

"But it was the money from my bestselling books that bought it in the first place. It is my house and I am not going to put it on the market."

Sell her house? Her wonderful, amazing dream house, the home she loved beyond all reason, almost as much as her fans and her writing and her students? Then Emma Jean remembered that she had lost her fans, didn't have any students at the moment, and wasn't doing any writing except in the form of angry letters to her fan club president. Was her life some sort of spiritual experiment? Did God or Buddha want to see how much misery they could heap on one woman? Because when you added on the loss of Riley, and her marriage, and Aunt Cleo, it was more than any one woman should have to bear.

"Emma Jean, don't be silly. The house is our major asset. How are we going to divide things if you insist on hanging onto it?"

"Well, I don't know. But I'll find a way. All I know is that I'm not going to sell my house, Peter. It is one of the few things I have left in the world."

"Hang on a sec," Peter said, and then all she heard for a minute was a lot of white noise. Then he came back on the line. "Now what were you saying?"

"What's that sound? Where are you, anyway?"

"On my way to Walla Walla. Had to get a spider out of the car."

"What are you doing in Walla Walla?"

"Looking at equipment."

"Peter, no. You've spent enough of my money on that stupid winery."

"It's not stupid—"

"It's expensive as all hell. And it's my money, what little I have left, that you are spending. I don't even know how you're going to buy it, since I can't get any of our damn credit cards to work."

"I have another solution for our money problems. Since you are not willing to move forward quickly with the divorce and selling the house—"

"*Our* money problems?" Emma Jean squawked into the phone. Ava reappeared with a bag of something, and a paper cup, which she set before Emma Jean. She took a drink of her decaf. Heavenly. Ava sat back down, opened the paper bag, and pulled out a chocolate bar, which she unwrapped and took a huge bite of.

"We should go through with the re-financing, then. I've taken the liberty of having the bank draw up some papers. It'll give us a chunk of money, Emma Jean. And you yourself just admitted we really need it. Once the winery gets on its feet, I won't need any more. It's only while I'm getting it established. Plus, it will give you time to figure out how you can keep the house in the settlement."

"Oh, for God's sakes, Peter, are you crazy?" Could you even believe him? She sat back in her chair. The last thing on God's green earth she was going to do was endanger her—and Claire's—home, whether by putting it on the market or refinancing it.

Now she had to add Peter to her growing list of worries. She'd been getting along just fine by pretending he didn't exist. She was going to have to cut him off somehow, which meant she was going to have to find an attorney. And that was going to cost yet more money. But certainly going into deeper debt by refinancing the house wasn't going to help the situation. Oh God, at the moment she didn't feel like she had the energy to deal with anything, least of all Peter and his adolescent idiocy. This was what she got for engaging with the world. It was far, far easier just to hide.

Emma Jean shook her head. "I'm not going to refinance the house, Peter. And I'm not going to put it on the market, either. I know we're having a bit of a cash flow problem, but I'm not putting my house at risk just for one of your whims. I've got a child's future to think about now. And that house is where little Claire is going to grow up."

"Fine, be that way. But you'll be sorry. Because I intend to win it from you in the divorce settlement, then."

"I'm hanging up now."

"You can make your life far easier if you just agree to it now," Peter said. "It'll be cheaper by far."

"Good-bye, Peter."

"You're sure you won't consider refinancing?"

"Oh, for God's sake, Peter, what part of no don't you understand? I'll give you a hint. This is what it sounds like." Emma Jean pressed the button to end the call. She closed her eyes, took a deep breath, and opened them again.

Ava stared at her from across the table. "Did you cast Peter asunder?"

"What book did you learn that phrase from? Wait, how did you know who I was talking to?"

"Cuz I heard you call him Peter. And it didn't sound like you were saying it in a good way, either." Ava shrugged. "I like Riley way better."

"You've never met Riley," Emma Jean pointed out.

"I've talked to him on the phone. And I can just tell from the way you were talking to Peter that I wouldn't like him. I'm a very good judge of character."

Emma Jean liked Riley a whole lot better at this particular moment also. At any moment, actually. She felt a sudden stab of missing him dreadfully. Better not to dwell on that.

Emma Jean looked at her watch. "Why aren't you in school?"

Ava looked at *her* watch and then gave Emma Jean a look that could melt a snowdrift. "It's 3? We get out at 2:30?"

"But you're supposed to be under armed guard at all times."

Ava shrugged and hooked a thumb over her shoulder. "Wendy's upstairs, at the goofy store."

Emma Jean looked at the store at the top of the stairs and saw that it was a needlepoint and knitting shop.

"She likes that needle stuff," Ava said.

Emma Jean now noticed again on the table in front of Ava a pink mug decorated with a tiara and the words *Special Princess*. It was full of small trinkets and wrapped in clear plastic tied with a red bow.

"Did Wendy buy you a present?" Emma Jean asked.

Ava glanced over toward the coffee shop, and following her gaze, Emma Jean saw that it featured shelves of similar mugs and other candy-laden knick-knacks. Ava slid the mug across the table and into her backpack, which sat on the floor beside the table. Funny how the girl always seemed to have some little treasure or another, wasn't it? And yet when Emma Jean asked about them, she always hushed up.

"My real Mom is coming."

"Oh, darling, that is wonderful."

A bird chirped somewhere nearby and Emma Jean looked around, confused. Ava reached into her backpack and pulled out her phone. Her face infused with joy when she read the caller display. "That's her calling me now!" She opened the flip and turned away, then wandered across the arcade floor and settled at a nearby table as she began her conversation.

Emma Jean watched Ava talking intently into the phone. Her stomach felt empty and raw. She reached for a cookie Ava had left on the table and tore a huge piece of it off. Lord, what a day this had turned into. That awful man who used to be her husband harassing her so and the profound exhaustion she felt. And now Ava's mother was returning. Not that it was any concern of Emma Jean's. The girl was a horrible pest anyway. Emma Jean stuffed a bigger chunk of cookie in her mouth and then another. Soon as Ava returned she would say her goodbyes and head for home. Thankfully, the girl was soon back.

"How's your mother?"

"She's great," Ava said. "She'll be here for Thanksgiving. She and I are going to look for a house while she's here. It'll be a big one. Really big."

"That's good, darling. I'm happy for you." In truth, Emma Jean felt murderously jealous of the way Ava's mother was planning to waltz back in and buy her daughter's affection, but she couldn't exactly say that. She stood up. "I've got to get started on the trudge back home. The way I feel, it might take me until dark to get there."

"Why don't you ask Wendy for a ride home? She loves to do stuff for people."

Usually Emma Jean hated to ask people for things. But asking Wendy for a ride home sounded like a pretty good idea.

"C'mon," Ava said. "Let's go find her."

Chapter Nineteen

Confession is Good for Her Soul

The spacious needlepoint store felt decidedly girly. Lace curtains covered the lower halves of windows that looked toward Mt. Baldy, and late-afternoon sun streamed through the top panes. Needlepoint canvases were stashed everywhere, on a freestanding display in the center of the room and in bins beneath the windows. One wall featured skeins of yarn sorted by color and hung on hooks, a veritable rainbow of it. Emma Jean sighed with pleasure. The act of creation always made her happy, no matter what was being made. And she loved an activity that necessitated actual equipment, because writing required mostly her brain power, and very little in the way of tools.

"Can I help you?" a voice sang out.

In the front, windowed corner of the store, two women sat around a round table covered with yarn and canvases. One of the women Emma Jean didn't recognize, but the other was Wendy, who looked up and smiled when she saw Emma Jean and Ava.

"Oh, hey, I haven't seen you in forever," Wendy said.

"She needs a ride home," Ava said and then promptly scooted to the other corner of the store, where a small play area populated with brightly colored plastic toys had been set up.

Emma Jean advanced toward the table slowly, her hand reaching out to stroke displays of specialty wool, her eye falling on a needlepoint canvas. At the table, she started to sit in an empty chair when she realized a black leather jacket and tan cashmere scarf were thrown over it. She took the empty seat beside it, and Wendy introduced her to June, the store's owner, whose job description apparently included spending most afternoons sitting at the table stitching.

"This is wonderful," Emma Jean said. "I used to do needlepoint all the time."

"No reason you can't start again," June said. She was petite and had dark hair flecked with gray.

Maybe Emma Jean would buy herself a needlepoint canvas. Maybe what she needed was a project, something to keep her busy over the long winter nights to come, when engaging with the world would be even more exhausting because there would be snow. She could stitch something for Claire. Although there was the wee problem that she was broke.

"Ava said you needed a ride. Is everything okay?" Wendy asked. She was wearing a yellow sweatshirt with bunnies on it. They formed a conga line across her chest, and one had a bow, made from real ribbon, while another one held a book, which was actually sewn onto the sweatshirt in the form of a charm. But Wendy's concern for Emma Jean cheered her and took the edge off her tiredness, and that counted for a lot. Emma Jean felt glimmers of her old self returning, and she was just mustering an Emma Jean Sullivan famous novelist response, when another woman appeared at the table.

Sally Marx, erstwhile *Vanity Fair* reporter, in an over-sized white fisherman's sweater and a green, black and gold silk scarf tied just so at her neck, clutched a hank of turquoise yarn. She slid into the chair draped with the black leather jacket and looked at Emma Jean.

"Well, look who we have here, the famous uber-novelist."

"What's an uber-novelist?" June said.

"Hi, Sally," Emma Jean said. She stared at the woman who had been responsible for much of her recent pain and tried to think of a cutting remark. "Thanks for spreading the word about my pregnancy."

Emma Jean cursed herself that she couldn't come up with something better. She was getting lame in her hormone-saturated old age.

"You're pregnant?" June peered more closely at Emma Jean. "Wow, congratulations, I wouldn't have guessed it at your a—"

Was it just her imagination or had Wendy slapped June's knee? At any rate, Wendy now shot June a murderous look and smiled at

Emma Jean. "I should have guessed that you and Sally would know each other, both being writers and all."

"I've been hoping to interview Emma Jean, but she's awfully good at eluding me," Sally said. Her mouth moved, but the rest of her face didn't. Emma Jean had never seen anyone who been Botoxed so close up before. The effect was fascinating, if a bit disconcerting.

"Are you doing a story on her novels?" Wendy asked.

"Oh no, "Emma Jean said. "Nothing so upfront as that. Sally prefers to work in more subtle ways. Don't you, Sally?"

"I'm all about the subtle," Sally said. "And sometimes even the not-so subtle. Wendy knows that."

"I do?" Wendy said.

Emma Jean was trying to discern all the nuances of the conversation. Sally and Wendy seemed like old pals, but two women couldn't be further apart in manner, appearance, and, well, just about everything. "Do you two know each other?"

Wendy nodded. "She comes into the library all the time."

"I have a vacation home here, darling," Sally Marx said. "And I'm grateful to Wendy for pointing me in the direction of the Marielle Delaney story." Sally smirked as she said this. There was no other way to describe it. The woman smirked.

"Oh, that poor woman," June said. She stabbed a needle threaded with white yarn into her canvas, which appeared to be a picture of Mount Baldy. "I can't believe what a big deal they are making out of it."

"It is a big deal. She said the story was all true and now it comes out that it's not. I think people should be held accountable." That was Wendy, the librarian speaking.

Emma Jean felt like a deer caught in the headlights. She searched her mind for a non-clichéd way to describe it but came up short. This was nearly as bad as being outed as a pregnant person. No, maybe this was worse, because she had to endure seeing Wendy and Sally face to face. At least Marielle wasn't here. How could it be possible that Wendy, who Emma Jean had blabbed to about Marielle's book in the first place, was sitting here at this very table? And clearly Sally had gotten the idea for the story from Wendy. So the whole Marielle debacle *was* Emma Jean's fault. Like a deer, perhaps her best bet now would be to flee, since she hadn't yet been flattened by the oncoming rush of the car. She scooted her chair back to leave.

"Where are you going?" Wendy asked. "I thought you needed a ride. If we wait just a bit longer, I can loop around and pick up my son without having to make two trips."

"I thought I heard Ava calling me," Emma Jean said.

"I didn't hear anyone," June said.

"You're looking really good, Emma Jean," Wendy said. "How far along are you? Are you feeling well?"

"Oh, pregnancy is so exciting at any age!" June clapped her hands together like the one autistic child Emma Jean had known. The boy had been like a dog in his enthusiasm for wherever life took him, and clapped often to show his appreciation. What if Claire, the amazing life force within, was autistic? After all, Emma Jean was considered an old pregnant person. And, dear Lord, which was worse, the conversation about Marielle or the conversation about Emma Jean's pregnancy?

The whole table was staring at her. She'd gone off on one of her pregnancy brain freezes again. Maybe she was suffering from early dementia. Maybe she wouldn't be able to care for Claire because she'd be crazy. If only she weren't so damn tired. "Do you know what the sex is?" June was asking.

Emma Jean took a deep breath and willed her attention back. "Why, darling, thank you for asking. I've not had an ultrasound yet, but I don't really need one because I'm positive it's a girl." Emma Jean scooted her chair back further.

Sally Marx cocked her head to one side. "How are your readers reacting to the news of your pregnancy? I'm curious, because you've been such a wonderful role model for those of us who choose not to have children."

Suddenly the exhaustion she'd been holding at bay since leaving the bookstore hit her, all at once, like a tsunami, or the car finally connecting with the deer frozen in its high beams. She couldn't deal with the pressure anymore, she just couldn't. And she couldn't handle the guilt she felt about Marielle, either. She felt a tear slide down her cheek. Jesus, Emma Jean Sullivan didn't cry. And yet she felt another tear, and then another, and her lip quivered and she just wished she could *control* herself but she couldn't.

"Are you alright?" Wendy asked.

"I'm fine." Emma Jean waved her hand in front of her face. The damn tears kept coming.

"You don't look so good," June said. "What's wrong?"

"I'm pregnant," she blurted.

"News flash," Sally Marx said.

Wendy shot her a dirty look and turned to Emma Jean. "Um, honey, we know that."

"I'm forty-eight years old and I'm pregnant and it's wonderful and awful at the same time because I never thought I could get pregnant and I wrote all that stuff about hating babies and now all my readers hate me and I've been trying to hide from it all plus be nice but I'm just so tired."

"I think you're nice," Wendy said.

Sally produced a tissue from her handbag and handed it to Emma Jean. June scooted up closer to her and patted her on the back. "It's okay. Old people have babies all the time."

"That's not the only problem," Emma Jean sobbed. She glanced at Sally. Oh what the hell. She couldn't do it anymore, couldn't keep trying to uphold her image. Give it all up and get it all back, one of her New Age books said. Yeah, right. Give it all up and lose it all would be more to the point. But it didn't matter. She'd lost so much already. She opened her mouth and told them all—Wendy, June, and Sally—the whole sordid story.

She told them how she'd met Riley, back in June, and how she'd not been able to resist him. How she realized that she didn't have any friends and began a Campaign to be Kind. She told them about her first trip to Sun Valley, and about learning that she was pregnant. She told them about trying to get an abortion, and how she dreaded telling Peter about the pregnancy. She related the story of the trip to Walla Walla, and the disastrous announcement of her pregnancy, how Peter had told her that he'd had a vasectomy. She told them about going to see Riley in L.A., and how he did not have time for her, and how they survived an earthquake together, and how that was the first time she'd felt Claire move. And how she'd moved to Sun Valley to hide, but instead she met Ava, and found Bob, her Fake Christian father sniffing around. How the story of her mother's death that she'd heard since childhood suddenly wasn't true and how she couldn't find out for sure because now Aunt Cleo wouldn't talk to her, no matter how many times Emma Jean called. She told them how Sally had announced to the world that Emma Jean was pregnant, and now all her fans hated her, and worst of all, way worse than anything, was that Riley had decided he could never, ever see her again. And, finally, she said how Peter had decided it was the perfect time to sell her house—her dream abode, the one place she truly felt at home. It took half an hour, at least, to tell the tale, and when she was finished, Emma Jean looked up at her listeners and said, "I've just been *so* bad."

June patted her on the back again. It was a gesture which if Emma Jean were writing it would seem clichéd and ineffectual, but in reality was strangely comforting.

"I don't think you've been all that bad," Wendy said.

"Well, adultery is bad," June said. She'd set her needle and her canvas down during Emma Jean's story. "It's a sin."

"Oh, stop. That's such an old world view."

"Really?" Emma Jean looked at Wendy with hope.

But there sat Sally, staring at her with that same damn reporter's gaze, not saying a word, just staring at her.

"Really," Wendy nodded, her fake blonde curls bobbing along with her head. "Life is too short not to spend it with the people you love."

"Riley says he loves me. But I'm not sure he does, seeing as how he won't leave his wife and now he's ended it with me."

"An honorable man," June said. "That's good."

"Good for her, not me," Emma Jean said. And for the five thousandth time over the last few days, she realized how much she missed Riley, that devilish grin, his sparkly blue eyes, the little cowlick at the back of his scalp.

"Emma Jean," Sally said.

Emma Jean sighed. "You know all my secrets now, Sally. You might as well write about it." Give it all up and get it all back, her ass.

More like get it all gone. But she was just too tired to care anymore. All she really wanted at that moment was to see Riley.

"Thank you. Can I call you if I have more questions?"

"Why not?" Emma Jean said. And she thought, why the hell not?

The setting sun cast pink and gold shadows on Mt. Baldy as Wendy dropped Emma Jean off at the entrance to the condos. The road looped around tennis courts, with the condos lined up along the other side. Cleo's condo was at the far end, but it was easier for Wendy to drop her off here. Her messenger bag was now laden not only with the books she had purchased but a bulging clear plastic zip bag containing a needlepoint canvas, yarn, and a selection of needles and needle threader. At least she had a project for cold, winter nights. She'd chosen a small one, not the big expensive canvas she'd wanted, and she'd decided to think of it as a tribute to the moment when she released all of her worries in one long blast of confession. She couldn't wait to read what the Christian books she'd purchased had to say about that.

At that precise moment, Emma Jean looked toward the condo and saw a car parked out in front, with a woman standing next to it. Was she having another pregnancy brain fart, or didn't that person look rather familiar? And then Emma Jean was running, in a clumsy, pregnant sort of way, because that person did indeed look familiar. It was Aunt Cleo, and suddenly she felt like everything would be okay again if she could just feel Cleo's arms around her.

Chapter Twenty

Sometimes It's Better Not to Know

"Oh God, it's so good to see you! I've missed you so much," Emma Jean said, throwing herself into her aunt's arms. Whatever had happened between them, Emma Jean hoped fervently that it was now history.

"Me too, baby." Cleo squeezed Emma Jean tight, then loosened herself from the hug, kissed her on the cheek, and stepped back. Swaddled in a purple and blue outfit that seemed to be some sort of two-piece caftan, Cleo stood next to an oversized SUV which Emma Jean didn't recognize, the back doors of which were opened wide. Up the stairs, the door to the condo was also open. Suddenly Bob appeared in the doorway. Bob, the evil adulterer, Bob the Fake Christian, *Bob* Bob, her father. He waved, and then started down the steps toward them.

Cleo cocked her head and inspected Emma Jean. "You're looking good, darling. Pregnancy suits you. Oh, by the way, I found you the most precious baby clothes in Seattle. I'm afraid I went a little overboard and ended up filling a suitcase full."

"Well, at least Claire will have clothes," Emma Jean said. She took a deep breath, still panting a little from her brief run. "At the rate I'm going, that may be about all she'll have."

"What's wrong, baby?" Cleo said.

"It would take a book to tell you everything," Emma Jean said. Besides, she'd just told the whole story in the most exhaustive and exhausting manner possible. And now here was Bob, standing beside Cleo with the most annoying expectant look on his face. So there would be no more confessions from Emma Jean's lips.

Bob wore a tan shearling jacket that looked like something out of a Norm Thompson catalog. Beneath the coat, a shirt collar the color of soft moss showed, and he wore finely cut wool slacks and expensive-looking shoes. The man had taste; she had to give him that. It was probably where she had inherited her well-known propensity for stylishness.

"Hello, Emma Jean," he said.

"Why are you here?" Emma Jean said.

"Be civil, darling, I didn't raise you to be rude," Aunt Cleo said. "Bob drove over to Seattle to pick me up. He is here because you and I need to talk. I came home for that precise reason, and darling, Bob needs to be a part of it."

Emma Jean groaned. She was growing to *hate* it when people said they needed to talk. It meant delving into very serious issues, and frankly, at the moment, she was damned sick of delving. She'd already done enough delving for fifty bestselling novelists, probably more.

"Let's go inside," Cleo asked. "I'm freezing my fanny off out here."

Emma Jean managed to forestall the talk for a little while, pleading exhaustion, which was true. But after a brief nap, she had no choice but to reappear in the kitchen and face Bob and Cleo. She suspected that this was not going to be a conversation she would like. There was the off chance that Cleo wanted to talk about something like opening another gallery or something. But Emma Jean didn't think so. After all, she'd called Cleo a gazillion times, pleading for information on her mother's death. Emma Jean sighed, and tried not to notice that Bob cut a rather dashing figure wearing a blue apron tied around his waist as he drained pasta.

Dinner, entirely cooked by Bob, was a simple, and yet delicious, Emma Jean had to admit, spaghetti, with crusty warm French bread and a green salad. Bob and Cleo drank Cabernet, Emma Jean water, though she cast a covetous eye on their wine glasses. Even with the delicious food, it was awkward. They sat in the dining room, which was dominated by a mammoth abstract painting above the sideboard. Heavy striped silk drapes of orange and purple and blue hung at the windows. Usually Cleo preferred to close the drapes to keep the cold out. Tonight, however, they'd left them open, because it had started to snow. Just a little, enough to be pretty without burying the town the way it sometimes happened in winter, according to Cleo.

Bob had insisted that Emma Jean and Cleo sit while he served them, and after they'd all gotten their food and he'd said grace, a silence fell at the table. When had Emma Jean ever felt awkward around Cleo? It was the presence of Bob and his booming preacher voice that was the problem, no doubt about it. When dinner was finished, Emma Jean cleared her throat and cast about for something to say to clear the air. But Cleo beat her to it.

"I came home today for a very specific reason," she said.

"And I thought it was just because you missed me so much," Emma Jean said. Her attempt at a joke, lame as it was, fell flat. Neither Bob nor Cleo smiled.

"Darling, this isn't easy. As a matter of fact, it might be the hardest thing I've ever done." Cleo took a gulp of wine, finishing her glass, then scooted her chair back and stood. She disappeared into the kitchen, her caftan sweeping behind her like an emperor's robes, and reappeared with another bottle of wine, which she made a great show of opening, tasting and pouring. Cleo poured wine for her and Bob, set the bottle on the table, and then stood behind Bob, placing one hand on the back of his chair. The folds of her gown fell just so, and she looked like she was waiting for the paparazzi to pop out from behind the kitchen door and snap a photo.

Aunt Cleo took a deep breath. "I killed your mother."

"No, it was the shellfish. I found out about it in those papers in your files." Emma Jean said. She eyed Cleo's wine and wished to high heaven that she could have a glass. Stressful times discussing delicate family matters definitely called for wine. "Unfortunately. I mean, God. How much better is death by goring than a stupid allergic reaction?"

But before Cleo had a chance to answer, Bob rose, and stood beside Cleo, and it only ruined a tiny bit of the drama that he stepped on the hem of her caftan and she had to rearrange herself before he announced, "No, Emma Jean, it was neither bull nor shellfish. And I'm the one who is responsible for your mother's death."

What was Bob saying? What was Cleo talking about? Emma Jean wasn't in the mood for all the drama. Plus she had little Claire to think about and protect. And so she scootched herself to the edge of her chair. Even though she couldn't move fast, she could move and it seemed to be the only solution, to get the hell out of the room.

"Stay here, darling," Cleo said. "I've been waiting forty-five years to tell you this and I have no intention of letting you not hear it now."

"It is time for us to come clean. You know the old saying, cleanliness is next to godliness? It doesn't just refer to physical cleanliness, you know. The Lord wants us to be clean inside as well," Bob said. "In my church, we have a saying—"

"Bob, she doesn't want to hear about your church right now," Cleo said.

Despite her better instincts, Emma Jean spoke. "I'm so confused. Are you telling me you actually, physically killed her? What about the allergic reaction to shellfish? Surely you didn't orchestrate that?"

Cleo shook her head. "No, we meant metaphorically. I thought you of all people would grasp that. Here's the story, Emma Jean. Bob and I fell in love, many, many years ago. It was—is—a powerful love and it took us both by surprise. We tried so very hard, but—"

"We were bad," Bob interrupted. "We fought a valiant battle, but we were sinners."

Cleo shot him a dirty look and took a step away from him. "Darling, Bob and I were having an affair and your mother found out about it. And that is why she went to Spain to meet her tragic destiny."

"I knew all that. I knew she went to Spain to escape Bob's adultery...wait, what? Did you say it was the two of you having an affair?" Emma Jean said.

Cleo nodded. Bob reached out his hand to Cleo and the two of them stood there, gazing at Emma Jean.

"I fear the Lord has punished us," Bob said, "He has blunted the light He shines on—"

"Oh shut up for a minute, Bob," Cleo said. "Emma Jean, listen. There's more you don't know."

"Let me guess," Emma Jean said, even though her brain still hadn't processed everything that Cleo and Bob had just told her and didn't really want to. "I'm not Claire's daughter, but yours."

Cleo sighed. "No, darling. Though I'm flattered you might think so. But life only happens like that in your books. No, this has to do with our lives right now." Cleo looked at Bob, smiled and reached out her hand to him. He smiled back, took her hand and kissed it.

Emma Jean's mouth dropped open.

"Bob and I are still in love," Cleo said. A shower of snowflakes hit the window, in that odd sound that only snow made when it fell.

"Our passion burned so brightly that even the weight of history and years could not extinguish it," Bob said.

"We hope that you will give us your blessing, darling, because we've waited so very long to be together. And we don't want to wait any longer."

"But…" Emma Jean sat back in her chair. She was having trouble focusing. "But, why now? Why didn't you tell me any of this years ago?"

"Oh, darling I wanted to," Cleo said. "I started to tell you so many times. But I just couldn't bring myself to do it. And then once you have kept a secret for a while, it becomes very hard to disengage it from its hiding place."

Bob stepped closer to her, and Emma Jean noticed that his tan had a faint tint of orange to it. "For me, it was the news that I am going to be a grandfather. I can't make the same mistakes I made the first time. I'm not getting any younger, Emma Jean, and neither is your aunt. We want to spend the time we have left together. And we want you and our grandchild included in that."

"Well, I just don't know if that is going to be possible," Emma Jean said. She had a sudden image of herself at age five, lost in the toy store, staring at a Barbie doll on the shelf in a deep pink package, after having followed some cute boy away from Aunt Cleo. She'd been following cute boys for years. And then it hit her.

"I've been searching for you, in one way or another, my entire life," she said to Bob.

"And I am finally here," Bob said.

"Oh, for God's sake," Emma Jean said. "Could you be any more inappropriate and sentimental? I didn't mean that in a good way. I meant it in a bad way. A very bad way."

"All we want is your approval," Aunt Cleo said. "I love you more than life itself, and even though Bob makes me the happiest woman on earth, part of me will always yearn for you if you deny us your love."

Emma Jean had to hand it to Cleo—she knew how to stage a dramatic scene. She herself might have inherited her sense of style from Bob, but she certainly got her ability to create drama from Cleo. But this event was not just about drama; it was about Emma Jean's life. Or more to the point, her mother's life. And how she had been told a complete wrong story about it, sold a whole bill of goods. And not just that, but she was being asked to accept Bob, not only as her father, but also as her uncle. And furthermore, the thought of her beloved Aunt Cleo together with Bob was nearly more than she could bear. On the other hand, did she want to be one of those women who held a grudge and carried on a personal vendetta that split apart the family for decades? Oh, Lord, her life had gotten confusing.

"But why didn't you ever tell me the truth?" Emma Jean said. "I would have liked to have known the reality of how my mother died before I wrote a bestselling memoir about it, for starters."

"Oh, darling, I wanted to. I wanted to tell you so badly. But you always got such comfort from the story of her dying while running with the bulls. Her bravery seemed to give your life a kind of purpose, an event for you to live up to. And so…I just never found the right time to set you straight." Cleo cast her eyes down modestly.

"Let's look at the positive here," Bob said. "Cleo has spent the last 44 years atoning for her behavior. She stayed away from me, despite my pleadings, and she did a damn fine job of raising you, Emma Jean. And now it is time for us to come clean, not only in the eyes of the Lord but with you, our darling daughter."

Emma Jean sighed. It was difficult to wrap her brain around not only the newly revised story itself, but all of the ramifications this new version held for her life. It would take her years to sort it all out. But right at this moment, she had a petulant Bob and a querulous Aunt Cleo staring at her, waiting for a response.

"Can you ever forgive me?" Cleo said.

"You know, in my novels, things change overnight," Emma Jean said. "Heroines have an epiphany, and suddenly everything is different."

"The Lord can work in miraculous ways," Bob said.

"But that's not how it happens in real life." Emma Jean raised her hand to silence him. "I don't think I'm going to be able to click my fingers and suddenly accept all this—either your relationship or the new story of how my mother died."

"You have to admit my story was much better. The truth seemed anticlimactic after all the drama that preceded it. All I wanted was for you to think that your mother was heroic, darling." Cleo suddenly looked wrinkled and old, her eyes dull as tarnished copper. "I'm desperate for your forgiveness. I don't know how many years I have left," she pleaded.

Emma Jean looked at her aunt, the woman who had raised her, the woman she loved so much. She looked at her aunt, and she didn't know who she saw anymore. She shook her head. "I don't know how to deal with this. So much has happened I can't process it all."

"Take your time, darling. We're not going anywhere," Cleo said.

She pushed her chair back and stood up. "I think I need to go to bed now."

"I know how hard this is for you," Cleo said. "And I'm so sorry that we had to spring it on you. But I knew the time had come. I was a wreck back in Seattle. I knew I had to come home to tell you."

Emma Jean stared at her aunt, wishing that she *hadn't* come home to tell her this news. And then it hit her—home. Home was what she needed. Her real home, in Portland, not this godforsaken mountain town. Peter was in Walla Walla now, she could have her wonderful house back and being in it would fortify her claim to it. She could see Trish, and that would make Emma Jean happy, even if Trish was sickeningly in love with Connor. She could be home in time for Thanksgiving, her favorite holiday, and she could invite everyone she had ever known for dinner that day. Oh, she was so excited.

"That's the one good thing you've said all night, Cleo. I'm going home. Tomorrow. And now I'm going to my room to book a ticket."

* * *

The next day, Emma Jean awoke to a world covered in white. She felt energized and eager to put her plan to return home into place. Her plane left that evening, and she was so excited she could barely stand it. She'd be home for Thanksgiving in Portland! She called Trish to tell her to pick Emma Jean up at the airport and also that they needed to start planning Thanksgiving dinner, immediately. Oh, wouldn't it be fun to host the dinner at her house! Suddenly she could hardly wait to get out of snow-covered, mountainous Sun Valley and be home in lush, green, rainy Portland. It would make her so happy to be home. Even if more problems than the word count of her latest chapter awaited her. Even if Riley was not going to be part of her life.

But before she could go home, she needed to do a couple things.

"What's wrong?" Ava had said when Emma Jean called.

"Why do you assume something is wrong?"

"Because you called and talked to Wendy first. I have highly developed intuition for these things."

Emma Jean wracked her brain, trying to think of what book Ava would be reading that she would get the bit about intuition from.

"*A Wrinkle in Time*," Emma Jean cried triumphantly.

"It's a good book, though a bit beneath me," Ava said.

"It is not beneath you. I re-read it every few years or so."

"I am reading Charles de Lint," Ava said, and Emma Jean knew that if they were together in person, she would have her chin in the air in the haughtiest of manners.

"Oh, honey, doesn't he write the same book over and over again?"

"He writes urban fantasies that are more to my taste than many kid novels."

Emma Jean pictured Ava shrugging. Damn, she was actually going to miss the girl.

"So why are you calling?"

And Emma Jean had explained that she wanted to make sure she was home, because she was going to come see her. It was Saturday, so Ava would not be in school. Wendy's house was south of Ketchum, in the adjoining town of Hailey, where the airport was located, and where there was an actual chain grocery store, and a movie theater (owned by some Hollywood actor whose name Emma Jean could never remember, the one who had been married to Demi Moore). There were also a couple of housing developments of the sort you might find in any city in the country, and it was in one of these that Wendy lived.

Emma Jean drove slowly and carefully, not being used to the snow, and feeling a grave sense of responsibility to little Claire. Someone had shoveled the stairs up to Wendy's front door, so at least she didn't have to worry about falling on the steps. A stocky teenage boy with a face full of acne answered the bell—the snow shoveler, no doubt—and vaguely Emma Jean remembered Wendy telling her about her son. Everything in Wendy's house was painted in hues of tan and yellow with touches of red. There were doilies galore on tabletops and pillows with bears and bunnies and kitties on them, or sayings like, *Bless this Mess,* even though the house was spotless. And yet, something about the home was cozy and comforting. Wendy, dressed in tight jeans and a turquoise sweatshirt with the Sun Valley logo on it, led her through the living room and into the kitchen in the back, where Ava sat at a booth-style maple table, reading a book.

She didn't look up when Emma Jean entered the room.

"Hi, darling," Emma Jean said.

Ava held up a finger and kept reading.

Emma Jean looked over at Wendy and covered her mouth to suppress a laugh. Wendy mouthed the words, "too precocious," and they both smiled.

Finally, Ava looked up. "Oh, hi."

"Hi," Emma Jean said. She slid onto the booth beside her. "I came to see you because I have to talk to you."

"I know," Ava said. "We went through all that on the phone. What is up?"

Emma Jean took a deep breath. "I have to leave Sun Valley."

The look of shock and horror on Ava's face would have been deeply satisfying if it weren't so sad.

"No, you can't go!" Ava cried. "My mother is coming and you have to meet her!"

"But, darling, you'll be so happy to see your mother you won't even be thinking of me. Honest."

"You can't go," Ava said. "Why are you going?"

"I have to take care of some things at home."

"That is so stupid." Ava's voice was rising and gathering strength.

"Ava, honey—" Wendy said.

"I can't believe you're leaving. Right when everything was starting to go well. Damn it!"

"Stop swearing right this instant," Wendy said.

"I'll be back," Emma Jean said, though she didn't know when she would be returning, exactly. Lord, was Claire going to be this difficult to deal with some day? Emma Jean felt completely out of her depth.

"When?" Ava demanded.

"Um…I'm not sure yet, but—"

"You're just like all the other stupid adults." Ava was yelling now, and she hopped up from the booth. "I thought you were different. I thought you were special because you were a writer and all, but you're not. You're going to be sorry when my mother gets here and she's prettier and better than you. I hate you. I never want to see you again as long as I live."

And then Ava ran crying from the room.

"Should I go after her?" Emma Jean said.

Wendy shook her head. "No. It's best just to leave her when she's like this. You might try calling her in a few days. She'll get over it. Now just keep fingers crossed that her wretched mother actually does appear on schedule."

Back in the car, Emma Jean turned the heat and defrost on full blast and leaned her head on the steering wheel while the car warmed up. *Breathe*, she told herself. She felt awful, absolutely awful. She'd had no idea that Ava would take her leaving so badly. It was because she had such a hard time forming attachments, Wendy said. When she did form one—as she had with Emma Jean—she held onto it something fierce. As Emma Jean sat in the car taking deep, cleansing breaths, the thought occurred to her yet again that motherhood was going to be one tough job. Worse, she'd be doing it alone. Well, she had a few months to get ready for Claire. At the moment, she was worried about Ava. Maybe she could buy her a present and send it to her, something pink and glittery.

As she steered her car onto the street, her phone rang. Her heart ker-thumped in her chest. Maybe it was Ava, saying she was sorry, asking her to come back so they could have a decent goodbye and Emma Jean could recommend some more books to her. She fumbled for the phone, keeping her eyes on the road, and plunging her hand into her messenger bag and feeling for it. But caller ID listed not Wendy's number but the number of the Angela Devine Literary Agency.

Emma Jean was tempted to ignore it. No, she told herself firmly, she was done hiding. She was heading home to Portland in order to start dealing with things. She needed to face Inga. At least she could tell her that she had talked to Sally Marx. Oh, had she talked.

"Hi, Inga," Emma Jean said.

"It's not Inga; it is Angela."

"Oh." Emma Jean jerked the wheel in surprise, causing the car to slide a little on the slippery street. Oh God, Angela was probably calling to ditch her as a client. Well, Emma Jean would surprise Angela by taking the news calmly and with dignity.

"You won't believe what has happened."

"I know, Angela. It's hard for me to believe, too. After all these years you want to give me up? But I understand. *Wife* just didn't do as well as we expected. It's that damn Peter's fault. It was his idea in the first place. I knew I shouldn't have listened to him."

"Emma Jean, hush. I'm not ending our contract. Listen to me. You need to get cracking on a proposal immediately. This pregnancy thing has blown up. Margaret posted the letter you wrote, which was hysterical, by the way, and it's all over the Internet. They tell me this is called going viral. I don't know what the right term for it is, I'm just grateful. I think it's going to nudge the sales of *Wife* to a respectable level so that I can get you a good contract for the new book."

"Wait, Angela, I'm confused. What new book?"

"The one you're going to write a proposal for. Something about being an old mother. I don't know; you'll think of something. You just have to build on this pregnant at age 50 thing."

"I'm not 50," Emma Jean said.

"Whatever, you know what I mean. And blog, Emma Jean. Write down every damn thought you've ever had about pregnancy and being an old mother. Blog like the wind."

After she hung up, Emma Jean practiced her relaxing breathing all the way home. Oh there must be a God, because he or she or it had prevented her from entering the poorhouse, just in the nick of time. And he or she or it had given her back her career. Emma Jean stopped at the red light at the intersection of the street that led to the hospital, and closed her eyes in a quick prayer. The possibility of money and a revived career was all well and good, she told God, but all she really wanted was Riley. And then she asked God to throw Ava back at her, too.

Chapter Twenty-One
Turkey Lurkey

Emma Jean opened the oven to check the turkey. She knew that every time she opened the oven door to look at it, the heat escaped and the oven had to turn itself on again and that this was consequently not so good for the turkey because it caused inconsistent heating, but she couldn't help it. She was a visual person, that was all there was to it, and she had to *see* the turkey to gauge its progress. The problem with cooking a turkey was that you only did it once a year, and thus never truly had the chance to improve your turkey-cooking skills. Emma Jean shut the oven door, opened a cupboard, extracted a glass and poured herself some water from the spigot on the outside of the fridge.

Rain beat against the window, as it had relentlessly for the two weeks she'd been home. Rain, glorious rain. Wet, cold, Oregon rain. She hadn't realized how much she missed it until she experienced it again. She loved everything about the rain: the way it sounded on the roof, the way you had to throw your hood up and run to the car to avoid getting soaked, and the smell. Oh Lord how she loved the smell of rain. Indefinable, indescribable, yet so familiar and comforting. This rain was a cold rain, much colder than usual, and the weather forecasters were intoning darkly about the possibility of snow.

She heard a burst of noise from the living room, where her guests had assembled for Thanksgiving: Cleo and Bob, Trish and Connor, Marielle and Julia. She drummed her fingers on the black marble countertop of the center island and pondered how much longer she should leave the turkey in. Trish kept telling her to wait, that they needed to hold off, but as far as Emma Jean was concerned, Trish was absolutely blinded by love, and therefore not to be trusted in any manners of judgment.

Emma Jean sighed. She wanted to be blinded by love the way Trish and Connor were together. Well, Emma Jean was blinded by love; it was just that her love had been painfully ripped from her through no fault of her own. She stared out the window at the rain and wondered where Riley was celebrating Thanksgiving. Lord, she missed having that man in her life. And yet, slowly she was accepting the possibility that she could create a satisfying life for her and little Claire without him. She had even decided that if worse came to worse, she could let go of her beloved home, too. After all, since Emma Jean was learning what it meant to let go of everything she held dear, she might as well go all the way.

Trish popped her head through the door. Her cheeks were pink and her eyes sparkling. It was amazing how good love was for one's looks.

"You're not getting it out yet, right?" Trish said.

"No, mother, I'm not getting it out yet."

Trish smiled. She had a funny expression on her face but she didn't linger long enough for Emma Jean to figure out what it signified. Trish just gave a little wave and headed back to the living room, where Connor waited, and where, by the sound of it, the wine that was being poured liberally was having a lubricating effect on the general level of hilarity.

Emma Jean wondered if she could sneak across the hall to her office and spend a few minutes working on her proposal. The new book was going to be called the *POM Manifesto,* POM being short for Pregnant Older Mom, and she had so many ideas for it she could barely get them down on paper. Angela loved what Emma Jean had produced so far, *loved* it, and so did the readers of her blog. New fans seemed to be finding their way to her, intrigued by her story of falling in love and getting pregnant at such an advanced age. Even some of the angry fans had come around. A couple of them had written her saying they were now seeing fertility specialists.

Oh, it was delightful to have such influence again. And the attention had resulted in a wee bump in sales for *Wife.* There'd even been a request for an interview from a couple of newspapers. Nothing big, but at least it was something. And Angela thought more attention would follow once the *Vanity Fair* article came out.

Of course it would be even more delightful if she could share this resurgence in her career with Riley. Emma Jean sighed, and then told herself for the millionth time that she was fine without him. And she was. There would always be a space in her heart for him, but she was learning to live with that space and let it be. Maybe she should check the turkey again. There were also the potatoes to deal with, and peas, and she'd made a butternut squash casserole that needed to be reheated. Better to think about food than Riley. Just one little look at the turkey couldn't hurt.

"Emma Jean, close the door," Marielle said, coming up behind her.

"I'm getting cranky and hungry," Emma Jean said. "I want this damn bird to be done but Trish says I can't take it out yet."

"I'd tell you to relax and have another glass of wine, but that won't work at the moment, will it? Why don't you go sit for a bit until the turkey is done? You've been working your butt off all day."

Suddenly it occurred to her that she and Marielle were having a civil conversation. Emma Jean's project to become friends with Marielle had failed miserably. They hadn't spoken, really, since Emma Jean returned home from Sun Valley. If Marielle happened to answer when Emma Jean called she eked out a terse, "I'll get Julia," and handed off the phone. No: *Hi. How are you, beloved teacher?* Not a single *Oh it's so good to hear from you*, or *I'm so glad you've returned from the frozen north.*

"Everything is going okay out there?" Emma Jean leaned against the counter.

"You bet. I'm just getting another bottle of wine to refill glasses," Marielle said.

Did that *you bet* sound a little forced, just a tad bit too perky? Emma Jean watched Marielle drill a cork with the squiggle of the corkscrew, then expertly pop it out and wished she could think of something brilliant to say that would stitch the wound in the air between them. The smell of fermented grape wafted by her, competing with the aroma of the turkey.

"There," Marielle said. She'd cut her hair in the months since Emma Jean had last seen her. Now it was fashioned in a real style, with short layers that fell around her chin and softened her angular face. And she was wearing real clothes, a tailored black skirt and jacket with a red camisole beneath. The outfit looked classy and hip, not like her old style, which had tended toward the writer-trying-painfully-hard-to-be-cool mien.

"You look good," Emma Jean said.

Marielle had picked up the bottle of wine and started toward the other room, but now a look of surprise crossed her face and she paused. "Thank you."

Emma Jean realized by the expression on Marielle's face that she didn't compliment her often. Well, hell, she'd been her student. She believed in supporting her students' work, not constantly approving their personal style. But now that they were moving to friend territory, perhaps she could throw some praise out once in a while.

Marielle looked at Emma Jean as if expecting the other shoe to drop. No, that was a cliché, but it was such a good one, how could you improve on it as a descriptive metaphor? Always push your brain harder, Emma Jean told her students. Marielle looked at Emma Jean as if expecting a bolt of lightning to fall from the sky. Another cliché. Marielle looked at Emma Jean as if expecting a chunk of sheet rock to fall from the ceiling and smite her. That was awful, and she didn't even know if they used sheet rock on the ceiling. The one bad thing about being a writer was how often it pointed out her ignorance. Of course the good thing about it was that then she had an excuse to research the most obscure of topics.

"I found a store that sells second hand designer clothing. Wonderful things at amazing prices," Marielle said, apparently tired of waiting for Emma Jean to say anything else. "My old look was a bit immature, I decided."

"I think being a bestselling writer suits you."

The truth of the matter—and Emma Jean couldn't decide if it was a good truth or a bad truth—was that Marielle's book was now selling in the millions, if not gazillions of copies, sales pushed ever higher by the speculation about its truthfulness. At any rate, her compliment, to say nothing of the actual recognition that her student had, dare she say it, surpassed her in the publishing sweepstakes, now caused a look of extreme surprise to cross Marielle's face, like a storm crossing the desert. An adequate though not great metaphor, Emma Jean thought as Marielle nodded gravely and said, "Thank you. It does suit me, I guess. I've even enjoyed the controversy."

"You have?" Emma Jean felt her heart pound a bit harder, like a drumbeat escalating to a crescendo. Okay, she really had to stop with the dreadful metaphors, though, as she always told her students, the best way to become fluent in metaphor was to force yourself to think in them a lot. Maybe it was time for her to go back to teaching. Trish said she had a list of people waiting to study with her. That was a lovely thought she'd have to return to later.

Marielle nodded. "Yeah. I made a decision early on just to relax and enjoy it. Before I got published, I always read these articles by known writers that said publishing wouldn't make a difference in their life. Well, to hell with that. It's made a huge difference. It's what I always wanted and what I worked for for years. So I just decided to go full tilt and enjoy every second of it, even the crap."

"Wow," Emma Jean said, deeply impressed by Marielle's speech. "Maybe you could write a self-help book next. That's pretty good advice for living."

A huge grin split Marielle's face. "Well, I have to say, having great sex all the time, helps, too."

Emma Jean didn't really want her mind to create a visual of that. Not that she had anything against lesbian sex, like most women, she herself had a bi-curious streak, but it was her stepdaughter that Marielle was talking about having sex with. The very same stepdaughter Emma Jean had nurtured as a young girl. It made her feel positively dizzy. She grabbed the counter to steady herself.

"Oh, God, Emma Jean, I've been chattering away and you need to sit."

"No, no, I'm fine."

"No, you're not." Marielle grabbed the wine bottle in one hand and Emma Jean's elbow in the other and guided her toward the grouping of furniture arranged around the big stone fireplace. "You sit and relax and I'll go be charming and entertain everyone so they don't miss you for a bit."

The good thing about being pregnant, Emma Jean thought as she watched Marielle head out the door, was how everyone fawned over you. People had fawned over her as a bestselling writer, but she'd gotten used to that. And this was fawning on a personal level, with her physical wellbeing in question. But wait.

"Marielle," she called.

Marielle popped her head back through the door.

"I think an apology is in order."

Her student's face crinkled like plastic wrap folding over itself. "From me?"

Emma Jean shook her head and rearranged herself on the pillows. If she wedged a pillow in just the right spot behind the small of her back, the constant discomfort she felt there subsided.

"No, no, from me."

The expressions on Marielle's face—puzzlement to shock to happiness—were priceless, and Emma Jean wished she had a camera, even though she was determinedly not a photographer, probably because she hated pictures of herself so much.

"I've not given you your due. You're a colleague now, no longer a student, and I've not entirely made the mental shift. I've realized that over the last few months."

Marielle smiled. "Thanks, Emma Jean. But you'll always be a teacher to me."

"No, I want to be friends with you now." Emma Jean took a deep breath and felt herself wincing. "Can't we be friends?"

"Okay." Marielle nodded. "I'd like that."

"And that's not all. I hold myself responsible for the story about the memoir coming out."

Now Marielle looked puzzled again. She set the wine bottle she'd been holding all this time on the cute, little side table Emma Jean had insisted on hauling home from that antique store in some depressing coastal town. "Why?"

There was nothing to do but just say it. "Because I got drunk on the plane to Sun Valley last summer and told a librarian my doubts. I couldn't help it. I was so jealous that your book was on the bestseller list and *Wife* was doing so poorly."

"Oh, Emma Jean, is that what you think?"

Emma Jean nodded miserably.

"But that's not what happened at all. Sally Marx read the book in galley and started investigating from the get-go. She grew up in Ohio like I did and got suspicious," Marielle said. "I love you to death, Emma Jean, but honestly? The world does not revolve around you."

Emma Jean ignored the dig, a very *friendly* thing to do, she felt. "So you knew before the book was even published that there was going to be a to-do about it?"

"Pretty much, yes."

Emma Jean cocked her head to one side and appraised her student. "So, what is the truth, Marielle? Did it really happen or not? I don't care one way or the other; I'm just curious."

Marielle's standard response through all of the controversy had been the same: that she stood by her story as her version of the truth, and if people chose to read it as fiction that was their decision.

"Just like I told you over and over again in class, it's all true."

"I'll take your word for it."

Marielle raised her eyebrows and offered a funny little smile that had the effect of making Emma Jean wonder all over again if she was telling the truth or not. But *c'est la vie*. If Marielle wanted the world to think it was true, far be it for Emma Jean to prove her wrong. After all, part of the attraction of Emma Jean's first book had been the stunning chapters she'd penned about her mother's death—none of which had turned out to be true. So now Emma Jean understood a bit better about the permeability of truth and fiction.

"I'm taking the wine in now," Marielle said.

Emma Jean waved her away. All of a sudden she was so damned tired. She'd been up since six, working on preparations for dinner and sneaking in bouts of writing on the proposal. She wanted to close her eyes for one brief moment. Just for one minute, she promised herself, and then she'd go tend to her guests. She leaned her head back against the soft plush of the velour couch and her eye fell on the pile of books, artfully arranged if she did say so herself, that were stacked on the coffee table beside Aku Aku.

The titles all had to do with various religious traditions, though Emma Jean wasn't sure if one could call *A Course in Miracles* an actual religion, but one or two were about the Bible. Yet the single most important volume was the one that held pride of place beside the towering stack—the Carter family bible.

Her father had produced the Bible a couple days earlier, the final rallying point of his campaign to make Emma Jean forgive him. She had to admit that it was a good strategy. The gift had also led her on a whole new path of her spiritual search into the roots of Christianity, which had always made her so nervous that she had up to now avoided it. Aunt Cleo had considered art her religion, and never taken Emma Jean near a church, and so she thought of traditional churches as oppressive, intimidating places. Now that she knew the backstory between her aunt and her father, Cleo's rejection of religion made more sense (though it wasn't as if it hadn't made sense to Emma Jean in the first place; after all she'd been in a spiritual desert, an absolute *desert,* before she'd met Riley and begun her quest). Seeing as how Bob, her father, had been a part-time preacher all his life, it was no wonder Cleo rejected religion—she had to reject everything that smacked of him in order to maintain her sanity and not go off half-cocked with missing him. And Emma Jean now fully and profoundly understood about missing someone.

The one good thing about Bob was that he was now studying theology at Emory University in Atlanta. "I decided it was time to get a proper credential," he'd told her, after gifting her with the bible. Emma Jean was desperate to learn more about what one might study at theology school, but she hadn't yet forgiven him, so she couldn't admit this. The thought of having someone with whom to have long theological and spiritual discussions, and an expert resource to ask questions when she got confused, was appealing, but that would have to wait until she had forgiven him. If she ever decided to forgive him, that is. Honestly, could you believe that the two of them had had an affair back in the day? And then gotten back together again without telling her? Emma Jean shook her head. In a perfect world, she would reject anything to do with either one of them.

But she couldn't help it. She was fascinated with all religions and family history, too. She reached for the bible. It had a red leather cover and thin pages, like the old onionskin paper she found in Cleo's files. Despite the thin paper, her father had written and underlined throughout the book, and there were Post-it notes stuck over many pages with more notes written on them. Also book marks—tiny little strips of paper with jagged edges, like they'd been torn from the bottom of a newspaper or notebook paper or just a scratch pad. Emma Jean loved this bible. It was like a reading her father's journal, a window into his soul, even though she was not yet one hundred percent convinced she really wanted to understand that soul.

She was trying, though. The night before, he and she had sat in this very room and she'd asked him about his beliefs. He'd gone off on a long tangent, and she'd stayed up way too late listening to him, which was why she was so tired at the moment.

Cleo had been there, too, of course. Despite Emma Jean's best attempts to ignore her aunt, Cleo had nosed her way into Emma Jean's life at every opportunity, which translated into every day. The previous evening, Cleo sat in the other room while Emma Jean listened to Bob orate and Emma Jean had not made any effort to include her.

But this morning had been a different story. Cleo had appeared at the house bearing gifts, a patently obvious ploy to win Emma Jean back over. Cleo brought a decaf soy latte, not nearly as good as a Bowl of Soul from Mountain Karma, but decent nonetheless, and a cinnamon and cashew scone. Emma Jean had not yet had breakfast, since she'd been up writing, so she was starving. Poor little Claire desperately needed some nutrition, so how could Emma Jean turn her aunt away?

It happened right after Cleo set out plates and forks and sat down across from her. As Emma Jean watched her aunt, today dressed in bright red and pink with a burgundy boa around her neck, she had an epiphany.

"Oh, Aunt Cleo, I understand it all now!" she'd blurted so suddenly that Cleo dribbled coffee down her chin.

"Do tell," Cleo said.

"It's the same thing as Riley and I—you and Bob couldn't help it, you just fell in love."

Cleo and Bob had done exactly what she had done with Riley—*fallen in love*. Nothing more, nothing less. So if she was angry with them, she was angry with herself. It was a bit of a duh moment, she had to admit. She had understood this with her mind, but she hadn't fully gotten it in her heart, the way all the spiritual traditions said you had to, until this very moment.

A sweet smile spread across Cleo's lips, cracking the erratically applied lipstick. "That's it exactly, darling. Does this mean you forgive us?"

Well, Emma Jean wasn't quite yet ready to make any rash promises. The idea of Bob and Cleo together still rankled. "I wouldn't go quite that far," Emma Jean said. "But, Cleo, you've always had that saying, step by step, we travel far. So let's just consider this a first step, okay?"

"Oh darling!" Cleo rushed to Emma Jean, nearly falling over the table in the process, and flung her arms around her. Emma Jean struggled not to be smothered by the folds of Cleo's red dress.

Even though she hadn't precisely admitted it, she felt that somewhere in the dim recesses of her mind she had forgiven Cleo. After all, Emma Jean had barely even known her mother, and had only one dim memory of her. It was Cleo who had raised her, Cleo who had made her into the adult she was today, Cleo who was her true mother. Emma Jean felt pleased with herself for this revelation, and was now certain that she was winning all kinds of points with God. She'd had a little chat with the Supreme Being just that morning, explaining that she hadn't quite managed to include Bob in her forgiveness campaign but was taking baby steps by being kind and gracious to him.

She had elucidated this to Trish later that morning when Trish came by to drop off extra chairs they'd need for the dinner. Grudgingly, she had admitted that she was enjoying having Bob around, just the teeniest, tiniest bit. "It's great having someone to run all my questions by. Though I'm not entirely certain about this whole Jesus thing yet. But it is interesting."

"Faith is about more than your latest interest, Emma Jean. You're supposed to believe it deep inside," Trish said.

"Well, maybe I do." She raised her eyes to the ceiling and pondered her feeling center, her gut. Truth be told, she wasn't yet sure what she believed. "Anyway, you're an agnostic, so how would you know?"

"It's my job to analyze human reactions, their crutches, and faith is one of them."

"Your problem is that you over-analyze, Trish. Let go and just feel for a change. That's what faith is about."

And as she said the words, Emma Jean realized that they were true and that she *did* have faith. She had faith in some sort of God even if she didn't yet have the theology to match it. Faith that she truly was learning to be less judgmental and more kind. And she had faith in a bright future, faith that little Claire would be born healthy, faith that she would be able to raise her properly as a single mother. After all, look how well she herself had turned out, and she'd been raised by a single parent.

Remembering all this, Emma Jean realized why she was so tired. First the late night the previous evening, then up early to write, and after that a full day of visitors and food prepping. No wonder she was exhausted. Emma Jean leaned her head back again. She'd just close her eyes for a brief moment to refresh herself, and then she could join her party. She breathed deeply and relaxed.

"Emma Jean." The soft voice penetrated her consciousness. Dear God, she'd fallen asleep. Oh crap, the turkey. And her guests. But it was hard to lift her head; it felt like it weighed two tons. Opening her eyes took more energy than she'd ever expended before, or so it felt.

"Emma Jean."

Apparently the pregnancy now made her dreams more vivid and real, because she could *swear* Peter was standing in the room with her. She opened her eyes. He *was* standing in the room with her, hovering above her in that annoying way he had of violating her personal space.

"What are you doing here?" Emma Jean said.

"How are you, Emma Jean? It is so good to see you, and my don't you look wonderful tonight."

She realized that in truth she probably looked like crap, with her hair askew and her mascara smudged beneath her eyes, the way it got when she fell asleep like this. Not that she cared, since Peter was a conniving, betraying bastard, but nonetheless she felt it important to look her best in any situation. But if she were writing this scene in one of her novels she would certainly not write it like this, with the heroine—Emma Jean herself—at her worst and Peter hovering over her in the power position.

"It is always a treat to see my lovely wife, especially on a special day such as this."

Emma Jean peered at him suspiciously. Peter was way too jocular to be sober. She positioned herself so she was sitting more upright and peered around his side to see if he was holding a wine glass. He was. Of course Peter would be holding a wine glass. It was just that he was so used to drinking wine that he rarely got drunk. So either he'd had a lot, or he'd been imbibing Scotch. Peter always got drunk on Scotch. But wait. He couldn't have been here that long, as she hadn't been dozing for but a few minutes or someone would have awakened her. Or the turkey would have caught fire. Or something. Her brain hurt from trying to figure out all the *or somethings*.

"You're drunk," Emma Jean said.

Peter raised his wine glass in a mock toast. "Perhaps, my dear wife, I am just happy to see you."

At that moment her cell phone, sitting on the table where she'd left it, started ringing. Emma Jean ignored it.

"Aren't you happy to see me?"

The cell phone quit ringing and a second later started again. Peter reached for it. Emma Jean lunged, got it first, and saw Wendy's number on the screen. Wendy could wait. Though maybe Ava was with her and had decided to start speaking to Emma Jean again. Peter loomed closer. No, she had to deal with her soon-to-be-ex-husband. Regretfully, Wendy and Ava would have to wait.

"I'm disappointed in you. So far all you've said to me is, 'you're drunk.' Is that the best you can come up with after all this time?"

"It's only been a little while, Peter."

"A month. But we had that charming conversation on the phone a mere week ago."

Why did Peter choose the day of her party to return? She wasn't happy about having to deal with him. But he seemed so drunk as to be difficult to handle and so she went for as soothing a response as she could muster. "You just caught me at a bad time. I think I fell asleep for a little bit. I've been so tired lately. Now, excuse me, but I've got to check on the turkey."

Emma Jean stood, swayed, touched her fingers to the table to steady herself, and then Peter was next to her and taking her in his arms. She stiffened, his brown sweater rough against her cheek, inhaling his usual smell of wine, a hint of lemon from his aftershave, a tiny bit of bad breath.

"Peter, don't," she said into his chest.

"Aw, c'mon, Emma Jean, tell me you are happy to see me."

It was *almost* good to see him—in the way it was good to see an old friend who hadn't been around in ages. She pulled her head back to look at him, really look at him, and he bent toward her as if to kiss her. Emma Jean stepped back, out of his arms. This was too much. Peter was going way too far. She'd made it clear she was done with their marriage, so he didn't need to be trying to kiss her, for God's sake.

"I've got to check that turkey," Emma Jean said.

"I miss you. We need to talk. I've got so much to tell you."

"We talked. On the phone, a week ago, as you just reminded me. And I made my position clear."

"I wanted to tell you, I've accepted a job in Walla Walla."

"Congratulations, Peter," Emma Jean said. "I think you'll be happy back in Walla Walla."

"I was hoping you'd come with me," Peter said. He gazed deeply into her eyes. "That's why I came here today."

Couldn't this very moment be a scene in her book, with her husband standing in the house they used to share, begging her to go with him to start a new life? For a brief iota of a second, she wavered. She *could* go back. She could take Peter back, and maybe he'd learn to accept little Claire. She was developing a whole new fan base, and, with luck, the *POM Manifesto* would hit it big. She could have the life she had lived with Peter before she met Riley. She stared into Peter's eyes. They were deep and limitless, and as she stared into them, she knew beyond a shadow of a doubt what she wanted.

"No. It's not going to work, Peter."

"I miss the way things were between us."

"You miss my money."

"Aren't all our years together worth at least some effort?"

Emma Jean nodded. "They are. I agree with that totally. But you're forgetting one thing. I don't come alone anymore." She pointed to her stomach. "There's two of us, now, remember."

"I'm even willing to forgive you your indiscretions, Emma Jean. Which, frankly, is damn big of me. I'm willing to accept your baby and live with both of you. I've missed you so much lately, and missing you makes me realize how much I love you. I am willing to fight for you. For us."

"More to the point, you vowed to fight for what little money I have left. You've talked to a divorce attorney and found out your threats to take me for every penny are pretty baseless, haven't you?"

Bingo. She could tell by the look on his face that she'd hit his motivation dead on. Emma Jean stood and walked to the oven, opening the door one more time to peek at the turkey. She didn't want to be near him anymore; she didn't want to smell his grape and lemon smell or look at his nubby sweater or see into his eyes. He was willing to forgive her? And it was damn big of him? Yes, she had been bad, very bad, and she had admitted that. But he had been too—and way earlier and for a lot longer than she had. The very basis of their marriage had been a lie, a lie he had maintained steadfastly for fifteen years. She couldn't stand to look at his sanctimonious, patronizing face any longer.

The open oven door let out a burst of heat to her face, and she closed it again. "What about me forgiving you, Peter? How about that, huh? Did it ever occur to you that might need to happen before I agree to move to some godforsaken town in the middle of nowhere with you?"

"It's not godforsaken," Peter said. "Sunset magazine called Walla Walla the premiere wine destination in the country."

"Oh for the love of Jesus, can't you think of anything besides wine?"

Thankfully, just then Trish poked her head through the door. *Sorry*, she mouthed over Peter's head. "I guess maybe it's time to pull the turkey out. Peter, we're about to eat so its time for you to leave," Trish said firmly. "I'll come back and help you with the rest of the meal in just a second, Emma Jean."

"But what if I don't want to leave?" Peter said. "What if I want to spend Thanksgiving with my wife?"

"It really is time for you to go," Trish said.

And then Bob appeared and grabbed Peter by the shoulder. "C'mon, Peter, its time, man."

Emma Jean had never been so grateful for her father. She sank down on the couch, staring after Peter, and felt a ridiculous stew of emotions roil about inside her—surprise, anger, relief, and most of all joy. This was it, the symbolic end of their marriage, if not the legal one. This was really it. Finally, she stood and squared her shoulders. Well. That was that. But there was still dinner to serve. Maybe she'd let Trish mash the potatoes, as that took a lot of energy. Dealing with Peter had been exhausting and hopefully Bob had thrown him out the front door, never to be seen again. The gall Peter had, appearing and upsetting her Thanksgiving dinner.

She decided she could manage putting the casserole in the oven and start the water for the peas. She puttered around the kitchen for a few minutes, trying to get her mind back to the last minute preparations and then the doorbell rang. Emma Jean looked toward the front of the house, puzzled. Now who would that be? Was it Peter, coming back to haunt her yet again? God, what did it take to get rid of that man?

She heard voices from the living room, the sound of footsteps on the wood floor in the hallway, the distinctive whoosh of the front door opening then a round of cheers. Apparently much drinking had ensued during her little doze. Someone yelled, "Good to meet you!"

Emma Jean skirted the marble-topped island in the kitchen, heading out to see who had arrived. But she didn't get very far because suddenly there was Riley standing in the door, smiling. Riley, in all his adorableness. Wait, Riley? She shook her head, closed her eyes, opened them again. First Peter appeared, and then Riley. She was having a difficult time processing it.

"Is it really you?" she said.

"It's really me," he said, and stepped toward her.

She flung herself into his arms. He wasn't wearing a coat—silly L.A. boy—and she pressed her cheek against the softness of his cotton shirt. Oh God, Riley! She couldn't believe it was really him, couldn't believe that she was in his arms, his strong muscular arms. She never wanted to let go of him. But wait. Oh God. Why was he here?

"Did you come to tell me goodbye in person?" she said into his shirt. She couldn't bear to see his eyes when he said goodbye, and she wanted to remain in his embrace as long as possible. She wanted to savor it so that when she was old and alone she could remember how wonderful it had been to hold him one last time. She could tell Claire about how romantic and tragic it had been, and they could cry together.

"No, Emma Jean. I did not come to tell you goodbye."

"You didn't?"

"I did not."

She still didn't trust herself to look at him.

"I came to tell you hello."

She broke away from him and looked into his eyes. They were twinkling, the way they had when she first met him, the way they always did when they were making love.

"I'm so confused," Emma Jean said.

"I know. I'll explain everything. But first I need this." And he bent down and enfolded her in his arms again and then kissed her. He kissed her long and hard and nations triumphed and withered, armies fought pitched battles and won and lost, and it felt like every garden everywhere in the world burst into bloom. This was what had been missing in her life; this was what she needed to make herself whole. Riley. But when the kiss ended and she stepped away, she suddenly felt shy.

"Your shirt is all wet," she said.

"It's starting to snow," Riley said. "I didn't know I should expect snow."

"It doesn't happen often. It's because you're so special," Emma Jean said.

"You think?" Riley nuzzled her, and aimed his lips toward hers again. Then she remembered her guests. The turkey. "Oh God we can't do this right now," she said, and stepped back.

"Why not?"

But she'd caught a glimpse of him, and now all she could do was stare. He was dressed in wool pants that hung from his waist as if personally tailored for him, and a light blue shirt of the sort that you spent lots of money on at Nordstrom. Not like his usual jeans and t-shirt.

"You look amazing," Emma Jean said.

"You look pregnant," Riley said.

Emma Jean suddenly remembered how she'd fallen asleep on the couch and woken only when Peter arrived, worrying even then about her hair and her mascara. She looked a sight, no doubt. And now Riley was telling her she looking pregnant, which could only mean one thing.

"Oh God, I look fat, don't I?"

Riley laughed and pulled her to him again. "You don't look fat; you look pregnant. You're glowing."

"You're such a liar."

"Listen, Emma Jean, we need to talk."

"Damn right. Why are you here, Riley?" Suddenly, Emma Jean was angry. Here she'd been miserable, positively miserable, without Riley for weeks and now he waltzed back into her life without so much as an apology only after she had decided she would be okay without him? "And by the way, how do you know I want you here? What if I was so pissed at you that I never wanted to lay eyes on you again? Don't you think it was a little presumptuous to make the assumption I was pining for you?"

Riley furrowed his brows as if he was trying to be very serious, but a smile played at the corner of his lips.

"Don't laugh at me."

"I'm not laughing at you. I'm smiling because it seemed impossible for me to imagine you not feeling the same way I have for the last few weeks. I've felt like a part of me has been missing, Emma Jean." Riley shook his head.

There were shouts and hoots of laughter from the front room, and Emma Jean glanced in that direction. The party. They really had to get dinner going.

"Oh Riley, that's exactly how I've felt, too. But...what about Carolina?"

"Hard as I tried with her, I just couldn't do it. I was living a lie, and I knew it. She knew it, too. But that didn't make it any easier when she found out about you."

"Oh, crap."

"Yeah. It's not been pretty."

Emma Jean tried to feel sadness for Carolina's pain upon learning that her husband was sleeping with another woman, particularly given her recent experience with Bob and Cleo, but all she could think about was how happy she was to see Riley.

"Does Carolina know about the baby?"

"Afraid so."

"How?"

"I told her," Riley said.

"Wait, what? You told her? About me? *And* the baby? You told her everything?"

"Because I was tired, Emma Jean. Tired of the lying and the sneaking around. Mostly, though I was tired of not being able to be with you."

Wasn't he the most wonderful man ever in the whole wide world? Emma Jean was marveling at his courage, telling Carolina about her and the baby, when Trish reappeared in the room.

"I hate to interrupt this reunion, but I think we need to get dinner going. The guests are getting drunk."

"Let's do it," Riley said. "I am a mean potato masher. And by the way, thanks for all your help, Trish."

Emma Jean looked from Riley, who she was having trouble taking her eyes off, to Trish. "You mean you knew he was coming? Oh God, that's why you kept telling me not to take the turkey out."

Trish nodded. Emma Jean felt a rush of love for her assistant, even if she was not going to technically be her assistant much longer. But Trish would be something better, Emma Jean hoped; she would be a friend.

Cleo burst into the kitchen at that very moment but paused in the doorway and glanced at Emma Jean, eyebrows furrowed. "Everything okay in here?"

"Everything is fantastic," Emma Jean said.

"Except we need help with dinner. You can start the peas," Trish said.

"I'd love to, darling." Cleo swayed from one foot to another, her wine glass held high in the air.

"Never mind, Cleo," Trish said, eyeing her with alarm.

"Oh, good," Cleo said. "I never was much of a cook. I'll just go sit back down until you tell us it's time for dinner, then."

Emma Jean wondered how Riley had gotten to the house as she put water on for the vegetables. She wondered, but there was no time to ask. Trish must have given him the address so he could take a cab. It didn't matter. All that mattered was that Riley was here.

"Well, then." Trish clapped her hands and walked over to the stove. "Let's get the rest of the show on the road. Not only is it snowing, but your guests are getting totally smashed. Who wants to pull the turkey out and carve it?"

"But it's not ready to carve yet!" Emma Jean cried. "It's supposed to sit for half an hour.

"Tough," Trish said. "If we wait, everyone will be passed out. You go call them to the table, Emma Jean. Riley can help me with the turkey."

"Hand me those hot pads; I'll get it from the oven," Riley said, holding onto the countertop and swaying from foot to foot. "And then I'll get the potatoes going."

"Go seat your guests, Emma Jean," Trish said. "Now."

Emma Jean did as she was told, not having the ability to think what else she could do, after all that had happened.

As she walked down the long hall toward the front room, she noticed a blurry shape through the glass of the front door and then she heard the doorbell ring, though it was muted beneath the sounds of the hoots of laughter and shouting that was coming from the guests in the living room.

"Oh Lord, what fresh hell is this?" Emma Jean asked of nobody in particular and strode to the door.

There, on the porch, stood a petite dark-haired woman wearing a hideous army-green parka with a fur-lined hood. She held the hand of a little boy. Before Emma Jean could open her mouth, the woman spoke.

"I'm here for my stupid asshole of a husband."

Chapter Twenty-Two

Was Lost But Now She's Found

Emma Jean stared at the screeching woman standing on the front porch. Water dripped off the overhang, and snow fell behind her in big gloppy flakes.

The woman let go of the child's hand and pushed him through the door. "Where is he? Where is the bastard?"

"You're Carolina," Emma Jean said.

"No shit," Carolina said, following the little boy into the house. "And who is this?"

"Kind of a dim bulb for being such a hot-shot writer, aren't you? This is Noah, bean-brain."

"This is Noah?"

Noah smiled at the mention of his name. Noah. This child was Noah. Emma Jean stared at him, entranced, ignoring Carolina's invectives, because the little boy who stood clutching a small, red car and staring back at her had nappy dark hair and skin the color of the coffee she was no longer supposed to drink. Skin the color of coffee. Not the color of a piece of fine ecru writing paper, like Riley. Noah's skin was coffee-colored. And, Emma Jean felt compelled to point out to herself, Carolina, too, was as white as a piece of plain, old typing paper.

Emma Jean remembered the conversations she'd had with Riley. *I've never been certain Noah is actually my child. Ya think?* She sensed movement in the hall behind her, heard voices, and turned to see Riley with a look that landed somewhere between panic and extreme anger.

"Oh God. Carolina, what are you doing here? You're supposed to be in North Dakota."

"Say hello to Daddy." Carolina pushed her child toward Riley. Noah ran to Riley and threw his arms around his father's knees. "And to his fat lover while you're at it."

Oh of all the nerve. "I'm not fat; I'm pregnant."

"Whatever. Translates to the same damned thing, doesn't it—one very large stomach." Carolina carried a gaily-flowered messenger style bag, the strap of which was looped around her neck and over one shoulder. As she unhooked it, Emma Jean studied her, the sting of her insults pushed aside by her utter fascination with this woman. Riley's wife. Not the lush, fresh flower she had envisioned. Far from it. This woman looked more like the meth addicts that had populated the streets—L.A. thin (she'd have to give her that), with a long nose and dark eyes that looked dead. She'd gotten the strap unhooked now and hurled the bag at Riley.

"Here's his toys. And some clothes." Carolina knelt to kiss Noah. "Have fun with Daddy, darling. I'll be home soon."

"Wait, Carolina, what's going on?" Riley said.

Carolina—she who Emma Jean had wasted many a sleepless night being jealous of—was already back out the door. Peering behind her, Emma Jean saw a yellow taxi waiting through the veil of snow, which seemed to be falling harder and starting to stick. "I'm going on vacation. Two can play at this game, Riley."

Outside, a car door slammed and Emma Jean saw a tall dark-haired man emerge from the back seat of the cab, holding an umbrella.

"I'm coming, Chester," Carolina called. She blew a kiss to Noah, threw the ghastly fur-lined hood over her head and pulled the door shut behind her.

Emma Jean looked at Riley, and the rest of her guests, who had crowded in behind him. "I'm so confused," she said, for the second time that night.

It was Trish, of course, who got them all seated at the table in the dining room, setting an extra place for Noah, stacking phone books on a chair which she pulled up beside Riley, ordering Bob to carry the turkey platter to the table and setting him to carving, shanghaiing Cleo and Connor to carry in bowls of mashed potatoes, stuffing, salad, and a huge basket of rolls.

Emma Jean had been so shocked at the appearance of Carolina and Noah that she'd not even had time to nurse her hurt feelings that Carolina had called her fat. Now, though, as Riley pulled her chair out for her, she thought of all the things she should have said. *Well, your husband prefers fat me to thin little ole you*, might have been good. Or how about, *eat your heart out, because this fat body is carrying your husband's baby. And clearly yours never did.* Whatever, it was too late now because Carolina was long gone, and Riley seemed to be trundling down the path Peter had paved—the one that led to the Planet of Extreme Drunkenness.

In truth, everyone at the table currently inhabited that same planet, except for the ever-practical Trish and Emma Jean. And she herself *would* definitely be shit-faced, not to put too fine a point on it, were it not for the consideration of little Claire. The fact that everyone had a good drunk on was why Trish had insisted they all eat as soon as Carolina had swept out the door.

"But I need to talk to Riley," Emma Jean had pleaded.

"No you don't." Trish had said. "I was afraid this wasn't going to work. I told you this wasn't going to work." They were standing in the foyer, the other guests having been led to the dining room by Cleo, who insisted they all form a conga line, hands on each other's hips, with Noah at the lead. Trish and Emma Jean's conversation was punctuated by choruses of "Cha cha cha cha cha, HEY! Cha cha cha cha cha HEY!" as the assembled hordes apparently continued their dance round and round the dining room table.

"It's working just fine. Look at them; they're having a blast. I have to talk to Riley before we eat," Emma Jean had insisted. "Have you seen his child?"

"It was just a little hard to miss that entrance."

"I'm talking about Noah, not his awful mother."

"He's pretty damned adorable, I'd say."

"And not white," Emma Jean hissed. Behind Trish down the hallway, the conga line snaked from the dining room across the hall into the kitchen. Noah was now riding atop Bob's shoulders, and Cleo was leading the charge, wine glass raised high in one hand.

"Since when are you racist?"

Emma Jean stomped her foot. "I am not flippin' racist," she said. "I couldn't care if he was purple. It's just obvious that Noah is. Not. Riley's. Child. And I have to talk to him about it. This has implications for our relationship."

"What implications?" Trish insisted. Behind her, the conga line trailed from the kitchen to the dining room.

"It absolves all my doubts about him. Don't you get it? This is huge! It means he's a good man, not a lying, betraying bastard like Peter. Clearly this child is not the fruit of his loins. And yet he's raised him as his own, taken a menial job he hates and subsumed his own desire to be an artist—"

"Oh, for the love," Trish said. "He's not one of your characters. He's a real flesh and blood man. And let me remind you that adultery, by virtue of its existence within a marriage, is evidence of lying."

"But that's my point! He had good motivation for it, just as I did! I need to talk to him," Emma Jean insisted.

"You can talk all you want after dinner."

And so now here they all were, sitting at the table together, and Emma Jean was learning that living on the Planet of Sobriety was definitely not as much fun as taking up residence on the Planet of Extreme Drunkenness. At this very moment on that other planet, Bob had his arm draped around Riley's shoulder and was giving him stock tips, though how her father knew the first thing about the stock market was beyond Emma Jean. Meanwhile, someone kept kicking Emma Jean beneath the table, and she suspected it was Cleo, clumsily attempting to play footsie with Bob. Marielle and Connor—now there was an unlikely pair—flanked Noah while Connor entertained the little boy with bizarre napkin tricks, Marielle and Julia were loudly debating the likelihood of the snow turning into a blizzard. Emma Jean thought they were talking about the weather, but she wasn't certain, something one of them had said made her suspect maybe the topic was a different kind of snow.

And so nobody but Emma Jean heard the phone ring. The first time it rang, she ignored it. After all the events of the day, she was tired, just so damned tired, and all she wanted to do was sink into her chair and watch the spectacle around her. Let whoever was calling wait. But then it rang again, quit ringing, and started again. She heard her cell ring, then the house phone again. Okay, someone was really trying to reach her. Perhaps she should drag herself into her office to answer it.

And so she did. Caller ID read Randall Mason. Oh crap, wasn't that Wendy's husband's name? And now she remembered that Wendy had called earlier, too.

"It's Wendy," Wendy said when Emma Jean answered. "I thought you'd want to know that Ava is missing."

"What?" Emma Jean shrieked.

"She went missing."

"But I thought she was all happy with her mother. I've purposefully been trying not to call her—to give her space. Besides the fact that she's not speaking to me."

"Same here. She was so pleased that that bitch of a mother of hers had finally returned. They had plans to go to dinner at the Sun Valley Lodge and Ava was thrilled."

Bitch mothers seemed to be the theme of the day, Emma Jean thought, remembering Carolina. "So what happened?"

"Vanessa—that's her mother's name—got pulled over for suspicion of driving drunk, only she didn't stop. So the cops chased her and when she finally stopped, she was belligerent and yelled at the cops, so they took her into custody. And she called me to bail her out."

"Oh, God."

"When I asked her where Ava was, she said she couldn't remember."

"Jesus, that's unbelievable."

"So I left her in jail and went to where they were staying. There's no sign of her, Emma Jean. I'm really worried."

"Where could she have gotten herself to?"

"I've been racking my brains. The only places she ever went around here were your gallery or the coffee shop and both are closed for Thanksgiving."

"I'm on my way, Wendy. I'm going to hang up and go book a flight right now. I'll call you back."

"I was hoping you'd say that."

Emma Jean castigated herself all the way into the other room. She'd *known* not to trust Vanessa, even though she'd never met her, and she had *never* felt right about leaving Ava the way she had. Jesus, when would she learn to listen to her intuition? All the books talked about that. It was practically rule one of being a spiritual person. And she had failed miserably at it. Well, she was going to do everything she could to make up for her failures now.

Emma Jean strode back into the dining room. "I have to leave. I'm going to Sun Valley. Ava's gone missing."

All the laughter and discussion from the Drunk Planet ceased.

"Way to ruin a party, darling," Aunt Cleo finally broke the silence. "What happened?"

Emma Jean explained what Wendy had told her. "That's as much as I know. I've got to go find her. I'm going to pack."

"I'll call the airlines," Trish said and leapt from the table.

"Wait, maybe I can get you a seat on my pass." Riley stood, and amazingly, stumbled only a little.

"We'd love to take care of Noah," Marielle said. Only then did Emma Jean notice that the two women had taken over Connor's entertaining duties. Somewhere they'd scrounged up paper and pen—of course that wasn't difficult in this house, she kept notepads and writing utensils in every room, in case inspiration struck—and were drawing funny pictures that Noah was attempting to duplicate. "We've fallen in love with this sweet boy," she said and made kissy faces at Noah, which caused him to scream and cover his face. His very dark coffee-colored face.

"C'mon, I'll call the airlines," Riley said.

"I'm going to pack my bag." And she turned on her heel and headed upstairs.

Emma Jean chose a small leather weekend duffle, really a glorified purse, even though she had no idea how long she'd be gone, and threw in a change of clothes, extra panties, and all five books on her nightstand. She ran into the bathroom to pack her toiletries, glimpsing herself in the mirror. Oh dear Lord, she did look a fright, but there was no time to worry about such things now. She threw her toiletry bag into the duffle and paused by the bed, trying to think of what else she might need. A couple warm sweaters. And maybe her wool socks. And boots—crap, there would be snow on the ground in Sun Valley, and she'd have to walk very carefully because of Claire. But it didn't matter. She'd do whatever it took to find Ava.

Downstairs, her father set the bag in the foyer, and she opened the closet to get her coat then walked to the back of the house. Everyone else seemed to have gathered by the fire in the family room, and luckily it appeared that someone had made tea and coffee so the wild drinking was over. She peeked in and waved but continued to her office where she heard Trish and Riley's voices.

There was a fire lit in her office, too. Noah lay on his stomach in front of the fireplace, drawing a picture on white computer paper. Riley sat at the computer, typing something into the keyboard, and Trish stood behind him. Emma Jean paused in the doorway for a minute. It was such a sweet little scene, like something out of a novel someone else would write but never her. Still, this was her lover, with his son, and her soon-to-be former-employee and they were looking for a plane ticket to go find a young girl about whom she cared deeply, maybe even loved if she had time to stop and think about it. Standing there, she realized she was looking at her future, minus Trish, of course. And furthermore, she couldn't imagine any future she'd rather have.

"Are you ready, Riley? Shouldn't we get going?"

"There's a plane leaving in a couple hours, and you've got a space on it," he said.

"I thought you were coming too," Emma Jean said as nonchalantly as she could muster. Suddenly she was terrified. Her heart pounded a staccato beat. She had made her choice, but what if Riley had changed his mind? What if he had decided it was all too much? What if he'd had enough of her crazy family and decided he should take his child and high tail it back to L.A.? She couldn't live through losing Riley again.

The smile that spread across his face was the best Thanksgiving present she could have asked for, and as far as she was concerned it took care of Christmas and all her future birthdays, too.

"You want me to come with you?"

Emma Jean clutched her heart, bit her lip and nodded, which was all she could manage without bursting into sobs. He stood and walked over to her.

"You're certain of this?"

She nodded again.

Riley started laughing. "You weren't exactly clear on that earlier, but I booked an extra seat for me, just in case." And then he put his arms around her and she nestled into his chest and felt like she was home. But then she thought of something.

"Hey, I do have one question."

"What's that?"

"Why did you stay with her?" Emma Jean glanced toward Noah and lowered her voice. "I mean, clearly, he is not your biological child. Didn't you know?"

"Of course I knew. It would be pretty difficult not to." Riley shrugged his eyebrows. "But I had one, big problem. I fell in love with him the minute he was born."

"Oh," Emma Jean said. There didn't seem to be anything else to say, as Riley's answer said it all. She couldn't think of a single thing he could have said that would have impressed her more.

"The same way I fell in love with you," he said.

She smiled up at him. "You're such a sap sometimes."

"Don't you think you two ought to get going to the airport?" Trish called. "It is going to take a while, the way this snow is falling."

"She hates unnecessary displays of emotion," Emma Jean explained. "And in Trish's world, any emotion is unnecessary."

"That's not true," Trish said.

Emma Jean ran across the room and kissed her. "I'll be home as soon as I can."

To her surprise, Trish stood and hugged her. "Good luck, Emma Jean. I'll pray for you."

"But you said faith was a crutch, so how can you pray for me?"

"Maybe I've reconsidered my position. Love has a way of changing people, you know. Now go."

And just as they made it to the front door, the entire party trailing behind them to say goodbye, Noah in Marielle's arms waving at all of them madly, the doorbell rang.

"Oh for God's sakes, who is it this time? Santa Claus?" Emma Jean said.

"Santa?" Noah asked.

Riley yanked open the door. On the other side of it stood a dark-haired man in a long overcoat. His shoulders and hair were flecked with snow. "Is this the home of Emma Jean Sullivan?"

"It depends on who's asking," Emma Jean said.

"I'm Kevin Marsh. From Delta Airlines," the man said.

"Wow, you must have pull at the airlines, Riley. They come pick us up and everything."

But Riley was staring at Kevin with a puzzled look on his face.

Kevin shook his head and laughed a little laugh. He was in his forties, darkly handsome in a craggy sort of way. "No, ma'am, I'm not here to pick anyone up. I'm here to deliver someone. At least I hope so."

"Oh no, we're not expecting anyone. And furthermore, we're running late for our plane. Maybe you need the neighbors."

"Ava Cameron?"

"What?" Emma Jean screeched. "Ava? Here?"

"Somehow she managed to buy herself a ticket and get herself on the plane. We're not exactly sure how it happened, as she's beneath the age where we let minors ride without authorization."

"How'd she buy the ticket?" Riley asked.

Kevin shrugged. "She said something about a credit card that she'd borrowed."

A puzzle piece went ka-thunk in Emma Jean's brain and she remembered the gallery credit card she thought she'd misplaced. Right. Misplaced it into Ava's hot, little hand.

"We've been calling and calling all night," Kevin was saying, "but nobody seems to answer the phone. So finally I figured I'd just deliver her on my way home, especially since this storm is getting worse."

But by now it had dawned on Emma Jean that Ava was somewhere nearby and she was pushing past Kevin and running down the steps in the snow, calling, "Ava! Ava!"

A car door slammed and there was a blur of movement and something slammed into her hard.

"Oh darling, you scared us so bad. We were on our way to Sun Valley to look for you."

"You were?" Ava looked up at Emma Jean. Even lit only by the dim glow of the street light, which was partially obscured by snow, she could see that the child's hair was a mess—Emma Jean would have to take her to the stylist ASAP—and she had dirty smears on her cheeks. Emma Jean had never seen a face more beautiful.

"I gotta tell you, you are one gutsy kid," Emma Jean said. "Come inside and tell me all about it."

"You're not going to send me back?"

"We can talk about that tomorrow. Wendy is really worried about you, and I know her family wants you home."

Ava shook her head. "I don't want to live with Wendy anymore."

"Then who do you want to live with, darling?" Emma Jean cringed inside. Lord, hadn't this child learned enough? Why would she want to go back to Vanessa?

"I want to live with you," she said.

And Emma Jean was struck dumb yet again. She stood and stared at the willful Ava, the little kleptomaniac. Ava, live with her? The thought had never occurred to her before. But now that Ava had said it, Emma Jean couldn't think of anything that felt more right.

Ava shriveled. "I knew you wouldn't want me."

"Did I say I didn't want you? No, I said nothing of the sort. Jesus God, child, when are you going to learn to quit leaping to assumptions? I'll make some phone calls tomorrow. But right now I have someone for you to meet."

"Riley?"

Emma Jean nodded. "And a whole bunch of other people, too."

"Do you have any food? I'm so hungry I could eat a damn horse," Ava said as she ran up the steps.

First thing tomorrow, Emma Jean thought, they'd start working on Ava's language. Wouldn't do at all to have the daughter of a soon-to-be-bestselling writer cussing like a stevedore. Wait, did stevedores still exist? And furthermore, what precisely was a stevedore? She'd look it up tomorrow. Maybe Ava could help. Emma Jean paused on the walk and watched the group of people—everyone she loved best in the world—standing right inside the door enfold Ava into their midst. There was plenty to worry about tomorrow. For the moment, all she wanted to do was go enjoy the first few moments of her future.

EPILOGUE

One Year Later

"C'mon darling." Emma Jean bent to lift her baby, groaning as a muscle pulled and her back nearly gave out. Damn it, this child was getting heavy, and she constantly forgot to lift with her knees. Emma Jean yelped when he yanked on her hair as she picked him up. He loved pulling on her curly locks almost as much as he loved grabbing at her earrings.

"No, Caleb."

He gazed up at her and smiled, then did it again. "You little imp." He was the cutest baby in the whole world, with apple dumpling cheeks and bright blue eyes and the sweetest button nose. And though she had read nearly every book on child rearing ever published and knew all about setting firm limits from an early age, when he smiled at her like that, she found it very hard to be resolute with him.

Emma Jean carried Caleb across the room and peeked out the front window. The snow which had started an hour ago was still falling, but the streets were covered only with a dusting so far. Thank God—tonight of all nights she wanted everyone to be able to make it to the gallery. At least Emma Jean didn't have far to travel. Her Sun Valley condo was in a luxury complex close to the mountain. Emma Jean loved the location. It was close enough to town to walk everywhere, which she did nearly every day with Caleb strapped to her chest. Thanks to their daily perambulations, she had lost some of the gargantuan amounts of baby weight she had gained. Of course part of the weight loss came from the increased activity level that taking care of Caleb demanded. Nobody had ever told her that caring for children was such hard physical *work*.

Emma Jean set Caleb on the couch and pulled a wool hoodie over his head, which took a considerable amount of effort as he kept waving his arms and trying to grab her hair. Next she'd have to go in search of a jacket to wear over the sweater, because it was damn cold outside. She prayed she could find something that wasn't pink. After Claire had turned out to be Caleb, she'd had to purchase a huge volume of baby clothes to replace all the girly outfits she'd collected. All those pink onesies were suddenly rendered useless, and though Emma Jean had told everyone repeatedly that two centuries ago, pink had been the actual boy's color, the current gender biases still stood. She was actually quite shocked by how firmly entrenched they were, and she was pondering writing an article about it for Salon.

Finally she got the sweater on, found a blue baby jacket and got them out the door and into the car. She only had to run back in once to grab Caleb's diaper bag. There was a place to park right in front of the gallery. Emma Jean was thanking the parking gods when the horrible thought occurred that the empty parking space might be a bad omen. If there was a spot available right out front, that meant not many people had mushed through the snow. She turned off the car and took a deep breath. It didn't matter. All was well. She was blessed in so many ways. The universe was abundant and so was she. Wait, scratch that last part, because what if the universe took her literally and made her abundance turn to fat again? But then Emma Jean remembered that the universe knew best what was good for her and she needed to relax and let go. She took another deep breath. At least she wouldn't have to schlep Caleb down several blocks of snow. Cleo's gallery had sidewalk warmers so that they were generally always clear, but other business owners weren't so considerate and Emma Jean lived in fear of falling with Caleb in her arms.

She was leaning through the open back passenger door, unfastening Caleb's car seat, when she heard a car door slam and someone calling her name. Before she even had time to turn, a blur of chocolate-colored movement slammed into her legs.

"Oh, darling, you startled me!" She looked down at Noah's curly black head, which currently was pressed against her knees. "But I'm so happy to see you. Did you and Daddy have fun in Twin Falls?"

Noah looked up at her and nodded. "I got a truck." He held up a red metal dump truck. "Daddy bought it for me."

"Oh, isn't your father the most wonderful man in the world? And where, pray tell, is he?" Emma Jean's heart pounded at the thought of seeing Riley. And then, all of a sudden, there he was in front of her, eyes twinkling, lips curved into that laconic smile. He pressed Emma Jean to him in a hug, squeezing Noah in between them.

"God, I'm so happy to see you," Emma Jean said.

Riley kissed her on the cheek and laughed. "It's only been since this morning."

"I know, but still. I miss you when you're gone. And so does Caleb."

Inside the car, Caleb chortled and kicked his legs in excitement at seeing his father. In his chubby, little fist he clutched his favorite teething toy, Aku Aku. Emma Jean looked from Caleb to Riley. Caleb looked exactly like Riley in baby form, and Emma Jean thought that was about the best thing in the world, unless you counted what a handsome young boy Noah was growing to be.

Inside the gallery, it was warm and cozy, a clean, well-lighted place as Hemingway would say, and Cleo, bless her heart, had made sure to set up the table the exact way she liked it. They'd placed it next to the largest Christmas tree Emma Jean had ever seen, which dripped with lights and ornaments. Emma Jean couldn't wait to take the family to get their own tree. Cleo herself was on a red kick these days, in favor of the season, she said, and she wore several shades of the color in her layers of skirt and tunic. When she saw them entering she yelled. "It's my favorite little ready-made family! How are you, dears?"

Emma Jean looked around the space, which, to her surprise, was packed with people. Cleo took Caleb from Riley's arms and kissed him all over his face, which sent him into paroxysms of giggles.

This gave Emma Jean time to greet a few fans and speak briefly—and munificently, she might add—about the state of the publishing world to one of them. She then sidled toward the food table in order to nab a glass of wine. The absolute best thing about having a baby as opposed to being pregnant was that she could drink again. Just as she was about to take a sip of wine, she heard the familiar voice.

"You're full of crap, Bob, and I'm pretty sure the whole Jesus-y religion thing is, too. I've just not had time to fully study it."

"Oh, there you are darling!" Emma Jean clutched her heart at the sight of Ava.

Ava had grown two inches and started filling out, much to her dismay, and all of a sudden, the gawky girl was blossoming into a beautiful pre-teen. She wore a short jean skirt over striped leggings and huge cowboy boots, and topped it all off with an oversized green sweater and a lacy scarf wound round her neck. Emma Jean shook her head. "What?" Ava demanded, ducking Emma Jean's kiss. "You're shaking your head at me."

"I'm just being glad you're you, is all, and it makes me shake my head in delight."

"You're full of shit," Ava said.

"Don't you go mouthing off like that tonight, missy."

"She's been spouting mouthfuls all afternoon," Bob said. "Hello, daughter." Emma Jean had learned not to recoil at his kiss. She had to admit, she was actually growing quite fond of her father. Ava seemed to enjoy him, too. She'd taken to spending the occasional afternoon with him in order to debate Christian theology, which try as he might, Bob could not convince her to believe in. That was another good thing about having Bob around; he came in handy when Emma Jean had questions about the sermons she heard at the church she and Riley had been attending.

"Ava is rebelling about going to church on Christmas Eve," Bob informed Emma Jean. "She wants to celebrate it at a Buddhist temple."

"The Buddhists don't celebrate Christmas, darling," Emma Jean said.

"That's the point," Ava insisted.

"Well, fine, but if we go Buddhist for Christmas we've got to do it all the way. So I guess we better cancel the tree expedition tomorrow. And I'll have to return all the presents I bought for you."

"Um, maybe I could be Buddhist after Christmas is over," Ava said. "Oh, hey, there's Wendy."

Emma Jean watched Ava race off to greet her former foster mother. God, she loved that child. And she loved that for as much as Caleb looked like Riley, Ava was actually beginning to look like *her,* with the same wild hair and oversized eyes that were too big for her face.

"That often happens with adopted children," Trish had told her.

"She's not officially adopted yet," Emma Jean reminded Trish. The good news was how smoothly the process was going, what with Ava's natural mother safely ensconced in jail and ready to give up her rights to the girl.

"God, quit being so literal."

"That's like calling the pot calling the kettle black, isn't it?" Emma Jean had said, and Trish actually laughed instead of rolling her eyes or tsk-ing the way she always used to. The fact that she and Connor were engaged and she had a job in a clinic had made Trish more human. She and Connor would be coming to Sun Valley next week, to spend Christmas with Emma Jean and Riley, and Emma Jean couldn't wait.

Aunt Cleo clapped her hands. "Darlings! May I have your attention please? Now that Emma Jean is here, *en famille,* I'd like to share a few words with you before we get started on the reading."

Emma Jean figured she didn't really need to listen to Cleo and wormed her way through the crowd into a corner and pulled out a compact to check her hair and apply lipstick. Could you even believe she'd walked out of the house and not checked her make-up? Lord, having children was so time-consuming, which had been the topic of her most recent blog. It was amazing and heart-warming how many of her fans had taken the leap from rabid baby-hater to devoted mother along with her, and they seemed ravenous for her ramblings on motherhood. She'd developed a fervent posse of new fans, too, who hung on her every word about child rearing. The *POM Manifesto* had just been published to rave reviews and damn good sales. Not bestseller status yet, but Angela said there was a good chance it would rise to the top.

She pulled out her lipstick and just as she was applying it, the crowd must have shifted because all of a sudden she could hear Aunt Cleo more clearly.

"People! I now turn the evening over to my beautiful and talented niece, Emma Jean Sullivan, who will be reading us a selection from her latest book."

She checked in her pocket to make sure she had one of her purple pens handy, for good luck. Then she walked to the front of the room where Cleo had set up a small wood dais. She took a deep breath, looked around at her audience and smiled. And then she began to read:

"Emma Jean Sullivan hated babies…"

About the Author

Charlotte Rains Dixon is a writer and writing teacher. She has published numerous articles and stories as well as three non-fiction books. Charlotte received her MFA in creative writing from Spalding University and teaches in the Loft certificate-writing program at Middle Tennessee State University. She lives in Portland, Oregon. Visit her blog at www.charlotterainsdixon.com.